Arise The Dead II: World War Two

MIROLAND IMPRINT 15

Canada Council **Conseil des Arts**
for the Arts **du Canada**

ONTARIO ARTS COUNCIL
CONSEIL DES ARTS DE L'ONTARIO

an Ontario government agency
un organisme du gouvernement de l'Ontario

Canadä

Guernica Editions Inc. acknowledges the support of the Canada Council
for the Arts and the Ontario Arts Council. The Ontario Arts Council
is an agency of the Government of Ontario.

We acknowledge the financial support of the Government of Canada.

A family memoir

Arise The Dead II: World War Two

Elizabeth Langridge

MIROLAND (GUERNICA)
TORONTO • BUFFALO • LANCASTER (U.K.)
2018

Connie McParland, series editor
Michael Mirolla, editor
David Moratto, cover and interior book design
Cover Images provided by Elizabeth Langridge
Guernica Editions Inc.
1569 Heritage Way, Oakville, ON L6M 2Z7
2250 Military Road, Tonawanda, N.Y. 14150-6000 U.S.A.
www.guernicaeditions.com

Distributors:
University of Toronto Press Distribution,
5201 Dufferin Street, Toronto (ON), Canada M3H 5T8
Gazelle Book Services, White Cross Mills
High Town, Lancaster LA1 4XS U.K.

First edition.
Printed in Canada.

Legal Deposit—First Quarter
Library of Congress Catalog Card Number: 2017955483
Library and Archives Canada Cataloguing in Publication
Langridge, Elizabeth, author
Arise the dead / Elizabeth Langridge.

(MiroLand imprint ; 14-15)
Contents: Book one. The Great War -- Book two. World War Two.
Issued in print and electronic formats.
ISBN 978-1-77183-281-6 (book 1 : softcover). --ISBN 978-1-77183-284-7
(book 2 : softcover). -- ISBN 978-1-77183-282-3 (book 1 : EPUB).
--ISBN 978-1-7183-283-0 (book 1 : Kindle). --ISBN 978-1-77183-284-7
(book 2 : EPUB) .--ISBN 978-1-77183-286-1 (book 2 : Kindle).

1. World War, 1914-1918--Personal narratives. 2. World War,
1939-1945--Personal narratives. 3. Creative nonfiction. I. Title.
I. Series: MiroLand imprint ; 14-15

D640.A2L32 2018   940.3   C2017-906410-X   C2017-906411-8

On April 6, 1915, in the face
of an imminent attack by the enemy,
a young French adjutant, Jacques Pericard,
seeing that his comrades in the trench
were either dead or wounded,
cried out: ARISE THE DEAD!

For James Langridge and May Wigley
and all the other 'ordinary' men, women and children
who suffered and endured through the two World Wars,
whose stories are seldom told.

✑ Prologue

Wraiths Of The Past

No longer does the Menin Road, dreary and squalid,
a tragedy of mud, weeds and shell craters, lead to the
Western Front. Now it is a trim provincial highway;
and sweaty, heavy-laden, sleepy-eyed men are wraiths
of the past ...

— Leon Wolff

Someone had placed two wreaths of artificial poppies under the flowering-cherry tree, leaning against the trunk. Long ago, in 1915, the predecessor of the tree, the Lone Tree on trench maps, had stood in the same place on the edge of No-Man's-Land. This tree had been planted in 1992.

That old tree had been destroyed by shell-fire from the German side on the night of September 25th, 1915, at the end of the first day of the Battle of Loos, Pas-de-Calais, north-eastern France. A first aid dug-out of the Queen's Own Royal West Kent Regiment nearby had been hit. Near the tree had been the British front line.

The poppies, made of red fabric limp with rain, had black plastic centres and were surrounded by a few green plastic leaves. Lizzie, seventy-five years old, daughter of a soldier, stood and looked at them, as gentle, cold rain fell on her head and shoulders and on two large framed photographs that stood next to the wreaths, black and white pictures taken over one hundred years before. Drops of water eased slowly down the glass, falling into silence. It was May, 2014.

One photograph was of a solitary young man in uniform, the other of a group of four young men, with names attached, almost illegible from damp. They were nameless to Lizzie and the others on the tour of the battlefields, yet still known one hundred years later to those who loved them by reputation, English soldiers of the Great War. *We are voyeurs only, unless we remember the tragedy of it*, she thought. Someone had been there before her recently to place the photographs and the wreaths, someone whose distant boy had been of the West Kent Regiment, or the East Surreys, the East Kents, or the West Surreys, or perhaps of the Scottish regiments who had been there on the first day of the battle, or the Irish Guards who came up later to the battle front.

A dirt track ran past the tree, the ruts moist with water, turning the soil to a clinging, reddish mud, while all around them crops grew as far as they could see over the vast plain that had been the killing fields. She could see seedling cabbages, wheat and potato plants. For mid-May the weather was unexpectedly cold that day, a change from earlier sunshine that had brought out the summer flowers prematurely, the roses in the cemeteries nearby where the soldiers lay. The sun hid now behind dense cloud that came almost down to the fields. Patchy mist hung over them. Nonetheless, invisible larks twittered above them, a litany connecting her and her companions to the past, drawing them in. They seemed to her to be asserting the power of life, descendants as they all were of the events of long ago, and hinting at the fragility of it.

They had just come through the small town of Vermelles, on the Vermelles to Hulluch road, a little west, where the soldiers had marched through in 1915, under shell fire at its east end. Fragments of stone had been chipped from around the church door on the main street. *Perhaps the upper part had been destroyed and then rebuilt*, she speculated. On such a dull day, there were few people about in the town; it might as well have been deserted.

The tour van, a suitable size for only ten people, stayed one hundred yards back from the tree, away from the water filled ruts. The four of them who had ventured out walked around in silence. Here one could find small balls of lead, shrapnel, that had sprayed out from shells, and sometimes little pieces of deeply rusted iron, difficult to identify.

Lizzie picked up one such piece, and a stone, flint, from the soil and put them in her pocket. Perhaps that stone had been there when her father, Jim, had walked this way. Perhaps his boot had pressed it down into the soil, and later it had been moved by the explosions of shells, and then by the farmer's plough in the time of peace.

She had longed to be in France again, her third time at the battlefields in ten years. Now she was here with her husband, James, and the others. The sense of futility seemed to wash over her with the fragments of mist. There was no language for it, for that exercise in pointlessness and murder.

Time like an ever rolling stream bears all its sons away, they fly forgotten as a dream dies at the opening day.

Fifty yards from the new Lone Tree, beside the Vermelles to Hulluch road, was the St. Mary's Cemetery, on the site of St. Mary's Advanced Dressing Station in September, 1915, to where the wounded had walked or crawled, or were carried, if they were among the lucky ones.

Her father had been one of the intended sacrificial lambs, the cannon fodder, of the 24th Division, 72nd Brigade of the New Army, the volunteers of Kitchener's Army, recruited to augment and replace the dwindling regular army that had not been sufficient for the onslaught that had overtaken them in Belgium in 1914. He had understood early on that his life counted as nothing to those who ordered the inexperienced boys into the firing line. There had been no way out, no way to live unless there was a wound sufficient to take one out and allow survival. He had told her that, many years before, in a moment of rare openness. Yet he had been a volunteer. Suicide had been a way out, to reserve the right to take one's own life before it could be taken by others, by the enemy or by one's own side, a summary execution for something called cowardice that was not cowardice. Many had taken that way. Censorship and silence had obscured the truth, hiding it behind banks of time and lies.

I am here again, Lizzie thought, as she looked at the framed photographs and then out over the plain of crops, an advocate from the future, moving back like a spirit into the past. *I will never be tired of France, because something of him and those others is still here.* Although he lived, he has something in common with these boys who fell in the plains and were never found, and those in the cemeteries and those who only have their names on memorials to the missing. An epitaph that she had seen read: "We know the loss but not the gain." Her boots were rimed with the clinging mud.

Somewhere here, very close, he had waited in a trench, the firing line, on the night of the 25th to the 26th of September, under shell fire. The colonel of his battalion was waiting for orders to come up to the front from the generals safely far behind the lines. It was the first time he, Jim, had been under fire. They were raw, having seen nothing of real warfare. They had been marched up to the battle front through congested roads chaotic with the traffic of war and men, mules and horses, those going up and the wounded going back. There had been thousands of marching men, going east. They were ordered to go over the top at 11 a.m. on the 26th of September. On that night the old Lone Tree had been destroyed. He might have witnessed it.

〜 Lizzie turned and walked slowly back towards the tour van. Not far behind her, at the other side of No-Man's-Land, had been the German front lines. Beyond those lines had been the impossible objective of the Royal West Kents and the other battalions: a gun emplacement to be disabled, behind banks of barbed wire and machine guns. That had been beyond the Lens-LaBassée road that ran from north to south. The slag heaps, like mountains, were still there in the near distance, from the coal mines at Lens where there had been fierce fighting and much slaughter, where civilians, coal miners and their families, had lived in underground tunnels, sheltering from shells and bullets, waiting for a slender chance to escape westward.

〜 Soon they, the pilgrims, would go on to the town of Arras.

〜 Isaac Rosenberg, artist and poet, soldier, killed in action on the 1st April, 1918, came into Lizzie's mind then:

Returning, We Hear the Larks

Sombre the night is.
And though we have our lives, we know
What sinister threat lurks there.

Dragging these anguished limbs, we only know
This poison-blasted track opens on our camp —
On a little safe sleep.

But hark! Joy — joy — strange joy.
Lo! heights of night ringing with unseen larks.
Music showering our upturned list'ning faces ...

Like the new Lone Tree, the flowering cherry, she had come back to occupy that place and had found the company and tributes of silent witnesses, and the power of memory.

∞ Chapter 1

War is so small, so sad, so inexcusable.
— Gregory Clark,
WW I soldier, WW II journalist.

The bomb dropped in the field behind the two houses where in spring wild daffodils grew among the tufts of coarse grass and around the old twisted apple trees thick with dark green English ivy.

It came out of a night sky that was like indigo velvet, with stars nestled in its folds like diamonds — as hard and impersonal as the cold rain. A weak moon illuminated a patch of the heavens, with its pale grey wisps of cloud against the purple-black.

Night rested uneasily on the meadows, shaws, spinneys and coppices of the land, on the pond and the stream, where moorhens and coots had trod through the moist clay banks in the light of day, and on the churchyard where the fence was broken down and sheep wandered in to crop the grass that covered the dead of the village. In the shallows of the stream, minnows, sticklebacks and tiny lampreys rested in the cover of the banks.

The blast from the bomb toppled the brick chimney from the nearest cottage, number two Bullrush Lane, so that it fell onto the grey slate roof. Glass from the back windows blew in. Masonry and bricks, lathe and plaster loosened inside the house and fell onto the beds, onto a child's bed, onto a baby's cot. Alien things, out of place, filled this homely space. Down, down the stairs the bricks fell, crashing, banging, in a mad orchestra of sound, bringing dust with them, into the front hall, loosening pictures, crushing ornaments, covering carpets.

In the small front sitting room the ceiling gave way, covering the beautiful ornamental Dresden porcelain lady, a wedding present, as she sat on the mantelpiece. She viewed her face in a hand-mirror, held out in front of her with a perfect, delicate hand, her stiff crinoline dress of sprigged roses spread around her. Her pale face with its fine eyebrows and perfect lips gazed out at the destruction as it fell and settled about her. Her light brown porcelain hair, arranged perfectly in ringlets and gathered back from her face with a bow, did not quiver as her lovely hand holding the mirror was chopped off neatly by a sliver of brick.

The sideboard, of veneered walnut with oak-leaf trim in solid oak, with its thick marble top and big oval mirror — late Victorian, received a direct hit by a clump of bricks falling from above. The mirror was wrenched from its screws but did not break as it settled in the space between the sideboard and the wall.

An exotic sea-shell, marked in tiny lettering "a present from Hastings," fell from the narrow mantelpiece above the Victorian cast-iron fireplace, together with a brass ashtray. The mahogany wall-clock with its mother-of-pearl inlay and Roman numerals quivered but did not fall. On everything a dust settled, thick and grimy.

In the main bedroom the mirror with the twisted cherry-wood finials atop the polished dressing table was knocked to the floor. Devastation and destruction passed through the house, as though it were struck by a giant malevolent hand.

⌒ In the kitchen a man and a woman were still awake, standing near the cast-iron range, where the woman was heating milk for cocoa and the man warming himself by the hot coals that showed though the grate. They had heard the whistle, screech and "womp" of the bomb; they knew the sound. In a few seconds, as in the holding of a breath, they braced themselves, their actions suspended, no time to run.

Cracks, wide and ugly, appeared in the walls around them. Automatically the woman reached for the saucepan and took it off the heat, put a lid on it and placed it on the floor. No point in wasting good milk. She wanted to cry out, but held it down by an effort of will.

The man, Jim, was wearing his work shirt, collarless, with a black weskit over top, and his working trousers.

"Get under cover," he said, taking her arm roughly and pulling her with him towards the heavy oak table where the children lay underneath. "Come on! Quick!"

The table, decades old and sturdy, shivered as plaster and lathe from the ceiling fell on it when they crawled under its shelter to sit beside the children who had been put there to sleep at half-past seven, as they had been for many nights now.

"Bloody bastards," Jim said. "Bloody, flaming bastards."

By the back door to the scullery, his leather gaiters, shaped to his calves, stood like sentinels that rocked back and forth.

The woman, May Harriet, fought down a familiar sense of panic. It wouldn't do to show fear in front of the children. The crashing went on, then began to peter out. May pulled the neck of her blouse up over her nose and mouth so that she could breathe without taking in the choking dust, then placed a sheet over the heads of the children, Jo and Lizzie.

Jo, short for Joanne, four years old, began to cry.

"Keep that over your face," her mother said. "There's a lot of dust." Her voice came out high-pitched with panic.

"No!" the girl said, pulling it off. She sat up, small in her pale blue flannelette nightdress. "What's happening?"

"Nothing much," Jim said. "Just a bomb out in the orchard. We'll be all right. Do you want some cocoa?"

"No!" Tears ran down the girl's face as she sensed fear, and saw behind her mother's shoulders the changed vista of the kitchen.

Lizzie, the younger girl, two years old, was wide awake now. As she lay on her back in a cocoon of blankets, she could see the brown, rough underside of the table with its swirls and patterns not very far above her head.

"It's all right," her mother said. "Stay there."

Jim looked at the stove, the fire still burning cheerfully, and wondered if the part of the chimney inside the house had been damaged, if sparks had got out into the bedrooms and set the place alight, what was left of it. He could smell smoke.

"Listen," May whispered, holding still. There was another wave of bombers coming over from the south, approaching with a muted roar. "That lot's on the way to London." They could hear the noise of many engines, feel the vibrations of the propellers as they made the remnants of the house tremble. They held themselves in against the desire to howl and weep. The baby's enamelled tin potty under the table went chink, chink, chink against a cocoa mug.

Through clouds of plaster and brick dust they saw the cat, Greysuit, squatting underneath the sink, moving nothing but his eyes.

"Come on, you buggers," Jim said. "We're waiting for you." Overhead the noise blotted out everything else; there was no past or future, only the moment, a moment in which one waits to die.

The grizzling of the kids filled the near silence as the sound of the invasion died away. It was replaced by another sound, coming from the north, their own planes, flying low. May Harriet Wigley, formerly of the Royal Flying Corps, 1916-1918, looked upward, as though her eyes would sear through the wood of the table and the remaining masonry.

"That's right, boys," she said. "Good luck, lads. Good luck."

Her faced crumpled as she squatted in undignified fear beside her husband and children. "Oh ... all those lovely boys, those lovely boys."

Faces, blurred by the passage of over twenty years, paraded in her head. Those faces that were never far from her mind, obsessed over, re-newed themselves in her inner vision, the ones who had not come back. In her imagination they smiled and joked, blew kisses, as they had done then. "Goodbye, May. See you soon."

They had departed from the aerodrome near Tadcaster. There had been the Americans and the English. Each smiling mouth had formed the same words as she stood outside the officers' mess to see them go: "Goodbye, May; goodbye, May; goodbye, May." Frederick George Decker of New Jersey had been one of them, out of place in Yorkshire, out of place in France from where he had not returned. Now he was seldom out of her mind.

Jim put a hand on her shoulder awkwardly, moved it round to her back, patted her one, two, three times.

"It's all right," he said. "It's going to be all right. We're alive."

"Sometimes I wish to bloody God I was dead."

"Don't talk like that in front of the kids," he said. "You stay here. I'm going to get the cocoa, then have a look round. The place could go up in smoke."

He eased himself out into the gritty dust.

"Be careful."

The saucepan of milk on the floor was still hot, but the cups with cocoa powder in them were sprinkled with bits of plaster. He carried them over to the sink where water still came out of the tap. It was good to have a task, to carry on while you collected your thoughts. This was tame, after all, from what he had known. If fate decreed that you were to die, that was it. Not a fatalist, he knew what you could do and what you couldn't do. It could have been a direct hit, just a few more yards.

The children were whimpering now. From outside he could hear someone shouting, Tom and Alice from next door. Deliberately, carefully, he rinsed and dried the cups, spooned in more cocoa from the tin, then a spoonful each of the precious sugar. A damn shame to have wasted the bit of sugar that he'd had to throw down the drain. Surprising that water still came out of the tap.

With a steady hand he poured hot milk into four cups, stirred up the mixture and added a bit of cold milk for the kids. Before he carried the cups on a tin tray over to the shelter of the table, he tested the kids' drinks to make sure they were not too hot. Already his nerves were steadying. The sound of the bomb falling, the whistle that it made, had brought back in those few seconds a peculiar kind of fear, a tightening of the whole body, a panic that he hoped he would never experience again.

Hard on its heels came that strange, detached alertness, as though he stood outside himself, watching himself as time stood still while he considered what he had to do — what he could best do to save himself and others. He recalled the sharp pain of the shrapnel as the shell exploded near him. Again he could remember the peculiar stench of the front line. It was a smell like no other, of smoke and exploded shells, of piss, shit and blood, of sweaty, unwashed, lice-laden bodies, overlaid with the overwhelming odour of the decaying flesh of mules, horses, rats and men, of the improperly buried dead. Later, he had come to know the smell of gangrene. More than anything, he feared gangrene. Over time he had come to love the smell of sweat, of dirty, stinking, feet, for it meant life.

Putrefaction was a sickly sweet smell that seemed to penetrate the very membranes of your nostrils, as though it would lodge there and never be expunged by any method known to man or nature.

May held the cup of cocoa for Lizzie to sip from while she held her own with her other hand. Panic and grief held her lips clamped so that she would not cry out, would not blubber like a child. Our lovely home, our lovely home. That was all she could think of, apart from the vague hope that Tom and Alice next door were all right. They ought to be, because they had been shielded by this cottage. As far as she could tell, the bomb had come down to the right, behind the house, in the orchard, closer to her and Jim.

"One of those bloody Jerries, gone up to bomb London," Jim said, standing in the middle of the kitchen on debris that crunched with every move. "On the way back. Got one bomb left and decided to drop it here, the buggers."

"We weren't showing any lights."

"There's a moon. Didn't have to show any lights. They know they're bombing civilians, killing children."

"They don't care," May said, letting the panic out, her voice high-pitched. "I expect we're doing the same to them. What's it all for?"

"People have been asking that question from time immemorial," he said. After swallowing the last of his cocoa, he squatted down, holding a candle, to find the mains tap in the cupboard under the sink, careful not to invade the sanctuary of the cat. "Just in case," he said, giving the tap several twists to the right, turning it off. "After I've looked upstairs, I'll put it on again."

When he flicked the electric light switch, beside the door to the front hallway, nothing happened. They had been making cocoa by candlelight earlier, and he had been reading a paper by firelight as he warmed himself. That was when they had heard the single enemy plane approaching from the north.

Outside, at the back, someone was shouting: "Are you all right? Are you all right?" The shouting was followed by a banging on the scullery door that led directly outside.

When Jim tried to open the back door that went out to the brick yard and the wash-house, he found that it was stuck in its frame, the structure warped.

"Can you push it?" he yelled.

The door came open in a shower of plaster, to reveal Tom from next door, white-faced, with his wife, Alice, standing behind him.

"You all right, Jim?" Alice said. "The little kiddies?"

"All alive." Jim said. "The house is in no great shape, I reckon. I was just about to go up and have a look at the roof, if the stairs are still there."

Tom wore trousers and a jacket over pyjamas. "Be careful," he said. "There might be some bare wires. I'll come up with you." By looking over Jim's shoulder Tom could see that this house had sustained more damage than his own. "Our place is not too bad. Chimney's down, and a lot of bloody soot with it."

"I'd appreciate some help," Jim said, standing aside to let them in. "Watch where you tread, there's broken glass."

"Bloody bastards," Tom said. "Do they think that killing us will win the war for them?"

Tom's surname was Katt. Indeed, he looked like a cat, with large, intelligent eyes of a light hazel colour that might have been too beautiful on a man had they not had a haunted quality about them, a percipience that spoke of a youth of hardship, something he would never have spoken of himself. There was an air of permanent exhaustion about his eyes, as though they had witnessed far more than any human should have to bear.

Quiet, sweet, unassuming Alice, who stood now in the candlelight, wearing a heavy wool coat over a flannelette nightdress, had also been with the Royal Flying Corps in the first war, stationed in Yorkshire. She was wearing rag curlers now, under a hairnet. There was a smell about her of camphorated oil. "How are you, May?" she enquired softly. "All right, duck?" Over her, like a wedding veil, was a sheen of raindrops.

May nodded, watching Alice crunch over broken plates and plaster towards her. "Got room for one more?" Alice said, ducking down.

They all shifted around a bit, the kids casting frightened eyes this way and that as they sat untidily in their small mound of blankets. Like Alice, Jo also had rag curlers in her hair, which was already curly of its own accord, having insisted on them. Never before had the kids seen Alice Katt in nightgown and Wellington boots, with a hairnet over her hair and a large metal grip holding it in place. "All right, duck?" Alice said to Jo. As with so many things, there was no reply to be made to that, as Jo shifted to make room for Alice to sit under the table, with knees drawn up.

"What about you, Alice?" May said. "The house and all that?"

"Still breathing, as you see. House not too bad, could be worse. It was a bloody shock, I can tell you. We broke our own rule for once, of never going to bed before midnight. And then going up stairs and all. We're lucky to get out." As she cast her eyes around the damaged kitchen she clicked her tongue in sympathy and anger. "Buggers! Buggers!"

The men had left the room, each carrying a candle, to go to what remained of the stairs, intending to explore the two bedrooms and the bathroom. Their departure was the signal for the two women to put their heads closer together and for Alice to place a hand on May's shoulder.

"It's a cruel shame, all this," she said. "You know, this makes me glad I did my bit twenty-odd years ago, simple though it was. I'd do it again if they'd let me. Perhaps they will, the way things are going. It makes you feel that you're going mad when you feel helpless, don't it? I wouldn't want to be in London at this moment, poor devils."

Alice's sympathy released May's tears, which she attempted to stem with the sleeve of her jumper. She never ceased to be grateful and amazed at the strangeness of certain life events, particularly those that had brought her and Alice together again after they had both been in Yorkshire with the Royal Flying Corps. Alice, having returned to Tunbridge Wells after the First World War, had married a local man. It seemed like a miracle that Tom also worked on the Calborne estate, that he and Alice had finished up living next to her and Jim in their tied cottages belonging to Lord Calborne.

Seeing their mother crying, the kids started to weep.

"Our lovely home," May whispered. "How will it ever be the same?

We've got no money to replace it. We're too old to start again." At forty-three she knew herself to be old as a mother of two young children. Jim was fifty-four. Tiredness made her feel twice her age, lumpen and weary. It was impossible to remember when any of them had last had an un-broken sleep.

"We're alive, that's the main thing," Alice whispered back, her own tears welling up.

"Where are we going to live? There's nothing else on the estate that I know of, and we may not be the only ones bombed out before the night's over."

"They'll find us something," Alice said.

May did not fully believe that, nor in the benevolence of "his Lord-ship." If there were no empty houses on the estate — and she didn't know of any — things were going to be hard. They might end up in a dis-used cowshed until these houses could be repaired, or in a barn, or in the wash-houses at the back. That was the trouble being in a tied cottage: nothing to call your own. She thought of a man she knew who lived in a garden shed at the bottom of somebody else's garden, where he seemed contented. No use being fastidious when there was no choice.

They would take a few moments to cry, to mourn what was lost, past and present, before they must be up and doing.

"All those lovely boys," May said again, obsessed.

"Yes. It helps to have a good cry. The trouble comes when you try to bottle it up."

That was not strictly true, May thought. You were left with a resid-ual sense of mourning, even after the cathartic washing of tears.

The sound of their weeping was drowned out by the frightened snuffling of the kids.

∽ Chapter 2

The men in the hallway facing the front door of the two-up-two-down house saw that plaster had fallen in patches from the ceiling, exposing the pale brownish-grey dried wood of the lathe. The light of the candle showed them a devastation that was heartbreaking. They coughed and spluttered, breathing through handkerchiefs.

They started up the stairs, with the crackle of broken glass underfoot from pictures that had fallen off the wall, while the steps themselves groaned and squeaked under the pressure of each footfall. At the top, garish shadows danced in the candlelight of things out of place. Part of the banister had been knocked sideways so that it leaned out into the hall below. Mostly the stairs were intact but splintered here and there, poking through a thin carpet.

On the landing itself the devastation was more thorough. Doors hung askew. Debris and heavier chunks of wood and masonry were spread over the colourful rag rug in the centre of the floor. A picture had fallen off the wall; it stood upright, its frame still intact, but the glass broken into many shards.

Jim picked it up carefully and looked at it, the lithograph of his army discharge, a picture of a seated Britannia holding a shield with soldiers standing to attention in front of her. "James Langridge," it read, "served with honour and was disabled in the Great War. Honourably Discharged, March, 1916." The thing itself was undamaged.

"I've got one of those," Tom said. "You don't want to lose that, Jim. Otherwise at times you'll think it was all a bloody dream."

We've got our wounds, Jim thought, keeping silent, placing the picture carefully against the wall. Wounds of mind and body. All his life since that war he had tried not to be bitter, because he had seen what it could do to people, how it could warp and destroy them like an acid working silently deep within. Now he felt a taste of bitterness, like gall in his mouth.

"You could have that re-framed," Tom said.

"I could," he said. It seemed to him that the Jerries, not content to do their damnedest to kill him in the past, had come after him here in this idyllic place, in the heart of the Sussex countryside, his birth-place, to finish him off this time and to kill his wife and children as well.

France had been idyllic too, green and beautiful, burgeoning with fertile nature that summer of 1915. That was until they had got up to the man-made charnel house that was the Front, where the contrast seemed calculated to deprive a man of his sanity. As it turned out, there was no sense in any of it. In fact, it had all been set up to make you think that what was madness in the extreme was honourable and glorious. He had never understood what was meant by glory, nor had he ever met anyone who knew.

From the pocket of his trousers he brought out a flattened packet of Woodbines. "Want a fag, mate?"

"Don't mind if I do."

They lit their fags from the candle before going into the small back bedroom that was the children's room. The pleasant scent of cigarette smoke went with them, disguising the newly released odours of old plaster and secret, bricked-up places that had not seen the light of day for decades.

"Steadies the nerves, doesn't it," Jim remarked, drawing on his fag, willing the smoke to help dissipate the tightness that had gripped his chest again.

"Yeah."

The small room before them, almost pathetic in its simplicity, was a scene of near ruin. Although the outer walls of the house there, and the roof, were largely intact as far as they could see, most of the ceiling plaster had come down, revealing a closed-in attic.

Pushed up against one wall, opposite a small fireplace, was an iron double bedstead, the spare bed, with a thin horsehair mattress and a faded cotton bedspread on it. It was now laden with debris.

"Careful, Jim. This floor might not be sound. If it gives way, we'll end up in the kitchen on top of Alice, your missus, and the kids."

In the remaining space of the room there was a child's narrow bed covered with bricks. Near it, on legs, was a large wicker cot, Lizzie's bed, that had been violated in a similar manner.

"A good thing you had the kids downstairs under that table. Makes you sick, don't it." Tom turned his haunted eyes onto Jim. "Where were you in the last bloody lot?"

Jim drew deeply on his fag, blowing out smoke before answering. "Loos."

"West Kents?"

"Yeah."

"I was at the Somme. Royal Sussex."

When they had first become neighbours, some years ago, they had both rather warily ascertained that they had been in France in the so-called Great War. That moment had formed a silent bond between them, that Jim reflected on now. They had not gone into detail, each had retreated into silence, with the certain knowledge that the other knew all there was to know.

"Did I ever tell you," Tom remarked, 'that my real name is Cyril?"

"No, you didn't," Jim said, taken out of himself for a moment.

"I was always called Tom, because of Katt, except by my parents. Why would anyone lumber a kid with a name like that?"

"Search me."

Testing the floor carefully, Jim inched forward into the room to extricate two of the children's toys, an eye-less and ear-less bear, and a worn panda. Then he and Tom stood at the bedroom door for a moment, as though they could not believe what they were looking at — a baby's bed in a battlefield. Yet at a deeper level, nothing surprised either of them anymore.

A siren sounded then, like a low grumbling, the air-raid siren that had been set up in the village. It started with a low sound, then went high quickly, until it was screaming out over the countryside.

"Here they come again, Jim. Better get down below."

Mingled with that sound, they heard the screams of the women. "Come on! Come on!"

The squadrons of enemy aircraft, dozens by the sound of them, were above them as they bent double to get under the kitchen table. The children were crying as though in mime, their cries drowned out by the overhead din.

They held hands, bracing themselves for God-knows-what, the adults bending over the two children, as though they could form a shield of flesh and blood. The diabolical ingenuity of man had ensured that flesh and blood were as nothing.

May leaned against her husband, his rough hand gripping hers. Feelings were too strong for words, as she wondered if he knew that she cared for him. He had not been her first choice; he had been her choice when the first was no longer there.

Yes, he knew.

The noise shook the ruins of the house as the squadrons flew over, on to London, the docks, the factories, the people of the East End, the shipping. They could hear then the deep, sonorous booming of an anti-aircraft gun that was positioned on a hill beyond the village. Boom boom! Boom boom! Boom boom! It was a sound, Alice thought, that made you feel protected, and yet full of dread at the same time, because big guns belonged in battlefields. It seemed to form an echo deep inside your body. Well, the battle was coming to them now. They were in the thick of it.

"God help us," May said.

As that noise subsided, they became aware of another sound, a siren of sorts, out in the road. "It's the powers-that-be," Tom speculated, from his cramped position under the table. "The Home Guard perhaps. Or it could be the blokes from the Air Raid Precaution, the ARP."

"They all do a good job," Alice remarked. "Though they're a bit late, in our case." She took off her hairnet and the metal clip, pulled out the rag curlers and stuffed them into the pocket of her coat. Her hair bounced about in tight little corkscrews, so that the kids stared at her and forgot to cry. "Now I look a bit more respectable."

They came to the front door, one from the Home Guard and one from the Air Raid Precaution, with their unbecoming uniforms and tin helmets set at angles. They came up the brick path to the front door, muffled torches in hands.

"You people all right in here? Anyone hurt?" the spokesman said to Jim when he opened the door and stood in a shower of dust.

Only in the mind, damaged forever. "No one's hurt," Jim said, knowing that he looked a sorry sight in his dust-covered weskit and work shirt. "We've got two young kiddies in here. We don't know where we're going to go, although the wash-houses look all right."

The first man looked at a notebook. "You're the man of the house, I take it?" He was young and looked as though he had only just started shaving. Even so, it was a mystery why he was not in the forces.

"You could say that."

"James Langridge? Wife May Harriet? Two children, Joanne and Elizabeth?"

"That's right. Our neighbours from next door are with us as well."

"Tom and Alice Katt?"

"Yes."

"What sort of a name is that? Sounds German to me."

"It ain't. You'd better ask him."

"Oh, I wouldn't do that."

"Are you here to help, or what? Or are you just collecting statistics?"

"If no first-aid is required, Mr. Langridge, we can get some help organized to clear you up, then we can drive you if you have somewhere else to go. Your wife's parents live about two miles away, I understand. The Wigleys, at The Stables."

"They do, you're right. But I don't think they've got room to take the four of us in. My wife's brother lives with them." What he wanted to say, but refrained, was that the brother, with the unlikely name of Cedric, was a miserable, selfish cuss who had never married because no woman would have him. Often he was called Ced, which became perverted to Sid, which he did not like. He was given to wearing posh brown suede shoes, and Jim distrusted anyone who wore suede shoes. No one could do an honest day's work in such shoes.

"Could we come in and look around, Mr. Langridge? We have to make a report about the damage. You might be eligible for compensation."

"And pigs might fly," Jim said, knowing he was being bad-tempered with this young man. "You're John Parson's son, aren't you?"

"Yes. And if you're wondering why I'm not in the forces, Mr. Langridge, I had infantile paralysis when I was a kid. Got a withered leg as a result."

"I wasn't wondering. I had enough people coming up to me in the street in the last war, after I was wounded and out of it, asking me why I wasn't in the Army. I used to put this in their face." He held up his left arm, the wrist bent permanently downwards, the skin shiny with pink scars.

"Shrapnel wound?"

"Yeah."

"Well, you did your bit. This is my way of doing mine."

"Fair enough. Come in." He stood back from the door to let them into the hallway. "We've still got water, but no electricity. I haven't had time to look at the bathroom upstairs. The lavatory might be cracked."

"Right you are, Mr. Langridge. I'll just have a word or two with the others." He and his colleague from the ARP, who so far had said nothing, crunched their way to the back of the house.

Faces peered out from under the table. "Oh, hello," Alice piped up. "It's young Parsons, isn't it? I don't suppose you know me, the younger generation not bothering much with the older ones, but I know you by sight because I know your Dad. I'm from next door."

Young Parsons blushed and straightened his helmet. "That's right. My name's John, too. Mrs. ... er ... Katt, is it?"

"Yes, that's right. You here to help us, duckie?"

"With the couple of strapping blokes you got here, I don't think you need us," the second young man said. "But there's plenty of grub and stuff up at the village hall, should you need it, and people there to suggest where you might stay if you can't make your own arrangements. This place looks unfit for human habitation to me."

"We haven't decided what we're going to do yet," Tom said. "Thank you for the offer of food. We're going to need that."

"And you're Mr. Katt?"

"Thomas Cyril Katt. Thomas being added on, like. Perhaps the name is German, I don't know. The story goes that my great grandfather came over here from somewhere in Europe."

Again young Parsons blushed. "Don't you worry about that. You're as English as I am."

"I should hope so. I was on the Somme. Do you know what that is?"

"My Dad was there."

"Now we understand each other."

"We're told to advise people," John Parsons said, "to search out their personal papers, family photographs, things like that, if they haven't already done so, and pack them up in a bag, in case a fire breaks out later."

May Harriet thought of where the children's birth certificates were, in a top drawer of her chest of drawers in the bedroom that she shared with her husband. She doubted that they were safe. Everything was such a mess, such a terrible mess.

They all came out from under the table, except Lizzie who remained swathed in blankets. Jim whacked the dust off her toy panda and handed it to her. Alice picked up Jo, wrapping a blanket round her as she held her.

"The kids can sleep in my front room," Alice offered. "There's not much damage, and there's the big table they can get under. Or there's the broom cupboard. Take our pick. We can have a cup of tea and then get them settled, May."

"Thank you, Alice. Much obliged." May clamped her lips together again to stop them trembling visibly. In the front room, in a solid trunk, she had some of the children's clothing, nappies for the little one, a few toys, safe and sound. Thank God for that. For now, they had food and water. There were potatoes in the shed.

"The 'all clear' hasn't gone yet," Tom reminded them. "We could be in for another lot."

"You're quite right there, Mr. Katt," John Parsons said. "Now, if you don't mind, Mr. Langridge, we'll take a look upstairs."

"By all means."

Outside, the night air was cold and fresh, with a smattering of rain.

The two women carried the children the short distance along the brick yard to Alice's back door. By the weak moonlight they could see that a branch from the oak tree that grew behind the wash-house had fallen onto the roof of Alice's part of the wash-house. "Look at that!" Alice said as they passed. "I was hoping we could live in there."

"Perhaps it's all right inside." That was where they did the laundry, where they lit the fires under the coppers to heat the water. May thought of the solid brick interior, the chimney that went up from the copper, the cosy warmth of a carefree, innocent world that had, in the space of a few moments, been taken away from them.

A desire took hold of May to run to the wash-house door, to fling it open to see if her copper was still there, the galvanized bath hanging on the wall, the clothes horses where she hung the laundry to dry on wet days, the tin bowls with the long handles for ladling out the hot water into the sink and washtub. She thought of the big, ungainly mangle through which she ran the washed clothes and bed linen, the small bath under the mangle into which the water ran.

All these things, simple in themselves, but strangely dear to her now, took on a poignancy as she imagined their loss. The mangle, with its two big wooden rollers, had been given to her by her mother. Only the weight of Lizzie in her arms, and the fear of perhaps making a fool of herself in front of Alice, prevented her from running over to the door.

God, how old she felt, with a weariness that would surely never leave her. All that beautiful Victorian furniture, the clocks and pictures, that Jim had brought to their marriage because he was a widower, had made her love their home with a quiet pride and satisfaction. It had made her feel so established. Before the birth of Jo, they had had friends and family to tea often, and she had never been ashamed of her home. Now all that was gone.

Those teas had often been served in the garden on summer days, from a circular table on which a white, delicate cloth billowed gently in the breeze. The days then seemed to be long and pleasantly warm, benign under dappled light. What lovely teas they had been, prepared with anticipation and something approaching joy. She had made water-cress sandwiches, from cress she had gathered herself from a stream where the water was pure and fast flowing, and tomatoes and cucumbers from the garden with the taste of sun upon them, thin bread and butter and gooseberry jam. Always she made two kinds of cake, the dark one, thick with fruit, and the sponge layer-cake with clotted cream and raspberry jam inside. Now she could picture herself pouring the tea into white bone-china cups of a delicate beauty. She could remember the pleasure of seeing her food devoured, her tea drunk with appreciation, the talk turning to world affairs and prognostications about the immediate future as they had taken their ease.

It seemed now as though that had taken place in another world. In those summers of 1934 and 1935, the possibility of another war had not overtly presented itself, although a creeping sensibility of threat was there. Shadows of the first war never left them. As they sipped their tea in the sunlight and squinted out over the lush countryside that surrounded them they could for a while emerge into that light.

Perhaps she was being punished for something, by fate or God. It was difficult to know what God was, what it all meant. The questions that were urgent in the first war had still not been answered; they went round and round in her head. Nonetheless, she prayed for help, to a nameless something.

As a child she went to church twice on a Sunday, under duress, walking a long way, because her father was a lay-preacher at the John Wesley chapel, as well as being a gamekeeper for Lord Calborne. Now she thought of the tedium of it. He had the gift of the gab all right, erudite and intelligent, had written his own sermons, though a modest working man. Religion was rammed down her throat then. Once grown up, she never entered a church. Now the warmth of her child's body against her chest kept her sane, as the presence of her family did when the panic threatened to pull her down, when she felt there was no help from anywhere.

Alice pushed open the back door of number one Bullrush Lane, which shared a common wall with the other house, to reveal a lighted candle in a brass candlestick that stood in the sink of the scullery. A heavy black-out sheet covered the small window.

"Come in, love. We'll see what we can get organized. I've got blankets and pillows under the table. We'll put the kids there for now until I get something organized under the stairs. I wonder what my kids are doing now. I hope to God they're all right."

May knew that Tom's and Alice's two sons, in the RAF, were stationed at Biggin Hill aerodrome, near London, and their daughter, Daisy, was working on a farm somewhere in Kent. Another daughter was working in a hospital, away from home.

"It doesn't bear thinking about," May said.

☙ Chapter 3

In the other house, Tom and Jim stood in the kitchen and smoked another cigarette each while the ARP man and the Home Guard man crunched about upstairs, their weight on the damaged floor sending little clouds of plaster dust into the kitchen and front hall.

Both men longed for a glass of beer; both imagined themselves walking up the road a bit to the village, across the village green, into the old stone pub and ordering a pint. Parts of that pub, an old cross-roads coaching inn, had stood since the 1400s. For all they knew, it might be a pile of rubble at this very moment, although they suspected that the boys upstairs would have said. Both men knew that they would have to make do with water or tea for now.

"Bloody cheek," Tom said, "what he was hinting about with my name."

"Yeah, asking if it was German."

"Perhaps it is, perhaps it isn't. How would I know? All I know is that I'm not one."

"He doesn't mean any harm. Just thoughtless. A callow youth, you might say."

"I do say. I'd like to ask him to roll up his trousers and show us his withered leg."

They could even find some amusement in it. "My old great-grandfather wasn't a Jerry, I bet. They were in the East End of London. Used to come down to Kent for the hop-picking. Some liked it so much they decided to stay. The ones who stayed behind up there won't half be copping it now, as we speak."

Although Jim felt sympathy for the unknown innocents in London under fire, the enormity of his own situation bore down on him. Where were they going to live? He thought of the market gardens and the kitchen gardens where both he and Tom worked, considering whether their jobs were under threat because there might not be anywhere for them to live on the estate. A few days off from work would be needed to clear up this place even superficially. It was not habitable, not safe. Any minute now the beams might give way, the roof cave in. It might not keep the rain out, the cold and snow that were coming.

"You'd better get out as many of your belongings as you can," Tom said, offering Jim one of his fags. "I've heard that people come in and pinch things from bombed houses. You'd hardly credit it, would you? Talk about kicking a dog when it's down. That's part of human nature, I reckon. Depraved, that's what it is, like a lot of other things."

"Yeah. Reckon his Lordship will re-house us?"

"He will if he can. I reckon he's a fair old geezer."

Perhaps he was, Jim thought. One thing was certain, his Lordship would not have to worry about where his next meal was coming from.

Jim knew that Tom was an exceptionally skilled gardener; there wasn't much about growing things that he did not know. But for his strong independent spirit and his hatred of giving orders, he might have been Head Gardener by now. They had both witnessed others giving orders, with seeming nonchalance, definitely with certainty, knowing that those orders would send hundreds of thousands of young men to pointless deaths, to maiming or madness. Neither he nor Tom would ever utter an order for which another man would have to salute or pull a forelock, if only mentally. He did not think it was cowardice or reluctance, a shirking of responsibility; it was a matter of principle, a distaste.

In some ways, Jim thought, *that first war had broken them, in the trenches of the Western Front; in other ways, it had taken away their illusions and made them stronger, those like himself who had got out.*

In the burgeoning French countryside of late summer, as he and his platoon of fifty men had waited behind the lines before the relentless march up to the Front, they could almost have deluded themselves for a while that they were on holiday, those lads who would never in the normal course of their lives have been able to venture outside their own country. Then, when they had started the march on the final leg of the journey up the line, those illusions had gradually been replaced by a reality that had no forgiveness or compassion in it.

Perhaps a person needed some illusions, needed them to stave off a kind of madness that could creep up unannounced.

Shortly after his arrival in the trenches, towards the end of September, 1915, he had seen a man of another section in his platoon throw away his rifle and run, yelling, towards the enemy who were bombarding them with heavy artillery fire. The name of that boy, aged eighteen, whom he had known, was William Partridge, a country boy.

Today he could recall exactly what Will had looked like, the details of his features, the way his soft fair hair had flopped over his forehead, the way his mouth turned up at the corners when he smiled. With that memory were the flashes of gunfire, the intolerable noise. Will Partridge had gone out to meet death, instead of waiting for it to find him. By so doing, he had kept a measure of self-respect, in his bitterness.

His own section of twelve men had hung together.

Now in the shattered house he and Tom Katt stood side by side, smoking silently. He was aware that they had each retreated into their own thoughts, half listening to the clomping above them, the exclamations and swearing. They were holding themselves ready for the heartbreaking task of clearing up, of seeing what could be salvaged.

When they were young in France, he remembered, there had been the fear of death, the reality scarcely comprehensible until it was staring them in the face. They had waited for it to come to them in many guises — a state of affairs that normally afflicted the old and the seriously ill. The world had been turned upside-down, the older generation devouring their young as though in an act of redemption for themselves. He had seen it then as a revelation, knowing himself to be in a trap that was waiting to be sprung.

It was an abnormal state, to be young and limber and to hold oneself in readiness for death, in all the beauty and sweetness of youth. It had been at the same time both real and difficult to imagine, a madness. To defend oneself and one's country was one thing, perhaps a necessary evil; but to go on the offensive, that was quite another.

The sound of the anti-aircraft gun on the hill beyond the village had unleashed emotions that he thought he had succeeded in keeping battened down. He and Tom smoked side by side in the shattered kitchen, both silent in thought.

Army discipline in a war, he knew now and had realized early then, was designed, ultimately, to destroy your individuality so that you would allow yourself to be murdered. On second thoughts, he did not think that "allow" was quite the right word. There had been the possibility of being murdered by your own side for some infraction of self-preservation, which was not sanctioned. That was if the enemy did not get you first.

It was more that you were caught up in events, not told what was happening. As surely as B follows A in the alphabet, you found yourself getting closer and closer to your own death without your explicit consent, until there it was in front of you, then all around you, with no way of escape, as animals that had been bred to be slaughtered came to the slaughter-house and could smell the blood of their own kind.

Here he was now, listening to other guns in another time. He had been through unspeakable madness and had come out the other side, not through any merit on his part that he could see, but by an arbitrary fate.

The hand holding the fag up to his mouth trembled. "What I would give now for a pint of beer," he said.

"Yes. I was thinking the same. Hang on a minute, I've just thought of something. Don't go anywhere."

"I wasn't planning to."

Tom went out smartly through the back door to the yard and presently came back with a large brown glass bottle of cider. "Forgot I had this, until just now." His face was animated.

From a cupboard Jim found two clean cups. They both watched in anticipation as Tom tilted the bottle and the dark golden liquid glugged out into the cups.

"Ah, that's a drop of good, Tom."

They had each drunk three cups of the cider by the time the Home Guard boy showed his face in the kitchen. Both old soldiers now thought of him as a boy. The other boy came in behind him. "This house is not safe," the formerly silent one said.

"Well, blow me down with a feather," Jim said.

"We'll send someone round in the morning to help you clear up, if you like."

"Much obliged, but we'll be all right. Others are worse off who need the help. We'll make a start on it now."

"Where will you sleep?" John Parsons said.

"You think we'll sleep? The all-clear hasn't gone off yet, for one thing. Don't you worry, if we're overcome by drowsiness we'll kip down in the wash-house."

"We should inspect that," the boy said.

"We've already inspected it, don't you worry. It's quite sound."

"Right ho, Mr. Langridge. If the Wigleys can't take you in until his Lordship can find you another place, you let us know sharpish."

"Thanks, mate."

"We'll take them in," Tom said. "Our place is not so bad."

"We'll have to inspect that."

"I thought you might."

"What time did the bomb drop?" John Parsons asked, taking a stub of a pencil from behind his ear and licking it.

"It was half-past eleven," Jim said.

"I lose all track of time in this job, working day and night as I do. Can't remember when I last had a decent sleep of more than three hours at a time."

"As much as that?"

"I don't know whether I'm coming or going."

Parsons wrote slowly in his notebook, balancing it in a cleared space on the wooden draining board next to the sink where there was a candle. "What's the date?" he said, looking up.

"The eleventh of November. It's Armistice Day, in case you didn't know." Jim paused. "Nineteen forty."

∞ **Chapter 4**

May looked around her as they entered Alice's house noting that, as Alice had said, the devastation was not as bad, but none-theless the destruction had entered this house and wrought its changes. Alice went ahead of May into the front sitting room where she had a big, sturdy oak table. In the front hallway they passed the polished oak hat and coat stand, noting that it was thick with dust, and that Tom's brown trilby hat, and all the others, were grey now.

"You settle the kids under that table, May, while I go and make some tea."

"I'll have to stay with them for a bit, to make sure they go off. As for me, I feel I'm never going to be able to sleep again."

"Steady, girl. Steady."

∼ Alice noticed that her hands were shaking as she reached up into a kitchen cupboard for the tea caddy. It must be delayed shock. It took you some time to take in what was really happening to you. There was a smell of plaster dust and smoke. She put a kettle on the Primus. It was steadying to do familiar things. The big brown teapot on the draining board was filthy with dust and its lid was broken. "Damn!"

In a cupboard above the sink was her best black teapot, nice china, with a picture of Queen Victoria painted on it, with lettering that read: "Her Majesty's Diamond Jubilee. Sixty Glorious Years."

There wasn't much point in keeping this teapot for "best," not much point in doing that with anything really. You could never tell when your number was going to be up. From now on, she was going to use the Queen Victoria every day.

As she got the tea ready, she thought of May, who had had the nervous breakdown all those years ago. It had taken some years to come on, but it had come relentlessly, after all the bottling up, the holding on. That's what came of not having anyone to talk to about things, anyone who would understand after it was all over, that last war. For some it was never over.

It had been fortuitous and strange that she and May should have met in the Royal Flying Corps, should have been sent to the same aerodrome in Yorkshire, where they had become friends. It was equally strange that they should have husbands working on the same estate and now be neighbours. Although, when you came to think about it, both their families came from Sussex and Kent, so the chances were high that they would be in the same vicinity when the last war ended. They had simply come back home.

How raw and innocent they had been when they had smiled at each other shyly in Charing Cross station in 1917, both conscious of entering an adventure that only war afforded, of doing their duty for their country. She had been Alice Randall then.

Some weeks or months after the end of that first war they had all been dispersed, the ones who were left, back to a so-called normal world, as though you could switch off your thoughts. They had left the camp forever, to get on trains that carried them down to London.

Only a few at the end had known May's sweetheart from New Jersey, Frederick George Decker, that sweet, laughing, golden boy at the aerodrome near Tadcaster. How vibrant with life he had seemed then. Alice had seen him hug and kiss May before his squadron had taken off for France in those flimsy craft, no protection to flesh and blood. "Goodbye, May. See you soon," he had called as he waved, lovely with his fair hair and blue eyes, handsome in his uniform.

May had stood outside the officers' mess, at the back, where they both worked, to watch his craft taxi away from her, then lift up into the sky.

Later, when bad news of him had come through, May had withdrawn into herself. Quietly she had gone about her work, grieving inwardly.

Of course, no official word came to May; she was only his girl-friend, bound to him by love which was not officially recognized. Only his next of kin could find out. It was only from the magnanimity of Tubby Tubbington, Frederick's friend and squadron buddy, that she had been told. May never saw nor heard from Fred again directly, although his one or two surviving friends told her that he had been shipped back to America. His commanding officer had expressed his regret to her, but had nothing further to add.

Now Alice thought of Frederick, of how he had loved to dance and to thump on the old upright piano in the mess. No wonder May had gone a bit mad.

She spooned tea carefully into the jubilee pot. Thinking of the old queen, long gone, recalled to her mind the tired, stricken face of the present king as they saw his picture in newspapers. A good, genuine man, he seemed to be, rallying the people in his own quiet way, standing among bombed-out buildings in London.

Just as the tea was steeped, May came into the kitchen. "The kids are asleep. I'd pray, if I knew what I was praying to," she said.

"Here's your tea, love," Alice said, handing a cup and saucer to May. "Have a bit of sugar."

"I don't want to take your ration, Alice."

"Don't you worry. I get a bit on the side now and again." They sipped appreciatively, standing side by side. "I was just thinking about Fred Decker, May, and all the other boys. Do you still think about him?"

"Oh, yes. We were living in abnormal times then, as we're living in them now. At that aerodrome in Yorkshire I thought I could have a normal life, that I could have a boyfriend who would perhaps always be with me. We were on the periphery, so we didn't realize. Those boys were sent there to die. We couldn't have them."

"It sounds so pitiful when you say it like that."

"It was pitiful."

The strange thing about love was that it did not go away when its object had gone, as it ought to do if there was any logic in anything. It went on, and on, and on, sometimes getting stronger from absence, eating away at you. In the normal course of events, that love might have weakened and died; now it would never die, its object transformed, unattainable.

Her weaknesses were known to her now. Strong though she might be at times, she could never take that strength for granted, that courage she knew she had; forever she must watch herself. Before she was ready, she had come face to face with the main fact of life — the impersonal and arbitrary nature of the world and its indifference to human life.

"Want another cup, May?"

"In a minute or two. I want to go out to have a quick look at the wash-house, while it's still quiet."

May went outside and into the dark wash-house where she groped on the window sill above the sink for the box of matches and a candle. The blackout material was already up on the window. She partially closed the door, then placed the candle in the sink and lit it. When the door was shut, she looked around the small room in the light that cast many shadows. As far as she could see, everything was as she had left it earlier in the day. In one corner the copper, enclosed in concrete, still gave off a little heat from the embers of fire underneath. The cosy warmth and orderliness of the room soothed her.

The two large clothes-horses, on which she had put sheets and towels to air, were still standing upright. She went over to the mangle and laid her cheek against the wooden rollers that smelled of cleanliness. If she closed her eyes she could almost imagine that the house outside was as it always had been, that everything was all right. But not quite.

She remembered how they had come to take her away, all those years ago, when she had broken down. It was an elderly man, a volunteer, who had driven her away in his own car, and it was the same man who drove her home weeks later. He took her through picturesque places, slowly, perhaps to cheer her. "Ashdown Forest," he said as they drove, "a beautiful place to walk in." Was she any stronger now that she had the children to live for and protect?

~ A faint sound of engines alerted her. Another wave of German bombers was coming over from the south, making for London. She put out the candle quickly and ran across the yard to Alice's back door.

"May! May!" Alice was calling her. "Get in here quick. We're under the stairs."

They were in the broom cupboard under the stairs, Alice and the two kids, with the brooms and other accoutrements removed.

"It's safer in here, I think," she said, as May looked in. She had brought blankets, pillows, and quilts, on which Lizzie was already asleep, curled up, while Jo had her eyes open. At the sight of her mother, she closed them.

May ducked into the cupboard, whispering: "The wash-houses are still intact."

Alice shifted to make room for her. "We'll wait it out," she said. "I have a feeling this is going to go on all night."

"I hope the men are all right."

"What, those two old soldiers? We don't have to worry about them."

May was not so certain. This was a different sort of war, a war against civilians more than anything.

When the planes were overhead, they put their arms around each other. Once you have lost, even for a short time, the integrity of your mind you are forever after living in fear that you will not be able to control an upsurge of emotion, that you will howl and scream when there is nothing to feel but your loss, when there seems no purpose to anything, to life itself. May closed her eyes as those thoughts went through her mind.

The roaring sound was suspended directly overhead, then began to recede. The exhausted children slept through it.

"This is getting monotonous," May said, relief at another escape making her flippant. "We mustn't let it get us down. That's what they want, the Jerries, to wear us down and break us, to break our spirit. It won't take much to break me, I know that."

"You'll do all right, May. I'm going to make more tea now, and get us a bit of bread and jam. You'd better stay here in case the kids decide to get out. There's broken glass." Alice struggled out of the cupboard. "I feel like a bloody mole."

May smiled. "I wish I had your spirit."

"I'm just as churned up inside as everybody else. As I said, you'll do all right. Don't think otherwise. It helps to know that others are worse off."

~ Next door all four men were under the kitchen table. Two abandoned brooms and a dust-pan and brush sat in the middle of the floor from where they had been clearing up. There was a mound of broken glass and crockery on a wad of newspaper.

"I told you we should have left while we had the chance," the boy from ARP said, chastising his colleague.

"What? Be caught out in the open in the van?" Parsons said scathingly. "With no bloody lights!"

"We could have got into a shelter or down in a ditch."

"I think we're safer here for now."

"Perhaps we should take turns with the tin hats," Tom suggested, winking at Jim. "Pass them round, like."

The two boys both gave him withering looks and retreated into silence.

"We're grateful to you," Jim said.

Chapter 5

The clearing up went on after the two young men had departed. Jim and Tom had bass brooms that they used to sweep up the debris. It was heart-breaking work. Neither man said much.

They finished the bottle of cider between them.

Jim could have wept, without much more provocation. You worked hard all your life, slogged away, then in a matter of minutes most of your material possessions could be taken away from you. Perhaps that was why you should not place much value on them.

The loss of the material value was not what made him want to weep. It was that each piece of furniture, each picture and ornament, had his personal history in it, much of it inherited from his mother. In this he saw his past destroyed. Not surprising that some people tired of struggling and, like drowning men, let themselves go under. He was not of that ilk himself, but he understood it.

~ Before too long there came another knock on the front door. Jim opened it to reveal an older man from the Home Guard, who had his helmet squarely on his head and looked deeply exhausted.

"Hello, Jim ... Tom," he said. "I was sorry to hear of your situation here." It was Arthur Pitt, a village man, who worked all day on the railway and then for the Home Guard at night, snatching sleep where he could.

"We're lucky to be alive," Jim said.

"I've come here because I'm looking for able-bodied volunteers to dig in the village," Arthur said. "They copped two hits there, and people are trapped under rubble. It's heavy work."

Jim and Tom looked at each other.

"The days are over when I could wield a pick-axe, I'm afraid, Arthur, to be honest," Tom said. "Or handle shovels full of broken bricks."

"I could come," Jim said, making up his mind quickly. "I'll have to clear it with the missus first. We've got two young kiddies here, next door now."

"I wouldn't ask you if we were not desperate," Arthur said.

"I know."

"I've got a lorry out in the road, though with no lights it might be faster to walk."

Jim went quickly to say goodbye to May.

Jo woke up then and put a hand on her father's jacket sleeve, gripping it tightly. "Dad, tell me a story."

"Well, I have things I must do," he said, taking in the desperation of his child.

"Tell me the one about the spider," Jo said.

"All right," he said, caving in. "Lie down now. Just settle down."

Sometimes he sang the story of the spider. Now he felt less than ever like singing. "Ready? Here we go then: 'A spider tried hard up a wall for to climb. Nine times he tried hard to be mounted, but each time he had a fall. The tenth time he tried without falling, and at last reached the top of the wall. So what is the use of repining, for where there's a will, there's a way, and tomorrow the sun may be shining, although it's been cloudy today'." This story had to be told in a sing-song sort of voice, so that the child would be lulled by it.

Jo lapsed back against her pillow, dreamily quiescent. Jim kissed her. "Go to sleep now."

From the wash-house he got an old raincoat and pulled it on over his jacket. Out in the lane, Arthur Pitt waited for him beside a dilapidated lorry. In the darkness they could see searchlights criss-crossing the night sky, looking for enemy aircraft from a search post beyond the village. "Perhaps it would be better if you walked ahead, Jim, to show me the way, until we get out of this lane."

"Right you are."

It was darker now, the moon behind clouds, and the night was damp and cold. The lane was narrow, with hedges on either side and ditches below the hedges. Although it was paved, there were pot holes. Jim had a torch, which he would use if he had to, the light muffled with a handkerchief. It was a crime to show a light in the blackout. He walked ahead, his cleated boots ringing on the surface of the road, while Arthur drove carefully behind him.

"Left, right, left, right," Jim said to himself. "Left, left, left, right, left." He swung his arms, striding along, his head up. That was how they had marched when they had been in training, all those young men, years ago, until they had got to France, near the battlefields, burdened with heavy kit. There they had stumbled along, heads bowed down, backs feeling as though they would break, exhausted beyond anything they had ever known.

Now he felt an unencumbered freedom, so that he could almost forget the bombed-out house that he had just left and the ones that would meet him in the village. If they were caught out in a raid, they would run ahead of the lorry in case it was hit and the petrol tank exploded, and they would get down in a ditch until it was over. God willing, if they did not receive a direct hit.

At the end of the lane was the bigger road. Jim got into the lorry then, and they moved along towards the village, going as fast as they could without lights. "It's the Pomfrett house and the one next to it that have been hit," Arthur said. "The men have been there digging for some time. The doctor's there. I hope to God they get them out. The mother's in there, and two of the kids."

The village was in darkness apart from two sheltered hurricane lamps where the digging was going on. The house was on the edge of the green, not far from the village hall where women from the Women's Voluntary Service and the Women's Institute worked day and night to provide food and innumerable cups of tea to those in need, as well as first-aid. The hall itself was in darkness, the blackout sheets over the windows.

Jim knew that a bomb shelter had been dug under the village hall, accessible from outside. It was a sort of dug-out, in case the hall received a hit and they had casualties in there.

There was a bomb crater at the front of the Pomfrett house, in the road. "It's round the back where they're digging." Arthur said.

Someone put a shovel into Jim's hand. Instructions were given and received. An ambulance stood nearby. Standing near the rubble was a boy of about twelve, crying. "What's the matter son? Is this your house?" Jim asked.

"Me Mum's missing." He wiped tears and snot on his jacket sleeve. "She's in there. They won't let me help."

"What's your name, son?"

"Charlie Pomfrett."

"Listen, Charlie. You go over there into the village hall and get yourself a cup of cocoa, and keep warm. I'll come over and tell you what's going on, from time to time. It's too cold out here. All right?"

The boy nodded miserably. Jim patted him on the shoulder. "Off you go then, son."

By the inadequate light of the lanterns, he joined the others in digging, soon adding the sound of his laboured breathing to theirs. They were shadowy figures, their jackets cast aside and shirt sleeves rolled up, their breath coming out in clouds as they panted in the cold air. "Whatch'er, mate," and "Hello, Jim," they said to him, not pausing. "Get stuck in."

Some of them he recognized, while some of the younger ones were not known to him. There were ten men, he reckoned, working on the Pomfrett house, while at least an equal number worked on the one nearby.

With their bare hands they shifted beams and other timbers after the bricks had been cleared from them. The woman's husband, Len Pomfrett, was there, panting and sobbing as he worked. "I was out on fire-watching duty," he said to Jim. "I'll never forgive myself if she's dead, and the two kids."

"You weren't to know your place would get hit."

They worked on, sweat pouring from them, even in the increasing cold. The shovelling reminded Jim of the trench digging and repairs that they had done in the last war when his platoon had arrived in the front line. This now was more shovelling, lifting and heaving broken bricks and mortar, flinging it out of the way. Two women brought them tin mugs of very hot, sweet tea.

In time, they made a hole big enough through which someone could crawl, into part of the house that had not immediately collapsed.

"Hello!" Len shouted into it. Silence.

Jim understood that the mother and two children had been downstairs under a table at the back of the house, much as his own family had been. This bomb had fallen closer than the one in Bullrush Lane.

Dr. Crane, who had been talking to the two ambulance drivers, came over to them. "I'm going to go in there," he said. "I have morphine and dressings, if needed.'"

Dr. Crane was in early middle-age, about forty-five, Jim thought, a good man and a good doctor who seemed able to turn his hand to anything of a medical or surgical nature, in a quiet and competent way. Not like some, who did not know what they were about and were sometimes partial to giving overdoses of powerful drugs to their elderly, ill patients, from which those individuals would not wake up.

"I'd rather go in there first myself, sir," Len Pomfrett said.

"I know you would, but it's better if I go, because I'm going to have to get in there anyway," Dr. Crane said. "What I want you to do is try to keep the passage that you've made from caving in. That would be the most useful. I've got a torch, which I'll put on when I get in there."

"Be careful, sir."

"I will." Dr. Crane spoke to the ambulance drivers. 'Be ready.'

On his hands and knees, the doctor disappeared through the hole, with the intention of getting to what had been the kitchen. "Bear to your left, sir," Len Pomfrett called after him.

Quietly, the ambulance men brought up two stretchers and several blankets. Unashamedly, Len wept at the sight of them.

Wanting something to do, Jim got on with clearing more rubble. When the mother and her two children had been brought out, if they were alive, he would go to get the boy Charlie. It would be better if the boy did not see them until they had been tidied up a bit.

In due course, the doctor crawled back out, holding his torch in one hand. "They're alive," he said. "They appear to have lost a lot of blood. They're still under the table, which has partly collapsed on them."

"Thank God," Len said, sobbing with relief.

"I'll need help to get them out," Dr. Crane said calmly, motioning to one of the drivers. "There's only space for one other person. We'll get Jean out first."

"Can't I go, sir?" Len pleaded, desperate to do something.

"No, man. You're better off out here."

They went in again, the ambulance man carrying a rolled up stretcher which consisted of a piece of heavy canvas, with two poles slotted into the sides of it.

Several pairs of hands reached to help with the stretcher when it appeared with the woman on it, the ambulance man crawling backwards, lifting one end as best he could in the confined space.

They laid her on the ground. There was a lot of blood on her face, matted in her hair and she was unconscious. "Jeannie, Jeannie." Len cradled her head and put his cheek against hers.

The other ambulance man attended to her, while his colleague and the doctor went back in for the boys.

When they were all out, Len looked around him, a sorry sight himself with his wife's blood on his face and all over his clothes. "Where in God's name is Charlie? Where the hell is my boy?"

"He's in the hall," Jim said. "Let me get him."

He ran to the village hall, knowing that the ambulance must be leaving very soon with the injured, that Charlie would want to go with them. They would be taken to the hospital in the town, about six miles away.

Charlie was lying on a bench, with a blanket over him, awake. At the sight of Jim he sat up, apprehension dawning.

"Your Mum's been brought out, Charlie, and your brothers. They're alive. Come on, give me your hand."

They ran back out into the cold night.

Jim's last impression of them before the ambulance doors closed was of father and son hunched together with the three stretchers, the father's face daubed with his wife's blood.

"What now?" he said to Arthur Pitt.

"We'll help at the other house. They're just getting people out of there now. So far, we haven't found anyone dead."

Stumbling about in the dark, he made his way with Arthur to the next house. "Watch out for that bloody great crater," Arthur warned. "Put on your torch." They saw smashed fences, uprooted hedges, then the house itself with a large gash in the roof, half the front wall gone. As they got close, a man came out through the shattered wall with a young girl of about ten in his arms. "Give me a hand here," he yelled. "There's another one in there."

Jim clambered forward over a pile of bricks and timbers and took the girl in his arms, while the other man turned back inside. There was blood on the girl's legs and on her face, Jim could see by the faint light of a hurricane lantern as he held her against his chest, yet her eyes were open and she made no sound. In his arms she felt as thin and light as a bird, her head against his shoulder. "Where are you hurt, dearie?" he said. "And what's your name?"

"I've got some cuts on my legs and head, that's all," she said, her eyes staring straight ahead. Jim has seen that expression in the eyes of shell-shocked men. "I'm Anne Clarke."

"I'm going to carry you to the village hall, to the first aid post," he said.

There were women from the Women's Voluntary Service hurrying about. "Should I take her down to the dug-out?" Jim asked one of them.

"Yes, the first-aid people are there."

More from memory than by sight he blundered across the corner of the village green to the first- aid dug-out and bomb shelter at the back of the village hall. "Please, Mister, my dog's still in the house," the girl said. "I don't want him to die. Can you get him out?" She cried then, muffling her face against his shoulder.

"Wait till I get you inside," he said, speaking gently, hoping that he would not have to be the one to tell her the news if the fate of the dog proved not to be good. "Then you can tell me where to find the dog."

"His name's Jock and he's only a pup really."

A tired looking woman in a makeshift uniform, with a Red Cross arm band, showed him where to lay the girl down in the bomb shelter, on a table softened by blankets. "We've got a doctor here," she said. "We'll take care of her."

"Right. Her name's Anne Clarke, and I don't know where her parents are," he said, putting the girl down and covering her with one of the rough, grey army surplus blankets, pulling it up to her colourless face. "Now, dear, where's the dog?"

"He's in a basket under the kitchen table."

"I'll see what I can do," he said.

A terrible anger and pity boiled in him as he made his way back to the bombed house, fixing his eyes on the pale light of a lantern. It was like a scene from hell. Figures bent and swayed as they heaved loaded shovels and spades, silhouetted against jagged, broken walls and gaping windows devoid of glass.

In his left arm and wrist the familiar ache began, from the deformity of the war wound of September 1915, brought on by the extraordinary physical exertion. Instinctively he rested his left arm against his chest and cradled it with his right hand, as he had done then.

At the house he walked straight through the shattered wall, intending to put on his torch once he was inside. "Where you going, mate?" another man intercepted him. "The roof could cave in."

"There's a dog in there, a pup. It's the girl's dog."

The other man grunted and said nothing.

Inside, Jim put on his torch, covering the light with his fingers as he played it over the shambles in front of him, in the sitting room where the ceiling was partially down, revealing large fallen beams blocking the door out of the room. Wallpaper of pale blue flowers and green leaves peeped through the debris here and there where the walls were intact. Matching curtains, still attached to a window frame, hung at an angle as the frame had collapsed. Furniture was smashed or laden down with debris from above.

Most of the houses in the village were of similar design. He reckoned he knew where the kitchen would be. In this case, the door that would lead out to a passage going to the kitchen was partially blocked by the beams, but would most likely open outwards into the passage, if he could get to it.

Sometimes, he thought, *it was an advantage to be short.* Only five feet, five and a half inches tall, but stocky, he could ease himself through spaces where a taller man might have difficulty. That had been an advantage in the trenches of the first war, he thought now. Snipers could not pick you off so easily.

He risked crawling under the crazily angled beams to get to the door which, with some persuasion, opened just wide enough for him to crawl through and to show him by the light of the torch that the passage was littered with masonry.

Then he heard the whimpering of the pup, the first really hopeful thing he had heard that night. Bending down under fallen beams, he traversed the narrow passage and entered the kitchen. The beam of his torch moved over the interior, to show a small table with two of its legs collapsed, up against a wall. It was here that the dog was trapped in its basket, covered with brick dust.

"Come here, mate," Jim said, leaning over to pick it up, a small mongrel that wagged its tail. "Come here, boy." He stuffed it inside his shirt, where he could feel it trembling.

With apprehension he made the return journey, as the damaged house groaned around him like a living thing as though it would shift and crash down on him at any moment. After he stepped through the hole in the exterior wall, he moved away from the house as quickly as possible.

Back at the hall, Jim handed the dog to the same woman with the Red Cross arm band. "Would you give this dog to the girl, Anne Clarke?"

"Oh, she'll be pleased to see him," the woman said. "Well done for getting him out."

Back at the bomb site, he and the others dug and shovelled until all people were out, until they could do no more with basic implements. Then they stood back, breathing heavily, wiping sweat from filthy faces.

Arthur Pitt came up to Jim. "Thanks for your help, Jim. Should I drive you home in the lorry?"

"I'll walk."

"Get some tea first, if you like. If there's anything I can do for you tomorrow, any shifting, I'll have the lorry."

"Thanks."

In the village hall he was plied with tea and sandwiches. Sweat was drying on him now and he was glad of the warmth of the coal stove. He knew most of the women there, but felt disinclined to get into any sort of conversation. The image of Jean's bloodied face was in his mind.

On the road again, walking quickly, it was good to feel the cold air on his temples. Left ... left ... left ... right ... left.

When he got back he would kip down for a while in the wash-house. He felt now that if he did not lie down he would collapse. They kept a small mattress, rolled up, hanging in the wash-house for just such an eventuality, with some army-surplus blankets and a pillow. The thought of that comfort kept him going.

He thought also of Len Pomfrett, a rough-and-ready sort of a bloke, but a good man through and through, who would do anything for you without the expectation of any sort of reward.

Tomorrow he and May would have to think about where they were going to live, clear up what was left of their home. There were things in the garden that they could eat, the Brussels sprouts still clinging to their stalks, gilded by frost some mornings now. It was yet another blow to have to leave that garden over which he had laboured.

For now, all he wanted to do was take off his boots and lie down for what was left of the night in the quiet and comparative warmth of the wash-house. Sleep would be another matter.

∽ Chapter 6

Lord Calborne came the next day in his Daimler, driven by the chauffeur, Reg Wheeler.

It was the latter who made his way to the front door, a door that would not shut properly because the frame had shifted.

"Hello, Jim," Reg said, looking natty in his dark navy blue uniform and peaked cap, fastidiously staying back from the plaster dust that was released around them. "Bloody hard luck, all this."

"You're right there, mate."

All morning he and May had been salvaging their possessions, searching out clothing, household linen, personal papers, bringing things downstairs.

Reg Wheeler jerked his head back when he talked, speaking of "his Lordship." "His nibs here wants to talk to you about where you're going to live," he said, sotto voce. "Sent me to see if you were in."

"Oh, does he!"

Lord Calborne got out of the car. Those who did not know his Lordship might have thought that he was an impoverished person who perhaps bought his outfits from church jumble sales or the garden fêtes of those who could afford to get rid of clothing. But by the obvious quality and cleanliness of his well-worn clothes, the shine on his old creased brogues, put there by someone else, he redeemed himself.

"Good morning, Langridge. What a terrible thing this is," he said, extending a hand for Jim to shake, something which he had never done before, to him or anyone else of the working class that Jim knew of.

Speedily recovering from his surprise, Jim took his hand. It was cold, firm, and very thin.

The exigencies of war had sparked in the old man, evidently, a touch of sympathy as well as a self-interest in the house that was his property, Jim thought sourly, even as he was glad at the same time that his Lordship had come. He wasn't a bad sort, that could be said for him; there was no apparent arrogance in him. Since the death of his wife two years before, who had chivvied him along in his many duties as Lord of the manor, he had become morose and silent according to those servants who worked more closely with him. No doubt, too, his army of servants had been seriously depleted since the outbreak of this war.

He wore the same type of clothes all the year round, more or less, with the addition of a squashed tweed hat and an ancient waterproof cape or trench coat in bad weather. Very occasionally he wore a silk cravat in hot weather, tucked into the open neck of his shirt, a thing which no working man would dare to put on, as it was a badge of the higher orders. All these things passed through Jim's mind as he surreptitiously looked the old man up and down.

They had in common their interest in the land on which they worked, lived, and earned their living, and a love of horses. His Lordship had been known to hold longish conversations with the lower orders about horses, once it was established that they knew what they were talking about. It was the same with dogs. Many dogs of numerous useful breeds raced and gambolled around the spacious gardens of the estate mansion, over the meadows and in the streams.

Jim knew a great deal about diseases of horses, about the treatments of ailments in them. Likewise, he knew about dogs, about mange, canker, worms, and, to a lesser degree, about fits. His Lordship valued a good dog man. Once he rode to hounds but now contented himself with keeping a few fox hounds as pets who might occasionally kill a rat to justify themselves. By all accounts, his heart had not been in the killing of foxes for sport.

"I would like to have a look around, if you don't mind, Langridge," Lord Calborne said, in his frail, breathless, upper-class voice, which made

Jim wonder if he had heart trouble, or something with the lungs. "Just the outside. I won't invade your privacy by going in."

"Just as well, your Lordship," Jim said. "It's not safe."

Lord Calborne looked at him sharply. "But you're in there. We must get you out of there as soon as possible. How is your wife? And the two children?" He prided himself on knowing about wives and children, although of course his dear late wife, Caro, had got it down to a fine art that he could never hope to emulate. At Christmas she had given every child on the estate five shillings as a Christmas box, and put on a party for them.

"They're all right," Jim said. "I'm hoping to get them up to the Wigleys' place later today." He felt awkward talking about his father-in-law's house as though it belonged to the man. Because that too was on the Calborne estate and belonged to his Lordship. It was a beautiful thatched house that stood on the edge of the estate forest, up a lane that afforded complete quiet and privacy.

Lord Calborne stopped in his tracks. "You mean they are still here?" he said, in apparent amazement.

Where else would they be? Jim thought. People like them had little or nothing to fall back on, as the old bloke should know, if he thought about it.

"Yes. I'm waiting to organize some transport, sir."

"Oh, Wheeler will take them. I'll get him on to it straight away after he's taken me home."

"Thank you, sir." Reg Wheeler wouldn't be happy about that, he knew. Jim got a quiet satisfaction from knowing that he himself had more in common with this old aristocrat than did Wheeler, who did nothing but drive around, polish the three cars, worry about getting himself dirty, and concern himself with trying to look and sound posh when he was obviously as common as dirt.

"We'll go round this way, sir,' Jim said, deferentially, not wishing to appear bossy, indicating the path around the side of Tom Katt's house. "There's less damage that way."

"Very well."

They walked around the side of Tom's house, stepping over bits of his fallen chimney. "Is Katt here?" Lord Calborne asked.

"They went down to the village."

At the back they could see the damaged roof and the walls with deep cracks in them, the debris littering the brick yard in front of the wash-house.

"I slept in here last night," Jim said, indicating the wash-house. "It's intact and warm." There had not been much left of the night by the time he had lain down there.

"Oh, dear, this awful war. It's wearing us all down."

There was a Calborne son, Henry, in the army, Jim knew. He wished he could ask after him, but knew it was not his place to do so unless the old man raised it first. There was a deep, deep sadness about Calborne, in his bowed shoulders, his dull eyes, as he mourned his wife from whose loss he would never recover. He was the sort of man who, in certain areas of his life, depended entirely on her. If he were to lose a son now, that would just about finish him off, Jim sensed. How are the mighty fallen.

They walked into the orchard after staring at the house for some time, and came upon a large crater with earth flung up from it, a further blight on this normally peaceful landscape. There was a powerfulness in this terrible fait accompli that took away speech, this invasion. In Jim there was a slow rising up of anger, which he sensed also in his companion.

"A great shame about those two trees," Jim said, referring to two downed apple trees. "That one's a Cox's Orange Pippin and the other's a Russet."

"Yes, indeed."

By mutual, unspoken consent, they tramped around the orchard in the wet grass, soggy leaves, and rotting wind-fall apples, looking at the crater from every angle, while Jim worried about his Lordship's brogues. He himself wore sensible leather boots.

"I shall have to arrange to have this fenced in as soon as possible," Lord Calborne said. "People could be falling in here. In the meantime, Langridge, could you see to it that the gate is kept locked?"

"Certainly, sir." It was as much as he could do to prevent himself from saluting, so ingrained was the habit from the past. Indeed his right hand and arm tingled from the urge to make the gesture so that he was forced to put his hand into his trouser pocket. Ah, his Lordship was a good sort, a decent old bloke, worrying about other people breaking legs and such.

The spirit of noblesse oblige was obviously alive and well in this man; it was second nature to him, and Jim found a grudging respect in himself for it, especially as he well knew those who would not lift a finger to help anyone, who would steal their last penny from them, and kick the dog when it was down.

No, "old Lordy," as he was sometimes called, would not let anyone starve, even though he was so rich himself that he chose to appear poor in some ways from fear of sparking a revolution. Most of his wealth, however, was tied up in land which was never sold. It did not, in fact, so much belong to him as to his family, in perpetuity.

It was ingrained in him never to flaunt his wealth, although the enormous "big house" was there for all to see if they cared to look. Almost all that he had, all that he used, was inherited. To him there was something almost vulgar about buying anything new, especially as quality tended to go down as time went by. Most of the food that he ate was grown on the estate.

His wife, the Lady Caroline Calborne, née Darrington-Hart, had played the part of the Lady Bountiful up to the hilt, so that no one else could have taken her place. She had fulfilled the role with such panache and grace that anyone who had received charity from her felt almost that they were doing her a favour in accepting it, because the pleasure was hers in the giving.

There was an art to giving, Jim thought, and an art to receiving. Only the gauche became huffy and bridled at it. You took what was offered you, graciously, against the day when you might be destitute, even though, badly given, there could be humility and shame in it. All the working people on the estate missed Lady Caroline, "Caro" behind his Lordship's back. The only daughter of the family, Elizabeth, had married and gone elsewhere. They had heard that she was doing useful war-work, a chip off the old block.

When they had walked back behind the houses, Lord Calborne paused. "I have good news for you, Langridge," he said. "And for the Katts. There are those two cottages empty at Badgers Gate where you both could live until I can get these houses repaired."

A surge of something like joy came to Jim, for he knew and liked Badgers Gate, a rural place of beauty, not far away. There were woods where one could gather firewood, fallen branches which could be dragged home and sawn up.

There was no road or lane right up to it, only part-way. Then there was a track up to the houses themselves. Or one could walk over a meadow for the last bit. There was nothing else there, apart from the two joined houses, although there was part of a Roman road nearby. He did not know how the place had received its name. In his mind's eye he could picture the houses, solid, several hundred years old, of mellowed red brick, with hung-tiles on the front and big stone chimneys at the sides. The last time he had seen it, the garden was overgrown, but there were masses of purple lilac in the summer and a weeping willow tree that stood beside a dried-up pond. One could be contented there.

"They are solid and sound," his Lordship said. "I was there myself this morning. They are quite dry and warm. I will get the chimneys swept for you."

"Thank you, Sir. That's a load off my shoulders, and no mistake."

"Of course," the other man said, "they have been condemned as unfit for human habitation, as you perhaps know. But that's only because they have no indoor sanitation or electricity. Otherwise they are perfectly habitable. There is a tap in the front garden, and the usual offices at the bottom of the back garden. The stoves are in good order so I have been assured. Perhaps, Langridge, you would like to go over there this afternoon and take possession. The doors are not locked. And would you please tell Katt?"

"I will do that, sir. Much obliged."

"One hopes it will not be for long. Of course, you know that the cottages don't belong to me. I have made the arrangement with Sir Otto Lind to let me have them for as long as necessary. He graciously consented when I asked."

"That was good of him." Jim tried to keep the sarcasm out of his voice. So Lind had not offered the houses of his own accord.

Neither he nor anyone else he knew liked Lind, a haughty, ungenerous man, who had, it was rumoured, inherited his vast wealth from former slave plantations in the West Indies, in sugar. The land he owned now had not been passed down to him, as had that of Lord Calborne; he had been able to buy it because another old family had died out, the three sons of that family having been killed on the battlefields of the Great War, in Belgium, the Ypres salient. Everyone in the village knew that.

If Lind had been a good man, he would have restored those cottages for use, when there was little spare housing to be had anywhere, when people were living in garden sheds and with in-laws who could not support them or did not want them. He was the sort of man who, had he been in the army in the first war, would have been shot in the back in No-Man's-Land by one of his own men.

Nonetheless, Jim was relieved about the house. It was unlikely that they would set eyes on Sir Otto Lind who, it was known, went up to London several times a week by train. It was assumed that he went there to take care of his vast business interests. Of the two farms on his property, one was run by a foreman and the other was let to a tenant.

Reg Wheeler was polishing the car with a chamois leather which he put out of sight quickly when they reappeared at the front of the house.

"I'll have Wheeler come back for your wife and children at about three o'clock," Lord Calborne said to Jim. "Would that suit you?"

"Yes, sir." He would like to have seen Wheeler's face when his Lordship told him that he was to pick up the wife and children, with sundry bags, and drive them to the Wigleys' place, but it looked as though he was not to have that experience.

The Daimler moved away, sedately, out of view. The old man had been kind.

All the time they had been talking, Jim had felt ashamed that he had not shaved that morning, that he was unwashed, even though he had rescued his razor, the strop, and the shaving soap and mug from the house earlier, and had ventured up the risky stairs to get a change of clothing from the chest of drawers that was still standing. He would shave now. Even in France they had been forced to shave most of the time, using rain water, clean or dirty.

His dirty shirt, weskit and trousers were an irritant to him. Ever a gentleman, Lord Calborne had not once glanced at his body, or even his whiskered chin, had only looked at the upper part of his face, at his eyes, man to man.

That morning at dawn he had got up and filled the copper in the wash-house with water, carrying buckets from the garden tap, had lit a fire underneath it.

May and the children had gone down to the village with Alice and Tom to get food from the shop and to see what they could get from donated food at the village hall. Now that most food was rationed, the garden was vital. If he did not pick the sprouts, someone might steal them.

In the wash-house he took the galvanized tin bath down from its hook on the wall. As well as a shave, he would have a bath, since the bath-room in the house was not safe to use. It was a tedious business, putting many buckets of water into the bath, first cold and then hot from the copper. Emptying it was even more tedious, but it couldn't be helped.

Facing the small mirror that hung in the widow above the sink, he sharpened his razor on the strop, then lathered his face using hot water from the copper.

As he drew the razor delicately and expertly over his chin and upper neck, he thought of the soldier from his platoon, Swifty Blake, who had cut his neck with such a cut-throat razor while shaving when they were on their way up to the Front. He had got what they called a Blighty One as a result, after nearly bleeding to death. It meant that he had to be sent home.

Swifty could have got into terrible trouble, as the men had been instructed to use a safety razor. Swifty claimed later that he had lost his safety razor, or had it stolen.

There had been such a commotion that the platoon sergeant had come running, while those nearby had, by various methods, tried to stem the flow of blood. The sergeant had looked suspiciously at the bleeding man, whose face was very rapidly losing colour. "What the flaming hell's going on here?" he had demanded. When given the facts, he had been beside himself with anger, then had been fearful that one of his men was rapidly bleeding to death in front of his eyes.

By direct pressure, using several field-dressings as padding, they had kept the man alive while four of the others hurried him on a stretcher along the trench to the regimental aid post, a dug-out. Before he went, before he lost consciousness, he managed to gasp out: "If I wanted to get a blighty, or kill myself, Sarge, I wouldn't choose this method."

Jim had been one of the stretcher-bearers for Swifty. In the aid-post, the MO, an exceptionally resourceful man, had stemmed the tide of blood and managed to sew up the artery that had been nicked. He had not asked too many questions. The platoon sergeant, by inventive lying, had managed to change the story so that no blame could be attached to Swifty Blake, while he had the razor spirited away. Nonetheless, Private Blake was considered a liability after that, liable to a sudden leakage of blood if subjected to undue stress, or physical trauma in the vicinity of the neck. In due course, he had recovered and been sent back home, from where the platoon had received a postcard of the seaside in Kent.

Jim found that he could smile at that memory now. How they had envied that postcard.

Lord Calborne gave the instructions to Wheeler about picking up May Langridge and the two children when they were back at Calborne House and the Daimler had been brought to a halt at the front door.

Wheeler managed to control his voice and his features as he said: "Very good, sir."

Calborne let himself in and went straight to his study, shut the door, and from the pocket of his jacket took a letter that had come that morning. Although he had already read it twice, he intended to read it again.

When he had first seen the letter, with its unfamiliar hand-writing, he had had a presentiment that it was from his son's commanding officer, writing to let him know that his son had been killed, a courtesy that was sometimes extended to the next of kin before the official pronouncement arrived. That had not been the case.

There had not been a letter from Henry for some time prior to this, so he had had to console himself with the idea that no news was good news and that his son was being moved around so that his own letters were not getting through to him. The last he had heard, Henry had been in Egypt. Now, it appeared, Henry was actually in England, something which strangely did not bring him much consolation because there seemed something odd about it all. If the letter had been in Henry's handwriting, he would have believed it.

After the retreat from Dunkirk, which had not brought his son home, he had lived with a constant sense of dread. Mental vignettes of his son as a little boy came to him all the time: Henry wading through streams looking for tadpoles to put in a jar; Henry standing in sunlight in the garden, conversing with one of the gardeners about how roses were grown; Henry learning to play the piano. He tried not to be sentimental and maudlin, but the images plagued him.

He read:

My Dear Father, As I cannot write, I am dictating this to one of the nurses where I am in hospital, who is very kindly writing it for me.

I do hope you are well, also Elizabeth and Richard, whom I have not heard from for several weeks. That is not surprising, as I have been moving around a lot.

At this time of writing, I am in a hospital near Southampton, with an expectation of being transferred somewhere inland, perhaps to Cornwall, when I am well enough to travel. As you can imagine, any dock area is not safe these days. So do not write to me here, or telephone. I shall write again very soon.

In North Africa I was wounded slightly in the left leg, which has become infected, and I have since contracted pneumonia. I was flown home in stages, by a circuitous route, as you can imagine, the Mediterranean being impossible.

Do not worry about me, father. I shall be all right and am being looked after very well.
With affection and all good wishes,
Your son, Henry.
P.S.: The nurse's name is Cynthia.

Lord Calborne feared that something was very wrong. If his son had been wounded in the leg, why could he not write? Perhaps he was wounded elsewhere, or was blind. Or perhaps he was so ill with pneumonia, or the leg infection, that he could not make the effort.

That there was no actual address on the letter of a hospital in or near Southampton indicated to him that Henry did not want him to come, to drive down there. That made him want to go all the more. Why should he not go? Or perhaps that information was not being made available to the general public.

So much was secret these days, as though there were spies everywhere. Perhaps there were, he didn't know. Certainly, some people he knew sympathized with the Germans, the Nazis. While he did not think they would stoop to becoming spies, to go against their own country, what did one really know of one's fellow man?

He had heard that Hitler actually had a respect for the English. Perhaps there was a little truth in it, as it appeared that he could have destroyed the larger part of the British Army before it ever got to Dunkirk. What some had called respect could simply have been a loss of nerve. What was happening now, with the blitz, with the terrible slaughter of civilians in London and elsewhere, did not indicate any respect but rather a mad desire to kill and maim as many innocents as possible.

There came a discreet knock on the door of his study, which was then opened to reveal Thwaite, his butler. "Is there anything you require before lunch, sir?"

"A cup of coffee would be very nice, Thwaite. And I don't think I want any lunch today. Would you apologize to Mrs. Leaney if she's got something ready? I'll have tea later and an early dinner."

"Very good, sir."

The butler had been with him for so long and had shared so much with him that he now thought of Thwaite as a friend, a confidant of the utmost integrity in certain things. Of course, he would draw the line at actually telling the man so.

Lord Calborne poured himself a small measure of whisky.

Thwaite made his way to the kitchens. "He doesn't want any lunch today, Agnes," he said to the cook. "He'll have tea at the usual time, then an early dinner."

"That's all right, Harold," Agnes Leaney said. "We'll eat it ourselves. I've got the coffee ready."

Unlike many cooks, Agnes was as thin as a rake and spare with it, had iron grey hair pulled back into a tight bun, covered with a white cap. Around her bony hips her large white apron hung loosely and reached down to her sensible black shoes.

Agnes had once been married, but her young husband, killed in Belgium in the first war, was a ghost-like memory now. Her greatest regret was that there had not been time for her to have a child, for she was at heart a maternal woman. There had never been anyone else to love. She had gone into domestic service at age fourteen at the big house, and had been serving more or less ever since.

Thwaite was back so quickly with the coffee that Lord Calborne knew he had anticipated his needs, as usual. Thwaite poured from the silver pot. "One lump or two, sir?"

"Two. Thank you, Thwaite. Would you mind asking Mr. Clark to come here, in about fifteen minutes."

"Very good, sir."

Thwaite went out quietly. Clark, his Lordship's secretary, would be having his lunch now, in his private room. Felix Clark, a consumptive sort of a bloke, Thwaite thought, had got out of being in the army somehow, by being declared physically unfit. No doubt he had coughed a lot at the time and had more or less starved himself for a few weeks prior to the medical, as he must have seen it coming. Of course, to be generous, and Thwaite thought of himself as a fair man, not given to hasty judgements, Clark might indeed have had tuberculosis as a kid. There had been a lot of it about.

Nonetheless, the other young servants of army age had been taken, leaving the part-time errand boys who were useless, so it seemed incongruous that Felix Clark should be pottering about taking shorthand and typing on a typewriter, getting his meals when he so desired in his private room.

Many other people of the aristocracy who employed secretaries, Thwaite knew, had had to resort to young women, and the rumours of the goings-on behind closed doors were legion.

In spite of his private thoughts about Clark, which he seldom vocalized, he went to Clark's rooms and respectfully passed on his Lordship's message.

⁓ Lord Calborne swallowed the remains of his whisky at a gulp. Not given to drinking much, he knew when he needed it and when he didn't. He carried his cup of coffee over to the tall window that overlooked the part of the garden that he liked best, where the white roses bloomed in the summer. When the window was open at that time of the year, the scent of them blew in to him as he sat at his desk. Now, all was sodden and bare.

He thought of Langridge, as the man had stood in the orchard earlier at the edge of the bomb crater, looking down into it. His face had been quite blank. He himself had known intuitively that Langridge, an intelligent, calm, and stoic man, honest to a fault, had been thinking of France. On the home front in the army himself, in the Great War, he had been too old to serve in France on the front line. It had been a slaughter of the young.

The fear for which he had tried to prepare himself, for which there was no real preparation, was upon him now. Irrational though some of his feelings might be, he had the most awful fear that Henry was dying. A little later, he would go over to the estate chapel, in that quiet place in the garden where his wife lay. There he would kneel in all humility and ask that his son's life be spared. Not knowing what he believed in beyond the reality of human life and nature, he yet believed in something, a nameless thing, that he sometimes thought of in his inner being as the Divine, as the Quakers did.

At this moment, he must think about what he had to do, then make arrangements. By the time Felix Clark came in, he would have decided.

Clark knocked and came in, as instructed, carrying a notebook and fountain pen. "You wanted me, Sir?"

"Yes, Felix." Sometimes he called Clark by his Christian name, as the man was in something of an anomalous situation in the servant hierarchy, neither here nor there, you might say, neither fish nor fowl. "Please sit."

He himself paced up and down.

"I've had a letter from Henry," he said. "At least, it appears to be from Henry. It's written from a hospital, by a nurse, apparently." Gradually, he was becoming able to convince himself that the letter was indeed from Henry; it was his terse style, and the postscript telling him that the nurse's name was Cynthia was pure Henry. No doubt she would be very pretty, probably besotted with him, as he was good-looking and had a rare natural charm.

Earlier, he could not seem to believe that Henry might actually be in England, not too far away, in fact, because he had thought of him for so long as being far away in the most terrible danger.

"What I want you to do, Clark, is this ...' Lord Calborne stopped his pacing and stood in front of Felix Clark, so that Felix hastily uncapped his fountain pen and opened the notebook. "Henry is in a hospital near Southampton, I don't know exactly where. It will be your job to find out. It will most likely be a military hospital in a requisitioned building, a school, or such like. Perhaps a public school, although I don't know of any likely places thereabout."

Felix Clark made a few notes, mainly to distract himself and to look business-like. Was that really in his line of work? What an awful job, like looking for the proverbial needle in the proverbial haystack. "Very good, sir. I'll do my best."

Clark refrained from making any personal remark then about his Lordship's son; it was not his place to do so. He had only seen Master Henry a few times, in his army uniform. He had seemed a pleasant sort, and of course Felix was very glad that he was in England, apparently safe. With all the bombing that was going on in the south of England he might not be much safer here than he had been in North Africa.

"Get to it, man," Lord Calborne said. "There is some urgency, as Henry thinks he might be moved farther inland soon, where it's safer, or even to Cornwall. You are relieved of all other duties. I'll get Cecily to help me until this is over. If I can get her, that is. I heard from her father that she's doing war-work locally."

"Very good, sir," Felix said again. Cecily, Miss Cecily to him, was the daughter of a former major who lived nearby. She came to Calborne House sometimes when there was a lot of work of a clerical nature. She was beautiful and tended to flirt with him. For his part, he would develop a slow burn and sometimes grin. One good thing to come out of this was that he would be able to stand next to Cecily for short periods as she sat at a table while he handed over some of the surplus work to her.

Cecily, he thought, had designs on Master Henry and would no doubt be overjoyed that he was back in the country. Unless he had been mutilated, of course. Cecily was not the sort of young woman who would saddle herself with anything other than a perfect specimen of manhood.

Such thoughts made him even more sympathetic to the old man, so he ventured a comment as he made his departure. "I'll get on to it immediately, sir, and may I say how glad I am that Master Henry is over here."

His Lordship nodded, an expression passing over his face that could only be described as bleak.

Back in his own work room, Felix shut the door and walked over to the window, giving himself a few moments of respite, not knowing how he might start the search. He wasn't a detective. Working with books, papers, accounts, writing in notebooks in his beautiful handwriting, keeping records, were what he did best. Those things were removed from the hurly-burly of the outside world, the war most of all, for which he was grateful.

If Master Henry had wanted himself to be found, surely he would have said so. Not knowing what was in the letter, he could only speculate. It was possible that Henry had been mutilated, perhaps about the face, and did not want his father or anyone else to see him yet.

Feeling restless and distressed, not having slept much the previous night from all the enemy activity overhead, Felix rang imperiously for

Thwaite. Let the man take away his lunch things and bring him some coffee. Although he felt sorry for Thwaite, with all the work he had to do, Felix nonetheless felt the burden of his own tasks that involved working closely with his Lordship in the running of the estate, even if it was just on the clerical side. Now he had this extra task.

With the younger servants gone to the war, the footmen and such, and the maids leaving to do war-work, Felix knew that Thwaite was running around like the proverbial flea in a fit, trying to do it all. Agnes Leaney, a good sort, was doing the same, while the old battle-axe of a housekeeper, Mrs. Taylor — never married, was becoming more infirm with each passing week and spent most of her time in her quarters. No doubt she would soon depart for unknown places, where life-long servants who did not have any family went. Somehow the household was muddling through.

Perhaps he would have to relinquish some of his war work, the fire-watching that he did in his spare time in the town of Burnham. For that, he was required to sit up in a cold church tower, or some such, and look out for fires started by bombs which he then had to report to the Fire Brigade. Spare time was becoming less and less, if he wanted to sleep at all.

"You called, Mr. Clark?"

Felix knew that Thwaite, a well-mannered man, was not given much to sarcasm, yet he detected in the other man's speech a very slight emphasis on the "Mister"; after all, he could have gone down to the servants' hall next to the big, sprawling kitchens for his coffee, which he often did, instead of making Thwaite tramp up the stairs.

"Sorry, Thwaite," he said. "I'm in a bit of a state. Would you mind getting somebody to bring me a cup of coffee." He did not actually know whether there was a "somebody" any more to run around the house with food, as he had heard rumours that the scullery maid, the last of the maids, had taken herself off to work in a munitions factory.

"Could I possibly be of help with anything, Mr. Clark?" Thwaite was genuinely concerned.

"Well ... please keep this confidential ... Master Henry appears to be back in England, probably in a hospital near Southampton, wounded.

His Lordship wants me to find out exactly where he is, so that he can go to see him. I'm not sure how I'm to go about that. It will be military information, I assume."

Thwaite's face had lit up at the mention of Master Henry, whom he adored. "Well," he said, thinking, "you could perhaps make a start by looking in the Southampton telephone directory for the biggest civilian hospital there, phoning them and asking where the military hospitals are. Even if they've been evacuated themselves, they'll have someone answering the phone, I should think, and they'll still have Casualty Departments. They would know."

"That's out of our area," Felix said. "Where am I going to lay my hands on a Southampton telephone directory?"

"I'll get you one, never fear."

"Thank you, Thwaite. I'd be very grateful."

"I'll bring that coffee at once, Mr. Clark." This time there was no emphasis on the "Mister". "Would you like a cup or a pot?" Thwaite allowed himself a rare smile at Felix Clark.

"Oh, a pot would be wonderful. I feel so much better for having talked to you. I was that worried."

When Thwaite had departed, Felix wondered whether he should have told the man about Master Henry, but then he knew that Thwaite was very discreet. If he had not been, he would have got the sack long ago and would not have been able to carry on in his career as a butler. Of course, he knew that Thwaite would tell Agnes Leaney — they were like an old married couple — but it would go no further with her.

Already he was feeling somewhat more at ease with the task that confronted him. A military hospital would perhaps not allow him, a mere civilian, to make enquiries, even though he was the secretary of Lord Calborne. Someone could pass information on to the Jerries and then they could bomb the hospital. There were spies everywhere. He would have to be very, very careful, and very tactful. When he was ready, when he had the telephone numbers, he would ring Southampton, put on his posh voice, and make a few genteel enquiries.

When the coffee came, brought by Thwaite himself, it was in a silver pot, and on the tray was a plate with four rare biscuits on a doily.

They were the type he liked, with sugar coating on them. As he took the tray, with a sincere "thank you," he reckoned that the biscuits were those sent down specially from London for his Lordship, from Harrods, or Fortnum & Mason.

Thwaite departed, carrying the used lunch tray. Back in the kitchen he thought about Felix Clark, warming somewhat to the other man. In these times of day and night bombing, which brought with them unremitting anxiety and irritability, as well as stark fear, there were few reserves of strength in anyone, he reflected. All the more reason that it was up to each individual to make a concentrated effort to let the best of themselves come to the fore, to be patient and kind with others.

~ His Lordship went to the gun room at the back of the house, near the door that went out to the stone cobbled yard where the horses were brought when he wanted to ride. He seldom rode now, all the grooms, bar one, having gone to the war. The one who was left, Walters, was old and bow-legged, too old to gallop about on horseback, although he could still feed and groom the horses. Sometimes a girl came to muck out the stables and exercise the horses.

Two of the dogs came up to him from the passage outside the gun room and sniffed his hands. "Not this time," he said to them.

Calborne put on his trench coat, the squashed tweed hat, and ferreted out a pair of Wellington boots. The place was becoming disorganized and dirty, the rows of riding boots unpolished. To one side was the gun cupboard which he always kept locked, the key hidden in his study.

He left the house unnoticed, to walk to the chapel. The weather was cold and blustery now, with a drizzling rain falling. It suited his mood perfectly. In his pocket he had the heavy iron key of the chapel door. The gardeners kept the chapel clean and relatively warm, put flowers on the windowsills and by the stone plaques embedded in the floor, commemorating the dead, with his wife's name among them. All the dead who rested there were encased in stone coffins in the crypt, which was entered by steps and a door from outside the main body of the chapel, so that inside the place of worship one could put the dead out of mind, when that was possible.

The narrow path to the chapel, once well-tended, was muddy and becoming overgrown. The thick oak door, reinforced with iron, was kept well oiled, so that it swung open with ease.

By Caro's engraved plaque there stood a vase of magnificent copper-coloured chrysanthemums that had been grown in the gardens on the estate. Sometimes he sat on a chair and talked to Caro, imagining what she would have said in reply. This time, he simply knelt down and touched a hand to the polished granite which held her name. Today he was here for Henry.

He took off his hat and knelt on one of the steps in front of the modest altar, bowing his head. "Lord, in thy infinite mercy and compassion, look with favour upon my son and spare his life. Forgive me my weaknesses and give me strength."

In that private place, he allowed himself to weep.

✆ Chapter 7

May Harriet lay on the floor under the big table of her parents' sitting room at The Stables, her two children with her, one on either side. Although she was dog-tired and it was one o'clock in the morning on the night after the bombing, she could not sleep. She thought of all sorts of things and people, including Jean Pomfrett and her two boys. Word had not filtered back to them to say whether they were alive or dead. Jim had described the scene for her, so she felt as though she had been there; the images were in her mind.

She thought of her favourite brother, Will, in his late thirties, married, who had joined the RAF, ground crew, and had been sent up to Iceland as a mechanic working on aeroplanes. From there he had sent home a photograph of eight of the mechanics in their uniforms. On the back he had written: "Me and some of the scruffs." They were grinning at the camera and all had fags in their mouths. Perhaps he would be safe up there.

In the house were her parents, Edward Wigley and Harriet, together with her miserable brother, Cedric, who, at age forty-one, was too old to be living at home. The army medical had not passed him as healthy enough to serve.

Jim had stayed behind at their house, sleeping in the wash-house so that he could prevent theft from the house, because neither door would shut properly, let alone lock. It was awful to think that some people would steal from bombed houses, but there it was. It was human nature, she supposed.

Alice and Tom Katt had been advised to go to the bomb-shelter in the village for the night, the one that had been built for the school-children in a field just beside the school playground. It was a squat brick building, with a flat roof, no windows and no doors as per normal, only an angled passage through which no light could show.

Earlier in the day Jim had paid a visit to the cottages at Badgers Gate with Tom, and declared them satisfactory. She was relieved that they would soon have a roof over their heads. But she dreaded the amount of work that lay before her, with no bathroom or indoor lavatory, only a midden at the bottom of the garden, no piped water in the house, and no electricity. Although this, her parents' house, did not have those things either, she had got used to having them herself. Her parents' house had a well outside the back door, one of those old-fashioned wells with a chain and a bucket that you had to wind a long way down to reach the water. It was a pretty house, altogether lovely, and required almost constant work in one way or another, heavy work. One must be thankful for safety, for what one had.

This room, this house, were known to her intimately. Now she let her mind wander around the room, seeing the pair of orange and white Staffordshire china dogs on the high mantelpiece above the cast-iron Victorian fireplace with its ornamental ceramic tile surround. Her father's gun rack was above them, where he kept two shotguns required for his work as game-keeper on the Calborne estate. There were other ornaments, the shepherd and shepherdess, that she loved.

Above the oak bureau there was an oil painting, dark and in need of cleaning, of Little Red-Riding-Hood, just her head and shoulders, and the face of the wolf with his teeth showing and his tongue lolling out. The girl in the picture had a Victorian face, large, beautiful eyes with a slightly fearful expression, and a cupid's bow mouth.

There was a chaise longue and other Victorian furniture, cushions, other pictures, ornaments. On the opposite wall was a small framed pencil drawing, a side-view portrait, entitled "Henry Irving as Dante." She had always supposed, but never asked, that long ago her parents had gone up to London to see the actor at the Lyceum Theatre.

Already tonight there had been three waves of bombers coming over, accompanied by the sirens going in the village, the anti-aircraft gun booming in the distance, then the planes of the RAF. They felt a little removed here, even though the house could not have been much more than two miles from the village. It was sheltered by the trees of the forest that grew up close to the house.

Tomorrow she would go back to her own house, with the kids, to clean, sort, and pack. The cottage at Badgers Gate would have to be cleaned too, before they could get a lorry from somewhere to take their belongings, along with the damaged and broken furniture, to the new house. Arthur Pitt had said he would help.

The one consolation on the horizon was that Alice and Tom Katt would still be next to them. They could go together, she and Alice, when they had time, to the Women's Institute to help in some small way with war-work, even if it only meant making sandwiches for the Home Guard men.

She must have slept at last because all at once there was her mother bending over her offering her a cup of tea. Her mother, seventy now, was grey and worn. "I'm going to fry some eggs and bread in a minute," her mother said. "And boil some eggs for the kiddies." They kept chickens, so had fresh eggs.

The kids got up and started to run about, while May rummaged in her bags of clothing to get clean things for them all to wear. Jim would come up later with a pram for the children, and they would all walk the two miles back to Bullrush Lane to carry on the work. She felt ill at ease here, worrying that the kids would disturb her parents' settled life and invoke the bad-temper of Cedric when he came home from work. There wasn't enough room for all of them. It was difficult to get hot water to wash with, or find privacy. When she got back to her wash-house she would give the kids a bath in the old galvanized tin bath.

Cedric had not always been mean-spirited, May thought. Something had happened to him, perhaps from being too much alone, perhaps from the anxiety of the war. At one time he had had girlfriends, yet had somehow missed the opportunity to marry, perhaps from a lack of confidence. Most of the time now she disliked him, yet knew that she still loved him as a brother in some strange way. One could not sever emotional ties easily.

Lizzie stood in her grandmother's kitchen, her wet nappy swathing around her knees. It was held to her bodice by two safety pins, one on either side. Because she had been running up and down the cold passage to the back door, her bare legs and feet were mottled blue with cold. Chilblains prickled on some of her toes.

The kitchen itself with its big cast-iron range was warm. Lizzie liked the kitchen.

"Where are your socks?" her granny said, busily frying things on the stove.

Her grandfather came in then, from outside. Seeing her, he picked her up and swung her above his head and held her there so that she could look down into his upturned face, which she did with adoration because she loved him and he loved her.

He was short and spare, with not an ounce of fat on him. On work days he wore a waistcoat that he called a weskit, over his striped shirt, a cloth cap, his work trousers and leather gaiters above boots that came up to his knees. On cold days like this, he had a jacket.

"Hello, Moggy!" he said. "How's my Moggy?"

Lizzie laughed, not knowing why he called her Moggy.

May came in and took her. "Come on, you've got to get dressed. Then Dad's coming to take us home."

"Hello, May," Grand-dad said. "Did you sleep?"

As Lizzie watched, May put up her face for a kiss and he kissed her on the cheek. "A bit," she said.

Grand-dad sat at the table and started to eat his breakfast. "We're getting used to that anti-aircraft gun," he said.

Lizzie went with her mother down into the larder where they could have some privacy — a cold room, two steps down from the passage, where milk and meat were kept — and there she was dressed.

"Oh, look at those chilblains!" her mother said. "Don't you take your socks off."

From where they were, Lizzie could hear Granny and Grand-dad talking in the kitchen. She heard them say the word "Hitler" a lot.

When they came out of the larder into the passage, Jim came through the back door, muffled in his heavy overcoat and cloth cap. "I've come to get you," he said. "I've got the pram."

The weather was raw now, May thought, as a blast of cold air came in with him, and they had not been able to have a fire in the bombed out house because the chimney was down . The kids would have to play in the wash-house while she and Jim sorted out the house.

"We haven't had breakfast yet," May said to Jim, sitting down with the two kids at the table, while Jim and his father-in-law stood in the centre of the room and talked about the war, the bombings in the village, the high price of things, when it all might end.

Then Grand-dad put on his jacket and said that he had to go out to his vegetable garden to pick what was left of the vegetables before the frost destroyed them.

"Want a cup of tea, Jim?" Granny asked, as she stood in front of the fire, her face flushed with heat.

"Oh, I would. It's raw today." They could hear the wind roaring in the chimney.

Before long, they put on their warm outdoor clothes and prepared to depart. "I'm cooking a rabbit stew later on," Granny said. "So you can have your dinner here, if you want to."

May hugged and kissed her mother. "Thank you, Mum. I don't know what time we'll be back. There's so much to do."

"I wish I had the strength to help you."

When they were in the passage, preparing to leave, Cedric came in from outside. May knew that he went into the forest to cut firewood early in the morning, then came home to have breakfast. On the Calborne estate he had an isolated job, clearing and cutting wood. May speculated again that the isolation was why he was rather odd, always thinking that people were out to do him down.

It wasn't normal to be alone for so long; then when he came home he had only his parents for company, she thought. With those girl-friends in the past he seemed never to have arrived at the point of asking one of them to marry him.

Perhaps he was too mean to marry, May speculated again, as she looked at her brother, muffled up in his outdoor clothing, his face red from the cold wind. Living with his parents was perhaps too easy, with his mother cooking for him and washing his clothes.

Lizzie did not like Uncle Ced, because he liked to tease her, would make fun of her when she was running around padded up with towelling nappies. He would squat down to her level, put his face near hers and say: "Knickerbockers, knickerbockers, knickerbockers." She did not know what he meant, only sensed that he was not a benign man in some ways and knew instinctively that it was not appropriate for a grown man to tease a child. Jo did not come in for his teasing, because he favoured her, while it was Grand-dad who loved her, Lizzie.

As they stood there in the passage, Cedric, without a word, took off his coat and unwound his long scarf, hung them on the wall hooks in the passage. Lizzie, in her mother's arms, looked at him as he looked at them, unsmiling, as though they were not related to him in any way.

"What are you lot doing here?" he said. "Sponging on us?"

Granny straightened up from where she had been bending over the stove. Lizzie saw that she put her hands on her hips and opened her mouth as though she would speak. Once, Lizzie had seen Granny slap Uncle Ced around the face with a wet dish-rag.

"Sponging?" Jim said. "What do you mean by 'sponging'? We've been bombed out." Cedric had not offered to help them clear up the devastated house. At that moment Jim felt anger as though it were choking him, and an awful kind of bleakness. Some of those who should be for them were against them. Not that he had expected anything at all from Cedric. In adversity, you soon found out what people were really like.

"You know what I mean," Cedric said as he turned to look at them. "We haven't got money or food to look after you lot."

"You are not speaking for me, or for your father," his mother said.

Going on instinct and spurred by his anger, Jim lifted his right hand and slapped Cedric hard on the face. "Come outside and say that, you filthy toe-rag," he said.

Cedric's head jerked sideways, and he fell back against the wall.

"You flaming coward," Jim said. "Come out and fight. Too young for the last war, and not fit for this one. How did you get out of that?

Other men have died for you in their hundreds of thousands, so that you can stand there and tell me we're sponging on you. Rivers of blood have flowed to keep you safe over here. Young boys have been blown to bits so that people like you did not have to fight on this soil."

Both men were breathing heavily. Lizzie was frightened in case Uncle Ced would hurt her Dad.

Jim opened the back door and bundled Cedric out into the cold. Although he was too old to get into a fight, and he knew it, his despair and anger drove him on so that there was no decision to be made; his body seemed to be acting of its own accord as he drew back his right fist and hit Ced full on the jaw. Although his age was against him, he had the benefit of training in unarmed combat, albeit over twenty-five years ago.

His injured left hand and arm from the shrapnel wound rendered his left hand useless for punching, so he followed up his advantage with another blow to Ced's chest with his right fist. They pummelled each other, fell to the grass beside the well.

Lizzie looked on, seeing the two men rolling over and over on the grass.

"Stop it! Stop it!" Granny shouted at the two men, flailing at them uselessly with a dish cloth.

May felt as though she had been struck dumb, as the two men grunted and punched each other before her eyes.

"For God's sake, May," Granny said, taking Lizzie from her, "go and get your father. He's over in the kitchen garden. Be quick about it."

May, as though waking up, ran round the side of the house, with the intention of going across the lane to the front of the house to find her father in the large garden that he had carved out for himself in the field opposite.

Once round the side of the house, she slowed to a walk. Her heart was beating fast from shame at her brother and she wished she could disown him, as she often did. Yet there was a regret in her, a sense of mourning for what he might have been in different circumstances.

She would be in no hurry to get her Dad, because she had come to the realization that it was time Cedric got a punch or two in the "kisser," as the local boys said of a fight. She felt confident that Jim would prevail, even though he had only one good hand for fighting.

Panting from the short run, she reached the lane. What an awful thing for her kids to have to witness. This war was such a strain on everyone; they rose to anger quickly; they lost control. She opened the gate from the lane to the fenced garden from where she could see her father digging on the far side.

There was a narrow, neat cinder path all the way round the edge of the garden, which had also been put there by her father. Everything he did was done with an economical expertise, wresting a living from the land, in a quiet, unassuming way.

As she walked slowly along the path, she felt the security of his life-knowledge drawing her in. That was one of the things that had attracted her about Jim too, she saw now, the quality that both men had of never being at a loss. From somewhere inside them they tapped into an infinite well of common sense.

"Dad, Mum sent me to get you," May announced, feeling child-like again, "because Ced and Jim are having a fight."

Edward Wigley put down his spade and brushed soil off his hands by rubbing them together. "What about?"

"Ced said we were sponging on you."

"Oh, did he! Come on, Jock," he called to his little brown and white terrier. "We'll sort this out."

In no great hurry, he picked up a birch gardening broom, one he had made himself, and walked along the cinder path to the gate, with Jock bouncing about between him and May.

Still taking his time, he walked along the side of the house. Jock ran ahead, his alarmed barking heralding their approach. Jim and Ced were circling each other on the patch of grass beside the well, fists clenched, bending at the knees, both gasping for breath. May thought they looked like two old-fashioned pugilists that you saw in old photographs.

The dog went wild, yapping, running round and round them. Both men had blood on their faces. May felt sick to see it.

Edward Wigley, gamekeeper and lay preacher, God bless his soul, May thought, took a swing at the backside of his son, using the twigged end of the birch broom, landing him a blow. "Lay off!" he shouted. "Lay off this minute!" The dog circled in closer, baring its teeth.

Ced swung round, his red and bloodied face ugly with temper, while May stood rigid on the other side of the well, and Granny, holding Lizzie, looked through the kitchen window.

"Give me that broom!" Ced shouted, grabbing the handle with both hands, trying to pull it from his father's hands.

Edward Wigley, although seventy-two and small, held on to the broom with amazing dignity. "Let go," he said quietly. "If you as much as lay a finger on me, you are out of this house. You can pack your bags and get out. This is my house. And I will never want to see you again. I'm ashamed of you, and you ought to be ashamed of yourself."

There were no sounds other than heavy breathing, a wind in the tree-tops, and the excited snorting and galloping of the terrier who was lunging now at Ced's ankles. May could see that the dog was confused, although its major loyalty was to her father.

"Let's behave like civilized human beings," Edward Wigley said. "When we're in a war, fighting for our lives, we don't want to have disagreements at home. We have to hang together and cooperate."

Cedric capitulated all at once, turned and ran into the house. As the others stood silently, they could hear him blundering up the stairs and then heard the slam of a bedroom door.

Jim dabbed at the cuts on his face, and the dribble of blood from his nose, with a handkerchief.

"Are you all right?" May said, faint with relief.

Jim nodded, his swollen lips pressed tightly together.

"I'm ashamed of him, Jim,' Edward said, coming over to Jim, "truly ashamed. Sometimes I wonder how I could have produced such a son, so different from the others. You'd better come in and have another cup of tea and let Mother see to those cuts."

Granny had already made more tea. May poured it out for all of them, feeling chilled to the bone. Before long, Jim was seated in a chair, his face tilted up, eyes closed, while granny bathed his face with warm water and dabbed iodine on the cuts.

May brought the pram into the passage to warm the blankets by the fire for a few minutes, then while she drank the tea, she settled the two children in the pram under the hood. It was drizzling now, and she put the waterproof covering over the other part.

The kids were silent, staring out at their father who had brown blotches of iodine on his face. Granny, under his instructions, put little bits of cigarette paper on the more recalcitrant cuts that would not stop oozing blood, as he did when he cut himself shaving.

"Dad," May said, "can Ced get at those guns?"

"He can get at those guns, but not at the ammunition. I keep it locked up."

"Perhaps he could get it from somewhere else. I'm frightened."

"I'll lock up the guns," her father said. "He's a coward at heart, you know. He's not a criminal, May."

"Coward or no coward, I'm frightened." Although she said that, in another way she wanted to go up the stairs and speak to Cedric, to say that they forgave him. It was unnatural and unwise to let resentments fester, to develop into full scale feuds, for then you often got to a point where you could not see your way back to something more reasonable.

She watched while her Dad took off his cloth cap, hung it on a coat hook in the passage, and scratched his thick, iron-grey hair. "I think Cedric will be all right," he said, "once he's calmed down. But if he isn't, I can always get in the police to talk to him. A warning would be enough to settle him down, I should think."

May thought of the middle-aged and tired constable who lived in the village and rode slowly around on a bicycle, who would most likely react after an event, not see it coming. If only her brother Will were here, sweet William, intelligent and sensible. It was very strange that two brothers could be so different.

~ It was a relief to be walking back to their own house, wrecked though it was, just as it was a relief to be going through the familiar motions of pushing the children in the pram. Even the rain gently pattering on their faces was calming.

On the main road she and Jim walked quickly, side by side, close but not touching. May did not look at his face because she did not want to see the tense despair that she knew was there, that he would be trying to hide from her. Like her, he would be wishing that she did not have to stay at The Stables; he did not have to say it out loud. They could not speak; events had outstripped any superlatives of speech.

Back at Bullrush Lane, Jim opened the door of the wash-house with the heavy iron key, where they were met by a wave of warm air. "I lit the fire before I left, and filled the copper," he said. May looked round with relief to see that he had also brought in the Primus, a small, rough table and three wooden chairs, as well as all the food that had been in the kitchen, some crockery and cutlery, pots, and the big black frying pan.

"Well, it's looking very nice," she said. "It's lovely and warm. Have you seen Alice and Tom?"

"I saw them really early. They were going to go over to Badgers Gate to clean their place and to take over some bedding. I've asked Arthur Pitt if he could come tomorrow with his lorry to help us shift some things, then come the next day as well."

They had to get out, of course they did, but she dreaded leaving this house. Jim had put two of their big wooden trunks out in the yard between the back door and the wash-house, and they were being rained on now. "You can put the clothes from the chests-of-drawers in those," he said. "I've dragged the chests-of-drawers out onto the landing, because it's safer. Be careful, anyway. I'll stay with the kids while you go and get some of your things. I'll find an oil-skin sheet to put over the trunks."

"Have you seen anything of the cat?"

"No. He's alive, that's all I know. He'll be all right."

The back door was open a bit, wide enough to admit a cat. May pushed it open wider and called out, "Puss, puss, puss."

Just when she thought there was no hope for the cat, he rushed out from the ruined interior and came over to her. How sweet and beautiful he was, she thought, with his fluffy grey coat and yellow eyes. She squatted down, putting out a hand to him.

"Greysuit, you poor old boy. We didn't feed you, did we? We didn't give you anything."

Greysuit rubbed against her knees. When he began to purr rustily, as though he had got out of the habit, she let the tears come. "You poor, poor old boy. Come in where it's warm."

With the cat safely in the wash-house, May went upstairs to bring down armfuls of clothing, bed linen and towels, from the chests on the landing, testing each step as she went, as the floor groaned and creaked under her weight. Cold air and rain were coming in through the roof here and there where tiles were off and beams had fallen.

From the airing cupboard beside the kitchen range she took out all the remaining linen. She knew that Jim had turned off the water supply at the mains and emptied out all the water pipes.

Back and forth she went, filling up the trunks as the rain drizzled down on her. Later, she would bathe the children, do some washing, wash herself, and cook vegetables on the Primus for dinner. They had potatoes and carrots in the shed, a tin of dried milk and one of dried eggs, as well as condensed milk, some treacle, bread, and Symington's soup squares on which you had to pour boiling water to make soup. They were, she thought, made of tomato flavoured corn flour. Jim had been up to the village hall to get a bag of food, mostly local produce and some home-made bread, fish-paste in a small jar, and some jam.

They would be all right. They were lucky to have a sink and cold-water tap in the wash-house.

Later in the day, Edward Wigley came to them, having walked from The Stables. "I've come to help you walk back with the children, May," he said, "so that you won't have to come back, Jim. You don't have to worry about Cedric. I've told him to sleep in the hut in the woods until you've moved out. We'll take his food up there to him."

"I'm grateful, Dad," May said. There was a substantial hut in the forest where the men who worked there could shelter from bad weather, warm themselves with a cast-iron stove, and rest. "I was dreading seeing him. I know we'll get over it; we'll be all right eventually."

"He'll apologize, if I have anything to do with it," her father said.

Chapter 8

J im remained in the wash-house with the cat when the others departed. He spread out his bed again on the floor. The place was warm and steamy from the hot water in the copper that was almost at boiling point. Clothes were hanging on the clotheshorses, the crockery was washed and dried. All was neat and tidy.

When he had gone up to the White Horse, the pub in the village of Fernden, a bit earlier, he had found the atmosphere tense. There was some bomb damage in there from the night before, broken glass and furniture. People came and went hurriedly. They downed their beer, as he did, and left, holding themselves in readiness for the air-raid siren to go off, to go to their duties.

Women, in uniform and out of it, were purposefully crossing the village green to get to the hall and the bomb-shelter underneath it, for their evening and night duties in first aid and other endeavours.

Jim had put the blackout cloth up over the small window of the wash-house to keep any light from showing, had lit a candle. The dark November evenings were depressing now, cold. There were the embers of a fire under the copper, giving off a red glow, which he would allow to go out, as smoke might be visible to the enemy.

Before going to bed himself, he would take a turn around the two houses to make sure that all was well. He intended to sleep with the upper part of his body under the small table that he had brought into the wash-house. It would not offer much protection if another bomb fell, but it was better than nothing. It had the effect of making one feel safer, like the rest holes, or "funk holes," as some of the men had called them in the first war, when they had to try to sleep in the trenches. You had the upper part of your body in a hole in the side of the trench, the one facing the enemy, while your legs stuck out for anyone to trip over as they walked by. Again, it made you feel better, gave you a sense of security, even though it was a false sense. With it had been the fear of being buried alive, if there was a direct hit on the trench above.

With the old raincoat on, and a torch in his pocket, Jim let himself out to walk around the houses, being quiet about it. The night raids had not started yet. Very soon they would come, the waves of bombers, heralded by the siren, making for London. The RAF boys would be going out too, thundering low overhead, to try to bomb the airfields in France. He had read that they had been taken over by the Jerries as bases for raids across the channel. *Bloody Jerries.*

Quietly he stood there listening and thinking, hearing the soft pattering of rain on the brick yard and on the wash-house roof. There was a scent of wet leaves, of cold freshness, a faint odour of rotting apples, and every now and then a whiff of smoke from the wash-house chimney.

From the time of the fight with Cedric he had felt very sober and low in spirits, almost in despair, yet with a certain satisfaction that he had had the guts to do what he had wanted to do for a long time. Yes, those punches had been very satisfying, he had to admit that. The stinging of the cuts on his face when he applied fresh iodine informed him that he still had a fair chance of defending himself, if he had to. He had had to do what he did. What could the future hold, when you seemed to be taking one step forward and two back all the time?

Slowly he walked round the side of Tom's house, as silently as the metal cleats on his boots would allow. Although his tiredness weighed him down, he felt the alertness that he had known in France, coming up to the Front. Once there, in the firing line, he had looked through a metal slit in the sand bags of the trench, out into No-Man's-Land. His rifle had been at the ready, a reassuring heaviness in his hands, as he had watched the pale flares shooting into the sky from the enemy lines nearby, illuminating the waste-land of shell holes and craters, the heaped bodies of the dead that could not be brought in.

Sometimes when he had looked out, there had been a few jagged tree stumps here and there, like broken teeth in a punched-in mouth. It had been a crime then to fall asleep while on sentry duty, punishable by being shot. That had not been a difficulty for him, for he could imagine the German sentry, his opposite number, watching for him to reveal his position, to give himself away.

Now, in 1940, in a different war, he was aware of the crater in the orchard on home ground, a travesty. The flower gardens at the front of the houses were dormant now, the rose bushes bare. In spring and early summer the fuchsia bush would bloom, with its drooping crimson and purple flowers, the lupines would come, the antirrhinums, the peonies, Solomon's Purse, the poppies, London Pride, love-lies-bleeding, the corn flowers, love-in-a-mist, *centurea montana* with its strange, ragged blue flowers, the montbretia. That was how he liked a flower garden to be, a profusion of different types and colours, all put in close together so that the weeds did not stand a chance. All those things he loved.

They would plant nasturtiums that would climb up over the hedge, with their subtle yellow, orange and red flowers brightening the green of the hawthorn. In the orchard there would be apple and pear blossom, the most ephemeral of all blossoms, he thought. Soon his garden would be trampled down by workmen repairing the stricken houses. With luck, it would regenerate.

Looking back, as he often did, he could not for the life of him recreate his own state of mind at the time all those years ago when he had joined up for the army in the first war. It was impossible to know now exactly what he had been thinking, why he had volunteered in October, 1914, apart from a vague idea of adventure and that he had wanted to do his duty by his country. Better that, than wait to be conscripted as it turned out. Yet now, in this new war, he had a greater insight into what he must have been thinking, because now there was a different and a greater desperation, a sense of evil that came, he thought, from the deliberate murder of civilians. The tentacles of that evil were moving now into his own land.

All of them, the young men of 1914, had had a completely false impression, or no impression at all, to speak of, about what it would be like at the battlefront. How could they have known? It was beyond imagination.

They should have been informed by common sense, he could see now. If he had waited for conscription he would perhaps have been too old, although he remembered a man of sixty-one in his regiment being at the front. In a very vague way, he had had an idea that he would represent his family even though they were not in the habit of thinking that way. It was more about a diffuse sense of duty and doing the right thing. That had not lasted very long once the action had started.

From a distance of twenty-odd years he could see his idealism, his naiveté, how they had been exploited, and how it had been all for a gross mistake. Easy now, of course, to say that. Standing in his own garden, that was not his own, he felt the depression and creeping hopelessness in the face of intransigent evil. One must not give way to that, because that was the beginning of the defeat that started in the mind.

He thought of the three medals that he had been given, one of sterling silver which he had had to sell later to make ends meet.

↬ As he stood there in the quiet night, there was a faint sound from inside his house. The front door was open about six inches, which was as far as it would close, being prevented from swinging open farther by several bricks propped against it on the inside.

When he walked up to the door, pushed it open abruptly, to surprise whoever was inside, he risked putting on the torch, shining it into the devastated interior. The place was better now for having been cleared up, yet the shock of confronting that devastation again constricted his chest and throat.

"Who goes there?" he shouted out, moving inside and playing the light up the stairs, over the hanging banister, back to the hall, into the broom cupboard under the stairs, into the front sitting room, then through to the living room cum kitchen at the far end of the front hall. Perhaps there was a cat in here, a stray dog, or a fox.

A dark figure ran out from a corner of the kitchen, where the Welsh dresser stood, where he and May had packed up their crockery into wooden boxes. The beam from the torch lit the man up as he dashed out through the scullery and the back door into the yard, then turned right.

"Hey!" Jim shouted.

The man looked familiar, but not enough that he could identify him by name. He played the torch over the boxes of crockery which looked as though they had been tampered with.

Seeing the man turn right, Jim had made an educated guess that he would cut through the orchard to get back to the village, rather than risk going round the front of the house where he might run into him. Even though the orchard gate was closed and locked with a chain and padlock, someone could climb over it. There was not enough light for him to see the bomb crater and, unless he had seen it earlier or had received word where the bomb had come down, he might fall into it.

Serves him right, if he did, for he was the lowest of the low, on a par with Cedric. People like him hated to be identified, hated having their deeds brought into the light of day for all to see. Like trench rats, fat and obscene, gorged on the flesh of dead men, they preferred to scuttle around in the dark.

Taking his time, he went towards the orchard. Before long, he knew that his surmise had been correct, as he heard scrabbling coming from the hole, which had sloped sides and would most likely not cause a man to break a leg.

With a handkerchief over his torch, he went up to the edge of the crater, then put the full beam of light on the man inside.

"Well, if it isn't Georgie Tanner," he said, recognizing the youngish man, whom he had seen earlier in the White Horse pub, the only one who had been sitting down to drink his pint of beer, while the other men present had stood about, ready to leave quickly. Jim knew Tanner to be unemployed, that he had got out of being in the forces because he had, appropriately, a lazy eye and couldn't shoot straight. A fixture in the village and in the pub in particular, he was known as work-shy.

"So you're here, Tanner, helping yourself to a few things," Jim said. standing near the lip of the crater, looking down. "Well, I'm going to get the constable, and if you can get out of here before he comes, good luck to you, but if you can't, you can take the consequences."

He had no intention of getting the constable, who had enough on his plate, but he would report this to him tomorrow. Georgie Tanner should not be allowed to think that he could get away with it.

Tanner reminded Jim of a water rat climbing up the bank of a river, but without the agility. The incongruity of the scene hit him and he began to laugh. The man grasped the crumbling sides of the crater and tried to get a foothold to get himself up. There was a little water in the bottom, so very soon Tanner was slathered in mud. The indignity was punishment enough.

Jim went on laughing, bending double, holding his right side where he had a rupture.

As though on cue, the air-raid siren started up, soon blaring out over the fields and the village.

"You can stew in your own juice," Jim shouted to the man below him, who was now unrecognizable. "If you show your face around here again, I won't be responsible for the consequences. And don't you count on lightning not striking in the same place twice."

"Don't leave me here!" Tanner said, speaking for the first time.

Still smiling, Jim made a dash for the wash-house, where he found the cat already under the table, on his makeshift bed.

"Hello, old chap," he crooned to the cat. "We're going to stick it out together." From a can of milk that he had stood in a bowl of cold water to prevent it from going sour, he poured a measure in a saucer for Greysuit.

It occurred to him that, if another bomb fell nearby, damaging the wash-house, and if he were still alive, he could be scalded by many gallons of very hot water cascading out of the copper. *Well, you took your chances where you were; there was nothing else for you to do.*

It was very unlikely that Georgie Tanner would not be able to get out of the crater; in a sheer funk, he would clamber out somehow. Because of his muddy state, Tanner would have to enter the village to get to his house by a circuitous route under the raid by enemy bombers. He could not risk showing himself and raising questions. Ah, it was good to have a laugh. That one would keep him going for some time.

He put out the candle in case a glimmer of light was showing under the door. It was a good thing that a branch of a tree had come down on the roof, not damaging it much, as it acted as camouflage. By the light of the embers under the copper he crawled beneath the table and lit a fag, pulling deeply on it, his knees drawn up, remembering how he had

had to be very careful about lighting up in the trenches and how matches had been in short supply. It was best to light more than one fag from
every match.

The cat crawled under his uplifted knees. With his free hand, Jim
stroked its head. There was no purring in the cat tonight; the roar overhead was inexplicable to it.

To him, the noise, his crouched position, the fag tucked into the palm
of his hand, the fear, the crater of revealed earth in the orchard recalled
more than ever the past so that the first and last wars blended into a
continuum in his mind, as though there had been no respite.

Underneath the din of the invading aircraft, he could hear that the
anti-aircraft gun had started up, with a deep and evil sound. Boom boom!
Boom boom! Boom boom! He wondered if it was having any effect, or
was like a pea-shooter against a pigeon.

Bile was in his throat and the remnants of the food that he had
eaten. Convulsive swallowing kept it down. He felt the urge to urinate
and for his bowels to empty. With his right hand, the good one, he
reached for the warmth and softness of the cat, who lay in unnatural
stillness in its shelter under his knees. Beneath his hand he could feel
the rapid fluttering of its heart.

May and the kids would be safer, sheltered by the dense conifers of
the Calborne forest. In spirit he was with them. As for Cedric, he had
no thoughts for him, one way or another, sheltering there in the forest
hut. When you faced death, you wondered who would mourn you. Perhaps Cedric, who might not be mourned much, would be in the safest
position of all. Granny might recall with some tenderness how she had
held him in her arms.

Georgie Tanner would be running home now, he expected, a man
of mud, running from tree to tree to find some sort of shelter. That was
the nearest he would come to a battlefield, the contemptible little shit.

To distract himself, Jim took out his cigarette papers and the tin of
tobacco to roll a couple of fags. Sometimes he only wanted two or three
puffs, for which it was more economical to roll his own.

Two bombs fell then, in quick succession, in the village, or on the
far side, as far as he could gauge the distance. The bile filled his mouth

again, so that he had to spit it out into a bowl. Too close. Too bloody close by half. Why were they bothering to bomb a country village? Only a perverse mind would do that. It could be that the RAF were on to them, in which case they might have to dump some of their load. He thought he had few illusions about human nature, yet still he believed in goodness, for he had seen it where least expected, together with courage.

In London now the sirens would be screaming, people would be running towards shelters, to underground stations, if they were not already in them, coming like rats from shattered homes, because they had nowhere else to live. The docks would be burning, the city would be burning, filling the sky with red, and the anti-aircraft guns would be spitting out their shells into the night sky where searchlights crossed and enemy planes released their cargo. Jim felt for them, those people, with an all-pervading mourning.

Later, he would go up to the village to see what he could do.

Chapter 9

Felix Clark found the military hospital near Southampton. At that, his satisfaction and relief had brimmed over.

They would not tell him, however, whether Captain Henry Calborne was there. They would, they said, only speak to his father, Lord Calborne, which indicated to Felix that Master Henry was indeed there.

"I'll inform his Lordship immediately," he had said. "He will contact you. Thank you so much."

He had been shunted through several people, then had asked to be put through to the Matron. In a very dignified and posh voice, she had informed him that she would be pleased to talk to Lord Calborne any time, if he cared to telephone her directly in her office.

Felix could imitate such a voice if he concentrated hard. He had a talent for it, which he exercised now while he wrote down her personal telephone number.

After giving himself time to calm down — felt pleased with himself, yet sweating with nerves, he brushed his hair, straightened his tie, dabbed a little 4711 Eau de Cologne on the insides of his wrists, and made his way to his Lordship's study.

It was part of his nature to be nervous, he thought, yet he did not know exactly where it came from. Orphaned at an early age, he had been brought up by an aunt, his mother's sister, who loved him devotedly. Childless, unmarried, she had lavished all her maternal feelings on him. There had been few men in his life, and now he felt ill at ease with swashbuckling masculinity which he saw as a sham. People were people, whatever their sex. Lord Calborne, with his quiet good manners, his propensity to understatement, his calmness, suited Felix perfectly.

Felix knocked.

"Come in."

"Good morning, sir. I am almost certain that I have found the military hospital where Master Henry is, but they won't give me the information and insist on talking to you personally. The Matron, that is, sir."

His Lordship looked at the piece of paper on which Felix had written the address of the hospital, together with various telephone numbers. "The hospital is well outside Southampton, sir, so it should be reasonably safe. In peacetime it's a boarding school, but the children have been evacuated."

"Well done, Felix," Lord Calborne said. He gazed out of the window at the bare rose bushes that were being whipped by the wind, to give Felix time to blush with pleasure and to get over it. "Of course, Southampton is being bombed these days. I wouldn't consider it safe. Henry said in his letter that he might be moved to Cornwall soon, which is why I want to see him as soon as possible."

"Yes, sir."

Calborne turned back to the room and walked over to his desk. "As soon as I've ascertained that it is the right place, I'll make arrangements to go there. I'll motor down with Wheeler. Perhaps the Matron would be willing to put us up for a night or two."

"Yes," Felix said, venturing an opinion. "You certainly wouldn't want to be driving back in the blackout, sir, in unknown territory."

"No, indeed."

When Felix left, Calborne sat for a while at his desk, considering what he should do.

It had been on the 10th June this year that Mussolini had brought Italy into the war and had moved troops to Libya, threatening Egypt and the relatively few British soldiers who were there to defend it. Vastly outnumbered and cut off from their supplies via the Mediterranean, they had seemed for a while in a precarious position. Henry had been in that place, at Mersa Matruh, near the coast, from where they had conducted raids on the Italian outposts in the desert. He was with a tank corps.

Letters had come fairly regularly at one time. Henry had explained that Mersa Matruh was about one hundred and twenty miles from the Libyan border and some two hundred miles from the Nile Delta. His letters were censored, so he could not say a great deal, but what he did say was amazing — about the desert, the heat and that he did not think the Italians wanted to be at war. It had been thrust upon them.

Names came to Lord Calborne then, from the Great War — Joffre, Foch, Falkenhayn, Ludendorf — particularly Joffre, who had moved hundreds of thousands of French soldiers about, like pawns on a chessboard, to positions of certain slaughter. Then there had been Haig of the British Army doing the same thing, after Sir John French.

One had to defend oneself, of course, but to send young men on the offensive, flesh and blood against machine guns and heavy artillery was more than madness, it was evil incarnate.

A heaviness came over him when he thought about that war. A glass of whisky was appropriate now — well diluted with soda.

~ He made the telephone call to the hospital, asking to be put through to Matron.

"Oh, Lord Calborne," she said, speaking slowly, very dignified, he thought. "I was expecting to hear from you. Your son is here."

"Can you tell me about his condition?"

Her very slight hesitation renewed his fear. "He's making good progress," she said, without giving anything away. "I've arranged for you to be put through to the Chief Medical Officer, Major Hall."

"Thank you. If I were to come down to visit my son, would you be able to accommodate me for a night or two, and my chauffeur?"

"I'm sure we could. We have several rooms put aside for the purpose."

The Medical Officer sounded a little abrupt, but not unkindly. "Well, Lord Calborne, I won't beat about the bush. Your son has been very seriously ill from a leg wound, from a machine-gun bullet. He developed a serious infection that went to the bone. The desert heat, you know, and not being able to get good medical care soon enough."

"I see." Calborne had not felt such fear since the time Henry had fallen out of a tree at age thirteen and briefly lost consciousness. "Is he expected to recover?"

"In my considered opinion, yes. But it was touch-and-go for a while. Those bone infections, once they get a hold, are very hard to shift. And, of course, his general condition was not particularly good when he arrived here. Very run-down, you know."

"I see. How was he brought home?"

"Well, they took him to a hospital in Alexandria, of course, initially. When the infection set in, in a serious way, and seeing as the Mediterranean was out of our hands, it was decided that he should be sent home. They managed to fly him to Gibraltar, where he was very lucky to be put on a ship that was heading for England, at Southampton."

"Thank God for that."

"Yes, indeed."

"Could I come to see him?"

"Yes. There is one other thing. He's blind, I'm afraid, so you must try to prepare yourself for that. However, it is, I believe, a psychological blindness. There appears to be nothing whatsoever wrong with his eyes. As for his brain, he does not seem to have sustained brain damage."

Lord Calborne found that he had lost his voice.

"I have confidence," the doctor went on, "that the blindness will resolve itself in due course. The sooner we can get him away to a place where he cannot hear enemy aircraft dropping bombs, the better."

"Yes." Lord Calborne managed that word. Clearing his throat, he went on. "I'm thinking of coming down to visit him, perhaps tomorrow."

"By all means, do come. I think he would like that, although he was initially apprehensive about letting you know of the blindness."

"I got that impression, because he said nothing about it in a very recent letter, not written by him, of course."

"When you are here, come to see me."

"I will. Thank you."

For a long time Lord Calborne sat at his desk, sipping the remains of the whisky and soda and thinking that his intuition had served him well. The image of Henry blind was very painful to him. At the same time, gratitude that his life had been spared brought with it its own peace.

Thwaite knocked on the study door and came in. "I've laid the table for your lunch in the morning room, sir."

"I'll be there in a few minutes. Thank you, Thwaite."

He liked to have lunch in the morning room, instead of in the big, cold dining room. The latter was magnificent at Christmas time or at the New Year, or when they had guests, when both fireplaces were blazing. For everyday use he much preferred the smaller morning room where Thwaite would light a fire and serve his lunch on a small cherry-wood drop-leaf table, from where he could look out at a different aspect of the garden.

"Would you tell Wheeler that I would like to see him in my study after lunch?"

"Certainly, sir."

"I'm thinking of leaving for Southampton tomorrow, and I may be there for two or three days."

"Very good, sir."

Thwaite felt an uplift of something like joy. The visit seemed to signify that Master Henry was all right and would perhaps be coming home on leave before too long. He said nothing and kept his face impassive. After lunch he would prepare his Lordship's wardrobe for the journey, then pack the suitcases, as his Lordship no longer had a personal valet.

There seemed to be no personal loyalty these days, for the footmen and valet had joined the RAF or the army, as volunteers, as though they could not wait to embrace change and a different employment.

As he walked away, Thwaite conceded that he too, had he been much younger, would no doubt have embraced a new kind of life. Being honest, he had to admit that he had not been immune to twinges of envy as the younger men had departed the big house, with no evidence whatsoever of nostalgia in their demeanour. The same had been the case with the young women and girls, who had departed with what had appeared to him a quiet sense of purpose and relief.

Arthur Pitt arrived as promised with the lorry that was for the use of the Home Guard for the duration, to move the Langridge family to Badgers Gate. He would also take some things for Alice and Tom Katt.

Lord Calborne had kept his promise to have the chimneys swept and the cottages cleaned up.

May was happy as she sat in the cab of the lorry with Jo and Lizzie, and Jim in the back with their belongings, as it bumped down the lane, then over a track in a meadow towards the cottages. Some of what they had in the back were poor, broken things. At last they could be settled for a while and she would not have to go back to The Stables until the unpleasantness with Cedric had blown over. No doubt her father would force Cedric to apologize to her and Jim eventually, and they would make efforts to repair the rift.

Alice Katt came out of the second cottage when they drove up.

"Hello, May! Hello, Jim!" she called. "I got a fire going for you in your range, and a fire under the copper." She reached up and lifted Jo down, then Lizzie.

"Hello, Alice," Jo piped up, looking sweet in her red wool coat and matching bonnet.

"Hello, dearie."

"That was good of you, Alice, to get the fires going," May said. "The house must have been cold."

"It was, but it doesn't take much to warm it up. I can keep an eye on the children while you're moving things in."

The children, at last released from the constraints of being in someone else's home, ran around the wet garden. They had their rubber boots on, hats, gloves and scarves against the raw November day. Round and round they went, in the rough lawn at the side of the house that was enclosed by tall, thick hawthorn hedges, the leaves gone now.

Through the hedge they could see the meadow beyond, which sloped gently downhill to a stream. In the hedge there was a climbing stile that they could use to get into the meadow, which was called the water meadow because it flooded when there was heavy rain. Lizzie and Jo stared over the stile into a new country.

"There's a quince tree by that stile," Alice said, pointing.

"Oh, a quince tree!" May said. "We can make quince jam, if we're still here when the fruit's ripe."

"Where's Tom?" Jim asked.

"He had to go to work," Alice said. "His Lordship's greenhouses are getting neglected, so he said. He's gone to keep the heat on."

Since the bombing, the head gardener, Bill Green, had been holding the fort by himself, May knew. Tomorrow Jim would have to go back to work in the market and kitchen gardens, and she would be left to sort out the house and look after the children. Alice would be there for company until she had to do her stint of war work in the village.

At least once a week May would go up to the Women's Institute in the village hall, where she would take part in the "make do and mend" drive to repair second-hand clothes that had been collected for those in need.

Jim, with Arthur, began to unload their damaged and undamaged furniture and other belongings. He felt contented that they would soon have an intact roof over their heads. Already he was planning what he would do with the dormant garden to prepare it for spring, even if they were no longer there themselves when it was time to plant.

At the bottom of the garden there was a brick midden, near to the climbing stile and the quince tree. Earlier, Jim had looked at the midden to make sure that it was serviceable. The large bucket was still there, the lavatory seat, of smooth wood, clean. It had a thick wooden lid over it, where one could sit to meditate, to escape, to listen to the wind in the trees, to read. There was even a small bucket on the floor, partially filled with soil, to be sprinkled in the larger bucket. The door to the midden was solid; it shut securely and there was a bolt. A ventilation brick let in fresh air near the sloped roof, and air blew through a two-inch gap under the door.

One of the first things May did in the living room of the house was to put the large, old black kettle on the range to heat water for tea. "It was good of you to light the fires," she said again.

"Well, it's such a raw day," Alice said, shifting things about. "What can I do for you, May?"

"Well, duck, if you can find a table cloth, in that bag, we can put it on the table as soon as the men bring it in. There are cups in that box," she said, pointing. "If we get that set up, the place will look lived in."

"Right you are, love."

The men shuffled by them, carrying a chest of drawers. "Where do you want this, May?" Arthur asked.

"In that room there," May said, indicating a small room that was off the main living room, which would be a bedroom all the time the bombing went on. "Could we have the table next, if you don't mind, Arthur?"

One entered the old house directly into the living room, the room with the kitchen range, an all-purpose room. It had a window looking out to the front garden. With the other small room off it, and the scullery at the back of the house, that was all that there was to the ground floor. At the top of a narrow staircase there was a bedroom with a second small room beyond it. The old house was sound and dry. The atmosphere of the house was welcoming, May thought. If there were ghosts here, they were contented spirits.

Before long, the men had the table in, having twisted it this way and that to ease it through the door.

"This will do," May said, looking at the fire with satisfaction, and at the tea cloth that Alice had spread over the old oak table they had sheltered under when the bomb had fallen. After tea she would put the dark golden chenille cloth over the table to hide its plainness.

Jim came in with a box of books under one arm and the bamboo what-not in the other hand, which he deposited in a corner.

The books, May thought, would keep the children occupied. They liked looking through the *Book of Knowledge*, at the pictures. Her big, old dictionary that she referred to often was on the top.

Alice rummaged through a box and put out cups, saucers, a jug and a sugar basin.

"There's a teapot in there," May said. "We've lost quite a lot of crockery. I'll make some cocoa for the kids; we've got enough milk."

"It's going to take some getting used to," Alice remarked, as she poured milk into a small jug that had a motif of violets on it, "having to go outside to get water in this weather, to have to heat up water on the stove for washing up or keep the copper going all the time."

"Yes, it's back to the past all right. Still, we must be thankful that we have a roof over our heads, a place to call our own. And we have the knowledge, Alice, we know how to do it."

"You're right there."

The kettle began to sing on the cast-iron range, as the flames roared in the chimney, both soothing sounds, the sounds of home. May poured a little hot water into the teapot that Alice had unearthed from the newspaper wrappings in the box.

"One good thing, there's plenty of firewood here," Alice remarked. "You just walk into the wood opposite and find a branch that's blown down, pull it back home and saw it up."

"We'll be all right," May said. There would be a lot of work, she could see that, but she knew how to live without modern conveniences. One got used to it. There was an art to doing without things, an art to being poor. There were different types of poverty; she had never been brutalized by it, as she could imagine one might be in a city slum.

Here, to a certain extent, one could live off the land. They were surrounded by natural beauty, the rolling green meadows, the hedges, the woods, birds, wild animals, flowers. There was a weeping willow in the garden, where there had once been a pond. At the side of the house there were masses of lilac bushes that would be alive with bees when the blossoms were giving off their evocative scent.

Never did she take that beauty for granted, for it constantly surprised her, could jolt her out of any self-pity, even though it brought with it reminders of mortality, of time passing. In her youth the sheer beauty of nature had highlighted her loss. When she was tempted to dwell on the discordant note that none of it belonged to her, she understood that essentially it belonged to no one. Lord Calborne would die as surely as she would, as would Sir Otto Lind who had only lent them the use of the house because he had been asked by the old aristocrat, a better man than he was in every way. The world belonged to the Divine, whatever that was. The idea brought a certain peace.

Yes, this would do.

In another box she found the tea, Brooke Bond, and spooned some into the teapot. When the kettle boiled, she poured water onto the tea leaves, a comforting action.

"Tea's up," Alice said to the two men, who were just depositing the sofa, shaped like a chaise longue, against a wall of the living room. Its brocaded cover was dulled now by ingrained dust from the bombing, although May had brushed it with a stiff-bristled hand brush.

"Ah, that's what I like to hear," Arthur said. "I'll just get a couple of chairs from the lorry."

The kids rushed in, breathless and ruddy of face. May eased off Lizzie's muddy boots. "There's cocoa for you two," she said.

"And how are you, my duck?" Alice said to Lizzie. "All right?"

Lizzie nodded, shy.

As they drank their tea, standing up, the men talked about the bombing in the village.

"Rabbits," Lizzie said, in a lull. "Where's rabbits?" In the other house they had been in the shed.

"In the lorry," May said. "There's no shed here. We'll have to put them in a place where the foxes can't get them. We'll have to keep the cat in, too, until he gets used to this place." The two big grey rabbits, the Flemish Giants, were meant to be eaten at some point, but had become pets. As far as May knew, they would go on being pets.

"I'll have to build a shed," Jim said.

"This place hasn't been lived in for quite a while," Arthur remarked.

"Condemned," Alice said.

"Where's cat?" Lizzie asked. Those animals were at the centre of her life.

"He's in the lorry and all," Arthur said. "We'll bring him in; he'll be getting pretty chilly."

"Put him by the fire,'" May said. The cat was in a wooden box with a wire-netting front over the door.

After tea Jim's gardening tools and the rabbits in their hutch were put at one end of the big scullery at the back.

~ As Jim and May lay in the big iron-framed bed that night, in the small side room off the living room, he stared in wakefulness at the unfamiliar ceiling, part of which was sloped, as they were under the staircase. The bed was covered with the big eiderdown and the patchwork quilt that May had sewn.

May was sleeping, the deepness of her breaths attesting to the level of her exhaustion. The children were again under the table, a few yards away, with the chenille cloth hanging down the sides so that they could pretend they were in a tent.

In this house, the bombers sounded farther away, a little, as it was at a greater distance from the village. The familiar siren had gone off; the raids had begun. They had heard the low-flying aircraft of the RAF, trying to intercept the bombers, driving off the fighter planes, or flying out to France and Germany. Now he felt himself straining to hear them coming, their own boys, from the aerodromes in Kent. It was surprising that they had any fighter planes left, after the attacks on the aerodromes.

∞ Chapter 10

Reg Wheeler drove the Daimler sedately through the wet, blustery countryside of lowering skies, heading south-west towards Southampton, going first towards Haywards Heath in Sussex. His Lordship muffled up in a camel hair overcoat, a scarf and tweed hat, sat silently in the back.

They were not used to going such long distances since there was little petrol to be had. Reg had cans of petrol and a food hamper in the boot, the latter prepared by Thwaite and Agnes Leaney. They had made up a separate pack of food for him. In addition, his Lordship had a decanter of whisky in a padded box with a handle, especially for travelling.

After this journey, they would have to be very careful about using the car. They might have to resort to a pony and trap around the village. Somehow his Lordship had managed to get his hands on enough petrol to get them to their destination and back.

Reg had studied maps carefully so that he could avoid Southampton. Between himself, Felix Clark, and his Lordship, they had planned the journey, which would take them several days as they could not drive after dark because of the blackout. They would stay at small country hotels on the way avoiding towns that could be bombed. Reg had planned several alternative routes, and had looked at railway lines and schedules so that they could proceed and return by train if something went wrong with the car. He favoured the railway lines and stations that were well away from the coast and from the big towns.

Directly north of Southampton was the city of Winchester, which he planned to avoid, driving north of it. The whole area was littered with tiny villages.

The temporary military hospital was north and west of there, out in the country about a mile and a half from a village, so avoiding targets for air raids should not be too difficult, Reg thought. Although there was often no rhyme or reason to the enemy's method of bombing — or why else would they bomb the village of Fernden, he made the assumption that they would go after docks and aerodromes if they could.

He would drive through West Sussex, then into Hampshire.

They had left Calborne House early in the morning, and stopped at cafés for coffee and tea. His Lordship seemed morose, thoughtful, and left the ordering of the coffee to him. At other times, they stopped in rural places to eat from their packed hampers. Felix Clark had telephoned ahead to reserve beds for them in small hotels. They would drive sedately, taking their time.

At each stop, Reg perused the maps carefully, marking with a pencil the place that they were currently at. It was an adventure for him, which he found he was enjoying, although he felt for his Lordship, who did not know exactly what he would find when he saw Master Henry.

In due course, on the third day, they found themselves on a narrower, winding country road, in an area of open fields and bare trees, driving towards the large country house that had once been a private dwelling, then a boarding school, and finally a military hospital. Reg speculated that, after the war, if the Germans did not invade and take over, the place would revert once more to a school. He was frightened at the thought of an invasion, tried to put it out of his mind as best he could. Inevitably, it crept up on him in idle moments. Now, out of familiar territory, and close to the Channel, the thoughts plagued him again as he considered how narrow was the strip of water that made Britain an island, no more than twenty-two miles from Dover to Calais.

There was a large sign for Playter House School, on posts, at the side of the road at the entrance to a driveway. The driveway itself was barred by a wooden arm that lifted up to admit vehicles, and beside it was a sentry box with a soldier inside. This, as much as anything, brought home to Reg the fact that there was a war on.

The soldier, dressed in the usual khaki, came out with his rifle pointed at them. "Good afternoon," he said, bending lower to look in the back seat at his Lordship. "Could I have your names and the nature of your business?"

His Lordship lowered his window and spoke up, easing himself forward. "I'm Lord Calborne from Fernden, Sussex, here to visit my son, Captain Henry Calborne. And this is Reginald Wheeler."

The soldier consulted a list. "Right you are, sir. We're expecting you." To Wheeler he said: "Drop off his Lordship at the front entrance, where there will be someone to meet him, then drive round the right hand side of the house to the back, and someone will direct you where to park."

The entrance to the school was a wide, arched stone porch that sheltered a heavy oak door with iron studs embedded in it. Two soldiers, with rifles, who were sheltering in the porch, came out as the Daimler came to a halt.

"Lord Calborne?" one of them asked, evidently having been telephoned by his colleague. "This way, sir." The house was a good three-quarters of a mile from the road along a private driveway.

Reg drove the car carefully round the side of the house, having watched his Lordship, who looked frail and slightly bent, walk up the steps of the house and disappear from view. Reg could find it in his heart to feel pity for the old man, whom the servants at Calborne House — when there had been any servants — had sometimes referred to as "the old bugger." It was affectionate more than anything, he assured himself. He himself was married but had no children.

~ Lord Calborne scarcely noticed his surroundings as he came into a wide entrance hall with very high ceilings and supporting pillars. As though she had been waiting for him, the Matron came from the nether regions of the hall, looking dignified in her immaculate uniform and triangular shaped cap that came down to her shoulders. It was not clear to him whether she was a civilian Matron whose services had been commandeered for the duration, or whether she was with the army. It did not matter. They shook hands.

"Could I offer you coffee, Lord Calborne?" she asked. A handsome woman, she was not intimidated by his title, it seemed, or obsequious.

"Perhaps later, Matron. Thank you. I'm rather anxious to see my son."

"Of course. We've told him you are coming, but not exactly when. He's concerned about his blindness, that he didn't tell you about it himself."

"Yes. It will be a shock when I'm actually confronted with it. I've tried to prepare myself." *Not enough, not enough.*

She took him up the central staircase and along a carpeted corridor off to the right. At the far end, the corridor turned to the left. Matron stopped at the corner.

"Captain Calborne is along there," she said. "He has room number six. I'll leave you to go there yourself. It's a private room, even though he did not want to be alone. He asked to be in an open ward, which we do not have here for the officers. We thought because of his blindness he could be looked after more carefully if he had his own quarters. Actually, he spends most of his time in the common room and the officers' mess."

Lord Calborne walked along the quiet corridor very slowly. It had been wise of Matron to let him proceed at his own pace, instead of knocking on the door, announcing him and ushering him into the room, he thought.

At room number six, he hesitated. All was quiet within. In fact, the whole place was quiet for a hospital. No doubt the receiving area where the ambulances came in, and the operating theatres, the acute surgical and medical areas, were at the rear of the building and would show more activity.

Deciding against knocking, he turned the handle of the door very quietly and went into the room.

At first he did not recognize Henry. The man who sat on a wooden, upright chair by the window, partially facing the room, was dressed in civilian clothes. He was very thin, the planes of his face sharply visible, the eyes sunken in their sockets. His hands lay loosely in his lap. The skin of his face was sallow, the colour of pale sand, faded sunburn.

The sightless eyes looked out with no expression in them, certainly no recognition. How could there be? Yet he was alert, aware that someone had come into the room.

Lord Calborne did not advance into the room. He stayed on the thick, patterned carpet beside the door, feeling as though he might collapse there. It was evident that he should have done more to prepare himself for this. But what could he have done? Perhaps he should have gone to see the vicar of the church that he attended sporadically, the Reverend Burroughs, or asked for a private audience so that they could talk about Henry and perhaps pray together.

He thought of the words from psalm thirty-one, that he had had to memorize as a boy: *For I am a stranger with thee: and a sojourner, as all my fathers were. O spare me a little, that I may recover my strength: before I go hence, and be no more seen.* For some reason, those words came into his head.

"Father?"

Lord Calborne opened the door and went out into the corridor, where there was no one. Turning left, he walked quickly until he came to some back stairs, servants' stairs, that took him to the ground floor and a door that went out into the garden at the back. There was a narrow gravel path, which he took, walking rapidly. Rain was coming down quite heavily, so he put up the black umbrella that he had carried in with him from the car.

Without direction, he walked away from the house, following the path, walking among very old cedar trees, then large circular beds of dormant rose bushes set in spacious lawns, into a spinney. There he rested against a tree, drawing breath.

"For God's sake, pull yourself together."

The sound of rain in the trees, on his umbrella, soothed him — and the cold, stinging air on his face.

After waiting for several minutes, he turned back, going the way he had come, walking slowly but with purpose to the door from which he had come out.

At Henry's door he knocked softly and went in. Henry was sitting as before, his face turned into the room, the thin, exhausted features strained with expectation. There was a walking stick hooked over the arm of the chair.

"Father? Is that you?"

"Yes."

Not giving himself time to think, Lord Calborne moved forward.

Henry picked up the walking stick and got to his feet, leaning heavily on it, to the left. Evidently, it was his right leg that had been damaged. Looking carefully, Calborne could see that the right leg was thickly bandaged and that the trouser leg had been slit at the seams.

A stab of compassion, as sharp and intense as it was uncontrollable, passed through Lord Calborne as he walked up to his son. Henry put out a hand towards him.

Instead of taking the hand, Calborne put his arms around his son and held him strongly. "My dear boy," he said. "Dear boy."

~ Reg Wheeler was in the kitchen of the hospital, in the servants' quarters, sitting at a table by himself having a meal that had been served to him by a woman who was now washing stacks of dirty plates and mounds of cutlery. Cheerfully she talked to him as he ate, and she plunged her red, swollen hands repeatedly into the sink full of hot soapy water. Suds from the soap spilled over now and then onto the floor as she piled the washed plates onto the large wooden draining boards.

"Terrible it is," she said, "the bombing that's been going on in Southampton. Thank God I don't live there myself. I'm in the village. I used to work here when this was a school. I'm lucky to keep my job, seeing as it's the army."

Reg had been given a very comfortable room in the servants' quarters, where he had deposited his overnight bag, and then taken Lord Calborne's luggage to the room that had been designated for him.

"Where's the nearest pub?" Reg asked, anticipating that he would have more free time than usual, at least in the evenings. During the day, in the two or three days that they would stay there, it was possible that his Lordship would want to take Master Henry for a drive, if he were up to it. Of course, the weather was rotten, and Master Henry could not see anything. Still, he might want to get away for an hour or two.

"There are two pubs in the village," said the woman, whose name was Gladys. "One at each end. There's The Crown, which I like best. More local people go there. Then there's The Black Swan. Some of the officers from here go down there to the Swan."

"How far?"

"Only about a mile. Of course, it's up hill and down dale, which is a bit awkward when you can't put on a torch and it's pitch black." Gladys laughed. "Some of our people have fallen into the ditch. A sorry sight they look when they get back here, if there's been any rain. There are usually other people on the road who can tell you where to go."

Reg could not risk taking the Daimler out after dark, not being able to put lights on. Besides, if he'd had a drink or two, he wouldn't want to risk anything with the car.

"Want a cup of tea, duck?" Gladys asked.

"Don't mind if I do," Reg said. "Much obliged. That dinner was very good."

"That was something left over from the Officers' Mess," she said.

~ Captain Henry Calborne and his father were sitting in a corner of the large and comfortable Officers' Mess, with a tray of tea things on a low table in front of them.

It moved Lord Calborne to the edge or tears to have to pour tea for his son, to lift the cup and saucer into his hands, with the handle of the cup turned so that he could grasp it easily. "Handle there to the right," he instructed. Then when the tea had been drunk, he took the empty cup and placed it on the tray.

"Biscuit?" He offered the plate, guiding his son's hand, so that Henry could pick up a biscuit. "When do you think you can get leave, to come home?"

"The infection isn't cleared up yet, by any means," Henry said. "It's very painful to walk, and I can't get to sleep at night without something for the pain. I've been worried about becoming addicted to the drugs. They change them from time to time, to try to prevent that from happening."

"I see."

"I would like to come home. How are the dogs?"

"Oh, in fine form. They miss you, I can tell. They always seem to be watching for someone, and I suspect it's you." He did not want to mention his wife, who had also loved the dogs. "I seldom ride these days. I much prefer just to walk with the dogs."

"How is Thwaite?"

"Showing his age a little, as we all are, otherwise very good. He's looking forward to having you there. No doubt he'll spoil you."

Henry laughed. "I'm looking forward to that. Dear old Thwaite. And Agnes?"

"She's well."

"I won't be able to come until this leg's better."

"And the blindness?" his father asked gently.

"They think it's psychological, what they sometimes call hysterical blindness. Not a very flattering term, is it? But I wouldn't be surprised if it were true. Living constantly with the expectation of one's death inclines one to a madness of sorts."

"Yes. I try to imagine it, but of course I can't know."

They drank more tea, then Lord Calborne ordered a glass of brandy for each of them.

"Cecily asks after you when I see her, which is not often, I must say."

Henry smiled. "Oh, Cecily," he said, with a gentle hint of a dismissive tone. "Sweet Cecily, so full of life and fun. Cecily would not want anything to do with a blind man."

Lord Calborne could have wept. "I fear you are right there," he said, getting the impression that Henry was resigned to that, accepting, because there was perhaps someone else. Cynthia? He did not probe. It was not that there had ever been anything formal between Henry and Cecily, not even what you could call an understanding. Somewhat flighty, although very pretty and well mannered, she would perhaps not make a good wife for a Lord of the Manor. Unlike Caro, Cecily was very absorbed with herself and what she wanted.

"Tell me about North Africa, if it's not all top secret. And, of course, if you want to. Perhaps you would prefer to try to forget it."

"No, I should talk about it, because it helps."

Lord Calborne was gratified to see that his son's face was more animated now. Thank God he had decided to visit him, not to wait.

"I said in my letters that I was near Mersa Matruh. Well, we made raids into the desert from there, mainly to the Italian outposts. There were about fifty thousand of us, and about half a million of them," Henry said, speaking very quietly, his sightless eyes fixed at a point where he thought his father's face would be. "Then when we knew that the Med was no longer hospitable to us, and our supplies had to come round Africa, round the Cape, up to the Red Sea, you can imagine what that did to our morale ... the sense, and the actuality, of being cut off."

"Yes."

"I was in an armoured division that wasn't up to full strength. We were constantly outnumbered. I was hit by machine-gun fire when I was out of the tank ... lost a lot of blood at the time. Then the infection set in. They took me to Alexandria eventually."

"The MO told me about it."

They sat for a long time, talking and sipping brandy. Mostly, Calborne listened, until it was time to go downstairs for dinner.

An orderly came up to them. "Dinner will be served in a few minutes, sir."

"Thank you," Henry said. He struggled to his feet. "Could I take your arm, Father?"

Chapter 11

At Badgers Gate, Lizzie had a stick and was digging beside the house in some old mole hills that were scattered on the rough grass that had perhaps once been a lawn of sorts. She thought of the other house and longed for it.

Especially she missed the warm kitchen with the fire in the range, and the mouse hole near the sink, in the skirting board, where she had several times seen a mouse dart out and in. It had been tiny, that mouse, with little sparkling black eyes, and it had moved so fast that she was not sure she had actually seen it until it reappeared. Then she was fearful that Greysuit would catch it and eat it, because her mother had told her that cats ate mice. For long minutes she would sit very quietly on the floor to watch for it to come out.

Also she missed the wash-house with its very old worn brick floor that you could sit on or crawl on without fear of damaging your knees. There was the steamy, warm air and the constant smell of soap.

She thought of the wooden shed behind the wash-house, next to the vegetable garden, where they had kept the rabbits in their hutches. It seemed to her a secret, cozy place, where she could stand on a wooden box and feed dandelion leaves to the rabbits. Often she and her Dad would go out into the field behind the garden, walk along by the hedges, to pick the leaves of plants that the rabbits liked. They would stuff those leaves into a large bag or a basket. That place was her; it told her who she was.

Jim was digging in the front garden, turning over the sod that had been taken over by grass and weeds. Lizzie watched him as he dug up a clump of earth from which weeds sprouted, then grasped the weeds to pull them out and release the soil back to the garden. The dirt was rich, dark brown. Before her eyes the rough garden was taking on the semblance of something tamed, something in which flowers would grow, potatoes, carrots, lettuces.

Her Dad was wearing Wellington boots, an old jacket and cloth cap against the drizzle, while she had on a little oilskin cape with a hood.

Tom Katt came out of the attached house, with a spade to dig. "We'll get this place in order, Jim, just in time for us to move back to Bullrush Lane."

Lizzie turned her attention again to stirring up the mole hills.

"Well, with the shortage of manpower these days, it could be a long time before we get back in there," Jim said.

"Perhaps if we get this place ship-shape, Sir Otto Lind will be inspired to modernize it. It's a crying shame to have two houses unoccupied," Tom said, starting to dig.

"He's not the sort to consider that. Otherwise he would have done it by now."

Lizzie went round to the back of the house to see the rabbits that her father had put in a makeshift shed until such a time that he could build a proper one. The two big grey rabbits looked at her expectantly, their noses twitching. She pulled up some grass from the wet garden and pushed it through the wire netting into the hutch, which she could hardly reach. She liked to watch them eat, to hear them crunching on the stalks.

Alice, next door, came up her garden path from the midden and walked though the gate to look at the rabbits with Lizzie.

"Feeding the rabbits, dearie?" Alice said, bending down to peer in at the munching rabbits. "What fine specimens they are."

It would be a shame to kill those and eat them, Alice thought. She would have to have a word with Jim about that. There were plenty of wild rabbits about, and Tom and Jim were experts at snaring them, sometimes using a ferret to drive them out into nets. She had seen Jim making his own nets to put over the burrows in the rabbit warren. All the burrows bar one would be covered up with the nets, then he would put the ferret down.

The ferret, in theory, and often in practice, would drive rabbits out into the nets or snares. Sometimes the ferret would kill and eat a rabbit underground and not come out. Alice smiled. In that case, the man would come home and say disgustedly: "Lost the bloody ferret."

"How are you, dearie?" Alice said to Lizzie, reaching forward and stroking her hair out of her eyes.

"All right."

What a world they were bequeathing to their children, Alice thought. What a bloody mess it all was. You tried and tried to make it all right, to give a decent life to your children, then someone would come along and knock it all down, as though they had an instinct to destroy.

"You'd better go round to the front where your Dad is, so that he can see where you are." At any time the siren could go off, the black dots of planes appear in the sky. "Come on, duck." She took Lizzie's hand and led her around the side of the house.

~ May and Jo were inside, where a fire burned in the old range. The high shelf, the mantelpiece above the range, held the remnants of the ornaments that had survived from Bullrush Lane. The Dresden lady, with her damaged hand turned inward, looked out impassively on her new surroundings. These familiar things gave May a sense of order as she looked around the room, as she arranged and rearranged, unpacked and sorted.

The table under which they had sheltered was undamaged, apart from dents and nicks on its surface. Covered now by the chenille cloth, it stood against the wall under the window that looked out to the front garden. The sideboard that had been damaged stood against another wall. Over the next few days they would sort it all out. For now, they had the table and a few chairs to use.

Jo sat at the table, drawing with crayons on a piece of paper, in the circle of warmth from the fire, hearing the singing kettle and the pots of water on the range.

May went out to get a bucket of water from the tap. "There's tea," she said to Jim. "Then I thought we would go wooding. Would you like that, Lizzie?"

"Yes." Lizzie liked to go wooding. They would tramp into the mysterious woods, where there were sometimes wild rabbits, and birds that flitted through branches, as though they were following you, and there they would look for wood. When they came upon a fallen branch, they would drag it home, each person putting a hand on it. Then her father would put it on a saw-horse and cut it up into small pieces. She liked to watch him saw, his shirt sleeves rolled up, to see the sawdust float to the ground, to smell the wood, and see the logs piled up neatly, showing their pale insides. She liked to see the branch disappear.

Sometimes they would come across a tree stump in the woods, where a large tree had been cut down, leaving a lot of small pieces of wood, which her mother called "chips," and which were, she said, from an axe, very good for starting fires at home.

~ They drank tea in the warm room. "We'll be in for some heavy frosts soon," Jim said. "I'll have to get a better shelter for those rabbits."

The cat, Greysuit, who had not yet been let out to his new surroundings, basked by the fire, on the rag rug of many colours. Only occasionally did he look at the door, furtively. Lizzie, with boots removed, plonked down beside him. "Cat," she whispered. "My cat."

∽ Chapter 12

Reg Wheeler drove Master Henry and Lord Calborne out to the country the next day. They were already in the country, of course, but he had consulted his maps and found some very minor roads that would lead to places even more rural.

As he drove, he was mindful that he should be thinking of Henry Calborne as Captain Calborne and not as Master Henry. Yet he found himself unable to make the mental shift from thinking of Henry as the rather dreamy, sweet and kind young man who had lived at Calborne House after attending university and had tried to learn the running of the estate with the estate manager, against the day when his father would be no longer capable of taking an active part.

They parked in a lay-by that allowed them a view over open country, where a blustery wind blew rain in their faces as they got out of the car. Dark rain clouds hid the feeble late autumn sun. They all wore trench coats, scarves, hats, and gloves against the cold.

Standing discreetly at a distance so that father and son could be alone, Reg looked out over the land and imagined hordes of enemy soldiers walking over it purposefully, as he had seen photographs of them in the First World War on foreign soil. Although it was hard to grasp, with each passing week of the war the possibility became ever more plausible. Bloody Jerries. He did not try to pretend that he was not frightened.

He was of an age that he could have been a soldier in the last war. The fact that he had not been considered fit, because of tuberculosis at age twelve, which had left him with damaged lungs, had kept him out of it. Although he was grateful now to fate that it had happened that way, and that he had recovered from the disease, he had at the time felt a certain guilt and humiliation. That guilt had been particularly acute when several of his school friends marched away and did not come back, when he had in due course seen their names appear on war memorials.

Looking at those names etched in stone or cast-iron, feeling the mourning, he had somehow felt less of a man for not having risked anything, especially as he imagined that others were looking at him and thinking the same. Women risked their lives in child-birth — he had known more than one who had died labouring with child, as it was sometimes called — yet he ... he had not risked anything. In this war he tried to make up for it by fire-watching when he could, and by digging out those who had been buried alive. Not particularly fit, he nonetheless forced himself and did not grumble.

Seeing Master Henry now in such a state, so thin and ill as to be almost unrecognizable, Reg recalled again that awful sobering guilt and mourning for his friends, and for those millions of others he had not personally known. Witnessing the old man caring for his son so gently and sweetly without being patronizing made his respect for the "old bugger" go up a few notches, so much so that tears gathered in his eyes, which he was forced to wipe away with a handkerchief, surreptitiously.

~ Henry held his father's arm as they stood on high ground looking over the landscape. As though he had been doing it for a long time, Lord Calborne described the scene, in detail, to his son. He described the dark and the light, the differing shades of green, the grey clouds that moved with speed against the backdrop of the sky, a squall of rain that he could see coming, birds floating and soaring in the currents of air, a path that wound down below them, going into a clump of trees. "It's wild and rather lovely," he said, summing up.

An expression of something like rapture appeared on Henry's thin face, where the skin was tight over the bones beneath, as though there were no flesh between. "It's so amazingly wonderful," he said, "to feel cold on the face, to feel rain. And to smell the familiar scents of one's own country. I never thought I would come back, you know. After a while, all you know is war and abnormality, as though everything else had been an illusion, a dream."

"Yes."

"But one of the most awful things I find now is that I worry, constantly, about the men in my Company, about my friends. I feel guilty that I'm not there with them. It's because I can't get news, I don't know what's going on there. I have the awful feeling that people I write to, people I think about, may already be dead. I think of them lying there in the sand, in that heat, disintegrating."

Lord Calborne was acutely aware that any facile remark from him would destroy the confidences of his son, the mood of openness. "Yes, I do understand," he said. "Or I try to. It's natural that you would feel that guilt, because your head is still there, your thoughts and emotions. It is disconcerting to have your body in one place and your head in another. Also, you feel a sense of responsibility, of your command. You cannot just drop that."

"Yes."

"We cannot control our thoughts and emotions. A lot of the time, we can control our actions, our behaviour, in spite of what is happening with our thoughts and emotion. It takes courage to do that, bravery."

"Bravery, you know, is the most respected and prized human attribute in a war, at the Front," Henry said. "And I've discovered that you can't predict who will be brave under fire, who will be the man to go out and bring in a wounded friend. The reality shatters all your prejudices. Sometimes it's the man who is the most slovenly, the most lazy on fatigues, who will rise to the occasion magnificently and do something so brave and selfless that you want to weep. It may be the quiet, unassuming man who is the hero ..." His voice broke.

"Yes, of course. That is why it's important not to act on pre-judgment where people are concerned. We all pre-judge, of course, because to do so is a move towards self-preservation when necessary ... but to act on that, without absolute tight evidence, is the mark of the unintelligent and the boor, whatever his rank, if I may put it that way without seeming like an old pontificating ass. I feel about that so strongly ... it is absolutely wrong. One must try to give a person the benefit of any doubt until he proves otherwise, not to condemn him out of hand because one does not understand him, or one does not know all his circumstances."

"Yes, I agree. I feel so relieved to talk, to know what you think."

"In the last war there was such an emphasis on dealing harshly with insubordination in the ranks, particularly of what was called dumb insolence ... you know, a man could be shot for dumb insolence ... that at the time I always thought the real problems with the army were at the other end, in the higher ranks. There was such arrogance, you see, such assurance of being right, such idiocy, so much pulling of rank."

"It has changed somewhat now, thank God," Henry said fervently, his voice shaking. "There is more realism, I think ... more cynicism, perhaps ... and more compassion. I think I have become blind because of that in me. Sometimes I am ashamed ... at other times I'm proud, if that is the case. You see, I have not been destroyed by having to act as a murderer. I have not let myself down, and let down my men, by making arrogant decisions. I have tried to preserve life."

Lord Calborne swallowed, his throat working convulsively, as he squeezed his son's arm. "My dear boy," he whispered. "I'm proud of you ... very proud indeed."

"Thank you. That is all I care about."

Rain beat about their heads, unheeded. Henry had taken his hat off and thrust it in his pocket. Lord Calborne noticed that his son's hair had become so sparse from his illness that the water plastered the thin strands of it against his scalp in such a way that the shape of the skull showed through. That reminded him of how close his son had come to death, that he was not yet free from its clutches. He knew then that in spite of army regulations, he would do all in his power to keep his son safe, short of "pulling strings," which he did not see as fair, when others had no strings to pull.

First of all, he would endeavour to get Henry permission to come home on leave as soon as he was fit enough, perhaps for Christmas, if Henry did not assert himself in the matter, for fear of seeming to have preferential treatment, to which he had always been very sensitive. They would light the fires in the big dining room; they would have a magnificent dinner; they would have a party there for the village children as

Caro would have done; they would give out food hampers to the poor and needy, the bombed out. They would, in essence, kill the fatted calf for the son who had returned.

They would go to church and give thanks. The Reverend Burroughs, who was weak and frail, probably on his last legs, as he was himself, would pound on the lectern and tell the story of the son who had returned. "That which was lost has been found!" he would cry in the impassioned way that held the congregation spellbound, even though they did not believe in anything much.

Yes, the Reverend Burroughs had the gift of rhetoric in full measure, and knew how to use it to great effect when he had to. Once, over dinner at Calborne House, Burroughs had confided to him that he had lost his faith, a far cry from the days of his youth when he had been a missionary in China, had been innocent and fervent.

It did not matter, he had confided further, that you no longer believed in something very specific. For he had found that the older and more frail his body, the stronger his mind, and he was thus able to fashion a meaning of sorts out of that which seemed meaningless, and out of his day-to-day physical work with others. He clung to that, he had said, against the day when his mind also would deteriorate. If indeed there was something that could be called life after death, and he hoped there was, it would be at one and the same time both much more complex than we had ever supposed and yet wonderfully, amazingly simple, as such things often proved to be.

While he waited to find out, or not, Burroughs flung himself into his pastoral work with as much vigour as he could manage, for which his parishioners adored him. Kindness, compassion, and empathy were human concepts by which he lived. In this he was supported by his three daughters, whom his parishioners called Faith, Hope, and Charity, behind their backs, in a benign way, even though their names were Sarah, Ruth, and Mary, the youngest being Sarah.

Lord Calborne knew he was being fanciful, yet he intended to do it all, if Calborne house was not bombed first. In spite of the enemy, they would carry on, as they were exhorted to do by government slogans at every turn. Yes, they would celebrate life while they still had it. The thought of Sarah, the youngest Burroughs child, now a beautiful and spirited young woman ... there was no other word for her ... made him smile

"The Burroughs girls are well," he said to Henry. "Sarah drives her father around the parish on a motorbike with sidecar, the father in the sidecar, of course. He thrives on it."

"Sarah? Little Sarah?"

"Oh, she's not little. She's a woman now. No doubt you think of her as the girl with the pigtails and the navy blue gym-slip, going off to school on the bus."

Gratifyingly, Henry laughed. "You mean that little Sarah rides a motorbike? With the old man in the sidecar?"

"Yes, indeed. It's a sight to see, especially as she goes much too fast. They were stopped once by the constable for speeding, so I heard from the man himself. He let them off with a caution because the girl said it was a matter of life and death."

Together they laughed, easing the sadness that hung between them, and the deep depression that Lord Calborne discerned in his son.

"Perhaps I'll see for myself when I come home ... in a manner of speaking," Henry said.

"Your sight may well have returned by then. Sarah could be persuaded to take you for a spin, I'm sure."

"That's something to look forward to."

"Let us walk a little along the road, if the old leg is not too painful. Might do it good to move the muscles a bit more. Lean on me."

The rain came on more heavily and Lord Calborne opened up an umbrella that was large enough to shelter them both. "The bravery that we see in civilian life may be less dramatic than that on the battlefields, but very much there," he remarked, as they walked very slowly farther away from the car. "There must be plenty of it in London and other cities, even in our little village. I am constantly humbled by it."

"You are already quite humble, father. All one can really say of war is that it's madness. That word is so hackneyed now as to have lost its power to move us. Language is inadequate, or our ability to use it is inadequate."

"You're right, of course. Have you much pain, Henry?"

"No more than usual. It's better when I'm distracted like this." He hobbled on, leaning heavily on his father.

"Apropos of what I was saying earlier, Abraham Lincoln is reputed to have said: 'Most men can stand adversity, but if you want to know a man's character, give him power'."

"Oh, yes ... the uses and abuses of power. There must be humility."

"So seldom is."

"The best people have it."

They walked on, then by silent mutual consent, turned back. "I'm so glad and so grateful that you came, father."

"Did you think that I wouldn't?"

"You were part of the world that I had thought I must give up forever, part of the dream."

"You must see about leave. Speak to the MO and your commanding officer on the home front. I don't see why you shouldn't come home at Christmas."

"I'm frightened of relaxing too much, father, in case I have to go back. If not to the desert, then to somewhere else. You know ... it takes a long time to get one's self into a frame of mind where one can pretend that the loss of one's life does not matter so very much ... that one is not actually in a funk all the time. It is a kind of operation of insanity that one must perform on the self. Those who cannot do it, do literally go mad."

Lord Calborne nodded, then remembering that his son could not see his nod, he squeezed his arm. "I do understand. I understand completely that when you are a soldier you do not belong to yourself ... as far as one ever does. But here you are, you are alive. Home is still there, although for a time you may not feel safe anywhere. Our illusions of absolute safety have been shattered. We must readjust ourselves. All of us."

Calborne House, in a prominent position, was just as likely to be bombed as anything else in the countryside, he thought. They had cellars that they could get into for shelter. He had had more exits dug out so that if the house collapsed above them they could get out, with luck, and not be buried alive. He prayed that the house would survive so that Henry could recuperate there.

Neither of them, he sensed strongly, wanted to think now of what would happen to Henry when he was well, whether he would be sent back to the desert. It was to be assumed that his eyesight would return. There was a certain strain between them as they avoided what they both wanted to voice, but were frightened of doing so. Neither one could speak first at this moment, Lord Calborne knew. Perhaps before he went back to Fernden they would bring it up.

"Thank you, Wheeler," Lord Calborne said as they reached the car and Reg opened the door for them. "You're a very patient man."

Jim went out the back door of Badgers Gate Cottages, number one, and walked down the wet path in the darkness to the midden, with a folded newspaper under his jacket. For a while he wanted to be by himself, to read the paper, before the raids started. At Badgers Gate they were farther away from the village and the pub, too far to just call in for a quick drink, and leave the family subjected to raids.

He missed the wash-house with its warmth, as did May, he knew. They had left the heavy mangle there, as it was impossible to shift unless they had two or three men, its base being made of cast iron, as well as the big ornate wheel to which the handle was attached for turning the two wooden rollers. They had locked up the wash-house and the shed, to which they would go back from time to time to get tools, and so on.

Inside the midden, he shut the door and lit the stub of a candle that they had there in a saucer. He sat on the closed seat and opened the paper, bending towards the candle, to read the headlines and the gist of the news. Everyone knew that it was censored, of course. You had to make assumptions about what was really happening. That was not difficult, especially for one who had seen such things before.

What was different now were the thousands of civilian deaths, in London and other cities, children blown to bits. Bitterness was with him more these days. What had the last lot been for?

As time went by, there was the increasing sense that they would have to fight to defend their homes and their lives, from the brick block-houses that had been built, and were being built, here and there in the fields, down country lanes. He thought of the small, squat, flat-roofed, hexagonal buildings, with slits on every facet, just wide enough to admit a rifle barrel.

Every man and every boy over the age of thirteen, and every woman and girl, he assumed, would be issued with a rifle, and they would fight for their lives on their own soil, as the French and the Belgians had fought. If there were not enough guns to go round, they would fight with farm implements.

The thought was distasteful to him, but they would not wait to be slaughtered if that appeared to be their fate. They would not provoke; they would not go out aggressively; they would patiently wait to defend. And if it be that they should die, their blood would seep down into their own gardens, their own fields and streams, their own ditches.

He was tired of reading about Churchill who had, a few months ago, exhorted: "We shall fight in the fields and in the streets, we shall fight in the hills." All well and good, for had he not been thinking about that himself? But he did not trust Churchill, whom he thought of as a war-monger, although he spoke well, one could not dispute that. He also spoke glowingly of the offensive and of nothing less than victory.

Victory was a ridiculous concept. What it meant was that, when hundreds of thousands of young men, millions, had been killed, when there were few left who could fight, the powers-that-be decided to give up.

Old men killing young men, that was what it was. Young men who had not had a chance to mate, to father children. From the safety of fifty kilometres behind the lines, from the underground bunkers, the old men issued orders that they would never have to watch being carried out. They would not see the blood, hear the screams. They could cloak it all in lies, in words such as glory, honour, duty, our glorious dead. They would bully and coerce.

He did not believe in the offensive, for that was criminal. He had seen what it did. "Over the top, lads!" On the other side of the coin, you had to defend yourself from madmen. What it took was readiness, ex-pertise, cynicism, realism and, above all, patience.

Forget glory, honour, a dead morality. They led to lies and coercion. Bring on the cynicism; stare the madman in the face. But do not take the offensive against him. Let him do that; let him batter against you with his madness until he spends himself.

Putting the newspaper aside, for the ranting words had disturbed him, he took out the pack of cigarette papers and the tin of tobacco, inhaling the aromatic scent as he opened it. Sometimes he took snuff, placing two tiny pinches of it on the back of his hand, inhaling first one then the other into each nostril. It was a disgusting habit, he knew, as it stained the handkerchiefs that May washed for him.

He remembered how he had rested in a field on the edge of Hucque-liers, Pas de Calais, in a rare quiet moment on the long march up to the Front, inhaling the scent of tobacco as he rolled himself a fag. At that time, and since, he allowed his thumb nails to grow long so that he could tie string more easily, as well as roll fags. Going through the motions brought the turmoil for which there were no words.

Inhaling smoke, he leaned back against the wall of the midden. In the quiet of the night an owl hooted nearby and he could hear the rust-lings of wild creatures in the garden, a hedgehog, perhaps, or a badger. Sometimes at night he could hear the coughing and barking of a fox.

Soon, he would lie down, fully clothed, to sleep, in the expectation that he might have to get up to go into the village to dig out the bombed. Always there was a sense of waiting.

His Lordship and Reg Wheeler stayed for two more nights at the military hospital, before leaving after breakfast to begin the long drive back to Sussex.

"You'll see about coming home for Christmas?" Lord Calborne said to Henry as they stood in the immense entrance hall of the main build-ing, hanging back while Wheeler packed their suitcases in the car.

"Yes, I will."

Now that the time of parting had come, the things left unsaid weighed on Lord Calborne. "We'll talk more then," he remarked, "about the future."

"At the moment I can't seem to see more than one day ahead. I know that's a reaction to what has happened to me. That's one way of coping, I suppose. It's nature's way, as the saying goes. I'll have to deal with the future when it's thrust upon me. Thank you again, father, for coming. I've enjoyed your being here so much ... I just wish I could see you."

"That will come."

"I hope so. I can't imagine a future as a blind man."

As they talked , they moved towards the large double doors of the entrance, Lord Calborne with his hand on his son's arm. "I want you to promise me that you'll write to me at least twice a week," Lord Calborne said, noting that a nurse was hovering nearby, waiting to escort Henry back to the Officers' Mess or to the safety of his room.

"Of course."

They embraced. "Goodbye, dear boy. Don't despair."

"Let me come down to say goodbye to Wheeler. And father, please give my best wishes to Thwaite and Agnes, and of course to the Reverend Burroughs and his daughters, especially to little Sarah."

"Oh, I will." They descended the steps carefully. "The nurse is waiting to take you back." He signalled to the nurse.

Henry shook hands with Wheeler. "I wish you a safe journey."

"Thank you, sir. Welcome home."

From the back window of the car that moved sedately away from the house, Lord Calborne saw Henry standing on the gravel driveway with the nurse holding his arm, and he felt the sharp stab of farewell. His son's sightless eyes were directed towards him.

That was what this war was about, saying goodbye to those people and things that one loved, not least the former self. One came into a new awareness that would never leave, like a curse.

Wheeler slowed the car down until it was almost at a standstill, so that Lord Calborne could look at the reality of his son. The nurse's hand holding Henry's arm was a reminder that his son was not free, that he still belonged to the army and to the war, even though he was incapacitated. Her touch seemed both benign and proprietorial, engendering in him, the watcher, a sense that his son had been taken out of his sphere of influence. It was not a good feeling for a father to have, for it heightened the loss that he found in Henry's blindness, in his abject weakness.

The words of the writer George Eliot, whose real name was Mary Ann Evans, and whose work he read when sitting in bed at night, came to him: "In every parting there is an image of death."

As the car rounded a corner and Henry was out of sight, a glimpse of the army barrier across the driveway through the trees created a further suggestion of a prison. Lord Calborne faced forward and let out a sigh. "At least I know where he is now."

Deeming the remark not to be addressed to him, Wheeler said nothing, but kept his back straight and his head up, as befitted the chauffeur of a respected man to whom the concept of noblesse oblige was so ingrained that he never brought it to conscious mind.

"Lord Calborne of Fernden, Sussex," he said, as the soldier at the barrier poked his head in through the window. "And I'm Reginald Wheeler, his Lordship's chauffeur."

"Very good, sir," the soldier saluted. "Please pass."

∞ **Chapter 13**

Christmas would soon be upon them, Christmas 1940. May, with Lizzie, made her way across fields and along footpaths towards the village, planning meals in her head, wondering what she could get her hands on, in the way of food that was not rationed.

There wasn't much money to buy presents for the kids, or much in the shops in the village anyway. Sweets were rationed. She kept the ration books safely in her hand-bag, where she looked at them from time to time.

When the weather became really bad, she could get things delivered, she said to herself, as her rubber boots squelched through mud. There were always cabbages, their own cabbages, until heavy frosts or snow came and killed them. There were still some in the garden at Bullrush Lane, if they had not been stolen.

There was sausage-meat at the butchers, mostly fat, she suspected, and sausages, too. Bacon was rationed, sugar, and butter. She might be able to get some vegetables to add to their home grown things. Some of the tomato chutney she had made that summer had survived the bombing. There was always rabbit stew and rabbit pie, the meat simmered gently with carrots, onions, turnips, parsnips, potatoes, and whatever herbs they had in the garden, and then she would add Bisto gravy mix to make the liquid brown and thick.

In the rough garden at Badgers Gate there was a patch of thyme, some sage, and mint, dying back now because of the winter, planted by someone long ago, before the house had been declared unfit for human habitation. Perhaps that same person had also planted the quince tree by the stile.

It always gave her a strange feeling to look at things in gardens that were now hers to use, that had not been planted by her or her own family, useful things like herbs, or beautiful things that she could just enjoy and admire. Whenever she reached down to pick some mint, for instance, to put with new potatoes as they cooked, she thought of those unknown people who had planted it, as though their ghosts hovered over the garden. She wanted to say thank you. It was a continuity of sorts, for them, an immortality.

She planned her visits to the village so that she could meet Jo outside the village school, where the girl had started in September, although she had been only coming up to age five in October. On the other days that she did not get to the village, an older girl, aged fourteen, who went to the school, brought Jo home.

Lizzie was in the chocolate-coloured pram, snug against the cold early winter rain, dressed in a wool bonnet, a coat, and jodhpurs that matched the blue wool of the coat. Once across the small meadow from Badgers Gate, there was a dirt lane going to the village that took them up to the church yard, where they had to walk through, and then into the winding High Street where the shops were, and where the bus went through, infrequently, to the nearest town.

There was a small drapery shop too, run by Miss Styles, who sold basic items of clothing for men and women, as well as curtain material, cotton thread, and umpteen small, useful items of which one might run out at any moment.

May heard the planes coming when she was near a few trees, the sound coming from the north, and then she could see them in the distance. There was time for her to push the pram off the lane and get behind two trees that stood close together. The planes came low, and as they got near she could see the circular emblem of the RAF. Although she had not really thought they were enemy planes, she felt relief. As they went past her overhead, a sense of pride mixed with other, darker emotions brought a tightness to her throat.

Out on the lane again, she pushed the pram fast in the drizzle, as fast as the mud would allow.

When she had been in the county asylum at age twenty-one, there was a woman there who had lost three sons in the war, the first war. Why that woman came to mind then, she could not say. Seeing the planes had, perhaps, made her think of it. There she was, that woman, her image vivid, as though she had materialized on the wet lane. Her name was Agnes, the same name as the present cook at Calborne House.

May had walked in the gardens of the asylum every day, feeling claustrophobic in the wards and corridors of the building that seemed like a prison, painted cream and green. The gates of the gardens were locked, the vast grounds frequented by gardeners pushing wheelbarrows, wielding sickles that they called "swaps," mowing lawns, crawling about on hands and knees grubbing up weeds from the numerous flower beds.

Round and round she would go, on a cinder path, in the summer sun and gentle heat, looking at flowers, breathing in their scents, even though she felt distanced from it all, as if she would never actually move into it all again, into the real world. Was there even such a thing, she agonized then, as a real world where she could trust that what she loved, what she wanted, was not an illusion? They gave her something to drink, the nurses, a potion, she assumed, that made everything more distant still.

Distractedly, in those days, she had walked, round and round. One day she met an old gardener, with a wheelbarrow full of weeds, who spoke to her and said his name was Pilbeam, with a face screwed up like a prune. He wore a black weskit over a striped shirt with the sleeves rolled up. His trouser-legs, of brown corduroy, were hitched up and tied with string just below the knees, so that the bottoms would not get covered with soil. From then on, he talked to her every day, and she sought him out.

Once he gave her a rose, a little beyond a bud, smelling sweetly, a white rose. "That's for you," he said. "And if you wait a minute I'll go into the shed and find a pot for you to put it in, then you can keep it on your bedside table."

He had brought her out a little glass pot that she recognized as having once contained fish paste, which one put on bread. From a garden tap he put some water in it, then the rose.

As they stood together, a woman came down the path, looking about her. "John! John! John!" she called, passing them as though they were invisible.

"That's Agnes," the gardener, Pilbeam, said to May, very quietly. "Lost three sons in the war. Every day she calls for them. I sometimes think I've had enough of this job."

Along the path, the woman sank down onto a bench and put her head in her hands, weeping and keening. A nurse came hurrying along the path, up to the woman. "Come along, Agnes," she said kindly. "It's time for your tea now."

She had gone on then, in those leaden moments, in those days, walking, walking, walking, as though she were really going somewhere, carrying the rose. Now, Agnes was one of those people who would forever stay in her mind, with the shadows of her three sons, who could not be taken out by any effort of will, any more than Frederick George Decker could be taken out.

~ May and Lizzie came to the churchyard and went through the iron gate that latched behind them. The ancient church looked as though it were sinking down into the ground. It had a substantial enclosed porch, where one could shelter from bad weather temporarily while passing through, and read the notices on the notice board about the goings-on at the Women's Institute and the village hall, about the local war effort and the church. Volunteers were urgently needed for this, that, and the other. There were jumble sales, of which May made a mental note. Some of her best clothes, and those of the children, had been bought for a few pence at jumble sales, the items coming from the homes of the wealthy, for the most part. There were always those lovely hats, but no place to wear them, usually. May touched a hand to her nice, navy-blue felt hat, her pride and joy, damp now.

She carried Lizzie into the post office cum grocery shop. "Don't touch anything," she said. It was dingy in there, with little natural light and sacks of potatoes and carrots here and there, and dog biscuits. There were big jars of sweets with glass lids, containing mint humbugs, gob stoppers, fruit drops, lemon drops, toffees, extraordinarily strong mints, aniseed balls, licorice, and so on.

"I can give you an extra bit of bacon, Mrs. Langridge," Mr. Wallis the proprietor said, since there was no one else in the shop.

"Much obliged, Mr. Wallis," May said. "I'll have our sugar ration, and the butter, and a tin of condensed milk, and Brook Bond tea, please."

Mr. Wallis poured loose sugar into the metal scoop on his scales, and moved the weights about, then he poured the sugar into a thick, blue paper bag. "The weather's not too bad for the time of year," he said.

"No."

"Have they started on your house yet?"

"No. I expect we won't get back in there until the summer. We can still go up there and do the gardening."

"I reckon this war will go on for a long time. There's no sign that it will end any time soon."

"How's you son, Mr. Wallis?"

"I thank God every day that he isn't flying, that he's ground crew. But then the aerodromes are not the safest places to be these days."

May clicked her tongue and shook her head in sympathy.

"Want a bit of cheese, Mrs. Langridge? I've got some nice Cheddar and some Lancashire. I could give you a sliver or two of each, if you like."

"Yes, please. Have you got anything in for Christmas, decorations and things?"

"Well, I've got a bit of tinsel left over from previous years. I could throw in a bit of that, free."

"Thank you. And I'll have a loaf."

May came out into the street, carrying Lizzie with one arm and her basket in the other hand. It was time to go down to the far end of the High Street, to the school, to get Jo.

Every two weeks someone came to the village, up from the coast, to sell fish, a man with a van who parked outside The Crown pub. There was mackerel and herring, good, fresh, and cheap. Jim would cut off the heads, gut and clean them, while the cat would liven up and beg for the heads. May would dip the fish in flour, with salt and pepper, and fry them. She thought of that now in anticipation.

~ Jim was in the greenhouses at the Calborne market and kitchen garden, pruning, cutting back, tying up the grape vines and the peach trees that had been trained to grow on horizontal wires attached to the walls. It was warm in there, quiet and peaceful.

The boy who was in training pottered about nearby, having been given some tasks that were within his capabilities. Often, Jim thought of the mess if a bomb dropped on the greenhouses of the Calborne gardens. He saw no reason why anyone would do that, unless it was sheer cussedness.

Somewhere outside, Tom Katt was harvesting the last of the autumn crops. They had come through this time.

~ May, with Jo sitting on the end of the pram and the basket in the middle to even out the weight, walked back through the churchyard to get to the lane that would take them back to Badgers Gate.

As she came out the church gate, an army convoy came through the village. She stood to watch the big, dark green lorries go by, each one packed with soldiers who looked ridiculously young to her. The lorries had canvas tops, pulled tight over metal frames, and open backs. The soldiers waved as they went by, and she and Jo waved back. They would be going south to the coast, not far away. May waited, mesmerized, until the last lorry had turned the corner in the High Street, taking it out of sight, and she tried to force her mind away, unsuccessfully, from the question of how many of those smiling boys would come back.

To distract herself, she obsessively checked her handbag to make sure that she had put the ration books in there, and she handed a toffee to Jo.

The rain had stopped, the air fresh and scented with sweetly rotting leaves. Clouds moved across the grey-blue sky. From the small farm near the church came the smell of cow dung, and rotting apples from the windfalls. Rooks flew about, cawing, from bare tree to bare tree, while here and there a magpie flitted. The distinctive, beautiful black and white birds made her think of the rhyme she had chanted with her friends at school when they would see magpies:

One for sorrow,
two for joy,
three for a girl,
four for a boy,
five for (she couldn't remember what five magpies meant)
six for a story that's never been told.

Although she did not believe the old lore, of course, she did feel a little odd when she saw only one magpie.

As she pushed the heavy pram, May thought of when she had first met Jim. It was the summer of 1932, in the gardens of the Calborne estate where he worked, when she was thirty-four and living at home with her parents. She had had jobs, mostly as a nanny to the children of the very wealthy. When her charges reached a certain age, the jobs would come to an end and she would find herself back at home with her parents. Although not yet ten years in the past, it seemed so long ago, a time when the shadows of the first war flitted in and out of her mind at will, uncontrollable. New images and sounds now imposed themselves on the old — the shattered house, their broken furniture, the roar of over-head bombers, rubble inside and out, the scent of old walls laid open.

She slogged over the last field towards Badgers Gate. The wheels of the pram were thick with mud, as were her boots. She would have to put the pram in the scullery-cum-kitchen and allow the mud to dry before knocking it off with a stick.

Once inside, she would put the pot of rabbit stew, already cooked, onto the hot stove, then she would make herself tea from the kettle that was always warm on the outer reaches of the cast-iron range. The kids would get cocoa and bread and jam until Jim came home from work and they would have the stew, eaten with crusty bread.

These days, the air raids were as numerous as before, just less directly overhead, for the most part. Yet they could not relax their guard. The kids still slept under the table, and since there was the small extra room downstairs for a bed, she and Jim still slept near them. In the other house, she had slept on the sofa to be near them, while Jim, in a fit of bravado, had often gone upstairs. He wouldn't do that again.

Ah, she was looking forward to the tea, and a biscuit or two. One's inner life had shrunk down to small pleasures in the here-and-now. One dare not look far ahead; indeed, could not.

Alice was looking out of the window of the attached house as May went through the garden gate, and she waved. "I'm making some tea," May called.

The front garden was dug up now, raked smooth. Weeds had been pulled up from around the place, and from between the bricks on the paths. Hedges had been cut back. Yes, it was looking less forlorn, more like a proper home.

Alice came in and helped May take coats and boots off the children. "I did my stint at the first-aid post in the village hall this morning," she said. "It was quite busy, with men hurting themselves clearing rubble, that sort of thing. At least I felt as though I was justifying my existence, instead of standing around in a uniform trying to look important. Let me make the tea, duck."

May went into the bedroom off the living room and brushed her hair, looking into the broken mirror at her tired face. She applied a little Tangee lipstick, and dabbed some Evening in Paris perfume behind each ear. She placed the navy-blue felt hat carefully on top of the damaged dressing table to dry. Later she would brush it with a clothes brush.

"When I was in the village," Alice said as they sipped tea, "I ran into my friend, Molly. You know Molly?"

"Oh, yes."

"She's expecting again. That will be her fifth. She's that despondent, she was almost in tears there on the street. They're short of money as it is."

"They do say," May said, "that if you do a lot of mangling, it will bring on a miscarriage."

"If that were true," Alice said, "there would be an awful lot of mangling being done. I can't see it being that easy."

"Mangles would be banned," May said, and they both laughed.

"There's gin," Alice said. "They say that can do it, sometimes. Wouldn't want to have tried that myself. Might do some nasty things that you're not banking on."

"Gin's expensive, too. I've heard of women using knitting needles and coat hangers, getting peritonitis and dying. It breaks your heart, that people are so desperate."

"Well, there you are, that's life," Alice said, noticing that Jo was very interested in their conversation. "Does she understand?"

"No," May said.

Lizzie looked back and forth at the two women, liking to hear them talk, not having the least idea what they were talking about.

All day, May had avoided looking closely at the newspaper, at the front page where she had caught a glimpse of pictures of London streets, the bombed-out buildings, the fires, the night pictures like something out of hell. They showed the firemen and other emergency workers struggling, with thick hoses, to fight back against all odds. They looked so puny, those men, against burning buildings that were storeys high, their gaping windows like open mouths that cried out.

Now, she let her eyes stray over the paper as it lay folded on the big table, to read words here and there, about districts damaged, about the numbers of civilian dead, people homeless, people sheltering in the underground stations, coming up in the morning to find their homes piles of rubble. There was a picture of children sitting in the rubble of their home because they had nowhere else to go.

May put a tea cozy on top of the folded paper. When Jim came home, he would read it, once the children were in bed, and then they would discuss it.

"Another cup, Alice?"

⁓ In the night they were woken by waves of German bombers overhead, droning on to London, more and more, as though there would be no end to them. They shook the house. Around on the hills, the anti-aircraft guns gave tongue.

Alice and Tom came round, expecting the worst, prepared to pool what resources they had.

Lizzie got out from under the table and stood by it, holding the fuzzy pram-rug that she liked to take to bed.

"What's?" she said.

"It's all right, dearie," Alice said. "Just a bit of thunder."

"That's not thunder," Jo said, struggling out of their shelter after her sister.

"I'd like to go out and take a look," Jim said, "when this lot has gone over."

They put on warm coats, hats, and boots. With the children wrapped in blankets, carried in arms, they walked into the meadow and on to the middle where it rose to a bit of a hill. Facing north, they could see all along the horizon a pinkish-red glow in the sky above black, bare trees at the far end of the field.

They stood, at a loss. "That's London burning," May said.

~ Later that night, in the early hours, as May lay on her bed, the words of the magpie rhyme came to her, as things do, unbidden:

One for sorrow,
Two for joy,
Three for a girl,
Four for a boy,
Five to remember a love of old,
Six for a story that's never been told.

When she watched London burning on the horizon, something had solidified in her mind, a certainty. If they were invaded, each person would do what he or she had to do. They would not be passive; they would not be fatalistic. She would defend herself and her children with kitchen knives. If that meant death, then so be it.

∽ Chapter 14

Captain Henry Calborne had taken several trains from the west country, Cornwall, to get up to London, and was now making his way from one station to the next, crossing a section of the west part of the city by taxi to get to Charing Cross station. From there, the trains went south to Kent and to parts of Sussex.

Although he could not see, he could smell and hear the familiar scents and sounds of London — as well as the newly alien — through the partially open window of the taxi. Eagerly, he tried to identify each auditory and olfactory stimulus. Over all hung a scent of smoke.

In the back seat with him was another captain, Basil Seager, also from the military hospital in Cornwall, to which they had both been transferred recently from the converted school-to-hospital near Southampton. Captain Seager was accompanying him to Fernden railway station, where they would be met, before going on to his own destination a few stops farther along the small branch line into the countryside of Sussex.

It was very fortunate, Henry reflected again, that Basil lived in the same part of the country and that both of them had been given leave to go home for Christmas, had both been declared fit enough to make the journey. Although not completely well, still seriously underweight, nauseated at times from the incompletely cured infection, and in some pain when he put weight on his injured leg, Henry hoped that the familiar atmosphere of home, with tender loving care of a different sort, would give him a greater will to carry on.

Home would be changed; his father had warned him about that. Many of the servants had gone, the men to the war and the women to munitions factories and to work on the land, to keep the farms going where the men had been taken away. Women drove tractors, ambulances, lorries and buses. It was rumoured, his father had said, that if things became worse — and all the signs were there that they would get worse — women could be conscripted for National Service.

At home, many rooms had been shut up. Women came from the village to work now and again, to keep the "big house" going. Once again, he thought that perhaps it was just as well that he could not see it.

Over the past weeks he had been depressed, on and off, sometimes to the point of not caring whether he survived or not. At those times, when despair was all that occupied his mind, he supposed he was shell-shocked, although no one had suggested that diagnosis within his hearing, and he had not asked for such a label so that he might be absolved from going back. Privately he knew it to be true. Only the visit by his father to the hospital near Southampton had lifted him out of that depression for a time.

Now his changed home would be continually under threat, because there was the constant danger of being bombed while what was being called the "blitz" on London was underway. Their village was directly on the flight path. That necessitated taking shelter in the cellars of the house, of having sleep disrupted, of living with fear and uncertainty. The letters from his father had been worded with care and tact, yet giving him no doubt that Calborne House, together with the village, was in the line of fire. With equal tact his father had expressed the hope that the anxiety engendered by the threat, or the actuality, of bombing would not be detrimental to the good progress he had made of late. He knew that his father was giving him the option to leave Fernden for a safer place, should he be unable to tolerate it.

After his father's visit, he had started to receive letters from Sarah Burroughs, youngest daughter of the Reverend Burroughs, who had informed her of Henry's plight. Sarah had told him this in her first letter, had asked if he minded her writing to him because she very much wanted to, and thought her letters would cheer him up. Delighted at the first epistle, he had immediately commandeered his nurse to write and tell her so. As time went by he became less self-conscious in his replies, especially as the nurse informed him that several of the other men there were blind, for whom she had to write and read letters.

On the journey up to London, he and Basil had been lucky enough to have a small, first-class compartment to themselves for part of the way and had taken the opportunity to talk, and share confidences. Once the flood gates had opened, as it were, they both found that they could un-burden.

There was difficulty in stopping, each pausing only to give the other a chance to speak. Basil had the quality of listening, of attentive silence. Henry could feel it, together with the empathy of the other man, as he strained his sightless eyes in Basil's direction.

Some men emanated a kind of inward, silent hostility to the confidences of others, Henry knew very well, having encountered them. They were fearful, perhaps, that they would be required to give something of themselves, a secret that they were keeping for their own use, like a young child who secretly hoarded sweets, not wanting to share. Or perhaps it was that they simply were not capable. He hated such constipated holding back, such blighted sensibility. Basil was not of that ilk, and Henry gave up a silent prayer that he was blessed with such a companion on the long, tedious, and dangerous journey home.

As for himself, he listened intently to Basil's voice. The images that Basil's words evoked exploded in his brain like coloured stars ... pictures of retreat, battle, explosions, the obscene booming of guns, rising soil and sand, maiming, spilled brains and guts, blood, death, fear, pain, agony. Basil spoke well, articulate and expressive, as though it were all coming up from a deep mine of former silence where it was forged, where no human ears had borne witness to it, where it had taken time to form and perfect itself, a distillation of all that Basil has seen, experienced, suffered, felt.

As Henry listened, he strained his consciousness to picture the compartment in which they sat, his body half turned towards Basil, to the other man's face that he had never seen, his uniform, their luggage on the racks above them, the grey winter countryside going by them, wanting to put the voice into some sort of context.

Neither man was embarrassed nor surprised by the emotions such conversations brought forth; they understood each other, and the relief was immense.

"Would you go back to the desert if they asked you?" Basil enquired while still on the train. "I doubt that they would order you back, after what you've been through. Not for active service, anyway. Perhaps a desk job in Cairo? Assuming that the tide will turn there in our favour, of course. I must say, it looks rather bloody awful at the moment."

"I don't know. That question has been in my mind ever since I came out of the coma, although not seriously at first, because I had other things more pressing ... I was relieved to find myself alive, then I started worrying seriously about losing the leg ... then about the blindness ... then about whether I was actually ... well ... mad."

"I can understand that. It was the same with me."

"If I don't go back in some capacity, assuming I get my sight back, I don't think I could live with myself after the war. It's not as though it's all going to end soon ... it seems to me it's going to go on and on. We may get to the day when we can't remember what the world was like with no war."

"I dread that. I dread eventually thinking that the abnormal is normal, or something like that."

"Yes ... frightful. Absolutely frightful."

When more passengers got on at Reading, breaking into their privacy, they dozed.

∽ Now in the taxi that negotiated the pock-marked streets of London, Henry listened as Basil described the scene around them. "There are piles of rubble everywhere. It's awful, the devastation ... buildings with no windows, roofs gone. I can see bomb craters." He leaned forward and spoke to the driver. "Is this destruction typical?"

"This is nothing, sir." The driver, prematurely aged, had an exhausted, weathered face, the lines deeply etched. To Basil, he seemed to epitomize the spirit of London. "You should see the east end, around the docks. It makes you weep to look at it. They think they've pre-empted us, the bloody bastards, but we'll get them yet. I was in the last bloody lot, over in France. They'll find out that we don't just lie down and die easily in this country, although we ain't got much. Excuse my language, sir."

"That's quite all right."

"They're arrogant, see, and we're not ... at least, not the ordinary working people ... and I'm not speaking for the generals and toffs of the last war, or the toffs now. I dare say you're not of that mould yourself, sir."

"I hope I cannot be accused of that," Basil said.

"We've got no 'side,' sir, because we've had it stamped out of us from the time we were babes in our mother's arms," the driver said, "but somehow we know our worth. We're slow to rise up ... we always do, eventually."

"I couldn't have put it better myself. There's more cynicism, more realism, in this war, less blind obedience to high authority than there was in the last war, thank God," Basil said, leaning forward to speak to the driver earnestly, as though he were still carrying on the protracted conversations with Henry that they had engaged in on the train. "More people in the army are thinking for themselves. You would notice the difference, I'm sure."

"I get that sense myself, sir. You're a good gent, sir."

"Perhaps we have learned something from experience."

"I hope so, sir. They don't know, them Jerries, that we won't stand by and see our babies killed. It says in the bible that those who sow the wind shall reap the whirlwind ... Well, they're sowing the bloody wind all right. Now we'll wait and see what happens to them. I don't believe, necessarily, in an eye for an eye, because that can go on forever, but I do believe that if someone's out to kill you, beyond a shadow of a doubt, that you have a right to defend yourself."

"You're quite right," Henry said, leaning forward. "That's the difference between vengeance and justice."

The flood-gates of emotion had opened for their driver, as they had opened for himself and Basil on the train. Now he felt an acute awareness of all that was around him, saw inner visions of the shattered city, his emotions so close to the surface that he did not know whether he could control them. People walked around, going about their daily business, holding in the terrible mourning, conscious of the burdens of others, not wanting to add their own until such a time came that they could no longer hold it in.

"I've got a son in the navy," the driver went on, as the vehicle crawled forward, "and two of my girls are in munitions factories. You don't know what worry is until your children are in the front line. I didn't worry so much for myself. Now I know what my poor old Mum and Dad suffered in 1914 and beyond, while I was running about in France."

"What's your name?" Basil asked.

"Chapman, sir. Sidney Chapman. I was a sergeant by the end of the last war, sir ... that was mainly because I survived, by some miracle, to see the end of it."

"Well done. It's our pleasure to meet you, Sidney."

There was the clanging of an ambulance bell near them, and Henry strained his eyes towards it, out of habit.

"We may have to do some detours to get to the station sir ... there's all that rubble in front of us ... so long as you don't think I'm taking you astray. There's bomb craters in the middle of some streets, as well as buildings down over the road, like. We get to know where we can go and where we can't, though it changes from day to day, of course."

"Dear old London. What a travesty. You live here, Sidney?"

"In Bethnal Green, sir, with the wife. The younger kids have been evacuated to Kent. I want her to go, but she won't, not with our big girls still here. There's war work for her to do here, so we take our chances with the rest of them. The station we're going to was bombed on the 9th September, sir. We don't know from one day to the next whether it can stay open. If it can't, we have to take our passengers farther along the line, in hopes that one of the stations will be all right."

"We tried to by-pass London,' Basil said, "but it was going to be too long-winded, and we decided it would be no safer."

"You can only do so much. You should be all right if you keep moving, sir. Take the first train out, in case you don't get another, like. It's murder in that station, I tell you."

To Henry, Basil said: "Perhaps it's just as well you can't see, Harry. It would break your heart."

Henry, silent, tried to picture it anew, as the taxi crawled along in places, then picked up a bit of speed for short distances. There was a stronger scent of smoke in the air, not clean smoke like that from a country bonfire, but smoke from charred timbers, old wood that had long been hidden from public eyes in ancient buildings. There was dust in the air, too, from buildings that had been reduced to rubble, from crypts and cellars laid open.

At the station the taxi driver ascertained that rail lines were still open, then he shouted for a porter.

"Just wait there, old chap,' Basil said to Henry when they were out of the taxi and he was preparing to pay the driver. "We've got a porter for the bags. He'll show us which platform."

"Right," Henry said, standing still, finding himself disturbed by the hubbub around them, sharply noticeable after the quiet of the hospital in Cornwall, the countryside, then the relative quiet of the enclosed world of the train compartment. Everyone around him seemed to be shouting. There was the clatter of vehicles, taxis and ambulances, he guessed, in the forecourt of the station, as well as cars and lorries out on the street. In his mind's eye he could see Trafalgar Square nearby, the ancient church of St. Martin–in–the–Fields that he had loved to visit in better times, the Strand, Charing Cross Road, Whitehall ...

With these memories came an emotion so poignant that he thought he would cry out, as he was swamped by a familiar fear that he might never see again. "Basil ... are you there?" he said tensely, his voice rising over the din that surrounded them.

"Right here, old chap." Basil touched his arm. "Not to worry. Our driver's helping our porter get the luggage on the cart, and I'm just going to pay him. The trains are running, so our porter says. We may have to change more often than we bargained for, though ... some lines damaged, but not to worry, we'll make it through."

There was a jingle of coins. "Thank you, sir. Much obliged. Good luck, sir, to both of you."

"Good luck to you, and your wife," Henry said, wondering where they would be, the taxi driver, his wife and their two daughters, when there was an air-raid.

"Now, the best thing is if you take hold of my arm,' Basil said, tucking

Henry's hand through his bent arm. "Then all we have to do is follow on behind our porter. This place is absolutely packed, a mad house, all trying to get out before dark. Not too many people just hanging about, I can tell you. They're all moving out pretty fast. Jerry would just love to bomb this place into the ground."

Henry, gripping Basil's arm, turned his head this way and that, willing himself to see. It did not work. He could see light and dark, faintly, nothing else. "This cursed blindness," he said bitterly. "My thanks, Basil, for being so patient."

"Think nothing of it. I know you would do the same for me."

They had army passes for the train, which enabled the porter to take them directly onto the platform. "You'll have to change at Tonbridge, sir," someone informed them at the barrier, "then you'll be told there where you have to change again."

They moved forward, stopping and starting. There were people saying goodbye, people crying. Bodies pressed against them; bags banged against legs. "Make way!" their porter shouted.

Henry carried a thin white walking stick to denote that he was blind, which he did not doubt helped them through the crowd. "Look out, we've got a blind man here, in uniform. Make way!" he heard more than once, as well as whispered words of commiseration and pity.

The station smelled of smoke and soot, together with that peculiar odour of ingrained dust and dirt that clings to city stations.

"Our train's in, Harry. Sit on this bench, just behind you, while we get the luggage in."

"Thanks, Basil. I'm desperate for a cup of coffee, although I'll make do with tea if I have to. With any luck, there'll be some on the train. I don't care how awful it is. We'll lace it with brandy from my flask. What do you say?"

"Just the ticket! I'll find us coffee, don't you worry."

When Henry was ensconced in a seat on a train, next to a window, from which he could discern a faint light, he allowed himself to relax.

"Sit tight," Basil said, tipping the porter. "I'm off to scout for coffee. Back in a tick. Don't let the train go without me."

Alone in a crowd, secure in his seat, Henry felt in his tunic pocket for the brandy flask, which he had filled before departing from Cornwall. With something tangible to hang on to, together with the white walking stick, he forced himself to keep down any stirrings of panic that he tended to feel when left alone in unfamiliar places. In total darkness it was worse, if by turning his head he could not encounter even a glimmer of the fuzzy pale light that he had become used to.

He distracted himself by trying to think how he would hold up the train if it started to move before Basil had returned. If he were to stand up and wave his stick out of the window, yelling "Stop," perhaps that would do the trick.

There were others close around him, which helped; other army officers, he thought, among the passengers. "Are you all right?" someone asked him. "Anything I can do for you?"

Then a cockney voice, presumably coming from a porter, said to him: "All right, sir?"

To all of them he replied: "Yes ... thank you so much. I have someone with me."

Carefully unscrewing the top of his silver hip-flask, he took a swallow of the brandy, held the liquid in his mouth for a few moments before swallowing it in slow increments.

"Excuse me, could I get through!" Basil was back. "Here you are, old chap. Coffee! Courtesy of the British railways canteen, in those wonderful china mugs, half an inch thick."

Henry laughed. "Good show! Well done, Basil. Is it hot?"

"You bet it is. Here, the handle's to your right."

"Would you pour the brandy, Basil? A generous dollop."

When that was done, Basil sat down beside him, the scent of the hot coffee and brandy between them.

"I can't begin to tell you what this station is like," Basil said, out of breath. "Well, it's what it is ... a bloody bomb site. You know, I asked one of the women in the canteen if she wasn't frightened of being bombed, this being a target, and she said: 'Not half, duck. When the siren goes, we just get under the counter and hope for the best. We turn the gas off first.' Then she laughed. She put me to shame, I can tell you. I won't be sorry to see the back of this station."

All around them people continued to talk and shout, engines chuffed, whistles blew. For now, they were in a secure little world, in which they would soon be transported out of the city — as secure as they could be in a war where the place in which they found themselves could be bombed from the air at any moment. Henry knew full well that any security he felt was illusory, yet he felt it all the same; it was irrepressible.

There was around them a certain desperation, expressed often as a kind of hysterical jocularity that, Henry thought, came out of the awareness and expectation of sudden and unnatural death or maiming in the midst of the mundane and the most mediocre activity. Henry could sense it, as though by osmosis, knowing himself to be part of it, and helpless.

In spite of that, he found within himself the ability to retreat into the moment. The coffee, a mixture of boiled milk and probably liquid "Camp" coffee, was surprisingly good, enhanced by the brandy. "This is heaven," he said, holding the warm mug with both hands. "Sheer bloody heaven."

"Couldn't agree more. We might as well eat our sandwiches, now that we've got something to wet the old whistle."

There was the rustle of paper as Basil fumbled about in their knapsacks for the packed lunch that had been put together for them at the hospital. "Yes," he said, "we're on the homeward leg. It's amazing to me. I never thought I would see it again, you know."

There were the sounds of slamming doors, shouted goodbyes and frantic admonitions, the chuffing of the engine.

With much noise, the train moved slowly out of the station.

⌁ It was dark when the train — a different one — chuffed into Fernden station and came to a stop. There had been delays, detours, more train changes than they had expected, for which they did not complain, understanding that the changes had been either because of damage to the lines or for safety reasons.

On the journey they had made telephone calls as often as they could, Basil getting through to Calborne House for Henry.

"I always forget your father's a lord," Basil said, after one such telephone call, when they were back on the train. "Then I'm reminded when someone answers the telephone and tells me so. You're such a modest sort of chap."

"I have nothing to be other than modest. It has no real relevance in the army, that title. Tell you the truth, I'm sometimes embarrassed by it."

"Some would say it has a lot of relevance in the army. You're not likely to be a private soldier, are you?"

"You're right, up to a point, of course, as far as rank goes. I prefer, as much as possible, to get things on merit. Some things have changed since the last war, I think. The idea that privilege and duty go together, therefore the high-born should hold high office, doesn't ring true, does it? When we see every day in the army that the private soldier has duty in spades, including the duty to give his life, without any privilege to balance it."

At Fernden station, Basil got up. "Stay put for now, old chap, while I jump down to see if your father's there with the chauffeur. I'll just take one of your bags with me. Not too many people getting off at Fernden."

A minute or two later, straining to hear, Henry could discern his father's voice and that of Reg Wheeler. With that recognition came the urge to weep. Weeks ago, when he had lain in that hospital in Alexandria, then later on a flight, then a ship, bound for England, he had felt that his chances of ever getting home, back to his village and the Calborne estate, were slim.

Out on the platform, where the early winter wind was cold, he felt his father's arms close round him. "Welcome home, dear boy. Welcome home for Christmas."

Basil, thanked and hugged, invited to the estate later in the holiday for a Christmas drink and dinner, departed on the impatient train.

~ In the car, outside the station, Reg Wheeler placed a blanket over Henry's legs, even though his uniform greatcoat was warm. "It's rather nippy tonight, sir," Reg said. "Welcome home, sir, if I may say so."

"Thank you, Reg," Henry said, deciding to use Wheeler's Christian name, as befitted the emotion of the occasion. "You certainly may say so. Good to see you again, in a manner of speaking. Actually, I love the cold, you know."

"I understand what you mean, sir."

"You must be exhausted, dear boy," Lord Calborne said, getting into the back seat beside Henry.

"I am rather. It's so amazing to be home."

In contrast to the fug of closely pressed bodies on the train and the odours of a bombed city they had left hours before, the unadulterated smells of the countryside assailed him in the cool air, and the quiet of the dark night encompassed him with a welcome peace.

"At the house," Lord Calborne said, as Wheeler drove the car away from the station, "you'll find that we have only a few rooms opened. It's easier that way, not least so that we can keep track of where everyone is when there's an air raid. A bed has been made up for you in the drawing room, and we've tried to keep the furniture and everything else in exactly the same places as when you were last there. You should be able to find your way around quite easily. Of course, you won't be alone very much. We all sleep on the ground floor, and I'm in the morning room. When there's a raid we go down to the cellar where we have beds made up, too, as well as a supply of food and water. Of course, you can go down there for the whole night if you want to. It's quite comfortable."

"I see. It will be quite an adventure. It's odd to think that civilians are going through all that ... all the people I know in the village ... people all over the country. London was horrendous."

"We see pictures of it in the papers, of course," Lord Calborne said wearily. "Some people go to the cinema to watch the news. I don't go. When Coventry was bombed I could hardly bear to look at the pictures."

❦ Chapter 15

Over the next few days leading up to Christmas 1940, Lord Calborne put all his plans in motion, with help from members of his diminished household staff and volunteers from the village, including the Women's Institute.

There was the party for the children, to be given in the Great Hall, a vast room in the house that had not been opened since Caro had given a ball for Elizabeth's coming out. After that, life for all of them had taken on a sober complexity that had not allowed for such frivolity. That sobriety had culminated in the death of Caro from cancer, then the advent of the war.

As the dust sheets were pulled off furniture that had been more or less forgotten, he felt a fresh upsurge of emotion on viewing it. He had always supposed that he would die before Caro, perhaps a long time before, as he had been considerably older. Now here he was, still moving about like a rudderless ship in the vast ocean of the house. At every turn he was reminded of his loss, the vibrancy of her presence. Only in his study did he feel that she did not linger, for she had understood that the study was his sanctuary and had seldom entered it, had preferred to corner him elsewhere if something serious had to be discussed in a hurry, or she had instructed Thwaite to draw him out.

Now he found that he could smile at that idiosyncrasy, one of many that he had found charming, and that he could rejoice at the safe return, for now, of his eldest son.

With a rare sense of joy, brought on by Henry's presence in the house, he allowed himself to consider the problem of finding enough food for the party, something that he could not just leave to Thwaite, the cook, and the volunteers from the village, who needed something to work with. Certain food stuffs were in short supply and rationed, especially sugar. While he did not usually concern himself with such things, he thought about them now. Through contacts in London and in certain country towns, he and Felix Clark had managed over the past two weeks to locate ingredients that they could buy without ration books, foodstuffs that the skilled ladies in the kitchen could transform into delectable edibles such as many of the children had never seen. Things had been delivered and fetched, having been found and ordered by telephone. The party would take place in the early afternoon the next day.

For their own use, the big dining room had been opened up as well, the furniture polished; a chimney sweep had come from the village to clean the chimneys of the two fireplaces in that room. God willing, they would have Christmas dinner there, as befitted the return of the son who had been lost, then all would be shrouded up again after the New Year, as the sound of the sirens continued and the war went on.

~ "Father?" Henry came through the open door of his father's study, his white stick tapping in front of him. Since he had come home, all doors to principal rooms had been left wide open, including the study. "Are you in there?"

"Yes, come in, dear boy." Lord Calborne was gratified to see that his son's face was animated, had even taken on a bit of colour.

"What plots are you hatching, father?"

"Oh, the various functions I was telling you about. It's all in hand."

"I thought we might have a glass of whisky together, if you have the time."

"For you I have all the time you could want. Other things I can give over to somebody else. Shall we go into the drawing room? Take my arm."

As they walked from the study, off the front hall, to the drawing room, there was a sense in Lord Calborne that he had captured in those moments the pure essence of time, such was his gratitude at his son's presence, and his sense that this was all he could hope for now. This was perhaps the culmination of his solitary prayers in the chapel. Regarding the answer to prayer, he preferred to keep an open mind, for that was what came naturally to him.

"I do wish you were home for good," he said, as they entered the drawing room, where Henry's bed was pushed against a wall, behind an ornate screen. "Although I can't delude myself that this war will be over even within the next year. We're fighting on too many fronts; we're fighting for our lives."

Lord Calborne poured whisky from a decanter that stood on the large oak sideboard, adding soda water. "They'll ask you to go back, I expect," he said, picking up his son's free hand, placing the glass into the palm and closing the fingers around it. "You have valuable training and experience ... too good to go to waste. You will get your sight back, you know."

"I expect I shall, though I can't speak for my nerve."

"I don't suppose they would put you in the front line. Perhaps instructing would be suitable ... the new men coming in need to hear from someone who has been there, not just the theoretical."

"Yes. Once I'm well, things will become clearer to me.'

'Perhaps a desk job in Cairo."

"That's what Basil said. Cairo might be too far away from the action ... at least for a time."

"One would like to think so. In which case, you could go farther west, perhaps somewhere on the coast."

"We're vulnerable without the Mediterranean, especially if the Germans come in," Henry said, his back to the fire. "What we're doing now, pushing the Italians back west, may not be so easy with the Germans. I don't feel optimistic about it."

"Will they come in, do you think? For Egypt?"

"They wouldn't want to give up that prize," Henry said. It was odd, in the extreme, to be talking about North Africa—where he had had such horrendous experiences—in his childhood home, with his back to the fire, holding a glass of whisky. The dissonance of it vied with the pleasure.

"We'll see what time brings." Lord Calborne took a large swallow of diluted whisky. "You haven't forgotten that Sarah Burroughs is coming to tea this afternoon? She's going to be one of the helpers with the children tomorrow."

"How could I forget that?" Henry smiled. "I've been looking forward to meeting her ever since you told me about her and her motor-bike sidecar, although God knows what she'll think of me, poor wretch that I am these days. Just as well that I can't see myself."

"In the circumstances, you look all right. Sarah's used to injury and sickness. She volunteers at several hospitals ... plans to train as a nurse, has got into Guy's, I believe. She's not taking that up until the future looks a little clearer. If unmarried women are conscripted, she wants to be in the war effort directly. Her father needs her for the time being."

"Why doesn't he drive himself, in a car?"

"Shortage of petrol. They find the motorbike more economical."

"Oh, of course."

"He's frail, too. She's his eyes and his ears, you might say."

"I wish I could be that for you, father. Here you are, still caring for me like a child."

"I cannot think of anything else I would rather be doing. Never think otherwise."

"I'm grateful, father."

"As for my health, I think I shall keep going for quite some time yet. Have you any interest in seeing Cecily?"

"God, no. Absolutely not.'

'I'm afraid you may run into her at the church."

"Then I shall simply pass the time of day and move on. Cecily will marry a solicitor, or a stock broker, who has somehow managed not to be called up, and not from any altruistic motives either."

Lord Calborne smiled. "I'm afraid you could be right, dear boy."

~ They heard Sarah Burroughs coming, the roar of her motor-bike moving along the driveway, then pulling up near the front door. Although Thwaite would go to the door, Lord Calborne left the drawing room to greet her in the hall.

Self-conscious and suddenly fearful, Henry moved away from the fireplace to put his drink on a side table near a sofa, and stood there to wait for Sarah. The furniture, as his father had said, had not been moved, so in his mind's eye he could picture the room in all its detail. Although he longed to meet Sarah, he dreaded what she would think of him, for surely he would hear it in her voice, the shock at the sight of his emaciated form, his gaunt face, his thin hair that had not long ago been thick and luxuriant.

Undoubtedly his father had told her how he was changed, yet the reality might still be a shock. No doubt she would notice the slight tremor that came on unexpectedly, out of his control. He could not remember when he had last seen Sarah Burroughs, although she had told him that they had met last at a garden party, of which he had no recollection.

There were voices in the hall. The Reverend Burroughs had come also, probably to talk to his father about something, as he and Henry had already seen one another and talked at length.

"Hello, Henry. A pleasure to see you." The Reverend Burroughs took Henry's hand. "I feel that I should be addressing you as Captain Calborne, so I hope you don't mind that I call you Henry."

"Not at all. I did ask you to use my Christian name."

"Then I shall. I've come to talk to your father, and I've brought some rather good maps that I have, atlases, of North Africa, as he expressed an interest in seeing where you have been. And Sarah has come to see you, so that you won't be bored by the old fogeys." He spoke with the slightly breathless voice of one who suffers from chronic lung disease. Last time, he had told Henry that every winter he had a bout of bronchitis, no matter how well he tried to take care of his health.

Henry found himself smiling, disarmed once again by the natural warmth and empathy of the old Man of God, as he liked to call himself, whose skills with people had been finely honed over years of giving of himself.

"Now, here's my daughter," the Reverend Burroughs said, "who has proved herself so able of late with unforeseen talents, not least in the handling of a motor-bike, and many other unusual and useful activities that present themselves during a war."

Putting forward both hands, Henry's apprehension dissipated somewhat, especially when those hands were grasped by Sarah.

"Welcome back. It's wonderful to see you again, Henry," she said. "We've all been following your progress, everyone in the village, you know, and of course we talk about you in the church hall when we have tea and cake after Sunday service. All the young women are in love with you, and every girl over the age of twelve, I should think."

"What!" Henry laughed, hanging on to her hands, thinking how clever she was to launch into such a tirade and take him off guard. "That can't be right. They don't know what I look like these days; they wouldn't want to see me now."

"They would! There's a photograph of you hanging in the church hall, from when you were first in uniform. You haven't changed that much; you look absolutely splendid. Considering what you've been through — we know a lot of it, and can imagine the rest, you are amazing."

"And you, of course, are in love with me, too!" he found himself saying. Any such banter would not have entered his head five minutes ago. Sarah had a pleasant, light voice that soothed and seemed to mesmerize him. Charmed and somewhat bemused, he clung on to her hands.

"Yes," she said. "Always have been, from the age of five, when someone introduced us. You were wearing your school uniform, absolutely dashing. I took one look at you and was so overwhelmed and totally tongue-tied that I spent the rest of the time looking at my shoes while you talked to me. You must have had a great effect on me because I was usually an awful little brat. Never shut up ... according to my mother."

"You haven't changed much, then," he said. "Except that you're not a brat any more."

"Hope not," she said. "You, on the other hand, are as charming and as dignified as ever, Henry."

"Dignified!"

"Yes. Always were. And I bet you put on that uniform just for me."

"I did."

"Wonderful! I do love it, I could swoon," she said, laughing.

"Don't do that, I can't guarantee to catch you."

"Oh, I shall swoon on a sofa, as there's one conveniently placed behind me, then someone could dash out and get smelling salts, as they did in the old days ... although my mother still has smelling salts, you know. In my case, I would just be pretending, to get your complete attention."

"You have it." They both laughed. "Do you usually talk so much, without pausing for breath?" he said.

"Only when I'm nervous."

"You don't have to be nervous with me, dear little Sarah."

"Yes, I do ... because I did so want to fling my arms around you ... because you've been so brave, fighting in the desert in a tank, in the line of fire ... then being wounded so far from home ... and I can only tell you this because you can't see how red my face is. I didn't know how I would restrain myself."

"You don't have to," he said, his spirits soaring.

"I do, in front of our respective paters ... I do love that word ... now that I'm grown up I can say to my father: 'Oh, do shut up, pater' when he's particularly obtuse and preachy, and he doesn't mind because the word pater, which is really comic, softens the indignity and the rudeness of it."

"I see," he said indulgently.

"It's funny, isn't it, how we've all changed in this war, how the fear of sudden death gets rid of so many inhibitions and allows us to say things that we would never have uttered before, because if we don't say then now there might never be another chance? You become more real somehow."

"Yes. Are you grown up, Sarah? My inward vision of you is of long pigtails flapping about when you ran, of sticking plaster on your knees."

"Yes, I am. I'm twenty-two; my hair is sensibly short; I wear riding breeches most of the time because they're practical on the motor-bike, and since this war began I feel I've aged twenty years." She talked rapidly and quietly, close to him. "It's taken away my youth. That's what happens when you can't sleep because of air-raids, then you're on fire-watching duty, or volunteering at a hospital, or helping to dig out people who've been buried alive ... when you're frightened most of the time and consumed with sheer terror at other times. I've seen some awful things ... although not to be compared with what you've witnessed and suffered ... I shouldn't be going on like this to you, Henry, in case you think I'm moaning."

"It's quite all right. I do understand, and I fully accept that you're a woman, dear little Sarah."

"When you say that, I could weep," she whispered. "So just call me Sarah."

She guided him to the capacious sofa near them. "Sit now," she commanded.

"I do wish I could see you."

"You shall," she said. Taking both his hands, she put them up to her face. "Here I am."

Henry could hear his father talking quietly to the Reverend Burroughs at the other end of the spacious room where there was a large table by the window that looked out to the front of the house. They would be looking at maps spread out on the table, he suspected, deliberately leaving him and Sarah to themselves, their backs to them, not even glancing over in curiosity. He could picture them perfectly.

Delicately, with a fine tremor in his fingers, he felt Sarah's features, the shape of her face, the short, soft, fine hair. His fingers, sensitized by his blindness, followed the outline of her full, well-shaped lips, then her straight nose, her closed eyelids, the orbits of her eyes topped with the arched brows, the high forehead.

"You're very beautiful," he said. "Like you, I could weep."

"Weep then, if you must. No one will mind here. We've seen so much of suffering. I'm so happy to see you, after all those letters."

"Those letters kept me alive. Tell me what I look like, Sarah. Tell me honestly. Forgive my vanity, if that's what it is."

"Well, you're very thin, Henry, you know that. But it's a thinness that suits you. There are hollows in your cheeks that make you look like a tragic actor who must play Hamlet, who has starved himself to do so. Your eyes are the same ... wonderful blue eyes. Don't be frightened about how you look, because you don't have to be."

Henry heard the door of the drawing room open and Thwaite say: "The tea is ready, your Lordship. Shall I bring it in?"

"Yes, do bring it in, Thwaite, and thank you."

"I expect I shall have to pour the tea," Sarah whispered to Henry.

"No. Thwaite will do it. Stay here with me and rest. You must be exhausted."

"I do live on my nerves. I run on adrenaline, although I must say that when I get a chance to sleep properly I go out like the proverbial light. That's the advantage of being young."

There was the rattle of crockery as Thwaite pushed a tea trolley into the room. "Miss Sarah, will you have tea? Master Henry? And we have fruit cake, strawberry sponge, sandwiches of various types, home-made scones, gooseberry jam, and clotted cream."

"Ooh!" Sarah said.

"Will you have something of everything, Miss?"

"Rather, Thwaite! That's positively decadent, especially after vicarage fare. Thank you so much."

"China tea, or Ceylon, Miss?"

"Oh ... make it China."

"Master Henry?"

"Exactly the same for me, please, Thwaite."

Thwaite dragged a small, low table up to the sofa. "Your tea will be directly in front of you, Master Henry."

"He persists in calling me 'Master Henry.' Dear old Thwaite, I do love him so," Henry whispered to Sarah when Thwaite had moved out of ear-shot.

"Yes, he is adorable. We have no servants at the vicarage now, only a woman who comes in to clean twice a week. Mary does the cooking, or we all take turns to slap something together. Even father can boil an egg and make a cup of tea. You know, you hear about men who can't do anything useful like that. I personally think they're just pretending, so they never have to do anything they consider menial, beneath their dignity."

"You're probably right, Sarah."

"Can you cook?"

"Oh, yes. Enough to stay alive."

"I say, after tea would you like to go for a walk? It's cold and brisk, no wind."

"Yes, I'd like that."

"Thank you, Thwaite," Sarah said, as the tea things were put in front of them. "This is a feast for kings, and we, as lesser mortals, will enjoy it all the more."

The Reverend Burroughs and Lord Calborne wandered over to the fireplace to drink their tea. "Your father tells me that you were in Mersa Matruh in Egypt, Henry," Reverend Burroughs said.

"Yes, I was in a tank regiment, the 7th. I was wounded fairly early on in September, when we moved out of there to go into battle." How cut and dried it all sounded now, as he found himself mouthing the words, shuttered behind his blindness.

"We've found it on one of the maps," Reverend Burroughs said. "I understand from the newspapers that the allied forces have advanced into Libya since then."

"It appears so," Henry said. "The news we get is out of date, of course, and censored. One never knows how accurate it is, or whether there has been a complete reversal before we actually get it."

"We must defend the Suez," Reverend Burroughs said.

"We may be forced to pull out and do more to defend this country, the way things are going," Lord Calborne said. "But let's try to forget the war for now, shall we, while we enjoy our tea. I understand that you've been accepted for nursing training, Sarah, and that you've put it off for war work and in case there's conscription for unmarried women."

"Yes, I have been accepted; Guy's took me. They've been evacuated ... parts of the hospital ... to Kent, so I heard. The medical school has been taken out of London, I think. Don't know about the School of Nursing. Perhaps the whole hospital will be bombed to smithereens before I get a chance to go there."

"Well done, anyway, dear girl," Lord Calborne said. "We live in interesting times."

"I would prefer them to be somewhat less interesting," the Reverend put in.

"We're talking about war again," Henry said. "Could someone please spread clotted cream and gooseberry jam on a scone for me? We didn't get those in the desert, so I'm going to take full advantage."

"Let me," Sarah said.

⁓ A fine snow was falling when they emerged, suitably attired, through a back door of the house onto the cobbled courtyard. One of the dogs, Marigold, a golden retriever, elected to go with them.

"That must be snow," Henry said, holding up his face to it as he walked, holding Sarah's arm.

"Yes."

"How amazing. In the desert you try to conjure up the feel of snow on your skin, the soft sound it makes as it comes down when you're alone in a wood. But, of course, you can't imagine it there."

"No," Sarah said, wondering if he could sense her looking at him. "I thought we'd walk over past the chapel, along the path, then through the woods, in a big circle, if that's all right. I'll tell you exactly where we are as we go along."

"Perfect. Now that we're alone, I want to say again how much I've valued your letters, as well as being able to write to you. They gave me the will to live, because there were times when I didn't care whether I lived or died. Often it seemed easier just to slip away."

"You didn't ... that's what matters," she said. "I try to understand ... but of course I can't, not really. There's such a vast difference between a civilian and a soldier."

"Not such a difference as in the First World War, of course."

They walked in silence then, towards the chapel.

"We're at the chapel now," Sarah said.

"How are you really coping with the war, Sarah, you and your family?"

Their breath came out in small clouds around them. They walked close together on the narrow path, where tall, wet grass slapped against their legs, against the Wellington boots that they wore, and where snow had covered the ground here and there with a thin layer. Marigold walked along behind them, making no sound.

"To be truthful, I'm in a funk almost all the time," she said. "It's such an effort to appear brave constantly. The siren fills me with absolute dread, and the sounds of planes, whether they are ours or theirs. The thought of our boys being killed by the thousands — it all sickens me. I fear that we'll be invaded, taken over. The reason I run around all the time like a flea in a fit ... apart from the obvious useful work that I'm doing ... is that I'm too damn frightened to sit still for five minutes to think. Sometimes I'm forced into it ... thinking ... when there's an air raid and we're sheltering in the cellar, or I'm out somewhere and forced to go into someone's bomb shelter in a garden."

"War does many things to you. It strips away the myths by which we all live, first by making us aware of them as myths, and then by taking away their power. In the army you're no longer an individual ... you get caught up in the machine of war, which conspires all the time to tell you that you're expendable."

"Yes."

"You lose your faith in the general goodness of mankind, when you're faced with such evil. As for faith in God ... you lose that early, yet you go on calling on God in extremis, for want of something else, for fear of the void. There's a camaraderie with your men, with your friends in the army, which keeps you going somehow. Our dilemma is that we must defend ourselves against madmen. In the future, if we get through this with anything left worth having, we must learn, as a people, to be at least one step ahead of such evil ... instead of several steps behind. We must learn to anticipate it ... the shape it will take. God knows, we've had enough practice."

Sarah sighed. "As a species we may be genetically incapable of learning enough from other people's experiences," she said. "Perhaps our three score years and ten are not enough."

"I don't know. On the other hand, little children often have enormous wisdom and common sense, before they've learned to dissimulate as instructed. They can be mean too, of course."

"Yes, absolutely beastly at times."

Sarah sighed again, and they walked in silence, enjoying the chirping of birds in the few conifers that were mingled with the bare deciduous trees around them.

"Is that why you didn't want to go into the chapel, Henry, as we passed it?" she asked. "A loss of faith?"

"No. My mother is there. Too much lately I've thought of my mother, of my grief. Young men call out for their mothers, you know, when they're dying out on the battlefields, in the dressing stations, in the hospitals."

"I know. Did you call for yours?"

"I expect I did when I was delirious. It's so common that no one remarks on it."

"There's a dip here in the path," she said. "We'll take it slowly."

Their feet crunched over small icy puddles on the narrow path. "It's beautiful now, with a little snow settling on the twigs," she said.

"I feel I know so little about you, in spite of our letters ... mainly, I suppose, because our letters were not private. What did you do after you left school?"

"I worked at my old school for a while, helping with the younger girls at first, then working in the office as a sort of secretary. For a while I thought I would be a teacher, like Mary, then I found out that I was really too self-conscious to stand up in front of a class. I decided I was more cut out for nursing. Father became rather frail, so to help both my parents, I came home when war was imminent. That's the whole story. Tell me about yourself, why you were in the regular army. You never really told me, you know."

"Well, I read law at Oxford, because I thought it would be a good basis from which to run an estate such as this, with what I have always been taught by my father. Then when I was finished, I longed for something different, out of the ordinary, so I joined the army for the adventure. No one had any idea, of course, that there would be another war so soon after the Great War. It was unthinkable at that time."

As they went on, he grasped Sarah's gloved hand, his arm still through hers.

"It's so wonderful to be with you, that I want to be quiet for a while. People tell me that I talk too much, so I want you to know, Henry, that I have the gift of silence too, that I can be part of a companionable silence."

"All right," Henry said, squeezing her arm, "although I do like you the way you are."

As they walked on briskly along the woodland path, Henry matching his pace to hers, with snow blowing into their faces, he felt something that he had thought with certainty he would never experience again. It was joy.

∼ They walked in a large circle, as they had planned. "We're almost back to the house," Sarah said.

"I've enjoyed it so much," he said. "Thank you, dearest girl. Where's Marigold?"

"She's behind us, at our heels."

Henry squatted down close to the ground. "Here, Marigold! Here, girl!"

The dog licked his face, her warm tongue going over his closed lids, his forehead, his cheeks. He took off his gloves so that he could run his hands through her thick coat. "Good girl," he said. "Such a good girl."

Ebullient Sarah was now silent, and Henry could sense her tears. She was, he thought, more moved by his appearance than she had allowed him to intuit, all her life having been given over to the learning of tact, empathy, service to others, and kindness, at the vicarage. At that moment he found that he did not care so much how he looked. "When we get inside," he said gently, as he stood up, "we'll go to the kitchens and ask Thwaite to procure us some hot cocoa, with National Dried Milk."

Leaning forward, putting his hands on her shoulders, he kissed her cool, wet cheek.

∽ Chapter 16

The children's party was successful beyond anyone's hopes, no doubt because all involved wanted it to be, with a certain desperation, it being the first such party for a long time. *A gesture of defiance, you might say*, Lord Calborne thought as he lay on his narrow bed in the cellar during the air raid that started not long after they had gone to sleep. He was fully dressed, with his overcoat at the foot of the bed and his shoes on the floor beside it.

For him, too, it was the first such party given at Calborne House since Caro had no longer been there to organize it. For him it had been a diversion from the stresses of running the estate, of producing food in the market garden, making his farms productive, finding good workers.

There had been much laughter and noise, a surprising abundance of innovative things to eat, a conjurer, a magician, songs, music from the piano and piano-accordion, then at the end a Charlie Chaplin film which had been enjoyed by children and adults alike. Men had laughed, with tears in their eyes, at the antics of the little tramp and he had watched them from the sidelines with a tender sort of satisfaction that had surprised him.

There had been ragged children, even in their Sunday best, some obviously mal-nourished, who had eaten the food in the way that a starving dog eats a meal — with a certain haste and disbelief at its good fortune, and a quiet demeanour of guilt, as though its habitual deserved state was to be hungry. Then there had been those who were well fed, used to everything that hard-working parents could provide in a time of hardship.

Surreptitiously he had also watched Henry with Sarah Burroughs: how they had been in sympathy with each other as she had dashed about helping with the party; how she had come back to him like a homing pigeon while Henry himself had listened to the joy and shouts of children as he had sat or stood on the sidelines.

Now as he lay on the bed, subconsciously preparing himself for the whistle of a bomb that would declare at least part of the destruction of Calborne House, if not his own life, the words of one of the old established songs that the children had sung went repetitively through his brain:

Ten green bottles hanging on the wall,
Ten green bottles hanging on the wall,
And if one green bottle should accidentally fall,
There'd be nine green bottles hanging on the wall.

Thus he distracted himself. The song went on and on, until there were no green bottles hanging on the wall. They had also belted out the other familiar party song, "She'll be Comin' round the Mountain when she Comes." That party stood out like an oasis in his mind. He smiled into the semi-darkness, mindful that Henry was also lying awake not far away. At least he himself could read if he so desired; Henry must enter the depths of his own thoughts and memories.

What, he wondered, *would the state of the world be in this time next year?* There was no confidence in him that the war would be over, or that his own life would be unchanged from what it was now. The question of where Henry would be was like a blight on everything that he thought and did. And if the country were invaded, even he himself must take up arms; that thought occupied him much also. He would go with other men from the village to make a last stand where they could. What a motley crew they would be, a ragged army, quietly mustering in their common fear and sense of inevitability.

There was a feeling in all of them that they must make the most of the moments they had. His two other children, Elizabeth and Richard, were to visit after Christmas, when they could come to see Henry without their families in tow, because travel was difficult and costly, as well as unsafe. That was something to look forward to, his three children together again, if only for a brief time.

~ Christmas came and went at Calborne House in a flurry of activity and good food, the best that austerity, rationing, and the black market could provide. It passed in a tableau of aural and tactile impressions for Henry. They went to church, the residents of the house, all social classes, to sing carols and hymns — "Oh, God, our help in ages past, our hope for years to come." Henry shook hands with well-wishers known and unknown, a steady stream of them whenever he appeared in public, as though they were pouring out all their hopes and repressed sadness. They hung on his arms, patted him on the back, kissed him.

The members of the family walked with dogs, listened to music beside log fires, while Henry was aware of each hour going by towards the end of his leave, aware of the day when Captain Basil Seager would come for him and they would be driven to the railway station to begin the long journey back to Cornwall. Once they were back, his progress towards health would be assessed, pronouncements would be made about his blindness and his future in the army.

The dark side of their life contained the air raids, the sirens, the shelters in the cellars, as the blitz on London continued. Bombers roared above them as the siren sang out obscenely over the countryside. With something like awe they listened to the young men in the aeroplanes of the RAF protecting them from above, and they strained their ears to detect their presence.

Henry moved about in the landscape of his childhood home, within and without, with a sense of holding himself in readiness for something that he could not name, a sense of always waiting. Everyone he spoke to about those feelings confessed to the same. It was, Thwaite said — to whom Henry had let drop something in a moment of un-abashed confidence — a constant mustering of one's dignity in the face of death if, after taking all the evasive action possible, death could not be avoided. Thwaite assumed that one would have time to see it coming, without any delusion to cushion one against the reality of it, so he told

Henry. In the face of this reality, class barriers broke down. You could not share a shelter with someone without seeing them as fully human.

Sarah Burroughs came frequently to the house, and Henry found himself living for those visits, for then he felt most intensely alive. During those times she gradually talked less and he talked more, pouring out like a torrent long dammed up, his innermost sorrow, as far as it was possible for him to find words. Like Captain Basil Seager, Sarah had the quality of listening, and she and Henry held hands while sitting on a sofa in the drawing room, or walking along paths near the house.

Henry particularly liked her to take him to one of the streams on the estate so that they could walk along its banks and hear the trickle of water over stones. They did not talk of the future then; the present pressed upon them in all its poignancy, its tyranny of responsibility to hold the moment, lest the remorse that lay in wait for them should overwhelm and push them to madness. For now their respective houses still stood, their families lived, they could glory in the sound of the stream in the shallows. All these thoughts passed through Henry's mind; and he knew that the only concession to the future either of them had made was Sarah's ambition to take up her nursing training, and her promise to continue to write to him when he left.

~ "I'm going out for a short walk, Thwaite," Henry said, three days before his army leave was due to end. "Would you please tell father, if he's asking for me? I believe he's having a nap."

"His Lordship has actually gone out, sir, to the village, with Mr. Wheeler and the car. He said he would also go on to see the gamekeeper and the Home Farm manager, sir."

"I see." Henry himself had slept for a while after lunch, in his comfortable bed in the corner of the drawing room. It had been a particularly disturbed night, as he had had to get up twice to go down to the cellar, the second time deciding to stay. They had hurricane lanterns there, eiderdowns and thick wool blankets on the beds against the damp cold, and two paraffin heaters which gave off a feeble warmth in the cavernous wastes of the cellars. Down there, he feared his blindness more, in unknown territory, where he would be completely dependent on someone else to get him out if the house crashed above them.

He had lain there sleepless, comfortable enough, with a hurricane lantern near him so that if he chose he could open his eyes and discern a faint yellow light. In the morning he had felt heavy with exhaustion.

"Are you thinking of going out by yourself, sir?" Thwaite asked tentatively.

"Yes, I thought I would take a short stroll down the driveway, since I know it well, then turn round and walk straight back. I'll take one of the dogs with me. Marigold, I think, because she follows on behind."

"Well, sir, we could possibly find someone to go with you, if you don't mind my saying so, because there are daytime raids sometimes, as you know. Perhaps Mr. Clark could go with you. You wouldn't want to be caught out in the open. It's only because you can't see, sir, that I'm suggesting it."

"Thank you, Thwaite, but I want to be alone for a few minutes, need some fresh air," Henry said, shying away from even the thought of stilted discussion with Felix Clark, who would feel a pressure to make conversation with him, would not know when to keep silent. "I don't want to bother anyone. I'll be perfectly all right, I know the territory."

"Well, sir, if there is a raid ... God willing, there won't be ... his Lordship has had the ditches deepened along the far end of the driveway, near the wooded areas next to the road for purposes of shelter if people get caught out. Some of the deeper bits have small fences along the edges so that people don't fall into them when it's pitch black. Mind you don't fall into some of the shallower ones, sir." There was an anxiety in Thwaite's voice, which he was trying to hide, for which Henry felt a tender gratitude. Yes, he was stupid, perhaps, to go out, but he needed to feel the cold air on his face, to breathe.

"I'll be very careful," he said. "I have my stick."

⁓ Henry could tell by the crunch of gravel underfoot that he was on the driveway, which was bordered by flower beds, he remembered, near the house; then these gave way to grass verges, which in turn were separated from meadows by fences. There were no ditches here near the house, as the driveway was on a slight decline which allowed rain water to run towards the road into lower ditches.

Every tree and shrub was known to him on that part of the driveway; there were tall, spread-out oak trees, very old, and many holly trees which would have berries on them now, as well as some ash trees, larch, and other conifers. He could picture all of them. The ground would be frozen hard.

As he walked slowly, swinging his stick from side to side in front of him, close to the ground, he could hear Marigold snuffling contentedly in the grass verges. They would be covered with frost or a light snow, he could imagine, because there was a scent of frost in the cold air that made his nostrils tingle. He was glad of the substantial leather gloves that he wore, the heavy overcoat, his leather riding boots, the cashmere scarf that he had pulled up to where his wool cap came down to cover his ears.

If he were sent back to the desert he would do his best to recall this sharp coldness, the scent of frost.

~ Out of that cold, still air, without warning, came the wail of the air-raid siren, starting low as it always did, then quickly escalating to a high-pitched shriek.

"Bloody hell!" Henry said aloud, standing still in momentary indecision for what must have been only seconds yet felt like long drawn-out minutes. The dog, near him, began to bark frantically, no doubt urging him to go back, he suspected, or at least urging him to action. Already it was too late to retrace his steps at the slow rate he was able to move, and now he estimated that he was beyond the halfway mark towards the road. It would be better for him to go forward to the shelter of the wooded area, to try to find one of the shallower ditches that Thwaite had mentioned.

Using his stick to feel the way, cursing his blindness and his own idiocy in coming out on his own, he found the edge of the verge and walked along beside it as swiftly as he dared. "Marigold!" he shouted. "Come here!" By the loudness of the dog's barking he could tell that she was close to him now. "Come on, girl, come on." He had not brought a lead for the dog.

There was the sound of planes coming towards him, then the first ones were overhead, a roaring, the turning of many propellers. There were hundreds, by the sound of it. Mingled with the call to shelter of the siren, it seemed to blot out thought.

Going on instinct, Henry began to run, bending double, knees bent, both to be less visible and to be closer to the ground. Sharp pain shot through his injured leg; he had not run for a very long time. Against the better judgement of a blind man, he blundered on, panting, his boots now moving over grass, now on gravel, as he desperately tried to calculate where he would be on the driveway. "God help us," he mumbled.

Suddenly his front foot encountered nothingness and he pitched forward, instinctively curling himself into a ball as he fell, bending his head down towards his chest, putting both hands in their thick gloves to the back of his neck, his elbows in against his chest to protect his head and neck. Nonetheless, he fell heavily against frost hardened soil in the bottom of a ditch, he reckoned, on a thin bed of rotting leaves. A sharper and awful pain ran through his leg as he hit, and he heard himself scream.

All around him was noise, terrible, obscene noise. As consciousness slipped away from him, he heard the frantic barking of the dog.

∼ In Calborne House, Thwaite and Agnes the cook went into high gear, following their usual routine in a raid. Stoves were turned off, saucepans removed from stoves. On their way to the cellar stairs, both took their mackintoshes, hats, and scarves from pegs in the narrow passageway near the stairs, and lifted up their Wellington boots.

"I'm going to have a look outside the door for Master Henry," Thwaite shouted as he ran towards the front hall, putting on outdoor clothing as he went, having already decided to leave the front door open so that Henry could get in, perhaps guided in by the dog. As he looked out, there was no sign of either.

Catching his breath on a sob, Thwaite ran back to the cellar stairs. Master Henry would be sheltering, he knew that; he was, after all, a soldier. He whistled to the other dogs who had gathered in a nervous, milling pack in the passage outside the gun room where they slept these days, waiting for the signal. They blundered ahead of him down the stairs.

"Master Henry's out there," Agnes said to Thwaite when he got down, her face crumpling up with her fear and the strain of helplessness. "What are we to do?"

"There's nothing we can do in the middle of all this." Thwaite forced a calmness to his voice that was far from the terror that had come on him like a madness. "We just have to wait for the all-clear. He's a soldier; he'll know what he has to do. I'll never forgive myself for letting a blind man go out on his own."

"Directly this is over, we'll go out to look for him," Agnes said, pulling on her rubber boots, having already put on her other outdoor things. "He's a grown man. I hope his Lordship and Reg are all right."

"Men like Reg don't get killed in air-raids," Thwaite said. "Too sensible." What he meant was that, of all the men he knew, Reg was the most astute in looking after himself.

"Settle down!" Agnes shouted at the dogs, some of whom were trembling. "It's all right! It's all right, I say!"

When Thwaite had put on his boots, he and Agnes sat side by side on one of the beds, bolt upright, waiting to go as soon as the all-clear sounded. The cellar door was open so that they could hear it. The muted roar of aircraft overhead was deadened somewhat by the thick brick walls and arches of the cellars.

When the noise seemed to have reached its zenith, Felix Clark came clattering down the wooden stairs.

"I thought you were out," Thwaite said.

"Just got back," Clark said, raising a laconic hand to them in greeting. "Just made it." He was smoking a cigarette and wearing a natty black wool overcoat with a tie belt, a cap, and black leather boots. Thwaite thought he looked like Lenin or Trotsky, especially when he wore his wire-rimmed glasses. Yes, he was one of a kind all right, was Felix Clark. Sometimes Thwaite wondered if Clark was one of those nancy boys, but it did not bother him one way or the other, as he believed in live-and-let-live.

"Did you see anything of Master Henry outside? He's out there ... went for a walk with one of the dogs?" Thwaite asked, not holding out much hope, as Clark would have said.

"Hell! No, I came in the back way, by bike. I was going like the wind,

I can tell you, so didn't look to right or left." Taking up residence beside them on the bed, he took out a packet of cigarettes, opened it, and shook two cigarettes out onto the flap. "Have a cigarette," he said, extending the packet. "It steadies the nerves. Master Henry will know what to do, blind or not."

Both Agnes and Thwaite accepted, although neither of them normally smoked, noting that the cigarettes were of very good quality, the brand that his Lordship offered to guests. It would be a shame to pass those up. Thwaite had to hand it to Clark; he knew how to ape his betters; he knew how to present himself to the world in the best of lights, and you had to admire a man, or a woman, who was not caught entirely in the strait-jacket of his or her own class.

It was a subtle thing, of course; one had to be able to carry it off, otherwise one could be seen as ridiculous, putting on airs, inappropriate. All in all, Clark managed it well, Thwaite considered, as Felix lit their cigarettes with a flourish, using a heavy silver-plated table lighter that Thwaite had seen in his room.

"That's a nice lighter," Agnes remarked.

"It was given to me as a present," Felix said, pocketing the lighter, intimating, but not saying, that it had come from his Lordship. They fell silent as the noise outside went on. Felix reached for an ashtray and placed it on the bed between them.

There was unbearable pain in his leg. Henry opened his eyes to a grey nothingness, aware that he must have been knocked out and shot in the leg, that his blood was seeping out into the sand of the desert. Overhead the sound of aircraft vibrated the air. As he pulled himself up to a sitting position, feeling around with both hands, he thought that he was in a trench and that for some reason he could not see. Perhaps it was nighttime, yet he could discern a faint grey light.

Abruptly, in the near distance a gun started up, heavy artillery, its booming sound reverberating through his head. Unfamiliar in sound, he thought it must be an enemy gun.

"Man the guns, Thompson!" he yelled. "Man the bloody guns, for Christ's sake!" He felt around himself again, attempting to crawl, without success, then with his back to the trench he eased himself up to a standing position, crying out with the pain of it. "Anyone there?"

Fighting the pain, he put weight on the injured leg, finding that it supported him. Panting from exertion, his face dripping sweat, he wavered in the upright position, and then found that he was wearing gloves. Slowly, feeling that his sanity had deserted him, not knowing where he was, he eased off the gloves and let them drop. Shaking with what he assumed was shock, he fingered his face and head, found that he was wearing a thick cap and scarf made of wool. And an overcoat. "Oh, God," he whispered. "God, help me."

He touched his injured leg, and felt something wet — blood. He must be lost somewhere in the desert, wearing inappropriate heavy clothing, having been in the line of fire. Nights could be very cold in the desert sometimes.

Absurdly, when he touched the sides of the narrow trench, they felt cold, like frozen clay soil. A he reached up above his head, he felt air. Men of the tank corps feared being burned in their tanks, unable to get out. Men in all corps feared being buried alive as shells exploded near them. He thought of that as the claustrophobic nearness of the trench walls crowded in on him. Then the booming of the gun ended; the sound of planes was receding.

In the new quiet he could hear the rasping of his own breath and was aware of the shaking of his body. Equally absurdly, he could hear the barking of a dog. In those moments, in a limbo, he could not remember who he was. "Is anyone there?" he shouted. "Thompson?" Again the dog barked, the sound coming closer, then receding again, as though the dog were running up and down at speed. It must be night-time, he thought again, because everything remained dark. At his back was the solid wall of a trench ... that was about all he could be sure of, the barking of the dog perhaps an auditory hallucination. "Captain Calborne," he said out loud. "Captain Henry Calborne."

There was a peculiar silence, in which he could hear blood pounding through his head. The dog, if indeed he had heard a real dog, seemed to have run off. "Calborne, sir. Reporting for duty," he said. There was no reply. The dark quiet bore down on him oppressively. It could be that he was trapped in no-man's-land, all others dead. "Is anyone there?" he shouted again. "Help! For God's sake, help me."

The dog was back, barking right into his face, at a level with his head, so that he recoiled, feeling its warm breath. Then the dog was down in the trench with him, brushing against his injured leg, so that he cried out.

"You're all right, sir," a voice said near him, and someone touched his arm. "You're all right." The accent was English, Kentish or Sussex.

"Thank you ... thank you," Henry said, turning his head towards the speaker, who was next to him. "I don't know where I am ... I think I've been shot. I'm not absolutely certain who I am either. Can you help me?"

"Yes, I can certainly do that. I heard you shouting, sir, from the road where I was sheltering in a ditch, and your dog came to find me. You're on the Calborne estate, in a ditch yourself. There's just been an air-raid. You, sir, are Henry Calborne, and I'm Jim Langridge. I work on the estate for your father. I assume you fell in here." The man spoke carefully, enunciating each word, as though making quite sure he was understood.

"Yes ... I must have. I'm on the estate? Oh ... yes ... Langridge, I remember. We've met before ... of course. It's a relief. I thought I was in Africa. My leg ... it seems to be bleeding. Am I blind?"

"Yes, sir. You've been blind for some time, so I heard. Don't you worry now, we've got everything in hand."

"I thought I was in a trench, you know. I think I must have been knocked out." His teeth were chattering so much that the words came out slurred.

"That's understandable. We're in a common or garden variety ditch, sir, which you could say serves the purpose of a trench. That's an easy mistake to make if you're blind. Once we're out, I can have a look at the leg. Do you reckon you can walk?"

"Yes, I think so."

"Right. Turn sideways, like this; put your hands on my shoulders; then I'll be able to guide you out. When the ditch becomes shallow, we can just walk out of it."

Together they shuffled forward awkwardly, the bottom of the ditch going up a slight incline, with Henry's hands on the shoulders of the other man, as he had seem photographs of men walking in single file on the battlefields, blinded by mustard gas in the Great War. Those pictures flashed through his mind, like the flickering pictures of an old film.

"We're out of the ditch now. There's a tree stump here," Langridge said. "If you sit on it, I can look at the leg."

Shaking, sick with shock and pain, Henry allowed himself to be guided to sit.

"I've got a flask of hot tea, sir. You'd better have some, while I see to this leg."

While Henry put his trembling hands round the metal cup full of tea and sipped from it, he sensed the man kneeling in front of him, felt him gently ease off the riding boot and roll up his trouser leg. "The wound's split open; you must have knocked it. If I put some handkerchiefs on it and tie them round with a belt, that should do it, that should stop the bleeding. Don't you worry, it's not too bad. No bones broken."

"Thank God. It's been badly infected, you know."

"A gunshot wound, sir?"

"Yes ... machine gun." Memories, again in pictures, were coming back now. "There's a clean handkerchief in the right hand pocket of my overcoat."

"All right, sir. You just rest there and let me take care of everything. You've had a terrible shock. You just get that tea down you as fast as you can. Were you on your own out here?"

"Yes ... I think so." He was shaking violently now, his teeth chattering against the rim of the cup as he sipped the hot tea.

"Good dog you have there. She came to get me."

Jim Langridge tied his own handkerchief and Henry Calborne's over the opened wound, an ugly, long gash that had all the hallmarks of a wound that had not healed properly for a long time — red scars and pockmarks deep in the flesh.

"You must think I'm an awful coward ... shaking like this," Henry said.

"That's the last thing I would think. You've not only had a bad shock, you're feeling the cold now, and you've lost some blood. I was in the last war. You don't have to apologize to me, sir, if that's what you're doing."

When the leg was tied up and the boot on again, Jim Langridge looked up to see three figures walking quickly down the driveway. As they got closer he could recognize the butler, the cook, and his Lordship's secretary from the big house, all wearing what seemed to him an ill chosen assortment of clothing, hats askew, flying scarves, that did not seem quite appropriate for the coldness of the day. With them was an unruly pack of assorted dogs that gambolled about over the frozen grass verges.

As they got closer, Thwaite broke into a shambling run, followed by the cook who still wore her long white apron beneath her open mackintosh that flapped about as she ran, while the secretary strode along, it being beneath his dignity to run, Jim assumed.

"We need a stretcher," Jim shouted, trying to forestall protestations of alarm. "Is there one at the house?"

"We have several." Thwaite was sobbing, falling on his knees beside Henry, babbling about never being able to forgive himself.

"It's just the wound that's split open," Jim explained to him. "Everything else is all right." He spoke reassuringly, for the sake of the injured man, doubting that Captain Calborne's mental state was all right. *Poor sod,* he thought, *poor, bloody sod.* Henry sat with his head and shoulders hunched forward, his hands grasped together as though he wanted to still the trembling in them, ashamed for others to witness.

"What a relief," Thwaite whispered, tears running over his lined face, as he took one of Master Henry's hands and covered it with both his own.

"Run up to the house and bring a stretcher," Jim called out to Felix. "Phone for the doctor while you're there. Tell him the wound's split open and bleeding. Look sharp about it." With satisfaction, he watched Clark turn on his heel and start to run back. Men like Felix made him sick, poncing about in lovely clothes, playing at war in spare time, claiming chronic ill health, no doubt. Perhaps he was being unfair, but he could not help what he felt just then.

While Thwaite clung on to one of Henry's hands, the cook held the other, having disengaged the cup from which Henry had been drinking. Both were crying.

Jim took off his overcoat and spread it on the ground. "You'd be better off lying down, sir," he said to Henry, noting his pallor, "until the stretcher comes. You need to keep warm, and keep your head down."

Wordlessly, Henry allowed himself to be guided to lie down. It was a relief to be flat, to feel blood returning to his head, faintness receding. Dimly he was aware that Thwaite and Agnes were placing their own coats over him, here on home ground, before he passed into a strange kind of sleep.

∞ Chapter 17

Before long, Jim Langridge found himself in the kitchens of Calborne House, sitting at a long table, spooning potato soup into his mouth, while upstairs the village doctor, together with the district nurse, attended to Captain Calborne. There was a hushed and shocked sense in the house of a terrible calamity having been averted. Even the dogs, alert and watchful, were silent. In spite of air raids and the sound of the anti-aircraft guns, it was as though the war itself had truly entered Calborne House for the first time; it touched them with fear and disbelief, in the way that one senses a spirit in a house reputed to be haunted. They walked about quietly, spoke in low voices, as though each one bore a heavy burden.

Between the four of them they had managed to carry the injured man on the canvas stretcher up to the house, arriving just as Lord Calborne and Reg Wheeler had driven up. Alarming for the old man to see his son lying pale, inert, he had staggered as he hurried over to them, where it was left to Jim to give an explanation. The others had been in various stages of shock and regret.

Having finished the soup, Jim was offered a generous slice of treacle tart by Agnes, who hovered about him like a mother hen with her chick. "I won't say no," he said, accepting the plate, as she also refilled his cup with tea.

"Mr. Langridge," Thwaite said, stepping into the room, "his Lordship would like to see you in his study before you leave. I'll show you where."

While Jim had been eating, the cook and the butler between them had been cleaning blood stains and soil marks off his overcoat.

~ "Come in."

Not many people ever saw the inside of Lord Calborne's study. As Jim entered, he understood that and resolved not to stare about him like a bumpkin. Accordingly, he had a general impression of tall windows, a high ceiling, oak panelling, comfortable furniture, and an impressive expansive desk. It was not ostentatious, more a place where a man who must he at the helm of a large working estate had to make his everyday decisions, so that it was functional as well as comfortable. That this was a sanctuary also was evident.

At the same time he felt self-conscious about his own working clothes, the stained trousers, the work shirt and waistcoat that were damp with sweat, from where he had been shovelling rubble in the village.

"You most likely saved my son's life," Lord Calborne said, coming over from behind his desk to shake his hand. "He could have bled to death before anyone found him. How did you happen to be in the vicinity?"

"Well, sir, I'd been up to the village, helping to clear bombed houses ... shovelling, and the like. I was walking back home, going to take a short-cut through some fields when the air-raid started ... got into a ditch. When it died down, I heard someone shouting for help. Then the dog came to find me and led me to where the Captain was in the other ditch."

Lord Calborne nodded, his face bleak with sadness. "It was fortuitous, to say the least, that you were there, and that you knew what to do. He's shell-shocked, you know. This incident will perhaps be a test of whether he is going to recover enough to go back to the army ... assuming that his sight comes back, which I am thinking it will."

They stood together in the centre of the room. "A good thing he's out of it for now, sir," Jim said. "What he needs is time." Platitudes were comforting, he knew that from long experience; the more, the better. From constant use, they were well-meant and understood. One did not stand about thinking of complicated words in times of trouble.

"Yes. We must be thankful for what we have, thankful that he's on home ground, while so many are not."

They talked for a few more minutes, then his Lordship offered Jim a lift home in the Daimler.

"Oh no, sir. Thank you all the same. I'll walk, I need to clear my head."

They parted on very good terms, Jim fortified for the home journey by the food and tea that he had been given.

~ As he walked away from Calborne House in the general direction of his cottage at Badgers Gate, intending to take footpaths and walk across fields, he noticed that rooks, flapping and cawing, had gathered in clusters in some of the tall oak trees near the house. They were starkly black, like works of art, against the blankness of the grey winter sky. They drew his attention back into present life from a place where the tentacles of 1915 had sucked him into a morass of dissonance, where sense was senseless and meaning lost. So it was with a certain gratitude that he concentrated on them.

Forcing himself back, he looked down at the ground in front of him, where each frost rimed blade of grass was held perfectly in his sight. Henry Calborne's hollow face had been as pale as frost when he had lain so still under the piled coats, as though he were dead in a shroud where only his face showed. It was possible that Henry, heir to the estate, might never inherit now that he was in the clutches of the machine of destruction.

How poignant are a man's hands in death, he had thought in 1915 as he had lain in a field looking up at the summer sky on the march up to the Front. Henry Calborne's hands, thin and white, had trembled as he had sat on the tree stump; hands that would have played a piano, perhaps plucked at the resplendent harp that had been visible through the open door of the drawing room in the big house, had played the violin. Perhaps he did still play; one could make music without sight.

No, do not go to that dark place of dead hands, put it out of mind, he told himself. Look instead at the mist that rises over the shaw ahead, the blackness of the rooks in bare trees against the grey winter sky, the hedgerow stiff with cold and replete with petrified hips and haws left over from autumn; hark to the sound of water in the nearby brook, the quiet scuff of boots on the frozen clay path. Think of firelight in a kitchen range, the crackling of coal, its blessed heat, the roaring in the chimney. Think of the warmth and smallness of a child's hand, like a young bird fallen from its nest, rescued.

His thoughts went to the cottage in Bullrush Lane that was slowly being rebuilt. The beams of the roof and the underpinnings of the whole structure were being shored up. Sometimes he went there to make sure that the shed where he had left some tools was still padlocked. On those occasions he unlocked the wash-house with the big iron key, to sit for a while, to think, perhaps smoke a cigarette. The place was forlorn without the warmth of the fire under the copper and the steam from hot water, yet as he sat there with the door partially open, he felt a kind of peace. Perhaps next summer, or late spring, they would move back there.

〜 As he passed near the mansion of Sir Otto Lind, and the farm that also belonged to him, he saw the foreman, a man by the name of Webber — as miserly in human compassion as his employer — standing in the farm lane beside his car. Their eyes met as Jim walked past, and neither man said anything.

Webber had once waylaid him, accused him of taking housing by accepting Badgers Gate that should rightly be for men working for Sir Otto, to which he had replied that the house had been condemned as unfit for human habitation. Because there was no satisfactory reply to that, Webber had given none, had simply stared at him with something like hatred in his eyes. At the time, seeking for an explanation of such animosity, Jim had understood it as a kind of envy, which was odd really, as he had been in dire straits. It was not worth thinking about, much less worrying over.

As he walked on, he began to sing: "Hinky Dinky, Hinky Dinky, Parley voo, Hinky Dinky, Hinky Dinky Parley voo, Mademoiselle from Armentières, Hinky Dinky Parley voo," which he kept up until he was out of earshot. Then, in among some trees, he sang as he walked, the plaintive, sentimental song which he sometimes sang for the children: "There's a long, long trail a-winding/Into the land of my dreams/Where the nightingales are singing/And a white moon beams." Men had sung that song from 1915, far from home. It seemed appropriate now, with the image of Henry Calborne's bloodied leg sharp in his mind.

~ "You've been a long time," May said when he entered the warm sitting room of the cottage, coming directly in from outside. She coming in from the kitchen, wiping her hands on her apron, and her face flushed from bending over the copper full of hot water. "I thought you might have been hurt in the air raid." What she meant was that she thought he might have been killed. That possibility hung between them, as it always did. Had he not come, she would have waited till near dark, then taken the kids and gone out to look for him.

Rubbing his numb hands together before the fire, he told her the story.

"Will he be all right?" They stood close together in the warmth, united in their pity, only a thin line of altered fate separating them from Henry Calborne.

"I should think so. He's being well looked after."

"The old man must find it difficult to bear," she said.

∽ Chapter 18

Sarah Burroughs was in her bedroom at the vicarage in Fernden, where she had lit a coal fire in the inadequate small Victorian cast iron grate. It had taken a while for the scrunched up newspaper and the few sticks of kindling to ignite the coal, and now it began to glow and give off a little warmth. During the air raid that afternoon they had all been down in the cellar, she and the rest of the family.

She felt the need to be alone for a while now, to take respite from her activities which had grown to a point where she had little free time to herself. Besides, she had a cold coming on, bringing with it a headache. Accordingly, she had told her mother and sister Mary that she wanted to rest for a while, not to be disturbed, and she had pushed the one armchair that was in the room closer to the fire. That part of the room was cosy, with a lamp on the side table near the chair and the book of poetry that she intended to browse, a cup of tea beside it.

The vicarage generally was icy cold in winter, with high ceilings and spacious rooms that belonged to an earlier age when the vicars of the village had had up to fifteen children, plus a few servants. This year, they had closed up some rooms and kept passage doors shut in a serious attempt to make the place warmer and to save on coal. So far it was working quite well. Lord Calborne gave them wood, already sawn into logs, from his estate.

Sarah, curled up in her chair, with a blanket over her lower body, stared dreamily into the fire and thought of the Bronte family in the vicarage in Yorkshire. They had all died of tuberculosis, except the elderly father who had outlived all his children. Sometimes she thought that she too would be consumptive, when even the fires and the hot water bottles and the paraffin heaters failed to warm up the house and the winter wind blew gustily around the vast open gardens and battered against the tall windows. Then the inhabitants of the house wore layers of jumpers, heavy tweeds, the women with long calf-length skirts and thick stockings.

These days she thought a lot about Henry Calborne, of how much she cared for him, although she had tried not to. He would go away again and she would join the ranks of those women — the girl friends, the wives, the mothers and sisters — who pined for their men. Up to then she had allowed herself to feel sorry for them, as one does who is standing on the outside. As she felt herself drawn in, she found that almost all the time now she was on the edge of tears.

It was not clear to her whether she would be acceptable to Lord Calborne as an appropriate consort for his son, although he appeared to regard her with interest and affection. There would be little money for her to bring to any union, for her father, one of eight children, had not inherited much, and he was a generous man who gave of his own money where he saw a need. "Money always marries money,",was a saying that was bandied about in certain circles, and generally understood where it was not voiced.

Often her parents commented that people in general now were more realistic, more cynical, than they had been at the beginning of the last war. How could they not be, when this was a war against civilians as much as about armies. Perhaps they would also be more realistic about marriage. Whatever the outcome might be between herself and Henry, Sarah felt that all vestiges of her girlhood had gone.

Had there not been a war, Henry would probably have been suitably married by now, perhaps with a child or two, and she herself might never have come within his circle. Yet there was a change in attitudes, she sensed it, an opening up.

Henry, she thought, must be eight years older than she was, and although general opinion informed her that she was mature for her age, she was nonetheless inexperienced in a broader way of life in spite of the forced maturing experiences of war. She hoped to rectify this by taking up her nursing training ... perhaps she should do that as soon as possible. What worldly man would want a young woman whose life had been bounded by a country vicarage and village.

Sarah closed her eyes after drinking the tea in a few gulps, pulled the blanket up over her shoulders and settled her head into the side of the winged chair. Soon enough the German planes would return from wherever in London and vicinity they had gone to bomb, making their way back to France; some would have a bomb or two left over, to drop on civilians in other places.

One must look after oneself as well as others, otherwise one would break down and be useless, she thought. Far away, down in the front hall of the house, the telephone rang. It was not for her to answer this time. She allowed herself to sleep.

∼ The siren woke her up sometime later, so that she automatically flung aside the blanket, got up out of the chair and made sure that the fire guard was firmly over the fireplace before walking calmly downstairs.

Her sister Mary, tall and slender, beautiful with her red hair and hazel eyes, was still in the kitchen when Sarah entered it. The cellar steps went down from there. Mary, taking off her apron, looked at Sarah speculatively. "How's the rotten cold?" Mary had trained to be a teacher, then had come home to be with her parents at the outbreak of war.

"I feel better for having had a little shut-eye."

"There was a telephone call for you from Lord Calborne. He would like you to telephone him, for some reason. At your convenience, he said, when I told him you were sleeping."

"Oh? I wonder what that could be about." Now that Christmas was over, the children's party, she did not have as many reasons to go to the big house, only if her father needed to be driven there, or Henry invited her. "Are you sure he wants me, and not Daddy?"

"He asked specifically for you."

They went down into the musty cellar, where her parents were already sitting on an old sofa. Early on in the war the place had been cleared out and aired out as much as possible and basic items of furniture hauled down. Sarah remembered the laughter and the joking that ensued when they had manoeuvred the sofa down the narrow steps, vowing then that they would never bring it up again.

What, Sarah wondered, did Lord Calborne want with her? The prospect of seeing Henry again set up a nervousness in her that had nothing to do with the impending German bombers overhead. There were only two full days of army leave left for Henry, so it was possible that Lord Calborne intended to hold a farewell tea for him and had telephoned to invite her. Several times Henry had telephoned her himself; it was a little odd that his father had done so on his behalf, unless it was to be a surprise. She and Henry had planned that she would see him off at the railway station.

Patiently they waited in the depths of the house for the German bombers to go over them, back to France. There would be fewer of them, Sarah speculated, than on the inward journey. How incomprehensible, mad, and pointless it all was.

~ "Would you be so kind as to call at the house, Sarah, if you possibly could," Lord Calborne said when she telephoned him, his voice calm and reasonable, as she had always known it. "Henry's had an accident, fell into a ditch during the air raid this afternoon when he was out by himself ... nothing too serious, so I don't want to alarm you. It's just an opening up of the old wound ... and he's asking for you, Sarah. We would all be so grateful if you could come."

Sarah felt as though her throat had closed up and that she could not breathe. Panic, such as she had never experienced before, seemed to take away all initiative from her.

"Sarah?"

"Yes. I'll come immediately, Lord Calborne ... of course I'll come. Please ... tell Henry I'm coming."

"Thank you. We could send the car."

"I'll come on the motorbike. Goodbye."

Sarah stood in the cold hallway. Already, in the space of a few seconds, she had entered that other world where women wait in dread. Her heart was thumping, her mind searching this way and that, as though she must prepare herself for a great feat and her body was gearing up for it automatically without any specific direction that she was conscious of.

"What is it?" Mary came up to her.

"Something's happened to Henry ... he's had an accident ... fell into a ditch and hurt himself. Would you tell father I'm taking the bike?"

Sarah ran up the stairs to change from her skirt into riding breeches, a clean blouse and warm jumper. As she did so, her mind was already projecting forward to what she would find at the big house, of how Henry would look. *I won't cry when I see him*, she thought, because that would give her away in front of all of them. *No, I mustn't cry.*

By the back door, Mary helped her into her warm outdoor gear. "For goodness' sake, drive carefully. You're all strung up."

"I'll be all right once I get on the bike," Sarah said, as she pulled on the leather hat that came down over her ears like a pilot's helmet, then put on a pair of goggles.

The two sisters hugged, and Mary kissed Sarah on the cheek. "Telephone us later if you can, so that we know."

"I will."

Sarah ran out to the carriage house where she parked the motorbike beside her father's car, a car that was seldom used these days. The doors of the carriage house were left open so that they could leave quickly if her father were called out. She started up the engine of the bike, and Mary came out to wave her off.

Calmness came over Sarah as she drove the motorbike through the main gates of the vicarage, then past the familiar few cottages on one side of the road and the churchyard and church on the other. That brought her into the High Street of the village, and there she made a right turn onto the country road that would take her to Calborne House. The engine made a satisfying loud purring noise.

~ There was no point, Sarah discovered, in vowing not to cry when faced with a certain situation, for where love was concerned emotion was stronger than will-power. As she stood in the doorway of the drawing room at Calborne House, with Lord Calborne beside her — from where she could see Henry lying in a half sitting position on a long sofa near the fire, his eyes closed and his head to one side on a cushion, she burst into tears and turned away quickly so that Henry would not hear her.

"Come," Lord Calborne said, taking her arm and leading her into the study where he shut the door. Sarah sat down and covered her face with her hands, sobbing and gasping for air. From the pocket of her breeches she extracted a handkerchief that was none too clean, and held it to her eyes.

"Sorry," she whispered. They had summoned her to be of some help, and here she was going to pieces. There could be no secrets now from Henry's father.

"Here, my dear," Lord Calborne handed her a small glass of brandy. "Take a few sips of that. Perhaps it was unfair of me to expect you to come at such short notice. You'll have to forgive me for that."

"Oh, no." Sarah looked at him with a little upward, darting glance, then looked down again. "It's quite all right. I wanted to come." It was no good pretending that she could be calm and sophisticated, because here she was with a flushed, soggy face, kneading her soiled handkerchief in her lap with her free hand while she held the brandy glass in the other, knowing that she would choke on the unfamiliar alcohol if she took more than the tiniest sip.

"He's all right, really," Lord Calborne said. "He needs to rest. He asked if you could spend some time with him, and it's so good of you to come. The last thing we want is for you to be upset."

"I'm so sorry," she said, staring down into the glass of amber liquid. "I thought I would be strong. It's because I thought he would be going away, too."

"Yes, I understand. Well, I've been in touch with the military hospital in Cornwall and he's had his leave extended for a further two weeks, as has Captain Basil Seager, who is to escort him back. Then we are to drive them down to Hampshire to get on a train there, to bypass London, and then when they get into Dorset they'll be met by a military ambulance for the remainder of the journey."

He went on talking of their plans, so that Sarah felt herself calmed as she sipped the brandy.

Lord Calborne walked over to the tall window where the view of the garden soothed him — a long vista that was enduring, immutable, except with the changing of the seasons. *We are alone*, he thought, as he often did when the knowledge struck him. *In this country we are quite alone. It is up to all of us, to each one of us, to endure.*

"I'm all right now," Sarah said, after a while.

Earlier, she had brought the motorbike round to the back yard of the house, near the stables and one of the back doors, planning to seek out Thwaite or the cook in the kitchens. That way she had given herself more time to prepare mentally, or so she thought. As it happened, they had given her a cup of coffee first, a delaying tactic, and still it had not worked.

"We'll try again, then, shall we?" Lord Calborne said kindly. "I know exactly how you feel, Sarah. The same thing happened to me when I went to Hampshire to see Henry in the military hospital ... I couldn't face it at first, because he was so changed, you see. Come on, my dear."

This time she walked through the drawing room door and Henry's father announced her presence: "Sarah's here, Henry. I'll leave you now. Ring for Thwaite if you'd like tea." After letting in Marigold, the only dog that was allowed into the living quarters, he went out and shut the door.

As he walked back to his study, where he intended to have a small glass of whisky and soda, he thought how nice it was to have a woman there, even one so young and inexperienced as Sarah Burroughs, to help ease the emotional burden that both he and Henry had to bear. With her sweetness and youth, there was a core of great common sense, intelligence and strength, as well as loyalty and integrity. Nevertheless, he must not expect too much of her; it was not fair to her. It helped that she loved his son. Neither was she unacceptable to him, he found then, if there should be further developments.

~ "Sarah!" Henry held out a hand to her, his eyes, very blue and clear, moving to where he thought her face would be. "Do come and sit beside me. I've wanted so much to see you."

There was a low chair placed beside him, as though it had been put there just for her, and as she sank down into it and touched Henry's hand, the tears began to flow again.

Two lamps were on in the room, the blackout shades were already down so that no light would show to the enemy when the night raids came, and the large room was mainly lit by the firelight. The dog, having sniffed at Henry's hand, clambered into the worn-down and much chewed wicker dog basket.

"Don't cry, dear girl. I'm not in any pain now, or in any danger. The doctor dosed me up with something that's very effective." When he took her hand, he was comforting her, as he held her hand rather than she his.

"How did it happen?"

By the time Henry had told her the story, Sarah had regained her composure somewhat. Still, she was tense with emotion, with the unspoken hopes that hung between them, and sensing the same tension in him.

"This war ... I hate it so much," Sarah said bitterly. "We must fight, because Hitler's a madman, and those around him are mad. Presumably the majority of Germans don't think so. Father says that he's evil personified, and father is certainly one to grapple with the nature of evil. I wish we didn't have to."

"It's not easy to change the momentum of war, once it's started. That may be why I'm blind. Because I can't bear to see the chaos that it's created, can't look at the death and suffering."

"You shouldn't feel ashamed of it ... if you do. It has a sort of logic to it." She bent forward, close to him, giving over her hand to him, that he held in both of his, firmly.

"You're right, it does have. I'm not ashamed, exactly. Mystified by it ... and sort of awed. The irony of it is that I can't see you, I can't see the house, the estate, things I want to see."

"Perhaps it's one of those rare instances of a perfect explanation of nature that we sometimes experience."

"Yes. One of the ironies is that actual blindness makes you realize there are other ways of being blind. When we can see fully, you know, we fail to notice what we don't want to notice sometimes. We dismiss things; we become blinkered; we become mentally and emotionally blind. Then when you are actually blind, your inner vision forces you to 'see' them."

"It must be a torment that you can't shut off that inner vision."

"I sometimes think that my sight will come back when my brain has processed all that I've seen and done in the war."

"That would be the logical thing," Sarah said earnestly. "Perhaps."

"We must change the subject. Enough about me and my poor, sick body. I want to know all about you. Shall we have tea? Then you can tell me. I know for a fact that Agnes has made cakes."

"Let's," she said, smiling. Unexpectedly, Henry leaned forward and kissed her on the cheek, then he fumbled about to press a bell that was fixed to the wall near him. "I'm starving actually," she added. "Sometimes I forget to eat when there's so much else going on."

Before long, Thwaite had looked in and taken the order for tea.

"Tell me what you've been doing since I last saw you, Sarah, every little detail about the people you meet in the village on your visits, because I miss seeing the village people."

"Well ... let me see. There's a woman by whom I'm very impressed and humbled, because she has seventeen children and, when she can't stand them any longer, all the noise, she declares that she's going to have a 'quiet time' and she sits down, throws her apron over her head and face. The effect on the children is miraculous. They tiptoe around and stop talking, while she can stay behind her apron for as long as she likes."

"How marvellous!"

"Apparently, she's told the younger children that if they aren't quiet while she has the apron over her face, she'll disappear in a puff of smoke."

It was good to hear Henry laugh, so Sarah wracked her brains for all the dramas of her life as her father's helper when people were in need, without giving away any confidences or identities. Most of the people she knew managed to find some saving grace, some humour, if only black humour, in the circumstances of lives that had become abnormal for the most part.

Over tea, they talked and laughed, succeeding in placing the war behind a superficial barrier of gaiety. All the time the fire crackled and the lamps threw a muted yellow light on the comfortable furnishings of the room, on the mellow reds of the Persian carpets and the rich green paint of the walls.

"I must get back before the blackout," Sarah said suddenly, remembering that she would not be able to put the motorbike lights on.

"Don't worry. Wheeler can take you back in one of the smaller cars. Then you can pick up the motor bike tomorrow, or I'll get Felix to bring it back to you. He knows how to ride one. Reg Wheeler can see in the dark, I swear. Besides, he knows the roads round here so well, he could probably drive them blindfolded."

"You're very persuasive," she said. It seemed to her then that the mood between them changed suddenly, in one of the many twists and turns that emotion can take between two people.

"If I were not blind ... disabled ... things could perhaps be different between us, Sarah. I care for you so much. On the other hand, you're very young ... perhaps I have no right to hope that you would care for me in the same way. I'm thirty, and feel so much older. You have a life that you must make for yourself."

"You mustn't feel those doubts," she said, bending her head down as though he could actually see the colour in her face. "This war ... as much as I hate it ... we wouldn't have come to know each other without it. Now I can't imagine not knowing you in this way, and when you go I don't know how I'm going to bear it."

"It's a mutual feeling," he said. "I feel as though I'm trying to take hold of something that continually slips out of my hands. Will you come to see me every day, Sarah?"

"Of course I will. I want to."

"God willing, I'll get one more leave before I have to go back to duty."

"If you don't, perhaps I can meet you halfway," Sarah said. "With the bike." As they both laughed, she had visions of herself careening across the countryside on twisting small roads with the trusty motorbike and sidecar, suitably goggled and helmeted, bundled up, going to a tryst with her lover at breakneck speed.

"I'll get Thwaite to speak to Wheeler about driving you home," Henry said.

～ In the car, Sarah leaned back into the corner, a wool rug over her knees. A twilight illuminated the way for them as Wheeler eased the car forward, without lights, slowly along the driveway from the house. Glad that the chauffeur could not see her face, she allowed it to fall into its inclined mood of misery. As she had said to Henry, she did not know how she would bear the separation to come. It loomed before her, so that she could see no end to it. On the other hand, she would spend two glorious weeks with him, between her duties.

A decision had come to her. During the next one or two days she would write to the hospital Matron with whom she had been corresponding to say that she would like if possible to begin her training at the next intake of student nurses. The thought of remaining in Fernden after Henry had gone was increasingly unbearable to her. At home they had always known she must go, so would have to manage somehow without her.

Chapter 19

The next two weeks seemed to go by with unprecedented speed for Sarah, who became so used to going to and from Calborne House on the motorbike that she often thought it would find its own way there if she failed to concentrate.

Inexorably, the time came when Henry was to go. Captain Basil Seager had come the previous day, had spent the night at the big house, and they were ready to depart early in the morning, in the Daimler, with Lord Calborne accompanying them. She and the three permanent members of the household staff would be left behind to wonder and to grieve at the parting.

It had been a restless night for her, in which her mind would not remain still for more than a few seconds, and as she piloted the motorbike up the driveway to the big house she could see the Daimler already in front of the main door and Wheeler putting luggage into the boot. The sight of it, a scene that would remain, she suspected, forever in her mind, brought that weighty sense of inevitability and helplessness to her, the marching on of fate.

The driveway continued on round the side of the house, and she took that in order to leave the bike in the back courtyard. An idea was formulating in her mind as she parked, that after Henry had gone she would go for a walk through the woods on the estate to try to contain her grief, before getting on the bike to drive home.

It was a crisp, cold day, and she exchanged her helmet and goggles for a wool beret that came down over her ears, and wool gloves for the leather gauntlets that she wore, putting her driving gear into the sidecar. A watery sunlight shone through pale grey clouds and illuminated the frosted grass and the stark trees of the estate as far as she could see. It was as though the world had been abandoned by all living things except herself. After the noise of the engine, the silence of the place descended on her like a cloak, as did a sense that she must live in the moment.

At the front of the house, Henry was coming down the steps, with Captain Seager at his side, holding his arm, their heads close together, talking earnestly, so that Sarah felt tentative, as though she were intruding, until Captain Seager saw her and waved. "There's Sarah," she heard him say, at which Henry lifted up his head as though he could see her, and the gesture filled her with a sharp longing that it might be so. They were both in full uniform now, the formality of it serving to reinforce in Sarah the sense of his moving away from her, back to something that he had left only temporarily. Fate had allowed her to have him for a little while.

"Hello again, Sarah," Captain Seager said, extending a hand. "So good to see you. I'll leave you two alone. I expect you have much to say to one another. I'll give a hand with the luggage."

"Shall we walk round the far side of the house so that we can be alone for a few minutes?" Henry said, putting his arm through hers.

There was a gravel foot path round the right hand side of the house below a substantial terrace, where they could be hidden from view. With only a slight limp, leaning on her and on his stick, Henry was able to walk well. Over the past two weeks a nurse had come to help him exercise.

"You'll know where I'll be for the next little while, Sarah," he said.

"Yes."

"Nothing will change for now."

"No."

"When I can see again ... assuming the positive ... as well as being physically fit, they might send me back to Cairo. I could possibly be of some use at the army headquarters there," Henry said, as they walked slowly along the gravel path beside a winter flower bed that was spiky with frozen lavender stalks. To their left the stone urns and balustrades of the terrace loomed above them.

"And if they want to send you back to combat?"

"I would have to consider that at the time. If I have a choice."

Sarah, distracting herself, could imagine that in the summer this garden would be redolent with myriad scents and colours of flowers, with the humming of honey bees and bumble bees, with the delicate flitting of butterflies, living things that had no consciousness of war. Although the bees understood danger, as she did, otherwise they would not be able to sting.

"What's the situation in North Africa now?" she asked, her head down against the cold wind. With Henry's arm through hers, their hands were gripped tightly together. "I haven't read much about it in the papers."

"Well ... we've managed to make a few clever, successful moves against the Italians, so Basil told me. Thousands have been taken prisoner. Apparently, we've got the Australians on hand to help, from Palestine."

"How does Basil know this?"

"He keeps his ear to the ground. Though I don't suppose it's secret. Father reads the papers pretty closely, and he didn't say anything to me. Quite rightly, I suppose. He thinks I want to forget it. Perhaps we'll be all right there if the Germans don't come in. They're very professional and ruthless."

"Aren't we?"

"Not in the same way. At least, I don't think we are."

"Well, I'll write to you, wherever you are."

"Write to me today, will you, Sarah? So that I'll get a letter very soon, and I'll do the same, to let you know I've arrived."

Out of sight of the others, he stopped, took her into his arms and kissed her. They clung on to each other. This tangible, physical thing was something precious given to them for only a flash of time, Sarah knew. The feel of his heavy greatcoat under her hands, the warmth of his face against hers, that even the winter wind could not obliterate, were things that she must hold on to in memory.

Before long there was a shout from someone indicating that the car must leave, for they had a strict schedule to keep to.

Henry took a small package from a pocket of his greatcoat and gave it to her. "Open this when I've gone," he said.

"What are we to do?"

"Darling Sarah. Without my exerting a claim on you in any way ... will you wait for me?"

"Yes." She fumbled in a pocket of her jacket for a package of photographs of herself that he had asked for, that he hoped to see one day when his sight came back. "I've brought the photographs," she said, putting them into his hand. "They're some that Mummy took of me in the garden at the vicarage this last summer."

"Thank you." With their arms linked, they walked back to the car, where all luggage was stowed, ready for departure.

With a last squeeze of hands, Henry got into the back seat with his father. "Bon voyage!" Sarah called out, forcing a lightness to her voice, then watched the car as it moved quietly away from her down the driveway towards the main road and disappeared among the trees of the small wood.

Sarah turned away quickly, away from Thwaite, the cook, and Felix Clark who stood near the door waving, and ran from the house towards the path that went to the chapel. Clutching the package that Henry had given her, as though it were a lifeline between them, she ran over the icy path and did not stop until she had gained the porch of the chapel. There she fought to catch her breath and ease the pain of exertion and grief that had centred in her chest.

The door to the chapel was locked. It had not occurred to her that it would be locked; she had wanted to go inside, for sanctuary, and kneel in front of the altar. Instead, she would go to her father's church, the church of St. Mary.

Sitting on the stone bench in the porch, she opened the package that was wrapped in white tissue paper and tied with a thin green ribbon, to find that it was a book of poems, leather bound, entitled *Poems from the Great War*. When she opened the front cover, she found a note, folded, and a photograph of Henry, head and shoulders, in army uniform. He had stared straight at the camera, his youthful, open face curious and happy, a pre-war face.

"Oh God," she whispered.

She opened the book at random, and saw a name, May Cannan,

beneath which the words: "We planned to shake the world together, you and I / Being young, and very wise ..."

Quickly she shut the book, the panic of separation rising in her.

The note read: "Dear little Sarah, Do not doubt that you will be in my mind in every waking moment, and I pray that you will be in my dreams. If I return to duty and must give my life, if there is a God and I am called to account by Him for what I have done in my life that was most honourable I shall say that I have loved Sarah. That will be enough. What is there left to say in inadequate human words? Except that I shall yearn with all my being to be with you again. With Gratitude & Love, Henry."

The note was written in very small, neat script which, she thought, must have been produced by Captain Seager.

Because there was no one to hear, Sarah gave vent to her grief, her sobs unchecked as she leaned against the stone wall, her eyes closed, remaining there for a long time. This was what had happened because Lord Calborne had spoken to her father and her father had suggested to her that she should write to Captain Henry Calborne who lay blind and injured in a military hospital. There had been a chain of events that had drawn her in. That chain was already going on into the future and would play out as fate decreed.

~ Someone was calling her name. Someone out on the path. Wearily she got up to investigate and found Felix Clark coming towards her.

"Ah," he said, "there you are, Miss. Thwaite was worried about you ... we all were."

"I'm quite all right." *What a terrible lie!*

Although Sarah scarcely knew Felix, she liked him and found him interesting. He seemed to be one of those people who was in the wrong life, deserving something more unusual, more cloak-and-dagger, perhaps, because he had a certain uncommon panache. She had seen him, spoken to him briefly with the fire-watching crew in the village.

As he got up close to her, it looked as though he also had been crying, his face was puffy and serious. "Thwaite wants to know if you would care to have an early lunch with us, Miss? Seeing as it's so cold and miserable, we might as well have an early meal."

Sarah nodded her assent, grateful for the invitation and the diversion that it provided. The warm, spacious and comfortable kitchens of the big house beckoned to her even though she knew that entering the main part of the house — where Henry's spirit would linger and his conspicuous absence taunt her — would pull her further into a morass of grief. Perhaps she would be all right if she kept to the servants' quarters. Obediently, like a child, she followed Felix back along the path.

∼ There was no one in the vicarage drawing room when Sarah eventually reached home, chilled to the bone, and drawn to the fire that she knew would be alight there. Apart from the kitchen that had the big cast-iron cooking range, this was the warmest room.

She stood as close to the fire as she could, and held her cold hands out to the flames. Never before had she experienced such an odd feeling of dissonance, as well as of distancing from the world that she knew. All the familiar things, places, people, seemed flat in her mind, as though they had no emotion attached to them. All was meaningless around her. The only person who held any meaning was Henry Calborne, who was now riding in the back of a car progressing through the wintry countryside towards the destination of a railway station, unknown to her, then beyond. Although only he seemed real, the fact that his physical, tangible being was moving away from her was unbearable. She feared that he too would soon take on the semblance of a wraith.

She wondered if she were going mad. It was a relief when Mary came into the room; sweet, sensible Mary. "So he's gone, then?"

Sarah nodded.

"I heard you come back on the motor bike so I thought I might make a pot of tea, if you'd like some. Or perhaps you'd prefer cocoa? Mrs. Burridge has been here and made a stew for us, mostly with vegetables and a bit of fatty mutton, but she's such a good cook that I think it'll taste delicious."

"I think I'd prefer cocoa for now. It was so cold on the bike."

"I'll make you some. Why don't you have a bath, there's lots of hot water? With that cold you've got coming on, you don't want to get pneumonia or bronchitis."

"Mary," Sarah said, turning to her sister, "I'm so frightened."

"I know how you feel, because I've got someone, too.' Mary gathered Sarah into her arms. "I didn't tell anyone at first because I didn't want people asking me about him all the time. I don't think I could bear that. He was one of the teachers at the school."

"You could have told me."

"You were so carefree, so young, that I didn't want to burden you. Eventually I did tell Mummy, because she guessed. I suppose I was moping about too much. Since Henry Calborne appeared on the scene you've grown up a lot."

"That's true all right."

"We shall be able to talk now," Mary said.

Later, when Sarah had been warmed up by a hot bath and a mug full of scalding cocoa, which seemed to have combined to stave off pneumonia, she sat down at the desk in the relatively warm drawing room to write letters. First, she composed a careful letter to the Matron of the hospital where she hoped to take up her nursing training, saying that she was available. By now, it was possible that the preliminary training school for probationer nurses had been moved to yet another former country house, somewhere that was deemed relatively safe from enemy bombers. With luck, it would not be too far from home.

Then she wrote to Henry. That letter, she had decided earlier, would not be falsely cheerful. With the new maturity that she felt she had, she would be truthful with him, which he would expect. When she had finished, she would walk along the High Street to post the letters at the post office where collections were made several times a day from the red post box embedded in the wall. For her now, with all those others, most of them invisible to her, that box would be the beginning of the line of communication between her and the man she loved.

"Dear Henry," she wrote, "I am bereft now that you have gone."

Towards the end of January 1941, Lord Calborne opened his newspaper as he sat at the small table in the morning room having his breakfast.

Thwaite always brought in a tray with the paper folded at one side. On the front page he saw the words: "British Army captures Tobruk." He felt a lightening of his mood. The sudden small optimism made him note how depressed he had become of late.

He would write to Henry about it, although no doubt someone at the hospital would give him the news. There was time for him to write the letter before he was to receive his farm manager, Hugh Dalton, to discuss the business of the never-ending work for food production. Felix Clark, who would keep records and take shorthand for any letters that had to be written, would be present.

Dalton had wanted to join the RAF, but had been persuaded otherwise, being in the vital reserved occupation of food-production. Accordingly Lord Calborne never failed to appreciate his own good fortune in having such a capable, intelligent, and decent man to run his estate. It did not do to take people for granted.

Later, he would get Wheeler to drive him over to the market gardens to see the head gardener and discuss their productivity. At least once a month he liked to put in a personal appearance in winter to see what was being produced in the greenhouses. In summer he went more often, walking there. While he was out he would drive to the various cottages on the estate that had been damaged by bombs, including the two at Bullrush Lane, to see first-hand what progress was being made in the rebuilding.

After breakfast he went to the small writing desk in the drawing room, the one that had been Caro's, to begin a letter to Henry, taking the newspaper with him so that he could quote from it. Henry had told him that Captain Basil Seager was still at the hospital, but might soon be sent back to duty. It was Basil himself who wrote Henry's letters now, and read the ones that he received, so his departure from the hospital would be a blow to Henry.

Later on, in February, the same newspaper told him that a German general by the name of Erwin Rommel had arrived in North Africa, at Tripoli, with the intent to rescue the beleaguered Italians there.

Thwaite, having deposited the usual breakfast tray on the table in the morning room, fussed with the coffee pot as he poured the black liquid, made from "Camp" liquid coffee and chicory essence, and placed the rack of toast on the table cloth. "The news from North Africa is a little disturbing, your Lordship," he ventured. "The Germans are in, by the look of it."

"Ah ... yes, so I see. Churchill moved some of our troops out of there to Greece, so I believe. That was somewhat premature." Any ebullience that he had felt over the victory at Tobruk melted like the proverbial mist before the sun as he scanned the newspaper.

"Yes, indeed, sir," Thwaite said, moving the marmalade pot off the tray.

"Such a move has left North Africa wide open. Thank God Henry isn't there, that's all I can say."

"Indeed, sir."

"It will be a big blow if we lose the Suez. We're fighting on too many fronts."

A heavy weight seemed to descend onto Lord Calborne's shoulders after Thwaite had left the room, as he went through the motions of pouring hot milk from the silver pot into the black liquid that passed for coffee and then scraped some butter onto the toast. There was to be no respite now for any of them, not a moment of mental peace.

Later that day a letter came from Henry, written by a nurse, telling him that Basil Seager had left the hospital for an unknown destination. "There has been a change in my eyesight," the letter said. "For a few days now I have been able to discern moving shadows. For now, I have asked the nurse not to say anything, in case it is not permanent."

"Thank God ... thank God," Lord Calborne whispered the words, crushing the letter in his hand. "There are still small mercies ... and some not so small." Tears of relief came into his eyes. Since the death of Caro he found it easy to cry.

Several times a day he added to a letter for Henry, as thoughts and news came to him, and then when it was of sufficient length he sealed it in an envelope and gave it to Felix Clark to take to the post-box. It was a mixed blessing, of course, having eyesight. All the time Henry was blind he would not be returned to North Africa, a place that appeared to be entering a stage of increasing ferocity.

↪ Chapter 20

'**N**urse Burroughs,' Sister Butt of Barclay Ward, at the West Kent General Hospital, addressed Sarah on a Friday near the end of January, 1941, 'you will accompany Nurse Cresswell on her rounds and duties. She will show you the ward and explain everything to you. As a probationer, you will not do anything of your own initiative. Watch, listen, and learn.'

'Yes, Sister,' Sarah said, chastened by the meekness of her own voice.

When Sister Butt disappeared into her office, Sarah and Mona Cresswell, a third-year student nurse, walked back along the corridor towards the utility rooms that were near the entrance doors of the ward. At the other end, the wide corridor became the floor of the big open area that contained twenty-five beds of a men's surgical ward.

Sarah was very conscious of being unattractive in the plain mauve dress that signified the probationer nurse. Its hem came to just above her ankles, showing the sensible black lace-up shoes and black stockings that she wore. A loose cloth belt did not accentuate her waist. She did not have the starched white apron that Nurse Cresswell wore over her white dress with a fine blue stripe. On the short sleeve of her dress, Nurse Cresswell had three white stripes sewn to the fabric, denoting that she was in her third year. *Like a sergeant in the army*, Sarah thought. They both wore simple white caps, held on with metal hair grips.

It was clear that the hospital was not going to spend money on uniforms for probationer nurses who might decide to leave before their three-month trial period was up.

Every Friday, over the next few weeks, the probationer nurses would come to the hospital for a day of work, a change from their lectures and practical work at the country house that was the preliminary training school. Part of the London hospital to which they were affiliated had been evacuated down there to Kent.

"Come on, I'll show you the sluice, then we'll make some beds," Nurse Cresswell said, deviating from the corridor into a side room. "As a probationer, the sluice will be your domain. It's where we wash the bedpans and the urine bottles. We sterilize them by boiling. I'll show you how the sterilizer works, because it will be your job to do the sterilizing and to make sure that we have a constant supply of sterile bedpans and urine bottles. Woe betide you if Sister discovers that we've run out of clean bottles. We used to have more male orderlies, but now the young ones have gone off to the forces and we're left with a few old blokes, not enough to go round."

"Is Sister all right to work with?" Sarah asked.

"Oh, yes. She's all right underneath. It's like the army here. We do almost everything as the soldiers in training do, except march, shoot guns, click our heels and salute. Don't worry. Just let it roll off you like water off a duck's back. Think of it as a means to an end, your end."

They stood next to an odd shaped porcelain sink with a high splash-back. "This is where you wash the urine bottles. Empty the bottle in the sink; put it over this nozzle thing; then turn on this tap to wash it. Just turn it gently. Otherwise the pressure will be too much and you'll get sprayed with urine and water. It's sort of like a baptism, for the proba-tioners, to get soaked."

There was another large gadget, metal, affixed to the wall. "This is where you wash the dirty bedpans. Put the used pan in here; make sure the cover is locked firmly in place, like this; then turn on the water, which will wash the bedpan. When you take it out, you put it into this sterilizer. Watch carefully while I show you how it works. You might want to take notes."

The sterilizer was a big square metal box on legs, run by electricity, that had to be filled with water and brought to a boil. "It's like a Turkish bath in here when this thing's going full tilt. We boil the pans for at least twenty minutes. Don't let it boil dry. The metal urinals are boiled, while the glass ones are soaked in disinfectant. We use Lysol or carbolic."

They went through the motions, while Sarah mostly watched. Already she was feeling somewhat overwhelmed and a little depressed, not least by the twenty-five or so men of all ages and with all types of surgical diseases, in the beds of the ward. All eyes would be upon her, and she felt shy.

"Another thing that's your job," Nurse Cresswell said, "is to collect and empty the sputum mugs. Tip the contents down this drain here. My advice is to turn your head aside as you empty them, especially if it's just before lunch." She laughed merrily. "And I'm not joking. Then fill this sink with hot, soapy water to soak the mugs in, so that, when you come to wash them, they've been divested of most of their slime. Wear a mask, as some of the men may have TB."

"I'll remember," Sarah said, trying to concentrate, already feeling a little sick, while she kept a vision of herself tearing around the countryside on the motorbike, a scene that was already taking on the connotations of "the good old days." A stab of nostalgia added to her slight depression. Buck up, she said to herself. This is real life; this is what you wanted.

"Then you boil the mugs in this smaller sterilizer," Nurse Cresswell said. "Before taking them back to the patients, put in an inch of disinfectant, no more than an inch, mind you. Otherwise Sister will go round with a ruler and measure it. Woe betide you if it's more, because we get through too much disinfectant that way. Everything's in short supply."

"I won't forget," Sarah said again, meekly. It was clear that Nurse Cresswell's favourite expressions were "woe betide you" and "I'm not joking." However, these warnings were mitigated by her sense of humour and good spirit. Sarah vowed then to let it all roll off her, as she had been advised to do. In that way she would perhaps get to the stage where she would have three stripes on her sleeve.

"When you walk around the ward," Nurse Cresswell said as they came out of the sluice, "you walk quickly, because there's an awful lot of work to get through. But you never run unless it's for haemorrhage or fire. It's undignified to run, and at all times you must think of your dignity and behave in a professional manner."

"It's hard to look dignified in mauve, with no waist," Sarah said.

Nurse Cresswell laughed. "Don't worry. I know. As far as the dignity's concerned, if you stay calm, the patients will stay calm. Never scream during an air-raid, and don't get under a bed before you've got your patients under beds. Later on, we'll have bomb drill. I'm telling you this before Sister Butt tells you, so that you can look wise. Come on, we'll make a few beds now. We'll made one empty, then some with patients in them. I know you've done this at the training school, but it's a bit different when you have a real patient in a bed who's had part of his stomach removed and is in pain, for instance."

Sarah nodded, as they walked briskly down into the main ward area.

"We have some patients here who've been dug out of bombed buildings," Nurse Cresswell went on, so that Sarah wondered if she were trying to scare her. "Many of those go to the orthopaedic wards, if they have broken bones, but we get some, too. Awful things we see here. Flying glass can do terrible things to a person's face."

∼ Later, at mid-morning, they put on their heavy woollen cloaks to go for a coffee or tea break to the dining room a few minutes' walk away from the wards. As Sarah walked, clutching her cloak around her against the sharp January cold, she soberly contemplated the three years of training ahead of her, unable to visualize the end of that time. It seemed to be impossibly far in the future and she a different person.

Later, she and her probationer colleagues would be driven away from the hospital in a small bus, back to the country mansion, and then they were free to go home for the weekend, those who lived nearby. Mary was to come for her in their father's car. The oasis of that weekend beckoned like a solace. In the warmth of the drawing room at the vicarage she would write a proper letter to Henry, other than the few lines she was able to pen each night.

"When we get back to the ward," Nurse Cresswell was saying, "we'll change some dressings. That's part of my job, so you might as well watch. We have a few incisions and bomb wounds that have become infected, so we have to irrigate and pack some of those wounds with ribbon gauze."

"What do you use to clean the wounds?"

"Well, we have diluted carbolic, the old standby, and we have some soap solutions. We have Lotio Rubra, acriflavine, gentian violet, and my favourite, Edinburgh University Solution of Lime."

Although Nurse Cresswell was friendly and helpful, she was conscious of her superior position, Sarah noted, having endured almost all the required training. So far, she had not invited Sarah to call her by her first name. A longing for Henry and her family settled on her as they entered the dining room, and she scanned the nurses there for some of her colleagues from the preliminary training school while Nurse Cresswell went to sit with some of her own friends.

In the pocket of her unbecoming uniform she had a folded letter from Henry. It kept her going, like a talisman, and from time to time she put her hand on it to make sure it was not just a figment of her imagination.

~ At the end of the working day, as Sarah walked to the rendezvous point for the bus to go back to the training school, she found that her feet hurt, and her legs ached in a way that they had never done before. Throughout the long day, she had only sat down during the fifteen-minute coffee break and the short lunch break. That was the way it was going to be from now on, once the three months were over. They would be thrown in at the deep end: long hours, night duty, bomb drill, air raids, study, exhaustion, examinations. The saving grace would be the friendships they would make, she suspected, and the hope and comfort they could bring to their patients.

Before she left the ward, Nurse Cresswell said to her: "You've done well today, Sarah. Call me Mona. I'll see you next week."

Although her spirits had lifted at that gesture of friendship, the sudden cessation of frenetic activity left her vulnerable to the creeping longing to see Henry Calborne.

The rendezvous for the bus was near the porters' lodge by the main hospital entrance, where there was also an underground bomb shelter, mainly for the nurses in the residences to go to in the night. She and the others had been taken on a tour of it. Near the entrance she noted a sign which read: "Keep calm and carry on." Yes, that was what she must do — carry on, if not keep calm all the time.

～ That evening, in her own home, she completed a letter to Henry, telling him of the amusing things that had happened to her in the hospital, of the saga of the sluice, her domain, not mentioning the news of North Africa, or the day and night bombing of Kent, Sussex, and London. So far, she had assumed that the worst of the news would be kept from the patients in the hospital in Cornwall, especially from those who were suffering from severe mental stress.

In her diary she wrote: "So many questions and seldom any answers, only an unnatural expectant silence that hums in the brain like an ear infection. It is an obtuse silence, for waiting somewhere in dark places is the answer. It must be. Retrospect makes some things clear, or it appears to do so to a certain degree. At the hospital I am called 'nurse' by the patients and other members of the staff, yet I feel as exposed and ignorant as a new-born baby. Will I come through? And will the country come through? I must do my bit to the utmost. The alternative is unthinkable."

～ Henry, receiving her letter a week later at the hospital in Cornwall, managed to decipher her large, neat, rounded handwriting, without having to ask his nurse to read it.

Some days before, shortly after Captain Basil Seager had been discharged from the hospital to report to local army headquarters, Henry had begun to discern moving shapes. At first he had told no one, fearing that it might be a temporary phenomenon.

It occurred to him that he had undergone a mental and emotional change with the departure of Basil, who had become like a brother to him. It was a change that forced him to confront his own sense of duty, one that had always been strong, instilled in him from early childhood. From time to time he recalled particular people in his youth who had authority over him, who quoted in certain situations in which he had been regarded as lax, the final words of Lord Nelson: "Thank God I have done my duty."

Although all that was amusing to him now, in a wry way, he knew that the admonitions had entered deeply into his psyche; he would never be able to shake them off.

Even though the onset of the blindness, and its continuance, had been entirely out of his conscious control, he felt now that his renewed sense of duty was vying with the hideous nature of all that he had witnessed on the battlefields of the desert. There were no adjectives to describe what he had seen and felt; in their place was an amorphous jumble of intense emotion that he dare not face directly.

∼ Days, then weeks, went by in which he lived for letters, missing the close communication with Basil. As he walked the corridors of the hospital, tentatively, with his white stick, his injured leg getting stronger each day, he picked up discarded newspapers here and there that visitors had left. Taking them back secretly to his room where he looked at the print with a magnifying glass, as he did his letters, he found that the glass did not help much, as the problem was not one of magnification.

Gradually, with time, he was able to write, through a fog, then to read.

Still he told no one in authority at the hospital, asking his nurse to read certain letters, as he pondered what would happen next when he could see fully. Then he wrote to his father.

Winter changed to spring. From news given to him by others at the hospital, and now with difficulty from newspapers, he knew that, after the battles of the Allies against the Italians in Libya, the Italians had been pushed back westward. Then Churchill, because of the successes and a certain complacency, had taken many Allied troops out of North Africa and sent them to Greece, instead of going on to capture Tripoli.

What they had all feared had taken place. The Germans had arrived in North Africa under General Erwin Rommel, who had entered Tripoli on February 12th. Then his tank regiment had landed on 11th March 11th, occupying Agheila, to the west, a bottleneck place.

Before Basil's departure they had talked long into the night about the situation, sleepless from the anxiety that it evoked. Rommel mounted his first attack in the Desert War on March 24th. Henry understood that the British had not been ready; they had fallen back and the Germans were able to move out of the bottleneck into the expanse of the desert.

Sick with apprehension, Henry wrote a letter to his father, then a similar one to Basil, without the help of anyone, seeing the words that he was forming through the usual fog. The idiocy of moving their own troops to Greece, of not securing Tripoli when they had the chance, was clear to him now. Neither he nor Basil had understood why that had been allowed to happen. North Africa had been left wide open.

~ Lord Calborne read in his newspaper that by April 11th 1941 the weakened Allied forces in North Africa had been pushed back east, over the Egyptian border, apart from a small force trapped in Tobruk. Then towards the end of April he read that General Erwin Rommel and his army had entered Egypt on the 25th.

In the cellars of Calborne House, sheltering from bombs, members of the household sat or crouched near the wireless to listen to the news in the evening, straining to hear the words. The reception down there was not good.

"Can things get worse?" Agnes remarked to Thwaite.

"We haven't been invaded yet," Thwaite said dryly. "I hope Felix is all right, fire watching in that church tower."

"If we've got to die, we might as well die doing something useful," Agnes said. "It makes you feel you've got some control over the situation."

These days, she kept several handkerchiefs in the pocket of her apron with which to wipe away tears when the news came on the wireless. There was a compulsion to listen to the BBC, Agnes thought, even though she felt bowed down by what she heard. As soon as the words "Home Service" came on, she felt compelled to stop what she was doing and mentally stand to attention.

They learned that some of their ships had successfully negotiated the Mediterranean and arrived at Alexandria. Because Master Henry had been in North Africa, they felt particularly sensitive about it, yet they knew of young men all over the world who were in danger. Agnes, with her hand frequently in her apron pocket around her bunched handkerchief, prepared to weep several times each day.

~ In May, 1941, Henry received a letter from Basil stating that he expected to be sent to Army Headquarters in Cairo in the very near future and expressing the expectation and hope that he would meet up with him there in due course. He finished the letter by saying that the situation appeared desperate for them in North Africa, that they were just managing to hold on to Egypt, as far as he could see. No one told him much of an official nature. If the situation deteriorated in a serious way, he said, he hoped that he would be able to escape by air, by ship, or overland to Palestine. There were supply lorries that regularly made the journey out and back.

After replying to the letter, Henry made an appointment with one of his doctors to report that his eyesight was returning. It was possible, he speculated, that they would discharge him from the army as medically unfit, or retain him and offer him a non-combat role. If they offered him Cairo, he would take it. To be out of it all now, when he was most needed, would be a failure of sorts that he would not want to look back on in future years. Nonetheless, it was clear to him that there was a limit to what, in himself, was under his control, and perhaps he was the stronger for knowing it.

∽ Chapter 21

The month of May found Sarah on the wards at the hospital, full-time, the preliminary training school behind her. They had had a party, she and the fourteen other nurses from her group.

"Hello, Sarah," Nurse Cresswell had said in the hospital dining room at lunch time on that day at the end of March when they had finished with the preliminary training school. "Congrats at getting through that awful prelim place. Anyone who can get through that deserves a medal."

They found themselves the centre of smiling attention, the fifteen girls, as they entered en masse in their new first-year uniforms of striped dress and starched white apron, and joined the queue for food in the canteen-style dining-room.

"Thank you," Sarah said, knowing how many of them had felt like leaving in the previous three months, going back home. Many had shared tears at night from the sights they had seen; the first deaths they had witnessed; at the often pointless discipline, the studying, the examinations, the interminable learning of anatomy and physiology.

On top of that, they had to endure the tutors at the school. Some had been embittered middle-aged women who had lost their boyfriends in the First World War, or since, and perhaps as a consequence disliked the young women they tutored, with a rabid, envious emotion that bordered on hatred.

Sarah knew that this was perhaps a simplification of the situation that she had endured, yet could think of no other. The prettier and more charming the girl, the more she seemed to come in for their disapproval.

The possession of more than average intelligence did not seem to please them either, or the ability to think for oneself. They seemed to like the obedient, stupid girl who came in at the bottom of the examination list when the results were posted on the notice boards.

Any rare exception among the tutors had been a pleasure and relief. Sarah was beginning to realize that one's own words and actions were not necessarily responsible for calling forth certain reactions and emotions in others. Such behaviour often came from within the other person, perhaps from past happenings, not related in any way to her. Sometimes when she thought about these things she felt so much older, with a strange, knowing weariness. She was learning, slowly, how to take care of herself.

"I shall never forget that the femur is a long bone with a shaft and two extremities,' Sarah had joked, thinking of the interminable anatomy and physiology lessons, the late night studying, while the others had laughed with the same relief. They were delirious with success. No one could think about tomorrow. During the coming evening they intended to pool their pathetic supply of money and go to a pub in the town for glasses of cider or shandy, where they would make eyes at any soldiers, airmen, or other young men who happened to be there.

Before coming to the dining room on that March day, they had all been taken to the uniform-cum-sewing room in the hospital grounds, where they had been measured and given uniforms. As Sarah stood in the queue waiting for her food, she was very conscious of the starched belt of the apron that was buttoned around her waist firmly, giving her at last a female shape. Now, also, each girl had her own tiny room in the nurses' residence. Hers was warm, with its large radiator, so different from the rectory at Fernden, that she feared she might get soft here. They were housed in long, single storey huts that had been built during the First World War.

The next day, after getting her uniform, she had reported for duty at a women's medical ward at half-past seven in the morning.

By May, although many aspects of hospital life were new and strange, intimidating in some ways, Sarah at last felt that she was part of the hospital, that she had passed a test and was accepted by the others above her. Soon there would be another group of hesitant probationers in their awful mauve dresses. More than anything, she wanted to be useful, to do something for her country.

~ Lord Calborne had, by wireless and newspaper, followed Rommel's progress across North Africa. He listened to the BBC in his study, the news of North Africa given no particular significance compared with the fighting in other parts of the world, the blitz on London, the bombing of other cities, of shipping. While the announcer's voice went on, Lord Calborne usually helped himself to a glass of whisky and soda, with far more soda than whisky, because he did not wish to become reliant on alcohol for his mental equilibrium.

It had become his habit of late to write to Henry as soon as he had news, disturbing or otherwise, to trigger a discussion with his son. And the act of writing, being a close substitute for a conversation that he longed for, relieved some of the helplessness that was so much a part of their existence.

Sometimes he met with the Reverend Burroughs, at Calborne House or at the vicarage, to talk about the progress of the war and to pore over maps. Often it seemed to both of them that the country, and civilization itself, had entered the proverbial dark tunnel in which there was no light visible at the end. Fatalism was not a characteristic of the British people. He felt that in himself and in the empathy that he shared with his countrymen, so that somehow he knew they would emerge from the morass of initial inertia that came from not knowing what to do. Somehow they would rally; they must.

~ In the kitchens of Calborne House the three permanent servants, Thwaite, Agnes, and Felix, stood or sat by their wireless listening to the news.

"I feel bloody sick," Agnes said.

"We should have seen it coming," Thwaite said.

Felix, having handed round cigarettes and lit them, said: "A spot of fire-watching is in order tonight. I don't feel so helpless when I'm doing that."

"Better watch out for Germans, and all," Thwaite said. "After what they've done to London, I reckon that, if they're going to invade this country, it's going to be soon, and it's going to be here."

~ A particular letter came to Calborne House in spring, with the address written in an untidy and somewhat childlike hand, the lines deviating downward. In spite of the dissimilarity between the writing and that of previous years, the identity of the writer was unmistakable. Lord Calborne, holding the letter, put his head into his hands and wept.

⧈ Chapter 22

When spring moved into summer, 1941, May and Jim Langridge, Jo and Lizzie, moved back to the cottage at Bullrush Lane, together with the cat — and the dinner rabbits that had become pets, secure in their hutches.

Their pathetic pieces of bomb-damaged furniture, their pots and pans, the remnants of their china, their linens, the axes and saws from the shed, the hurricane lanterns, the tins of paraffin, were duly loaded onto a lorry and taken back. There the family found the house mended, echoing hollowly to their exploratory footsteps, smelling of new wood, plaster, and paint.

May went into the wash-house and laid her cheek against the big wooden rollers of the mangle, closing her eyes as she had done on the night of the bombing, taking in the faint scent of soap and cleanliness, willing her thoughts back to pre-war days until she felt a sense of peace.

When they explored the orchard they found that the bomb crater had been filled in, as promised by Lord Calborne. It formed now a slight mound, which would eventually sink down to create a flat surface, Jim assumed, as he stood and looked at it. Sod, green and healthy, had been placed over the obscene excrescence, so that, apart from the stumps of destroyed apple trees, neatly cut now, it looked as though nothing much had happened.

So are the dead buried, tidied up, hidden, he thought under the green apple trees. *The earth receives us, the unsung, unrecognized. Thus is truth denied, remaining only in the unreliable memories of those to whom it was memorable, in those who mourn, in those who witness others, and the self-destroyed in body and mind.*

They distributed their altered furniture throughout the rooms, positioning the pieces where they had, more or less, been before. There were gaps on floors, blanks on walls where pictures had been, on shelves where ornaments had stood. The wooden-cased, boxy gramophone, one of the few things unscathed, was perched on an occasional table accompanied by a few records.

"Do you want to cover the ground, Jo?" May asked, lifting the lid of the gramophone, when they paused to make tea, to take respite from their efforts.

"Yes," Jo said.

May cranked up the gramophone, turning the handle at the side, put a record on the turntable, switched it on, placed the metal arm with its needle on the smooth edge of the record, eliciting a hissing sound. Jo got ready in the centre of the kitchen-cum-living room. The reedy, male voice of the singer filled the room:

> *You should see me dance the polka,*
> *You should see me cover the ground,*
> *Oh the rollicking, rollicking polka,*
> *It's the happiest dance in town.*

Jo ran around fast, in circles, waving her arms, while her family watched her, Lizzie ensconced in her high chair, clapping and laughing.

"See me dance the polka," Jim and May sang. "See me cover the ground." Jo ran faster and faster, her dark, curly hair flying behind her, until she collapsed onto the sofa.

May turned the record over. "Skip Mazurka, skip again," a different voice sang, a tenor, seductive and mysterious, singing from another world that had disappeared from their reality. In truth, they had only been on the sidelines of such implied opulence.

"Skip Mazurka, skip again," May and Jim sang for Jo as she got up to skip around the room on the blue and brown patterned linoleum that had just been put down again. "Skip Mazurka, skip, skip again."

Lizzie, laughing in her perch, entered into that world of make-believe.

∼ Later, Alice and Tom Katt, who had moved back in next door, came in bearing a rabbit stew in a dish, and a loaf of bread that they were to share.

"Have you seen the shelter yet?" Alice asked.

"No, haven't had time," May said.

"His Lordship has done us proud. He said he would get one built before we all moved back, and he has. It's at the bottom of our garden, partly hidden under the plum tree, well dug down, with a double corrugated iron roof."

"He's had some drains put in," Tom Katt said, "because those things flood too easily. There are six bunks, so we can all get in there."

"Good," May said. "I'll take the bedding in there directly, before dark."

"I've got a small table in there with a Primus," Alice said, "so that we can make tea for ourselves and cocoa for the kids."

"Jolly good," Jim said. "Just like the old days in the trenches."

"No rifles though, Jim," Tom said. "I'd feel happier with one in my hands."

"Let's have another record," May said, wanting to hang on to their moments of merriment. "Not much choice, I'm afraid. It's either 'Oh, Play to me, Gypsy', 'Red Sails in the Sunset,' or 'The Gold and Silver Waltz'."

They all laughed, standing around the table. "Where did you get that lot?" Alice said.

"A jumble sale."

"Someone must have died," Tom said. "Give us 'The Gold and Silver Waltz,' May."

∼ After dark, they lay in the bomb shelter at the bottom of the Katts' garden, the men in the lower bunks along the sides, the women in bunks above them, the children at the end of the small space. The women had rigged up curtains over the fronts of their own bunks. There was a damp coolness in the shelter, even though it was a warm night.

Jim lay cosily under an old eiderdown and two ex-army blankets, listening to the light patter of rain on the corrugated iron roof and the quiet breathing of the others. Although the nightly blitz on London had at last stopped a few days ago, that was by no means the end of the bombing. If anything, it was now more unpredictable. The country seemed to have entered a new dark time from which it was not possible to predict the future, even a week or two in advance.

The shelter was like a dug-out, smelling of newly turned earth, without the stench of putrefaction that hung around a battlefield; so much so that when he closed his eyes he did not know where he was for a few seconds, until he forced himself to imagine the shape of the shelter, the curved roof above his head. Unless there was a direct hit, they should be safe here.

There was a sense in him of the changing world that was discernible beneath the dissonance of war, bringing with it an intuition that, if they survived, their lot in life could be more hopeful. He could not have said how he knew that, except that constant fear forged a new honesty, a perceptiveness. Or so he imagined.

What he had always wanted from life at a basic level was a wage that was commensurate with the effort that he expended on work for others, and a roof over his head that could not be taken away from him on a whim. For so long now he had stood on the edge of the abyss and looked down into it, remembering his father's toil, his mother's weeping when his father had come home and declared: "We're moving, Mother!" Over them had hung the threat of the workhouse, inhuman, impersonal, with its indignity and its connotation of abject failure and worthlessness.

He pulled the army blanket over his head, willing himself to sleep. With the smell of fresh earth in his nostrils and the roughness of the army blanket against the skin of his face, it was easy to conjure up the images of the front lines he had been in, however briefly, before the pain of wounds in abject fear, before the long move back from the battlefront to something approaching a spurious safety.

Only the fact that he was able to stretch out his body on a thin mattress, under an eiderdown that was reasonably comfortable, anchored him in the present. It was a luxury to straighten out the knee joints, to have one's head on a pillow, the whole body in a place of comparative safety, to have a certain faith in the shelter of corrugated iron above.

A few weeks ago, on April 19th, Primrose Day, he had passed his fifty-fifth birthday. He had lived long enough to know how thin the line was between life and death and, equally, between sanity and madness. Man was courageous and extraordinary, altruistic and evil. The terrible dichotomies and dilemmas that confronted one each day could only be faced, he found, in the light of one's own intention of goodness.

He did not delude himself that one could ever relax one's guard; it seemed to him that there was always a Hitler or a Mussolini waiting in the wings, or a Webber close at hand waiting and watching, to accuse him. "What are you doing, living in this house?" As though he had no right to a roof over his head, he who had always worked like a dog, had walked knee deep in the young dead of his country, had seen their blood in puddles of rain water, their limbs torn from their bodies piled up in mounds, his own blood dripping from him as he had walked.

Secure now in the shelter, he could think of rejoinders to Webber: "Where were you in the last war? Now you drive over the land on which others toil. You sack men on a whim, who live insecurely in tied cottages, who have children to support and little food." At the time, emotion had choked the words in his throat.

Old age was coming upon him fast; he was too old to recoup the losses of the bombing. Sometimes now he felt breathless when he dug in the soil and chopped wood. "You silly bastard, don't you know you've got heart trouble?" the orderly had said to him in the makeshift hospital in Étaples when he had crawled along the floor of the ward to see Frank.

Yes, he knew. He had no illusions. His children would live out his ambitions, and his own father's ambitions, such as they were. He did not presume to know exactly what his mother and his grandmothers had wanted of life. Sometimes when he looked at Lizzie and talked to her, when he held her hand and walked around his gardens with her, he knew that she would have it in her, would have the spirit to speak out for the kind of justice that had never been allowed him, even if she in her turn would be punished for insolence, dumb or otherwise. It was a lot, he knew, to put on her. It was mitigated by the fact that he would never voice it. Merely by observing, she would know.

If you look at what actually happens in a war, if you put aside all heroic words, all heroic imagery and symbolism, all reference to God and His will, you see that it has to do with the murder of young men on a mass scale. And there is no answer to the question "why?" They die until there are few left. Often those who are left, those who love the dead, go mad. It involves a forced abdication of the self.

In the first war, his war, there had been the concept of "dumb insolence," mainly on the part of the ordinary soldier in relation to his officer superiors. At the time he had not understood whether that phrase had been coined for that war, or whether it had been there in earlier wars. A man could be shot summarily for dumb insolence.

Conscientious objectors had been treated badly as well, threatened with execution. What was a man to do? The question tormented him, as it had done since he first had an inkling of the ways of men. "They" could not control your mind completely, although they tried; they could not take away the freedom of your thoughts.

Now, in this war, women and children in large numbers were joining the ranks of the prematurely dead.

In the dense blackness of the shelter he tried to give himself over to sleep, to still his unquiet mind. Beside him was a torch, just where he could put his hand on it, and at the end of the bunk, his shoes, trousers, and jacket which he could pull on in a matter of seconds. He half waited for the siren, and for the rain to stop, the soft early summer rain that would nurture the garden here and at Badgers Gate, where he would go from time to time to harvest whatever had grown to fruition. Thoughts of the harvest gave him some peace.

∽ Chapter 23

Sarah Burroughs, with another student nurse, was behind privacy screens around a bed in their ward changing the sheets. Their patient, an elderly woman propped up in the bed, had bronchitis.

A screen was abruptly pushed aside and the ward Sister came in. "Nurse Burroughs," she said, "someone has just telephoned from the porters' lodge to say there's a man waiting there to see you. He gave his name as Lord Calborne."

"Oh." Sarah's hands stilled from tucking in a blanket at the bottom of the bed. "Oh dear." At various times, and in books, she had learned that under shock a person could feel the blood draining from their face, yet she had never experienced it. Now as she stared at Sister, the phenomenon asserted itself.

"Sit down, nurse, quickly." Sister propelled her to a chair beside the bed. "Put your head down between your knees."

When Sarah was able to sit up again, she knew that her lips were bloodless. A terrible fear lodged in the middle of her chest.

"What is it, nurse? Tell me."

"He's the father of my ... my fiancé. It must mean that something has happened to him. Oh God, oh my God." She knew that she had a better chance of being allowed to leave the ward if she claimed to have a fiancé rather than a young man who was not in any formal relationship with her.

"Pull yourself together, dear," Sister said, not unkindly. "The porter distinctly said it was a young man. Now, get on your cloak and go down there. Nurse Partridge will go with you."

It was a pleasant day, in the afternoon, and Sarah and Nurse Partridge walked quickly in the open air the several hundred yards to the porters' lodge. As they approached they saw a young man in army uniform come out of the lodge and stand beside a motorcycle.

"Oh my God," Sarah said. "It's him, it's Henry." Sobbing, she stood still.

"Dry your eyes, love," Nurse Partridge said, squeezing Sarah's arm. "otherwise you'll look all red, puffy, and peaky, and he won't recognize you. I'll leave you now, and I'll tell Sister that your long lost boyfriend has come back from the battlefront. If she doesn't let you off duty early, I'll eat my cap. Bring him back to the ward to thank her for letting you come out. Sister's very susceptible to male charm, especially when it's coming from a Lord, I should think."

Although Sarah tried to dry her eyes, the tears flowed freely as she moved forward to meet Henry, who had seen her coming. Even from a distance she could tell that his health had improved, that his face, although pale, had filled out, so he looked more like the young man in the photograph in the poetry book.

As he walked towards her, she started to run, so that he spread his arms wide to receive her and she ran into them. Regardless of any watching eyes, they kissed. "Darling, darling Sarah," he said.

He was wearing a trench coat over his uniform, with a leather helmet and goggles pushed up over it. Sarah clung onto the front of his coat. "We're not supposed to run," she said, looking up into his face. "Only for fire and haemorrhage." It was funny, the things that came out of your mouth when you wanted to say something else entirely.

They laughed then, helplessly, holding on to each other.

"I'm on my way to Aldershot for a few days," he said. "Just thought I'd make a detour to see you, as I phoned the vicarage and your mother said you were on duty. There wasn't time to let you know. I'll get orders soon. When my sight came back, I asked to be sent to Cairo, if I had a choice. Things are moving fast for me, Sarah, because the situation in North Africa isn't good for us now that the Germans are there. We've retreated to Egypt, and the Germans are over the border."

"Oh dear. Some of it has been in the papers. I've been dreading this, that you would go."

"It will be all right, I'll be behind the lines, I expect. They need me."

"I knew you would have to go. Getting to Cairo won't be easy. Will you fly?"

"I expect so, at least part of the way. We won't worry about that now. They've given me ten day's leave, after Aldershot," he said, gripping her arms. "So I'll go home. Can you come to Fernden for a day or two?"

"I'll try."

"I can stay here for a few hours, then travel to Aldershot after dark. It's safer anyway. Can we go to a pub when you get off duty? I could meet you there."

"There's a pub just along the road, the Coach and Horses. Come up to the ward with me and I'll see if I can get off duty a bit early. I can hardly believe it's you ... it's like a dream, because I wanted so much to see you." Desperation made her determined at the prospect of having to face Sister and ask for a special concession.

'Don't cry. Look, Sarah, will you marry me when I get back on first leave from Cairo? Please. I intended to ask you this evening, but I can't wait. It's as though everything has speeded up, and if we don't do certain things now, this minute, there won't be another chance. We would have to keep it a secret, because I understand that student nurses can't be married. Please say 'yes'."

Sarah nodded. "Of course ... yes. I love you."

They smiled at each other, awed by the occasion that was only one among many auspicious happenings, yet this one belonged only to them in a way that nothing else could.

"Father gave permission, and sends you his very best love. He absolutely adores you, you know, and admires you tremendously for what you're doing here."

"It's nothing much," she mumbled.

"Don't say that. It is admirable."

"There are young woman in munitions factories, and worse. At least I'm not going to get blown up, unless this place is bombed. Please send your father my best wishes. I adore him, too."

"You'll be seeing him before too long, if you can get time off. We'll walk in the woods and meadows on the estate, through the buttercups, and listen to the cuckoos. We'll go into the chapel and plight our troth to one another, just you and me."

"We will," Sarah said.

"When I was in the desert, I used to long for those things. This time I'll long for you."

"We'll paddle in the stream," she said. "There's nothing more I'd like in the world, except that you didn't have to go away in the first place."

"I know. Our lives don't belong to us any more, if they ever really did. You do understand? That I'm compelled to go?"

"Yes, I've always known that. It's our duty; it's why I'm in this place. We're doing it for ... for goodness."

"Will you let me buy you a ring? I'd like to, before I have to go."

"I'd love to have a ring." Sarah smiled up at him. "Then I could wear it on a chain round my neck, to keep it a secret while I'm on duty. Some of the other girls do that."

"What's your birth stone?"

"Opal."

"I know I'm asking a lot, that you should commit yourself to me when I have to go away," he said.

"It's something precious to hang on to. And there's no one else, nothing else I'd rather do. Besides, I have to finish my training. That's going to keep me busy."

~ Later, in the public house, they held hands and sat at a table for two, while around them others milled, laughed and talked, creating again that air of time passing at great speed, of opportunities that, if not taken up now, would be snatched away without warning. The atmosphere in the pub was dense with cigarette smoke, the scent of beer, and a kind of desperate merriment among those in uniform, both men and women.

"The Germans have got Rommel in Africa," Henry was saying. "He's making things hot for us. There's a lot of fighting, so I've heard. He's advanced a long way east, while we're trying to hang on to Tobruk. We've been pushed back towards Egypt several hundred miles."

"Is the news censored, do you think? I've been reading about it in the papers."

"Probably. I get mine from people I know out there, and some chaps who come back on leave."

"What about Cairo?"

"I doubt that he'll get that far, because we'll throw in everything we've got," Henry said.

"Are you saying that just to reassure me?"

"No. I believe it. And if Hitler takes on Russia in a big way, he might decide largely to forget about North Africa."

"I wish he would forget about us. Perhaps if we keep on chipping away at him, we'll get somewhere. Most of the time I'm so frightened."

"He's like a man with too much rope."

Their clasped hands lay on the table in front of them, hers red and chapped from the work, the fingernails short from having broken off at the tips, while his hand was pale and strong, softened by the long recovery from his wounds. Sarah tried to imprint the image of their hands on her mind, so that when he was gone she could conjure up this scene to remind herself that it had been a reality.

"How will I survive without you?" she said, very quietly.

"Write to me every day, a diary letter, like the ones you've been sending me at the hospital. I'll do the same. We'll be in unison then."

～ On the Calborne estate when Sarah and Henry entered that quiet place over a week later, the chapel doors had been flung open to let in the warm June air. One of the gardeners had put flowers all around inside, not funereal flowers for those dead, but summer flowers of many colours and scents both wild and cultivated.

Summery in a flowing gauzy dress and a straw hat with a ribbon, Sarah walked into the chapel beside Henry, still with the feeling that she was moving in a dream. Sometimes when you wanted something so much, when you felt that it was absolutely right for you, there was a sense of awe and unreality when it came to pass. Henry was dressed in an off-white linen suit, casual, with an open-necked shirt.

I love him so much, Sarah thought as they knelt together in front of the altar, *that if he is killed I will not want to go on.*

From his pocket Henry took a small red velvet box and opened it to show her the ring, an opal circled with small diamonds, set in gold. With it was a fine gold chain, the sight of which brought tears to her eyes because he had remembered that she wanted to hang it round her neck when she was at work.

"It's so beautiful," she said, while he took the ring out of the box and held it in the palm of his hand.

Henry took her hand. "Will you marry me, Sarah?"

"Yes."

"I, Henry Calborne, promise to marry you, Sarah," he said solemnly, "at our earliest mutual convenience. I honour and love you, and therefore with the giving of this ring I plight thee my troth."

The ring sparkled in the summer light that came through the stained glass windows of the chapel as he put it on the third finger of her left hand.

"By accepting this ring I, Sarah Burroughs, declare my love and my promise to marry you, Henry, and therefore I plight thee my troth," she said, making it up as she went along.

They came out into the sunlight. With arms around each other, they slowly walked along the path that bordered a meadow, away from the chapel and Calborne House. Tall wild flowers and grasses brushed against their legs; butterflies hovered in the summer haze; birds called.

In the near distance, two barrage balloons were tethered in meadows, floating this way and that cumbrously in the yellow and blue air like whales out of water trying to release themselves. They were obscene above the hay fields that were resplendent with wild flowers. Yet they reassured Sarah as she looked at them, as they glinted silver in the sunshine. They could save them, and the house and farms, from a strafing run by the enemy in the air. At least, that was the theory; she had not heard where they had been put to the test.

As they walked on, a squadron of RAF planes flew over, heading south, and almost to the horizon where there was a main road, they could see a convoy of army lorries with canvas tops — troop lorries, heading south.

Sarah looked away from them, down at the sun-dappled earth of the path where their feet moved forward in unison.

∞ Chapter 24

Innt had been a nightmarish journey, by ship and then by air from Gibraltar. A bumpy landing at an airfield near Cairo brought an incipient nausea back more forcefully to Henry's awareness as they touched down. There was a collective sigh, felt rather than heard.

It was dusk now, a time of comparative coolness that he remembered from his previous time in the desert. There were six other passengers on the plane, plus the crew and some unidentifiable supplies.

Nonetheless, it was better by far, he thought, to come this way than to spend two months going round the coast of Africa by ship, a journey that had its own dangers. Stiffly he got to his feet and made his way with the others to the exit, carrying his attaché case. A rickety metal staircase was being pushed up to the side of the aeroplane so that they could descend.

As he came out into the muggy air, Henry could see that they were at a military landing strip. After he had claimed his bag and had been checked off by an army sergeant with a list and a torch, he made his way in the half-light towards the only building in sight, a small, square, flat-topped, utilitarian edifice that showed no lights. Far off to one side he could just make out a line of army lorries. The lack of light made him think of home and the blackout, wondering if they were in danger of being bombed from the air this close to Cairo. More than anything, this was a war of the air.

Some familiar scents came to him, yet ones that he could not necessarily identify. Beneath the immediate smell of fuel, he imagined he could smell filthy water, dung, and an odour of death blowing in from the desert. As he walked, he ruminated on whether his sight would let him down again, or would hold up for the duration of the war. No one knew how long that would be, least of all himself when all he could imagine of the future at that moment was the next few days.

Inside the building, where the windows were covered with dark shades, he found a few other people milling about. As he dumped his bag on the floor, he saw no one whom he immediately recognized. He assumed that he would be given a lift in a troop transport vehicle with others to be driven into the city, to the Army Headquarters first, as he had been instructed. Or perhaps he would be taken to the hotel near headquarters that had been taken over by the army for the duration, to house its personnel.

It would be good to have a bath, or even just a wash, then a drink and a meal, and he found himself looking forward to it. Sweat had gathered in his arm-pits and was trickling down the sides of his chest. The air in the building was warm and close, scarcely moved by the ceiling fans. He recalled then the sweltering heat of noon in the desert, the oven-like atmosphere in the army trucks and tanks, the mirages on the roads of sand that gave one the impression of moving through hazy water.

On his previous visit, if he could call it that, he had arrived at Suez and been taken with his division to a base depot for acclimatization before being sent to a camp for movement orders and to take up his command. Now that the Germans were in North Africa, very close at hand, it was doubtful that any men going to the front could be allowed the luxury of more than a few days, if that, of what could be called acclimatization.

Familiar doubts assailed him as he stood looking around him, doubts that he could be of as much use to the army behind the scenes as he had first hoped. Indeed, he felt like a very small cog in a big machine that he could not at that moment comprehend fully. The situation in the desert was fluid, ever changing. His field experience would no doubt be of some value, he assumed, in his understanding of the news from the various battlefronts that would be coming in to headquarters, and of the information that would be going out.

It seemed to him in this ramshackle building that served as an air terminal that there was a palpable sense of fear, manifest in the quiet deliberation in the movements of those around him, their lack of speech, their quick, suspicious sizing-up of strangers. Most were in uniform.

"Captain Calborne, sir?"

"Yes." Henry swung round, confronted by a soldier, who saluted

"Private Clarkson, sir. I'm Captain Seager's driver and batman. He's here to meet you, sir. Sent me in to get you." The private was short and stocky, dressed in desert uniform, his hair bleached blond by sun and his skin red. Out of his weathered face, eyes of startling blue summed up Henry in a matter of seconds. No doubt, Henry assumed, his months of illness were evident. Not much cop for active service, the other man must be thinking.

"You mean Captain Seager's outside?"

"Yes, sir. We have a staff car, for you and three others. Let me take your bag, sir."

"Good show. Lead on."

As they walked towards another door, it opened and Basil Seager came through, wearing the same sort of uniform as his batman. He seemed fit and well, although close up Henry could see that he looked very tired and somewhat strained. Seeing a familiar face dissipated some of the doubts that he had about being there.

"Henry!" Basil came forward, holding out a hand, grinning. "So good to see you. How are you, old chap?"

"Better for seeing you. Thank you so much for coming. It continues to amaze me that we've fetched up in the same place."

"Indeed. I'm sure it's been a bit of a hellish journey," Basil said. "But here you are, safe and sound. We'll soon get you fixed up."

The car, with five of them in it, plus the driver and a fair amount of baggage in the boot and inside, was still comfortable and spacious.

While the other three men started a quiet conversation of their own, Basil, seated next to Henry, turned to him and spoke.

"I want to fill you in about what's been going on. This has not been a good time for us over the past weeks. We've lost most of the territory we gained with just the Italians here. We've been short of men and supplies until some of our ships managed to get through to Alex in the last month or so. It's a bloody mess, if you ask me."

The strain showed on Basil's face as he spoke, quickly and tersely.

"Our chaps were instructed to fall back if attacked, and that's what they did. No other option really. They couldn't risk being too far ahead of their supply lines, particularly when supplies were short and they didn't know when the next lot would come up."

Henry nodded, knowing the scene only too well. He was beginning to feel faint now from lack of food.

"That's better than in the first war, in my view," he said, "when it was attack and be damned, a lot of the time."

"We've still got Tobruk," Basil said. "We're in a sort of stale-mate at the moment. Things could go either way. I hope this holds until we can get some reinforcements. The Jerries have got some very good anti-tank and anti-aircraft guns. We can be all right if we get our reinforcements soon and they don't get theirs in time. All in all, this has been a rotten year for us, but we're still holding on, as you can see."

"I hope I can be of some use," Henry said. "I feel a bit guilty that I'm not out there with the chaps of my division."

"Don't be. Everyone is of some use here, particularly those with experience of the desert. It's possible that they'll get you doing some instructing. In the meantime, you'll be at headquarters, helping to keep track of what's going on out there, in Communications with me, I expect. The major who's in charge of us is a decent bloke."

"Thanks for filling me in."

"I'll tell you more later when we're alone," Basil said. "We'll go first to the hotel where you can dump your bags, then we'll have dinner, which I've ordered already. We eat at the hotel where we live. Grub's pretty good, considering there's a war on. You must be bloody hungry."

"I am rather."

"My room's close to yours, on the same corridor. We'll have a drink and a smoke while we're waiting for our grub to be served. I'm afraid I've taken up smoking again in a big way. Filthy habit, I know. And I've become somewhat addicted to whisky and soda. A lot of chaps in the city drink like the proverbial fishes. It's the war on the nerves. So long as you don't let it get out of hand, so long as you do your job well, it doesn't seem to matter. The higher-ups turn a blind eyes, perhaps because they're doing it themselves." He attempted a dry chuckle.

"How have you been, Basil?"

"Oh, pretty good. I don't mind admitting it's a strain ... not knowing when all this is going to be over. If it goes on much longer we won't know how to cope with normal life when it comes."

"Our understanding of normal might be different," Henry said.

"I know one thing. I won't take anything good for granted again, if I get out of this alive. Sometimes I drive out into the desert, if I get a bit of free time, as far as to where I can hear the guns. It reminds me of why we're here in this stinking place, and it stops me being tempted to feel sorry for myself. Then I go back to my cushy desk job and the whisky and soda."

"Sounds as though you're suffering from a spot of guilt yourself," Henry said.

"I expect you're right. Bloody business all round."

"It makes me think of that First World War song: 'We're here because we're here, because we're here, because we're here'."

The car came into the city, showing the streetscape seedy and dirty, everything shabby, with street lamps casting a blue light and men in white robes flitting around like ghosts beside the roads. The air coming through the open windows of the car was hot and burdensome. During the day these streets would be teeming with people and vehicles of various types, Henry recalled. There would be beggars in every state of decrepitude, and street vendors, dogging anyone who was obviously a foreigner, persistent and annoying, yet eliciting pity.

As they came into the centre, there were small groups of soldiers walking along slowly, and civilians in European dress getting in and out of taxis. There were bars and hotels open. "What are all those soldiers doing here?" Henry remarked.

"Some of them have been on leave and been cut off from their units, don't know where they are," Basil said, peering through the window at the passing tableau. "It's a mobile war, more than most, and they can't always get transport out. Part of the job of headquarters is to locate units for those men. Mostly we send them out to a depot, then they go on from there, if they can. We keep track of where the front is." Again he chuckled, like a mental shrug. "There are so many rumours floating about, that sometimes we believe the rumours ourselves when we can't get enough information from the front. The most prevalent one is that Rommel could be in the city within a day."

Although Henry smiled, he felt the apprehension that so obviously weighed upon his friend.

"Do you think that's possible?"

"Doubt it. He would outrun his supplies. But we can't be complacent. If you're complacent, you're dead. Best to think the worst and try to prepare for it as best you can."

"Are we prepared?"

Basil laughed. "In theory, more or less."

~ The hotel, Henry speculated on entering a vast lobby, would in peacetime have been classed as "luxury". It had a splendour that was still evident, even though the furnishings had obviously been pared down and what was left provided a rather pathetic and seedy glamour, like a woman of the night past her prime who still looked beautiful in dim light.

A single potted palm decorated the space, standing on the elaborately tiled floor. A long, polished wooden reception desk was staffed by a man in uniform.

"Good evening, Wright," Basil said, addressing him. "This is Captain Calborne. I believe you have his room ready."

"Yes, sir. Here's the key. Shall I tell the dining room you're here, sir?"

"Yes, do. We'll be there in five minutes. And would you order my usual from the bar, for both of us."

"Yes, sir."

The room, which they reached via a small, creaking lift, looked more than adequate, with its own bathroom. A ceiling fan did something to shift the warm air. Henry washed his hands and splashed cold water over his face and hair, before meeting Basil in the corridor to go down to the bar.

Two drinks waited for them at the bar. "Your usual table is ready, sir," the barman, a local man, addressed Basil deferentially.

"Thank you," Basil said. He downed half his drink at one gulp, while Henry picked his up and carried it to the table in the large dining room, following on behind Basil. The furnishings were dark and formal, opulent in a quiet way. From here they heard nothing of the life in the street, the hush creating an illusion that there was no war on, save for the few people in uniform sitting at tables here and there. Some of them raised a hand to Basil.

They were seated by a window that was draped with closed curtains. "This place could be a target," Basil said. "I expect the Jerries know where we are. I'll explain the bomb drill later, then I thought I'd take you over to headquarters for a quick shufti of the place, so that you'll know what to expect in the morning. That's if you can stay awake that long."

"Oh, yes, I'll be as right as rain once I've got some food inside me, together with the whisky," Henry assured Basil cheerfully. Privately he hoped that the whisky would not knock him out, not being used to alcohol these days. Not that he ever had been, really, apart from wine with a meal now and again. If he sipped it slowly, between mouthfuls of food, he should be all right. It was funny, he smiled to himself, how men never wanted to admit that they couldn't take drink. He sensed that Basil would not mention his former blindness, and he would not bring it up himself.

"We plot troop movements on maps, try to keep track of everyone, and supplies, of course," Basil said. "There's an awful lot of work, in one way and another. All specialized, of course, each to his own."

"I'm looking forward to it," Henry said, and meant it.

"Two admonitions you'll hear a lot here," Basil said, smiling, "and you'll start saying them yourself — 'Don't you know there's a war on?' and 'You're not here for a bloody holiday'."

"Those sound familiar," Henry said.

A waiter, formally attired, brought covered dishes on a trolley.

"We can order our food in advance," Basil explained. "It saves a lot of time. You just tell them when you're going to turn up and they have it ready. I took the liberty of ordering for you, old chap. Hope you don't mind. We have to be careful what we eat here, as you know. Some of the chaps have been hellishly ill with jaundice, hepatitis, you know, as well as dysentery ... and much worse, which I won't go into here. Don't want to put you off your grub."

More relaxed now, Basil was prepared to describe life in Cairo in detail, and Henry could see that the alcohol was having the desired effect. Their meal, he could see, was mainly of vegetables in various sauces, on rice.

"Best to avoid any sort of meat, fish or shell-fish," Basil said. "Or anything uncooked, or anything not served hot. Milk has to be boiled. We get some of our food from back home, of course."

"I'm going to enjoy this," Henry said, taking a swallow of his drink, followed by a forkful of his dinner, which proved to be delicious. "Beats bully and smoky boiled tea."

"Sometimes I hanker after that desert tea. Once in a while I have my batman make it for me. You'll be sharing Clarkson with me, I expect."

~ Back in his room, Henry ran a bath for himself and unpacked his writing case and a framed photograph of Sarah. He was beyond tiredness, moving as though in a stupor. Disorientated, yet oddly at home at the same time, he was beginning to get a sense that he would be useful here.

After the cool bath, dressed in light cotton pyjamas, he sat at a small narrow table that served as a desk to write a quick letter to Sarah, using the hotel note paper. "Darling Sarah, have arrived safely in Cairo. Am at a hotel, address above, where I will be living. This beats kipping down in the sand, although the desert nights are spectacular under the stars. You can write to me here, as well as at Headquarters."

He went on to explain what had happened to him since leaving England, and asked her about herself. Wanting to get it off in the post as quickly as possible, he put on dressing gown and slippers and went down to the lobby where he had spotted a mail bag for outgoing mail. There he found the same soldier, Wright, on duty.

"That's the bag, sir," Wright said helpfully.

"Thanks, Wright. What time's breakfast?"

"Well, it starts up at five ack emma, sir, so that those who like to get going at dawn can do so. That's the best time of the day. You can get breakfast up to about half-past ten, then they start into lunch, sir."

"I'll remember that."

"To tell the truth, you can get food more or less any time, sir."

As Henry made his way back to the main staircase, he noticed steps going down below ground level, and a sign saying 'bomb shelter.'

"There's a siren, sir, if needed," Wright said. "The hotel has its own."

◯ Chapter 25

High summer. Lizzie, not yet three years old, sat in a field in sunshine by the house in Bullrush Lane, among small pats of dried cow dung. The cows themselves were far away over the other side of the field. The grass was warm and prickled her legs.

Beyond a wood in front of her, she could see a line of silver birch trees with leaves that shimmered and sparkled in the sunlight as they were moved by the breeze. They seemed to dance. Her father, who sat on a wooden chair near her, in the shade of a tree, had told her the name of the trees. He was reading a newspaper, having recently come home from work. He had rigged up a tent for her, of a blanket over a pole supported by two forked sticks. Near her, on the grass, was a plate of Victoria plums picked from Mrs. Katt's tree. They were large and juicy, those plums.

As she looked at the trees, as she basked in the presence of her father, Lizzie had a sense of being very old, of belonging there in that place, as though she had always been there, that there had never been a time when she was not there. Although she could not have put it into words, it was there instinctively in her mind, strong and powerful. She was separate and yet not separate from her father and from all of this around her. She was one with the little insects that crawled through the grass near her, with the birds that flew down from the hawthorn tree to settle on the side of the plate that held the plums. They looked at her cheekily with their shining eyes before they pecked at the plums.

Sometimes a plane droned in the distance and, when it became visible, her father would look up from his paper and watch it.

Once he put the newspaper down on the ground in order to take snuff. With fascination Lizzie watched him take the small rounded-topped tin out of his pocket, then place two pinches of snuff on the back of his hand and draw the powder into each nostril.

"Filthy habit!" Lizzie recalled her mother's voice as she washed the handkerchiefs that her father had used, brown with snuff. Lizzie had no idea why he took snuff, when it made him go into fits of sneezing, yet she liked to watch him take it.

When his bout of sneezing had subsided, her father turned and looked at her, smiling, his eyes running with tears. "Silly old me," he said.

The cat, Greysuit, wandered out into the field and lay down to watch insects.

The year of 1941 wore on. Sarah Burroughs had a few days off for Christmas. The student nurses on her ward had put names into a hat to draw for two of them to have time off over the holiday — and her name had been drawn.

As she sat on that bus with a small week-end bag beside her, it wended its way through twisted country roads, and she thought of the news. Earlier that month, the Japanese air force had bombed the United States naval fleet at Pearl Harbour. At the time she had supposed that they were taking advantage of world chaos to exert an old claim to the territory. She had not known where Pearl Harbour was, had had to study the maps that appeared in newspapers. People were saying now that the Americans would come into the war.

Then a day or two ago had come the news that the government had passed a National Service Act that conscripted unmarried women for service. That, more than anything, signified to her the seriousness and precariousness of the situation in the country. If she herself had not been a student nurse, she would be conscripted to work on a farm, or in a factory. Mary would have to go. In fact, there were no women she knew who were not doing work of some sort connected to the war effort.

It would be a strange Christmas with Henry still in Cairo, and the possibility of the destruction of their country as they had known it up to now. Certain things, certain aspects of life, became sweeter and dearer as they took on the quality of the ephemeral. Through the frequent letters that they exchanged, she and Henry were getting to know one another in a way that no peace-time letters would have allowed. Disaster brought out an honesty, a putting aside of a reticence that would have otherwise plagued them. They had agreed to marry quietly in a registry office when he could get home on leave, then they would have a service at her father's church in Fernden later when she had finished her training and when, perhaps, the war might be over.

"Then the bells will ring out in Fernden for us," Henry had written, "as they will ring out when the war is over."

Thinking of his words now, because she so wanted them to come true, they took on the quality of myth. The church bells would ring out now as a warning of an invasion, a call to defence, to arms. They did not ring out in joy.

When the bus stopped in the High Street at Fernden, she got off and walked towards the vicarage.

~ The holiday came and went. The church was full, yet no one could rejoice.

In North Africa and elsewhere, battles raged back and forth.

~ Three weeks into the New Year, 1942, in North Africa, Rommel made a counter-stroke which went more than 250 miles deep and pushed the Allies back from the western border of Cyrenaica, two thirds of the way to the Egyptian frontier. A new front was established on the Gazala Line, on the Mediterranean coast, just a little west of Tobruk.

Sarah read, sitting in the staff dining-room of the hospital for a fifteen-minute coffee break. As always she quickly scanned the newspaper for news of events in North Africa among all the news of fighting in Russia, bombing and sinking of ships in the Atlantic, the bombing of Germany and home, the Japanese attacks in the east. Her eyes lingered the longest on the news from North Africa, although she saw that the Japanese had captured Kuala Lumpur, the capital of Malaya. Hong

Kong had already surrendered, on Christmas Day, and before that, the Japanese army had captured Manila.

Sometimes Sarah wondered why she read the newspapers, when the news brought an increase to a residual sick anxiety that never left her. At the same time there was a compulsion to keep abreast of events, for ignorance, she felt, might in some way contribute to defeat. As it was, the news was censored, she did not doubt, as well as biased. They did not see photographs of the dead and dying on battlefields, or the dead and maimed civilians in bombed cities.

Other student nurses around her were scrutinizing newspapers too, with a quiet intensity, between taking mouthfuls of the rather awful coffee made with boiled milk and Camp liquid coffee. There was little sugar to be had, and the milk was generally reconstituted from National Dried.

As Sarah left the dining room, with the folded newspaper in her hand, she felt sick with worry because there had been no letter from Henry in the mail slot marked "B" in the dining-room. Three times she had gone through the pile of letters, finding one from Mary who was now a Land Girl working on a farm in Sussex.

Mary wrote that she got up at dawn, helped to milk the cows, fed them hay, let them out to the fields when the weather was decent, mucked out the cow sheds and transported the dung and straw by wheelbarrow to the dung heap. Sarah, in spite of her own depression at the war news and no letter from Henry, was able to smile at the visions she could conjure up of her beautiful, normally elegant sister dressed in old riding breeches, gum boots, old jerseys and jackets, pushing a loaded wheelbarrow full of dung. In a previous letter, Mary confided that her own boyfriend, somewhere in Palestine, was well, although she lived in fear that he would be sent to Egypt.

Nineteen forty-one had not been a good year. Now 1942 had started badly, as though a crescendo of destruction were building up, especially now with the Japanese in the war. They had, she sensed, made a mistake in attacking the Americans. And that mistake was a ray of hope for the Allies.

It was a good thing that her work was so intense and exhausting. In the evenings when she was not on duty, she and her friends and col-leagues often went to the bomb shelter when there were air raids, being on standby to help evacuate patients if necessary. They worried when there was moonlight, for the hospital was spread out over a wide area consisting of many single storey buildings that would be clearly visible from the air in spite of some large trees here and there. She had heard that large red crosses painted on roofs were often ignored by the enemy.

In the shelters they talked about the progress of the war as they hunkered down, fully dressed, to doze. There was a kitchenette where they smoked and made cocoa. Some of the girls whose boyfriends and brothers were overseas shed tears as they talked, trying to gain comfort from one another. The ones who did not know where their men were showed themselves the most distraught, their faces pale and eyes wide as they sat in the candlelight. Although there was electric light in the shel-ter, they preferred the soft, intimate light of candles as they sipped cocoa from their enamelled mugs and shared confidences in quiet voices. Sometimes a girl would turn her face to the wall and sob.

On a wall in the kitchenette someone had tacked up another one of those experimental government posters which admonished them: "Keep Calm and Carry On."

~ Weeks went by. Singapore was surrendered to the Japanese, who then bombed Darwin in Australia, so Sarah read in her newspaper and heard on the wireless in the sitting room of the nurses' residence, where the nurses crouched around it in the early evenings.

Towards the end of March they heard that the Royal Air Force had bombed Lubeck, in Germany, and in early April the Germans captured Salonika in Greece. Then on April 18th, the United States Air Force bombed Tokyo.

To counteract the tension, the hospital administrators held dances for the nurses in a hall in the grounds, to which off-duty soldiers and airmen were invited. There was a poignancy and a frenetic quality to the friendships and romances that the girls made with the young men who were really boys about their own age. Sarah, asked by some if she would write to them when they went overseas, explained that she was engaged.

She could scarcely sleep these days either in the bomb shelter or in her own room, and she lost weight, becoming pale and thin to the point where her ward sister remarked on it and sent her to the staff doctor. He prescribed cod-liver oil and malt, a dessert spoonful to be taken twice a day indefinitely. He tut-tutted at her weight, ordering her to see him once a week to be weighed. If she did not put on weight, he said to her, she might have to give up her nursing training, for if her health became too run-down, there was the danger that she could contract tuberculosis. Her ration of butter, fresh milk, and cream was to be increased temporarily until she had gained at least ten pounds.

In the shelter that evening, Sarah found that at least half her friends and colleagues were dosing themselves on cod-liver oil and malt on the doctor's instructions.

May and Jim Langridge, together with Alice and Tom Katt, listened to the wireless at number two Bullrush Lane in early June, 1942, and heard that Air Marshal Arthur Harris had ordered the bombing of Cologne by over 1,000 bombers on May 30th. This had been duly carried out. Six hundred acres of the city had been devastated.

"Revenge is a terrible thing," Tom Katt remarked. "What happened to: 'Vengeance is mine; I will repay, sayeth the Lord'?"

"It's all sickening beyond belief," Alice said.

"It is a terrible thing," Jim said. "But perhaps it will hasten the end. Do they care what they've done to us?"

After the news, music came on the wireless. "If you were the only girl in the world, and I were the only boy," someone crooned.

May got up, images of fire, noise, destruction in her mind, conscious that her lips were closed, pressed tightly together.

"Can I help you with the washing up?" Alice followed her out to the kitchen. "Don't let it upset you. I rather think, May, that at the moment it's either them or us. It's all madness. Think what they've done to London already ... and they haven't finished."

"I know. It's just that it's all done without our consent. One feels so helpless," May whispered, as she filled an enamelled bowl with cold water. "Would you get the kettle off the stove, please? I don't want to go in there again and let the men see that I'm losing my nerve."

Letters came from Henry to Sarah, confirming and enlarging on the news she had read and heard, although he played down the dangers of his own situation. It was unlikely, he said, that he would get leave to Britain in the foreseeable future.

In turn, Sarah wrote telling him that the Luftwaffe had started to bomb historic cities in Britain, among them Exeter and Bath, while she played down her own experience of enemy bombers passing over the hospital.

Sometimes their own fighters, Spitfires, flew over the hospital in squadrons, or just a few together beside the big heavy bombers.

Henry sent her photographs of himself in the desert, wearing shorts, hatless, his hair blown by the wind, his eyes squinting against the sun. Although still thin, he looked wiry and healthy, his face having filled out somewhat.

In contrast, even the most flattering photographs of her that she intended to send him displayed her unnatural thinness, her prominent cheekbones and hollow eyes.

~ Early summer came, and Sarah was given two weeks' leave from duty. As she packed, one bag with textbooks and lecture notes, another with clothes and personal items, she knew how close she was to tears when there was no letter from Henry for days, or even a week or two, though she knew that several letters from him often came at once.

Mary, who had managed to get some time off from the farm, was to pick her up with their father's car. Lord Calborne had got wind of her imminent arrival, no doubt having been told by her father, and wrote to invite her for tea and then for lunch on another day. They would, he said, talk about the progress of the war, because it didn't do to keep things bottled up. With that she agreed.

~ The days were warm and beautiful at Fernden, reminding Sarah of when she and Henry had gone to the Calborne chapel. Aeons ago, it seemed, and yet it might have been yesterday when she remembered the day's details and admired the opal ring that she had transferred to her finger now that she was home. Her longing to see him was constant, a physical ache. Since that day at the chapel she had matured and changed. Their time together had taken on a mythical quality, the only tangible things left, that ring, his photographs and letters.

It was wonderful to be home for more than a day or two, where her parents fussed over her and fed her, where she sat in a pew in her father's church, where she walked alone or with Mary through fields in sunshine.

~ Mid-way through her first week she sat under a tree in the Calborne garden, waited upon by Thwaite, who looked at her, when he thought she was not noticing, with a certain shock on his face. The bonny girl has gone, he must be thinking as he pushed a jug of clotted cream near her, with scones and blackcurrant jam, and solicitously moved her cup of tea close to her right hand as though she were too weak to lift it far. He himself had taken on a new weariness.

"Lovely to see you again, Thwaite," she had said, upon her arrival at the house.

"Likewise, Miss," he had said. "I hope this visit finds you well." Schooled as he was in the art of the poker-face, Sarah thought, he could not hide his shock at the sight of a very slender, almost bony, young woman. Also, she had grown her hair longer, had twisted it into a loose bun at the nape of her neck, and this made her look older and perhaps a little stern. Heaven forbid! There was a self-possession about her now, she knew, that was different from her more youthful self-confidence which, she had to concede, had been largely based on ignorance.

"I'm as well as cod liver oil and malt will allow, Thwaite," she had said, smiling, with something of her old spirit.

"I hope they're not overworking you, Miss," he said.

"Oh, they do that as a matter of course. There's nothing else for it. I've got two weeks to recuperate."

She and Lord Calborne talked about the Allied offensive that had taken place in North Africa near the end of May. It had been forestalled by Rommel and his army, and that part of the front had been forced to retreat quickly to the Alamein Line.

"The Germans," Lord Calborne said, "went three hundred miles deep in a week."

As he spoke, he encouraged her to eat the homemade scones and cakes, the tomatoes and lettuce from the kitchen garden, the cucumber sandwiches. He kept passing her things or moving them closer to her. "Eat up, dear girl. Otherwise we'll all be disappointed in you."

The fresh air, the sunshine, the relaxation increased her appetite, so to please Henry's father she piled clotted cream and jam onto scones and chomped her way through them while he talked. It did occur to her that she might be sick later on, as she had sometimes been sick as a child after eating too many sweet things at a party. With that in mind, she turned her attention to the cucumber sandwiches, the watercress, and the tomatoes.

"Our army was defeated at Gazala," he said thoughtfully, looking off across the vast lawns, "on the 14th. Bad show, that. They've had to retreat."

"I'm not sure where El Alamein is, although I do have a map that I look at."

"El Alamein itself is a small place on the Mediterranean coast. The line goes south from that. Too close to Cairo by far."

Sarah, her mouth full, nodded.

Thwaite came across the lawn bearing a fresh pot of tea, a silver pot covered with a white linen napkin. "More tea, Miss Sarah?" he said.

"Mmm ... please." Something approaching happiness assailed her. This was so civilized, so peaceful, and the constant alertness she had to maintain at work was creeping away.

"Henry seems more real here," she blurted out when Thwaite had departed. "Sometimes I feel he's like a ghost."

"Exactly. Would you like to read the letters that he sent to me? You could take them home with you, then bring them back when you come for lunch next week. They say a lot about what's going on in the desert and in Cairo itself ... all censored, I assume, but still good, without giving away military secrets."

"Thank you, I'd like to read them."

∼ A week later, Sarah was back at Calborne House to return the letters and have lunch on the terrace that looked out over the fields and the chapel.

"Miss Burroughs, sir," Thwaite announced to Lord Calborne who was standing near the table on the terrace, hands in his trouser pockets, looking out over his land resplendent with summer.

He came forward to take both her hands. "Glass of wine? It might help to temper the bad news, one item among many, I must say. We are rather focused on Henry, aren't we? Have you listened to the news this morning?"

"No, we deliberately didn't turn on the wireless," she said, accepting a glass of white wine. "Sometimes we have a news-free day, just to get our spirits up a bit."

"Sit down, dear girl. We have a cold soup, already here."

Tension mounted in Sarah as she drank the soup and ate the bread. If the bad news had to do with Henry directly, she assumed Lord Calborne would have said so immediately.

"Do you mind if I smoke?" he asked.

"Please do." He offered her a cigarette, which she accepted. Then he deftly fitted his into a cigarette holder before lighting both.

"Rommel and the German army have captured Tobruk," he said.

A sharp indrawing of breath was all that Sarah could muster at that moment.

"The Australians were there. Our men have been isolated for a long time, as you know. About thirty-five thousand of them, I believe. So the Germans have got them, and an immense amount of our stores. Some people are saying this is the worst disaster of the war for us, so far, apart from the fall of Singapore."

"Oh, God," Sarah whispered.

They sat in silence, smoking, until Thwaite came out with the main course, a spinach and mushroom flan, accompanied by a variety of vegetables.

"Is Henry ... ?" Sarah started. "I haven't had a letter here ... he knows I'm here, I think."

"I'm expecting a letter any day," Lord Calborne said. "You can bet there's something of a panic in Cairo. Henry won't let us down; he'll get something in the post. They have good escape routes. The rest of the 8th Army has had to retreat eastward."

"What now, do you think?" Sarah managed to get the words out before drawing on the last of her cigarette.

"In my opinion, there will be a lull, because the Germans have come on too fast. They will have out-paced their supply lines."

"Let us hope so," she said.

"With good planning, we can recoup, I think. That's my feeling. Our chap, Richie, perhaps decided to retreat because he had divided his forces. It's not clear. The BBC doesn't have the information on that, apparently, or they're not saying. It's doubtful that Cairo is under immediate threat."

Lord Calborne passed Sarah a dish of vegetables, so she piled some onto her plate and helped herself to a generous slice of flan. While allowing Thwaite to replenish her wine glass, she dwelt on the comforting words of Henry's father, the voice of experience that Henry would, for now, be all right.

"Tuck in, dear girl." Lord Calborne placed his packet of cigarettes and silver lighter closer to her. "Smoke any time you want to."

How dear he was, she thought. Just lately she had been thinking a lot about him as a father-in-law and, sometimes, as a grandfather.

They were both in the dark tunnel that everyone talked about now, she and he, together with everyone else in the country, where there was no light at the end. When she was with him, held together in their common anxiety, it seemed a little less dark.

✑ Chapter 26

What Henry did not tell his father and Sarah in letters was the extent of the panic in Cairo after the fall of Tobruk. The staff received information that Rommel was on his way eastward and was only one hundred miles from Alexandria on June 30th.

After the defeat of General Neil Richie at Gazala, there was much confusion and fighting on many small fronts. Some British and South African divisions managed to escape by circuitous routes east to the frontier with Egypt. This much they knew at headquarters in Cairo as information came in.

Henry stood in the communications room at HQ in front of one of the detailed maps that they more or less constantly perused, plotting army movements. Beside him stood Major Paynter, his colleague, short and stocky, with an open, plain face that belied his sharp intelligence and his competent understanding of the situation. Taller by a head, Henry was forced to look down to him, a gesture which seemed to put them on the same level professionally.

"I reckon," the major said, pointing at the map with a stick, "that our strongest division is the 1st South African, here on the coast at El Alamein. Then we've got the newly formed 18th Indian Brigade here at Deir el Shein ... my sources tell me that Rommel doesn't yet know they're there, although I must say, there's not much he doesn't know. Wouldn't be surprised if he's not listening in to every word put out on our wirelesses."

The major had been in the First World War, under fire, in a much more junior capacity, and not much fazed him now.

"Let us hope not, sir," Henry said, staring at the map. He was inclined to agree with the major, whom he respected enormously, his admiration confirmed daily. "That would explain a few things, if he is on to our communications."

Henry could picture perfectly what it was like out there in the desert, the images in his mind nagging at him more or less constantly, no doubt because he was not out there himself. Someone had to be behind the lines, but most of the time he felt that it should not really be him. "Considering the awful lot of armour we've lost in the retreat, we can use any element of surprise, assuming they don't know about Deir el Shein," he commented.

"Yes, there is that. See what we've got here … seven miles beyond the Indian brigade we've got the 6th New Zealand Brigade, at a place called Bab el Qattara … here." He moved the point of his stick around on the map, following the Alamein Line south from the village of El Alamein, which was now the battlefront. "Then there's a fourteen-mile gap … here to here … then we've got the 5th Indian Division at Naqb el Dweis. So, Captain Calborne, that's more or less what we've got between them and us."

"What have we got in these gaps, sir?"

"I can't quite say bugger all," the major said, staring fixedly and gloomily at the map. "We've got some small mobile columns, some from other divisions and the remnants that were garrisoned at Mersa Matruh."

"That was my lot," Henry said.

The major nodded. "Good luck to them. I expect they're going to need it. We've lost a lot, but I suspect that Jerry hasn't got a lot either. We've had some intelligence that Rommel plans to try for a breakthrough in the north, between El Alamein and Bab el Quattara."

Both men stood staring at the map, as though willing their defenses to be able to act according to plan. The shapes and lines of the terrain, the abandoned and ruined villages, the railway lines, the few roads, the impassable depressions in the desert, were as though burned onto Henry's brain. Some of it was hateful to him, the names he knew well. These days he looked at sunrises and sunsets whenever he could, enjoying them from the relative safety of the city, marvelling again at the gift of sight.

Telephones were ringing and staff were quietly moving around, conferring with one another, moving markers around on maps.

"Take a break, Calborne, while you can," the major suggested. "I'd like everyone to have a break before the balloon goes up, if it's going to. Go back to the hotel, get a drink and a meal. Then come back here. There won't be any rest for us tonight, let alone sleep. This is something of a showdown, by the look of it. Rommel's on the move. Fierce fighting, so I'm told, but I'm not going to spread that around too much yet. It might create a panic, more than we have already. The people in the street will know soon enough."

"Very well, sir. Thank you."

As he let himself out into the street past the guards at the entrance, showing his security pass, he paused to light a cigarette and inhaled deeply of the smoke. Walking quickly yet easily, he hardly noticed the people around him, especially those who accosted him trying to sell something that he did not want. At the same time he was alert, conscious of himself moving in the landscape, with that familiar odd feeling between his shoulder blades, the expectation of a bullet in the back.

All he wanted was a glass of whisky, well diluted with soda, followed by a good meal, then another cigarette. He might get a taxi back, if one were easily available. It was doubtful, he thought, that their army would be defeated, that Cairo would be overrun. There was a quiet conviction in him about that. Nonetheless, there was much confusion, especially as news came in about the many Allied soldiers taken prisoner and the amount of artillery and supplies captured.

Because it was hard for him to say where his quiet, stubborn optimism came from, he had to allow that he could be wrong, very wrong perhaps. He had certainly felt fear, a foreboding, when someone at headquarters had announced recently: "The bloody Jerries are close to the Alamein Line." That was still with him.

Often he and Basil drank whisky late at night with others in the hotel bar, where they discussed what the outcome might be of the war in general and of their own situation. There was always a sense of fear and awe at the impersonal nature of events that had been started by human action, at the spate of destruction that seemed to have a momentum of its own. They hunched together, speaking in hushed voices, fearing spies, those figures both real and conjured up, who would sell their souls to anyone who had the right price. There was also the fear of inadvertently spreading rumours through eavesdropping individuals at the hotel, people who worked there but were not part of the army.

After those discussions he would often fling himself down on his bed, fully clothed, to sleep while the soporific effect of the alcohol was at its peak. Sleep otherwise was difficult, when they felt themselves to be in a trap on which the door was slowly closing. The ceiling fans and the open window brought some relief from the heat. Through his open window he could hear noises from the streets, fewer as the night crept on.

As he strode into the hotel lobby and put out the stub of his second cigarette in a large pedestal ashtray, he took a sort of perverse pleasure in knowing he would not even have to make an attempt at sleep that night. There were still hours left in the day, as well as the whole evening ahead. Anything could happen.

~ After a meal and a drink, feeling fortified, he nonetheless allowed the soldier on duty at the lobby desk to get him a taxi for the return journey.

"It's a bit of a nightmare out there, sir," the soldier informed him. "I've had word that the station's packed with people trying to get out, and the roads jammed with lorry-loads of people getting out to Palestine. It's a bit premature, if you ask me, but I can understand it. We'll stick it out until we see the whites of their eyes, eh, sir?"

Henry laughed. "Well, Wright," he said, "perhaps until we see them on the horizon. What do you think of it all here so far? How are we doing?"

"Well, sir." Wright looked at him as though gauging what he could say and what he had to keep to himself of his opinion. "I talk to my mates ... what's left of them ... when they come in here on leave. The boys in the infantry up at the front say they're often cut off because the supporting tanks, and other armour, don't come up on time. When they're isolated from their back-up, they have no choice but to surrender when the enemy comes on. Then they get blamed for not putting up what is considered a good show by people safely back, well behind the front. It sounds fundamental, sir, but in reality, out there in the bloody heat, it's a bloody nightmare."

"Yes, I've been hearing about that, and I know it first-hand ... I was out there in 1940. Got shot in the leg." Out here he did not mention his blindness, which only Basil and the major knew about. It was always in his mind that he might wake up blind one morning. A glass of whisky and soda might at times be the only thing between him and the debilitating anxiety that could instigate the blindness.

Wright, nodding his understanding, looked at him with an added respect. "On the other hand, sir, the tanks get caught in mine-fields, or orders don't get sent forward in time. Sometimes the field HQs are too far back behind the lines. I know I don't have to tell you that, sir. I hear it from the other angle, see? You can see why cock-ups happen, but that doesn't make it any easier for the boys on the ground." Wright had become so animated that Henry considered him wasted standing there behind a desk in the lobby of a dilapidated hotel.

Reading his mind, Wright said: "I expect you're wondering why I've got a job that looks pretty cushy, sir? Well ..." — he reached behind the desk and brought out a rifle — "it's part of my job to defend this place, and to keep very close track of who goes in and out of here, so this hotel doesn't become more of a target than it obviously is. Spies and subversives, and all that, sir."

"I appreciate your job, Private Wright," Henry said. "And you're certainly doing it well."

"At the beginning of the war I was a crack shot, then got a splinter in my eye which damaged the cornea a bit. I'm still all right, just not as good as I was ... see, sir?"

"I certainly do. That would sum up things for a lot of us."

As Henry made to enter the taxi, Wright saluted him.

Inside the taxi, stifling hot, Henry turned his thoughts to their well-rehearsed escape plans, step by step. At headquarters he had all his personal documents in his attaché case, ready to pick up.

When he got back to HQ he found that news had come in of heavy fighting at Deir el Shein. Basil was at his desk talking on the telephone. He held up a hand for Henry to wait.

"Things don't look good for the 18th Indian Division," he said. Others were hurrying about looking grim, consulting maps, making telephone calls, conferring with each other in twos and in small groups. "It sounds as though they've been defeated, near enough. We're planning to send in the air force tonight to bomb the Jerries' supply columns because it's moonlight and Rommel could decide to come on. As a precaution we've sent out some more armour to make a showing, just in case the Jerries decide to come on anyway."

"Bloody hell," Henry said, standing side by side with Basil staring at the map, visualizing the routes that the Afrika Corps would take to Alexandria and Cairo.

"Precisely," Basil said grimly. "I could do with a drink."

"What we need to know, is whether Rommel would have the strength to hold what he captures ... assuming he could make a break-through," Henry said. "Our chaps are, after all, giving him a run for his money."

"Yes, if we can knock out some of his supplies and armour, we have a chance. My educated guess, based on our intelligence, is that he wouldn't be able to hold it."

The major was walking around to each group and each individual. "Gather together all your important papers and communications, anything that you wouldn't want to get into enemy hands," he said. "Start burning it."

There were fireplaces and stoves in the building that were soon in operation, bits of charred paper rising up the chimneys. The place took on a surreal air, as people hurried about with armfuls and boxes of papers. Heat from the fires added intolerably to the heat of the rooms.

Someone came in from outside, informing them that the charred paper from the chimneys was causing panic in the streets and people were asking if the British Army was abandoning Egypt. Crowds were gathering at the railway station, he confirmed. Cars were moving out to the coast road east.

Their shipping had moved from Alexandria through the Suez Canal into the Red Sea.

"From our point of view, the exodus is a bit premature," the major said. "Don't panic. Keep calm and carry on, as the people in blighty are being told. A showing of our tanks should help to put the kybosh on the Jerries. If it doesn't, I'll let you know if we have to resort to prayer."

A few people smiled feebly; no one felt like laughing. Telling people not to panic was one thing, while trying to achieve calm was quite another. Henry went to his desk to receive and make phone calls, in between sorting through papers. Through a nearby window he could see clouds of smoke hanging about from their own chimneys.

~ The next day, July 2nd, they learned at headquarters that Rommel was continuing his attack, but intelligence informed them that he had less than forty active tanks left and his troops were exhausted. The staff at HQ had taken turns to doze on cots in anterooms for an hour or two, most being exhausted but too keyed up to sleep. Food was brought in, and there was a pervasive smell of sweat, cigarette smoke, and various edibles. Coffee and tea were constantly on the go.

Henry and Basil stood with others in front of a wall map, where the major briefed them on the whereabouts of the two large bodies of British tanks that had been sent out as a warning to the German army. One was moving straight out towards the enemy, and the other moving round their flank. "We think, and bloody well hope," the major said, "that just the sight of the tanks will be a deterrent, seeing how exhausted and depleted the enemy is. Otherwise, some of our tanks will go round their flank and attack from the rear. We've calculated that Rommel will pull back when he sees what we're up to. Our air force has done a good job on his supply lines and armour."

"Are they as exhausted and depleted as we are, sir?" someone piped up.

"Any news of our men at Deir el Shein, sir?" someone else added.

"So far, the word is that most of them have been captured," the major said. "However, they have succeeded in delaying the enemy long enough for us to get our tanks out, under General Auchinleck, facing the enemy. As for our being depleted, I assume that we are about evenly matched. Let us hope that will be enough for now. Rommel won't give up until he absolutely has to ... we can count on that. You know his tactic under pressure ... pull back and disappear. He's not called Desert Fox for nothing."

260 • Elizabeth Langridge

The men around the major exchanged glances. The enemy was formidable and generally far from predictable.

"We haven't got much wireless security, by all accounts," Henry said to Basil when they were back at their desks. "I suspect the Jerries are able to intercept our plans of attack."

"Very likely," Basil said. "We just have to hope that we can initiate our moves before they can organize a countermove. If we could outflank them, and move in from the south to attack from the rear, we could perhaps trap him."

"Drink?" Henry offered. From the bottom drawer of his desk he took out a hip flask and two very small silver beakers.

"Won't say no."

In a narrow back corridor they took a quick drink, together with tea. "If this all blows up, old chap, and we manage to get out," Basil said, "I'll meet you in Jerusalem, by the wailing wall. I'll be there every afternoon at four o'clock. Assuming we get separated, that is."

"Done!" Henry said, knocking back the last of his miniscule drink. "That sounds like something out of the *Great Adventure Book for Boys*."

"A good thing we've both read it. Back to the burning."

"We should have an alternative plan," Henry said, as they went back to work.

"I'll think of something ... if you don't think of something first."

~ The enemy attacked the next day, but were kept at bay. Having got word of the outflanking movement, Rommel then ordered his dwindling troops and armour of the 21st Panzer Division to move back. As the British tanks moved towards them, the scanty troops and armour of the 15th Panzer Division also began to move back.

The staff at HQ in Cairo were exhausted. "There's word that they're moving back," someone stood up and announced.

"Thank God." There were collective exclamations, yet no one relaxed. It was too soon. Red-eyed and nervous from lack of sleep, they smoked and spoke in undertones, going about their business.

~ Over the next days, Henry learned, reinforcements were coming in, for them and for the enemy. There was a lull of sorts. Some of the Allies had been waiting in Palestine and now moved into Egypt. The 9th Australian Division came in, plus two fresh regiments, bringing them up to a strength of more than two hundred tanks. Plans for attacks were made.

Some of the men at HQ, Henry and Basil among them, continued to sleep on cots in the anterooms. It was some days since he had been back to the hotel. Their batman told them that expatriates were getting out of Cairo if they could, some having already gone. Those left behind, and the local population, he said, were living in fear at the closeness of the battlefront. People were referring to the burning of documents at army headquarters as Ash Wednesday.

"Perhaps one colonial master is much like another to them," Basil speculated.

Over the next days there were some ill-fated attacks by their own men, often running into mine-fields which held them up. What they succeeded in doing, by their presence, was to halt the enemy's advance. Their plans were good; the execution of them was not. Yet a sense of relief moved tentatively over the city.

Some of the officers were given time off to return to the hotel.

Eventually, word came in to HQ that the 8th Army had suffered over thirteen thousand casualties in July. Although the Allies had taken prisoners, many of their own men had been taken.

~ Winston Churchill decided to fly out to Cairo on August 4th to size up the situation. When he arrived, Rommel stood barely sixty miles from Alexandria and the Nile Delta. Information filtered through to Henry and his officer colleagues that, while Churchill was keen for a new offensive as soon as possible, General Auchinleck wanted to wait until September to allow new troops to become acclimatized and have some training in desert conditions.

"I've heard, sir," Private Wright said in the lobby of the hotel, "that his nibs is in town to size up the situation."

"How did you hear about that, Wright? It's supposed to be top secret."

"I'm not at liberty to say, sir. Don't suppose I could get his autograph?"

"You suppose right. Might get into the wrong hands."

~ On August 13th, 1942, they learned that new commanders were to be sent out to Egypt, one being General Harold Alexander, while General Bernard Montgomery was appointed Commander of the British 8th Army, North Africa. Montgomery was to be brought out from England. The wave of change brought in two new corps commanders also.

"Now," Major Paynter said in a briefing some time later, 'my latest information is that General Montgomery is being firm in deciding to wait until preparations and training are complete for our new troops. Very sensible. Success before impulse is the motto here, I think. Churchill is impatient, of course. My view is that Rommel will still try to come on while we're preparing for an offensive. However, it could be a case of giving him enough rope so that he'll hang himself. In the meantime, we're building up our strength."

~ "It's common knowledge, sir,' Wright said to Henry as he handed over his mail in the hotel, "that his nibs in London is gung ho to attack as soon as possible, while Monty is going to wait."

"Common knowledge, is it? You're in the wrong job, Private Wright," Henry said as he stood at the desk sifting through his letters. "You should be a spy. Perhaps you can tell me when he's planning to attack?" Every day they had these exchanges, so that Henry looked forward to them to break the monotony.

"I wouldn't go as far as that, sir. But I bet Rommel knows."

They both laughed. "I'd like to buy you a drink, Wright, when you're off duty."

"They won't let me drink at that bar, sir. Officers only."

"Well, you tell me what you want and I'll buy it, the moment you're off duty, then you can drink it in the kitchens."

"Much obliged, sir."

～ August wore on.

"We have, gentlemen," the major said at a briefing, "brought our complement of tanks up to seven hundred. The Germans and the Italians between them have, as far as we know, about four hundred and forty. Some of Rommel's new tanks have long-range guns. Our intelligence tells us that he appears to be planning an attack any day now." He pointed his stick at the main large map. "Up here in the north we have the 9th Australian Division, west of El Alamein itself, then we have, here, the 1st South African Division inland and a little farther east — as you can see. South of the South Africans, we have the 5th Indian Division, and the 7th Armoured Division in the south-east."

"Those areas are still heavily mined sir, by us, I take it?" one of the young officers asked.

"Yes, they are. In my opinion, those may prove to be vital in our defence. South of the 5th are the New Zealanders. This, gentlemen, is the front. Now, behind the front, we have all these other armoured brigades and divisions." He proceeded to reel off the names and the details of the men and armour behind the front line, the Alamein Line.

The staff stood or sat, and listened to him. There was a tentative mood of optimism.

"We are, I am confident, well set up, with our mine fields and our air force to back up our infantry and armour. When we are attacked, it is my understanding that we shall take a defensive position."

～ General Rommel attacked the 8th Army at Alam Halfa on the night of August 30th, where his army found that the British minefields were much deeper than they had expected. By daybreak he had not made much headway. His vehicles were heavily bombed by the British air force, and the men of the Allied armies on the ground kept them back.

～ That night, in his room, Henry sat down to write a letter to Sarah:

Darling Sarah. As I sit here in my room, there is the fragrance of an unknown blossom wafting through my open window from the hotel garden, a rare pleasure in this crowded city, so that I think of you with yearning and wish you could be here to share it with me. England seems so far away, with so much dangerous terrain between us. One must be thankful for what one has, and I am certainly that in the face of all we hear coming in to us from the desert day after day.

I pray that you are safe and well also, dearest.

We have just finished dinner. Basil sends his very best regards to you. He and I will meet later in the bar, where we all get together to discuss the progress of the war. It appears that we are approaching a showdown of sorts here, because the enemy is very close, perhaps something big, about which I cannot go into detail, of course. You will hear it on the news soon enough.

Do not worry too much about me, we have a lot of armour and good men between us and the enemy. Take very good care of yourself. All my Love, Henry.

Over the next weeks Henry learned that the new commanders were making plans, training their men and getting them and their equipment in place, forging new communications and strategies with the air force.

General Montgomery ordered the counter-attack at El Alamein for October 23rd.

At Calborne House, Lord Calborne turned on the wireless in his study to listen to the evening news on November 4th, 1942.

"The German army in North Africa is in full retreat after suffering a comprehensive defeat in Egypt at the hands of the 8th Army under General Bernard Montgomery," the announcer stated, causing Lord Calborne to get to his feet, glass of whisky and soda in hand, as though to run somewhere to impart the good news. Instead he stood stock-still, a sense of relief so powerful he thought for a few seconds that he might pass out.

"News of the victory came in a special joint war report from British Headquarters in Cairo this evening," the voice went on. "It described the retreating columns of German soldiers as 'disordered' and said that they were being relentlessly attacked by our land forces, and by the Allied air forces by day and night."

Lord Calborne raised his glass in silent tribute to those who had carried out the victory, who had fought, died, been wounded and maimed, who had survived; those unknown young men far away who were there so that he himself might be safer in his own home. In those, he included his son.

Then, taking a decanter of brandy, he made his way to the kitchens where the members of his scanty household staff would be gathered around their wireless. He would offer them a drink, and together they would raise their glasses.

$\sim$ In Bullrush Lane the residents of the cottages sat on bunks in the air-raid shelter listening to the news broadcast.

"Allied troops have captured more than nine thousand prisoners of war. Casualties among the German troops have been high. It has taken twelve days and nights of fierce fighting around the desert village of El Alamein to drive back the massed forces."

In the shelter, Jim and May, Alice and Tom looked at each other tentatively smiling. "A ray of hope," May said.

"Long columns of enemy transports began to build up along the coast road as the retreat began."

"Hallelujah!" Tom Katt spoke for all of them. "Halle — bloody — lujah!"

Four days later, on November 8th, Sarah listened to the news in the hospital shelter. "American and British forces invaded French North Africa in Operation Torch. This is the first major joint Allied offensive of the war."

∼ A week later she received a letter from Henry. "You will have heard the news," he wrote. "The enemy is in retreat westward, where they will be met by both our forces and by the Americans, who landed from both the Atlantic in Morocco and from the Mediterranean. Thank God. The relief we feel here is indescribable."

∽ Chapter 27

It had been a good summer, May conceded, if one could discount the war.

She eased off her rubber boots and put on slippers, having just come into the house from the garden with a basket of Brussels sprouts. Outside the air was crisp and pleasant with the smells of autumn, decaying leaves, wind-fall apples, and the scent of soil moistened by drizzle. She took off her old coat and the scarf that she had put over her head, shaking off rain drops and draping the garments over a chair. The house was quiet, as Lizzie was having a nap and Jo had been taken to the village school earlier that morning.

Now she would do the ironing that awaited her in the large wicker basket in which she kept the washed laundry. The three irons were heating on the range. The sprouts she placed in a colander in the scullery, then went into the kitchen to spread a blanket and an old sheet on the table for the ironing; with a pot holder she lifted one of the irons onto the trivet.

Ironing was a peaceful pastime, allowing her mind to go to other things as she smoothed over the clothes and pillow cases that had dried on the line in the garden and gave off the scent of soap and fresh air.

Over the summer, she and Alice volunteered at the Women's Institute in the village and had done work of all types, including the giving out of used clothing and household items to people in dire need, people who had been bombed out, people even worse off than she was herself. They all bought clothes at jumble sales and church bazaars, so there was no stigma attached to taking used clothing. Indeed, some of it was very good quality, coming from the wealthy people of the area, scarcely worn. All the volunteers had prepared food for them, the homeless families, and for the men of the Home Guard and the Air Raid Precaution.

They had done so much, with still so much left to do. The nature of it was that it was never-ending.

While ironing, she turned on the wireless to listen to the news. Those words — "This is the BBC Home Service" — made her pause in whatever she was doing, stilled in anticipation to know what was happening overseas and at home, yet fearful of what might be revealed. Always she was in two minds about switching on, then usually gave in. Hope mixed with dread, with many emotions in between, assailed her waiting.

In that way she knew about the Royal Air Force bombing of Hamburg on July 26th, and the German army entering Stalingrad on August 24th, the fierce hand-to-hand and house-to-house fighting that was going on there, the workers who had been issued with guns with which to defend themselves while waiting for the army to come up. The Russians were fierce, unbelievably courageous, she understood, fuelled by an overpowering love for their motherland, and a determination that the enemy should not make inroads there. How she admired them!

Would the English fight as fearlessly when they saw the enemy walking over their fields of Sussex and Kent, and through their villages? Would they fight behind piles of rubble, from underground holes? Yes, yes they would, she knew it in her heart. For if one saw death coming, one might as well go down fighting for all that one loved.

And now there was the hopeful news of North Africa. There had been something on the wireless about the American General, Dwight Eisenhower, leading the invasion of Tunisia, planning to squeeze the retreating Germans from the western end of the desert. The British army had already recaptured Tobruk. There was pride in that, mixed in with a pervasive sadness at the many who must have died. On the other side of the coin, Adolf Hitler had ordered the occupation of Vichy France.

She went out to the scullery to fill the kettle to make tea, catching sight of her face in the small mirror that hung in the window above the sink. Her skin was unhealthily pale, from poor nutrition and not enough sunlight, she assumed. These days she seldom smiled because she had lost so many teeth. And she only forty-four. Vanity it was, of course. So many people had rotten teeth, or gaps in their mouths, that they did not remark on that in others. Her grey-green eyes stared back at her with an abject weariness, the lids drooping. Only her hair, which had always been lovely, dark brown and naturally wavy, was still the same, more or less. She wore it pinned close to her head in little wavelets, to keep it tidy when she worked, a style that she knew was out of date.

When clothes were rationed, and no money for new ones anyway, fashion did not matter much, or the hair to go with it. Yet women were objects of mild contempt if they let themselves go. "She's let herself go, all right," people would say of a slovenly woman who had given up the fight. And one did not even have to be slovenly, she mused, just badly put together.

You could do a lot with a nice felt hat, in dark brown or navy blue, with a brim, pulled down over one eye in a sort of rakish gesture together with a little clutch bag held under the arm. It did not matter if your coat was old, so long as it was clean and brushed, and your shoes were polished.

May sighed as she put the old, sooty kettle on the range to heat up, then went back to her ironing. Not only was she saddened by a ravaged face that had once been beautiful, she hated the look of her hands as well, red and swollen from work, the nails broken. At night she rubbed Vaseline into them. Thinking about the way she looked, trivial though it might be, had something to do with self-respect, and took her mind off war for a few minutes at a time, like the hats that one could sometimes buy at a jumble sale for a penny.

She and Alice knew where to go for the good jumble sales, where one could find a lovely hat for next to nothing, discarded by a wealthy lady perhaps after only one wearing. But, the question arose, where could one wear the more elaborate concoctions of head gear, the ones with tulle and artificial flowers, without looking pretentious? Sometimes they wore them in the house while drinking tea and discussing their library books, their work, and the events of the war effort, the never-ending question of how to make ends meet.

Most of the time they bought more utilitarian items, of course, the knitted jumpers, the blouses, the good wool skirts, the coats. "I've got a lovely skirt for you, May," a friend would say in a conspiratorial whisper, while rummaging in a box under a table. "I've kept it just for you, duck. And there's a nice blouse that would go with it. There you are — tuppence ha'penny for the lot."

What fun they were, those sales. Once home, she would carefully wash and iron her washable purchases. Now she thought how much she loved the ritual of making tea, because it was something to do with your hands when the worst of the news came on, when you knew that you were getting a sanitized version of events and your imagination informed you of the real. When the tea was made and poured, she would sweeten it with a spoonful of condensed milk from the tin, while listening to the authoritative voice.

Often when listening she had such a sense of dissonance that she wondered if she were going mad, losing that mental equilibrium that kept her going, that fine balance that could tilt too far the wrong way. Both sides in the war were bombing places that had no military or strategic significance, places full of civilians. It was a tit-for-tat retaliation that in itself seemed criminal, pointless. Presumably, the side that could inflict the most damage, on innocent people or otherwise, would be the "victor". It made no more sense to her now than events of the first war had done.

She dipped a biscuit in her tea to soften it, the few good teeth she had left in her head not always enough to cope with the food she ate. Now that Jo was in school she had a little time to herself, which often meant the time to think in peace, or the time to look through a magazine once in a while, or look up a word or two in the old, heavy dictionary that she kept on the dresser. That dresser, which was built-in and belonged to the house, had by some miracle received only minimal damage from the bombing, perhaps because it was anchored to the wall, she thought. All the plates and cups on its shelves had been smashed.

The insatiable appetite for reading that she had had in her youth had become tempered by the constraints of time, and she had to be content with the occasional magazine and light reading from the lending library in the village. Now frustration nagged at her when she could not understand a word, or had forgotten how to spell something. In the general scheme of things, it was petty, she knew. They must live from day to day, from moment to moment, because one could not count on a future. Each little thing that gave pleasure was grasped, pored over. A bottle of cheap scent, a lipstick, or an unexpected poem in a newspaper were treasures to be hidden away in a safe place with the impractical hats.

That was reality after all; sooner or later one must die. The tragedy of it was that one so seldom had a life that could be called "living". The awareness of mortality was always there, just out of sight, like a haunting. They were too old to regain what they had lost, she and Jim.

Another Christmas would be upon them soon, with no end to the war in sight.

Dragging her thoughts back to the moment, she planned what she had to do in the next hour or two. After the ironing she would put on a pair of old cotton gloves and clean the pieces of silver plate and cutlery, some of it wedding presents that had not been damaged in the bombing. There was pride in keeping the beautiful embossed serving spoons clean and sparkling, and the set of "apostle" coffee spoons that harked back to a previous life, difficult to recall now. With the passage of time, that life took on more and more of a dreamlike quality, increasing her feeling of dissonance.

~ There was no respite for them, because in the middle of January, 1943, the Luftwaffe renewed its air attacks on London. Out in the garden bomb shelter they slept the sleep of the mentally and physically exhausted.

Towards the end of January, Jim Langridge read in his newspaper that the Allies had captured Tripoli, which he understood to be an important port for both sides in the fighting in North Africa, and then later on in February there was news that their own Air Force, together with the Americans', was bombing Germany day and night.

As he sat by the fire in the evenings and he rolled himself the occasional cigarette, he ruminated. There was a sense that a renewed resistance and a revenge were setting in against the Germans. The Russians had defended the heap of rubble that had become Stalingrad, fighting house to house, until what was left of the German army was forced to surrender, eventually, on February 2nd, because of starvation and intense cold, mainly, towards the end. The Germans, had lost 600,000 men, while the Russian defenders had lost 400,000. That did not, he assumed, include all the civilians who had died. Civilians had fought side by side with the army. Those who could not get away had retreated to underground cellars or holes in the ground, like moles or rats, starving.

Was that to be their fate in this country? In the vulnerable southeast where they were? He drew in smoke from his makeshift cigarette, which soothed his nerves, trying to visualize yet again what it might be like to be attacked in a civilian setting, with women and children there. They had no guns.

When you were old enough to look back on your life, you could see patterns that you had created, or had been created for you. They were patterns of what you had done with the time and the circumstances that had been given to you. Sometimes you were able to see something of what you had done to try to change those circumstances. And from those patterns you got some idea of who you were. When you are very young, a kind of inner sense informs you of who you are, an innate self-respect, as though that were your birth-right. But it is tentative, that impression, a fragile thing, open to destruction by people and events.

Events had conspired to destroy him, yet here he was, with a sense of self that was strong. How he had come by it, he could only speculate.

Sarah Burroughs lay on a camp bed, wrapped in blankets, in the bomb shelter at the hospital. Beside her she had a torch, a small framed photograph of Henry, and several of his letters which she read obsessively by the beam of the torch when she could not sleep, her head under a blanket. Things were looking up, he had told her, because the Germans were in retreat and the Americans were organizing themselves in the western end of North Africa.

On the sleeve of her uniform dress she now had three stripes. Against her neck the opal ring rested, warm from her body. From the ebullient girl she had been transformed into a thoughtful woman, mature before her time, desperate for normality, always waiting.

This was the last year of her training, the time seeming to stretch into infinity. She could not visualize the end of it.

～ As the weeks of 1943 went by, Lord Calborne duly noted that Rommel was replaced as commander of the Afrika Korps, in early March. What that meant was not clear to him then, except perhaps that Hitler was not pleased by events. On May 7th the Allies captured Tunis, then on the 13th the German army surrendered in Tunisia.

Walking around the gardens in spring sunshine, hearing the calls of birds, he felt a lightness of spirit that had hitherto departed from memory.

～ On July 9th 1943 a German aeroplane bombed the small town of East Grinstead, not far away, and May knew then that they, the local people, would do what they had to do to defend themselves. Bombs had been dropped along the High Street in broad daylight, and one on the cinema, which had killed two hundred and thirty-five people. There had been photographs in the local paper of firemen and others digging and pulling bodies out of rubble. It was as though the enemy knew that people went to the cinemas to watch the news. She had wept then, looking at those pictures.

❦ Chapter 28

Although the official age for starting school was five, Lizzie was still only four years old when she started at the Fernden village school in September, 1943, because her fifth birthday fell on October 31st and the powers that be decided that she could not wait another year. Thus, some children found themselves starting with children who were months older than themselves, which could make a big difference at that age in the maturation of the brain. May thought of these things as she entered the school at the beginning of the school year to deposit her two children.

As the school doors loomed in front of her on that first day, Lizzie sensed that the act of walking through them signalled the end of her freedom as she had known it. Even in her tender years she knew that.

May looked around her to see if there had been any changes wrought over the long holiday. There were the rows of sinks in the front hall, each sink with its chunk of red carbolic soap, then the rows of coat hooks.

The school, built of red brick, was at the far end of the village. Opposite was the playing field which was also the cricket ground, the football field, the site of the annual flower show and gymkana. A cricket pavilion, of wood, graced the playing field. The school itself consisted of two classrooms — one for infants and one for older children, some of whom were as old as fifteen, after which they were expected to leave — and a large hall where concerts and various other activities took place. Food was served here at mid-day.

Lizzie, with Jo trailing behind, was handed over by her mother to Miss Botting, an elderly lady with grey hair scraped back into a sparse bun. With her long black skirt and white blouse with long sleeves, she wore pale gray gaiters above her black shoes, which were done up with many tiny black buttons.

Lizzie, clothed in her brown Harris Tweed coat, stood sturdily by her mother and stared at this apparition who was so different from her mother, who managed to dress stylishly. At that moment May had on a navy blue felt hat with a brim pulled down to one side over her forehead, à la mode.

Miss Botting showed them a coat hook and a wooden cubby hole where Lizzie could leave her things. Outside they viewed the lavatories which were earth closets, and on the other side of the playground, the bomb shelter which had a flat roof and no doors or windows, just an angled passage for entry and exit. "As soon as we hear the air-raid siren we come out here," she informed May and the other mothers of new children.

Then the new children were to sit in the classroom for the infants and thread coloured glass beads onto lengths of string.

When the mothers left, a boy, John, began to cry loudly. Over a long time, this deteriorated to a steady grizzle. Miss Botting ignored him. In her, Lizzie observed the first intimations of indifference and cruelty, for Miss Botting was a bully in her own way, Lizzie discerned. Not a word of comfort passed her lips.

The children watched in fascination as Miss Botting undid the shiny black buttons on her gaiters by means of a special hook. Flick, flick, flick, her wrist moved as she manipulated the hook. The gaiters were removed to reveal thick black stockings.

∼ For the first week of school May accompanied Jo and Lizzie both ways, and then they were left to go home by themselves, a journey through the church yard and across fields, over a spindly bridge that spanned a stream.

The stream, babbling prettily through its steep banks for much of the year, could become a dangerous torrent in late spring when heavy rain sometimes fell day and night. Then it would overflow its banks into the fields around, washing away the yellowish clay soil so that the waters that lay over the fields were the colour of old mustard.

At these times, the children had to go a different route home, on higher ground.

"You little kiddies shouldn't be walking home by yourselves," Gladys Turk, a woman who lived near the school, said one day as she intercepted their progress. "Not with all these bombs about."

From that time on, she walked with them to within a short distance of their house — not so close that May, perhaps glancing through a window, could see her with them — in case that action might cast aspersions on May's mothering skills. Not wishing to get into a verbal altercation with May, to whom she might have given a piece of her mind, Gladys retreated when she thought it safe to do so.

From the woman's kindness, the girls — in the perspicacious and vague way of little children — came to understand something of an emotional and practical abandonment by their mother who had preoccupations of her own that had to do with both the distant and recent past. They were different from many other people, because they had had their home bombed, had barely escaped, had lost so much of a material nature that they could not afford to replace.

With this perception came the beginnings of that anxiety which besets children when they know that they are out of their depth, when their dependency comes home to them, when burdens are placed on them for which they do not have the maturity. Gladys drew them in, within the radius of her warmth and strength.

One day, in the last field on the way home, an aeroplane came down to land. "It's all right," Gladys said. "It's one of ours." They could see the circular red, white, and blue emblem of the RAF painted on the side. When the plane took off again, bumping over the uneven terrain of the field before rising, skimming a hedge, the pilot waved to them. They watched until it was out of sight.

"He's doing that for us," Gladys said.

Their Dad had told them to get down into a ditch if they saw or heard planes coming over, and thus inevitably they found themselves crouching in one, which was fortunately dry, one morning on the way to school. They were accompanied on this occasion by a neighbour, John Braithwaite. It was with amazement that Lizzie stared at John who was crying with fear, for if her Dad had told them to get down into a ditch it meant that they would be all right. Dad's well of common sense and innovation knew no end.

~ And so the days went on, with much threading of beads and drawing of pictures, until one day Miss Botting began to teach them the alphabet. "'A' is for apple, 'B' is for bat," she said, pointing to pictures. In due course they advanced to sounding out simple words. " 'C' is for cat, C-A-T," she said. " 'R' is for R-A-T.'" With each word she had a picture.

They did not like Miss Botting. A boy, Jeffrey, who did not seem able to grasp those basic rudiments of reading, was derided by her to the point where he was constantly in tears during reading. He would bunch up a soggy handkerchief in hands that trembled as he bent over his book that he could not decipher. Lizzie longed to put her arms round him as he sat next to her, but dared not make a move; indeed, did not know how to.

Sometimes Jeffrey's mother would come to the school, and at those times Lizzie was also moved to tell her how her son was being bullied by Miss Botting, in case he was too inarticulate or ashamed to tell her himself. In that she failed too, as shy as a fawn in a wood in some things, she could not bring herself to make the approach.

On the other hand, they loved Miss West, who came at least twice a week to teach them singing — doh, ray, me, fah, so, la, ti, doh! — and to thump on the piano with much enthusiasm as though she were pounding butter in a churn. The children responded to her like the proverbial flowers before the sun, for they sensed that she reciprocated their muted adoration. With bent, arthritic fingers, she would point to words of songs on the blackboard:

> *Coo, coo, we love you,*
> *Coo, coo, love us too,*
> *This is what they seem to say,*
> *Pretty pigeons, soft and grey.*

This chorus Miss West taught them in the dimness of the bomb shelter, where there was another piano.

"Cherry ripe! Cherry ripe! Ripe, I cry! Full and fair ones come and buy!" Miss West would bawl out over the tops of their heads.

With the air-raid siren sounding from the village, she would thump on the piano and lead them in: "All things bright and beautiful/ all creatures great and small."

The significance of one of the verses was not lost on them: "The rich man in his castle/ the poor man at his gate/ He made them high and lowly/ and ordered their estate." For they were, without exception, of the lowly.

It was not that they accepted the ascribed niche. From somewhere, mysterious and unidentifiable within them, the seeds of rebellion were sown on fertile ground, biding their time until nurturing showers would cause them to sprout.

Yet the implication that their inferiority was God-ordained was made manifest in many overt and subtle ways. Taken in with one's mother's milk, as it were, it wore one down, day in and day out. How could one hold out against it, except at great cost. To be ever watchful against it exacted a price.

There was no bad intent in Miss West. Someone else had written the hymn. She could be severe when necessary, and they understood it was for their own good. They were in the classroom when she introduced a new song: "And a two-ran-nan-nanty-nah!" she sang. "And a two-ran-and two-ran and two-ran-and two-ran nan-nanty-nah!"

What a silly song. Lizzie's spirit, still not cowed by circumstance, rose up and left the room, searching out open spaces, soaring over the school buildings and playground, passing down the lane next to the school, down to the village allotments where the men grew vegetables, over the stream. It went on over the green meadows and up to the beech woods where, in her imagination, she alighted and put her feet on the bronze-brown leaves that covered the soil under the trees. Here rabbits hid under bushes, birds flitted and called. In spring the leaves of the beech were the most tender green.

The air-raid siren forced her to leave the woods in a hurry, to be back in the classroom, where she seemed to be frozen, as it were, in her seat.

They heard the sound of planes almost immediately; no time to run across the playground to the shelter. "Under the desks, children! Hurry up!" Miss West stood at the front of the classroom, the blackboard on its easel to one side of her with words on it for "Two-ran-nan-nanty-nah," and her desk to the other side.

The children's desks were made of sturdy oak and cast iron, just big enough to shelter a child sitting on the floor with knees drawn up, arms around knees, head down sideways facing front.

The planes were suddenly overhead, low, shaking the building. Lizzie crouched down, keeping her eyes on Miss West for the next cue.

"John Braithwaite!" Miss West shouted against the noise, pointing a finger. "Get under your desk! And stop that grizzling at once. It serves no useful purpose at this moment. Now, children, keep your wits about you and your eyes on me."

When all children were under shelter, Miss West crawled into the narrow space under her own desk, beside the waste paper basket, facing the classroom, where the children could see her face and her sparse grey hair standing out from her head. They kept their eyes fixed on her, as a devout suppliant might regard a portrait of Jesus Christ, for if anyone could save them it would be Miss West who had never, so far, been at a loss.

Womp! Womp! Glass tinkled into the classroom from a window that had been inadequately taped.

"Bastards," Miss West said. "They've got the playing field ... and the cricket pavilion, I shouldn't wonder." Her usually ruddy face had gone pale and blotchy.

When the bombers had passed and the all-clear had sounded, Miss Botting came rushing in from the other classroom. "We've got broken windows," she said, her words tripping over one another. "They were clearly trying to target us. They can see it's a school. Oh, the wickedness of it. Thank you, O Lord, for this deliverance, for your mercy ..."

Miss West crawled out from under her desk. "Stay where you are, children, until we decide what to do next." He turned to Miss Botting: "Oh, do shut up, Elspeth. There will be time for prayer later. Have you left your brood unattended? The best thing we can do is to get all the children out to the shelter while we clear up the glass and see about mending the windows."

Mrs. Hooper, the headmistress, came in from her small house that was attached to the school building. "A good idea," she said calmly. "That was a close shave."

So many things were happening, Lizzie thought, clutching her knees in the cramped space under her desk, listening to the dying sound of the all-clear siren, the crying of John and a few others. She was frightened, but not enough to cry. She focused on a scab on her knee, from where she had fallen over while running the week before — and on her sense of surprise at the realization that Miss Botting had another name.

There was no point in questioning why this was happening, she knew instinctively; it just was. As far back as she could remember, there had been planes in the sky, dropping bombs; people had slept in cupboards and under tables, in garden shelters; grown ups were frightened and cried easily; there was not always enough food. Hunger was a feeling in the stomach that was a familiar accompaniment to life. Clothes were often bought at jumble sales, which were fun.

Over all was a pervasive anxiety, from which the sweetness of youth escaped now and again, bearing her away. That sweetness came in the shape of a baby bird, a new primrose, the discovery of a clump of celandines under a hedge, with their tiny yellow flowers like stars, the sound of a cuckoo in late spring and early summer, the first sweet violets, books. It came with Jim Card, the road-man, who gave them sweets from a crumpled brown paper bag when they walked home, with the words: "Take the poke and all." They understood his language; they knew the phrase of a pig in a poke. They knew he lived in a wooden shed at the bottom of someone else's garden, because he was poor and had no wife to care for him. Lizzie admired the economy of his life, as he rode about on a bicycle, and the generosity of the truly poor.

Mixed in with the incomprehensible was the sensible. There were people to approach and people to avoid; there were those who were innately good, who would remain good, she sensed, whatever the circumstances, while there were others who would never be good.

∼ Over the next days they were allowed to go into the playing field on the other side of the road from the school, with adults, to look at the two bomb craters there. The windows and doors of the cricket pavilion had blown in, while the wooden building itself had remained standing. What did it mean, this destruction? There was no answer.

One evening, two men came to their house with a box of gas masks, made of black rubber for her mother, father, and Jo, while she had a very small one made of red rubber. The men showed them how to put on the gas masks, which fitted very tightly around the face and back of the head, with unbreakable glass eye pieces. There was a big, heavy snout on the mask, made of metal, with a filter inside. With her face inside the mask, Lizzie felt that she could hardly breathe. What it all meant she could not understand. Looking at her parents, who accepted the masks readily, she sensed that understanding did not matter at that moment.

~ And so the days and weeks went by, so that Lizzie came to recognize the words for "cat" and "rat" without having to look at the pictures. "The cat sat on the mat" came next; then: "The cat sat on the mat after eating the rat." Even so, that was not the end of the rat.

One day, Mrs. Hooper, who was keen on drama, English literature and poetry — with a beautiful speaking voice, without being too la-de-dah, read to them from a book called *Old Possum's Book of Practical Cats*, that she said was by T.S. Eliot. Here, Lizzie thought, was something more interesting about cats, other than about the one who simply sat about on the mat and then ate the rat that they had clearly not finished with.

"McCavity's a mystery cat, he's called the hidden paw," Mrs. Hooper read.

A light went on in Lizzie's mind, as it were, creating a spotlight of rapt attention so that all else in her environment was in darkness around her.

"McCavity, McCavity, there's no one like McCavity." One day, when I grow up, Lizzie thought, I am going to write poems and books.

As the weeks went by, other stories and poems were enunciated enticingly by Mrs. Hooper. Most of all, Lizzie liked the poet Anon, who had written a lot in the books they used. It was peculiar that Mrs. Hooper never spoke to them about Anon, although she talked a lot about Walter de la Mare.

As this was all going on, they hurried out many times to the bomb shelter like the proverbial rats leaving the sinking ship. The shrieking siren came to instil in Lizzie the first intimations of dread.

Before they were allowed to go home each day, they had to recite the Lord's Prayer, then lift up their chairs to the desk tops, so that the cleaner could more easily wash the floor. The crashing of the chairs signalled the coming freedom.

There were dramas and pageants, plays and concerts put on at the school. They sang *Waltzing Matilda*, not their own anthem, Lizzie understood. What fun to sing about a jolly swagman.

Over all, questions loomed that remained unanswered.

~ The children collected waste paper for the "war effort." Two of them went together, from house to house, carrying a large sack between them. "Got any waste paper?" they piped up whenever someone opened a door to them. The paper, combined with the smell of sack, emitted a scent when it was sorted later that they knew they would never forget.

~ Her parents, who did not themselves darken the door of any church at that time, sent her and Jo to Sunday school where they had to learn certain verses from the Bible by heart and repeat them word-perfect the following week. "For all have sinned and come short of the glory of God," they recited dutifully, feeling guilty for something mysterious and unaccountable. Or: "Behold I stand, I stand at the door and knock." And you were a terrible one, a miserable sinner, if you could not find it in you to open the door of your heart to the Son of God. Perhaps her parents were simply allowing her and Jo to make up their own minds about God,

~ In the fullness of time, a day came that was called V.E. Day. Grown-ups cried in the streets and hugged each other; people waved from buses that crawled through the High Street of the village where there was a party. Tables were set up on the road. There was pink and white blanc-mange to eat, with red jelly, jam tarts, and cake. "Jelly on the plate, jelly on the plate, wibble wobble, wibble wobble, jelly on the plate!" a fat woman sang out as she brought round plates of jelly to the children seated at the trestle tables in the street.

There was music, a maypole, dancing. Men got drunk. The two pubs, the Crown and the Black Swan, served free beer. Musicians cried and laughed as they played their trumpets and piano-accordions for the maypole dancing. People stood about with handkerchiefs clutched to their faces.

Gypsies came into the village in their horse-drawn wagons, parking them where they could, joining in with the singing and clapping.

"The war's over," Lizzie's Dad said to her, swinging her up in the air.

Gladys Turk said it, too, over and over again.

The church bells of the Anglican Church rang out, having been silenced for a time, only to be used in the event of warning about an invasion. Now, unfettered, the bell-ringers pulled on the ropes of the ancient bells until they were exhausted and others took over. Through the open doors of the Presbyterian chapel, which had no bells, the reedy voices of parishioners could be heard out in the street: "Now thank we all our God, with heart and hands and voices." All the sounds combined together as though they would drown out the buzz of mourning that assailed those who had known terrible loss. No one was untouched.

The bomb craters in the playing field had been filled in.

~ Not long after, there was a wedding at the church to which all were invited. May stood outside with the children as the bells rang out over the village, the nearby fields and woods when the ceremony was over, as Sarah Burroughs, beautiful as all brides, on the arm of her husband Captain Henry Calborne, came out of the church into the sunshine. How handsome and how happy he looked. It was common knowledge that they had married before in a registry office and had wished to wait until the war was over before this celebration. Sarah, the daughter of the Reverend Burroughs, was a trained nurse now, had done war work and was already the mother of a child, a daughter. She was one of them now, as was he.

They threw confetti, May and the children, as the bride and groom walked slowly along the path from the church to the gates into the High

Street where the villagers were waiting. They broke into applause, and some were unabashedly crying for the happiness of these two people whom everyone knew. Their story was a living vindication for the suffering that they had all endured. They had come through.

~ After the war there was an examination at the school called the "eleven plus," which children were supposed to take when they were over eleven years of age, and which would give them a shot at going to a grammar school in a large town about twelve miles away. This school was an alternative to the common-or-garden variety Secondary Modern School, closer to home, that was a recent innovation and designed for all comers from the village schools as well as the town schools.

Lizzie was ten when she sat this examination — she did not pass — and was still ten when she started at the Secondary Modern in September of 1948. Some of her new teachers remarked on her age, but did not actually take any action, because necks that were stuck out very often were chopped off. So entrenched was the old order that even the innovative tendrils of the Labour Party could not reach far enough into the depths of the conservative countryside to make changes that could bring relief and a certain hope to the poor.

Two English teachers, both men, saved her. They admired what she wrote and how she wrote it, encouraged her. There was Mr. Wright, who lived an unconventional life in a caravan with his wife and baby son, and who encouraged each member of his English class to keep a diary, which he read from time to time. "Elizabeth's diary is particularly good," he wrote in one school report to May and Jim. She wrote about her walks with their dog, of watching men in the haying season building hay-stacks, then the skilled craftsmen putting thatched roofs on them made from straw, to keep out the rain. She wrote of the flowers and birds she saw along country footpaths, in woods and meadows, of the foxes, rabbits and stoats.

The other man, Mr. Pool of the fiery red hair and the loping gait, for whom she harboured a secret passion, encouraged her to read Shakespeare, while the other children were doing something more mundane. But he did not have time to teach her how to write a critique. All in all, she blossomed under his appreciation. The plays of Shakespeare, she thought, were too full of circumlocution to be enjoyable, although she liked the poetry therein. As she walked in summer through fields of buttercups and tall grasses, his words came to her ... *fear no more the heat o' the sun, nor the furious winter's rages; thou thy worldly task hast done* ...

As she paddled in the shallows of streams, these words assailed her ... *golden lads and girls all must, as chimney sweepers, come to dust.*

They confirmed in her a tentative knowledge that she had a skill, that she felt herself to be more than a girl who was destined for a dead-end job. It was a power that came to her in odd moments when she thought herself to be powerless.

∾ Chapter 29

"Well, Jim, what have you decided about giving up work? Have you come to any conclusions since we were talking last week? You said you're coming up to sixty-five next April when your old-age pension starts. I'll be sorry to lose you, and no mistake."

Bill Green, head gardener, walked across the floor of the potting shed where Jim was squatting in front of the stove to get it going, carefully lighting parts of the newspaper that was scrunched up under the kindling. He placed several small lumps of coal on top of the wood, then stood up. The shed was cold, with frost sparkling on the single small window that looked out over the market garden. As the flames caught the wood, both men stretched out their hands towards the warmth. It was early in the morning, with only the two of them there to service the coal furnaces in the greenhouses to keep the grape vines alive along with the other vulnerable trees and plants of an exotic nature. By the time the other gardeners arrived for work, the cast-iron stove in the shed would be giving out heat and they would warm themselves, make tea and drink it, before going out again to harvest the last of the Brussels sprouts and anything else that still survived outside, to take it up in baskets to the kitchens of the big house. The surplus would be stored in the windowless cold shed that was attached to the potting shed by a narrow passage.

"To tell you the truth, Bill, I can't go on much longer with the heavy work. I'm sure you know that; you've seen how I am."

Jim pushed his cloth cap further back on his head and loosened the wool scarf that he had around his neck. He and Bill had talked several

287

times about his increasing breathlessness, his gradually failing heart, the first signs of "dropsy". He thanked God every day that Bill was a good man, not likely to recommend that he be sacked if he could not keep up his fair share of the heavy work. "If it's all the same with you, I'd rather not go until I get the pension. We would starve." It was unnecessary to tell Bill that, he knew, but he wanted to articulate it anyway, to make sure that there could be no misunderstanding over the coming months.

"I have a very small disability pension from the Army, a token gesture," he added. The words hung between them in the cold shed, where their breath came out in little puffs before dissipating. His was a common problem for all those who lived in tied cottages on the estate, on any estate, where one's home went with the job.

"You go at your own pace, Jim. I'll give you the light work, in the greenhouses, as much as I can, and I'll give you the boy, too, to give a hand. He asked me the other day if he could spend more time with you."

"He did!'"

"Yeah. He said he was learning more from you than from anyone else, including me." Bill laughed. "You have more patience and understanding, so he said."

"That's all right with me, any time."

The boy, Terence, their apprentice, fifteen years old, had attached himself to Jim. Now he was grateful for the boy's youth and strength. "He could help me with the seeding when the time comes, and with the pricking out of the seedlings."

"Done! He can be the one to get down on his hands and knees."

Jim added larger pieces of wood and more coal to the stove, watching the flames. With the poker he lifted off the circular hot-plate from the top of the stove and placed the old, sooty kettle in the aperture, directly on the flames. This week it was his turn to service the greenhouse furnaces early in the morning, to get their own shed stove going in what was their sanctuary in the cold months. He would make tea in the brown enamelled tea pot, put out the mugs. Bill Green brought milk from the home farm.

"I'm worried about having to get out of the cottage, not having anywhere to live," he said.

"Yes, I can understand that," Bill said. "If you like, I'll sound out his Lordship about you staying on there. He must have thought about it; he's always up-to-date with what's going on with all of us, and he's a generous old bugger, we can't complain about him."

"I'd be much obliged, Bill. Lizzie's still at school, she's only fourteen. Jo's already working."

"Have you got your name down for the Trust houses? That's the best bet."

"I have, yes, but I don't suppose I'm near the top of the list." He thought of the maiden lady, Maude Histcott, who had inherited a lot of money in the late 1800s and had used some of it to build a row of very good, substantial houses near the far side of Fernden common, in trust for the elderly poor. During the remainder of her long life, Miss Histcott had given away most of her fortune to benefit the poor of the village and its surroundings. But for individuals like her, he considered, more of the poor would be housed in those ancient cottages which had been condemned as unfit for human habitation, those places like Badgers Gate, beautiful in their way, in rural places, dating back four hundred years or so, with no running water or modern sanitation or electricity. In such a place might Shakespeare have dwelt. In recent times, some people could be housed by the council. In the past, it had been the workhouse, or the poor house. The possibility of it hung over them like a cloud of shame.

"Get old Dr. Ramsay to put in a word for you with the Vicar, who's the main trustee of those houses, since your health is failing, Jim, and you have a legitimate reason for needing one of those houses. Make the old doctor good for something, as I understand he's not very good at his job these days ... too out of date, so I've heard."

"That's a good suggestion, I'll ask him." Jim poured boiling water onto the tea leaves in the pot. "I haven't got the guts to tell the old man I want to change to another doctor. It's misplaced loyalty, I know."

"You're right there, Jim, it could be a matter of life or death. It's time the old bloke hung up his coat anyway, although we can't talk. He must be getting on for eighty. It's not really to do with age ... a lot of people get better with age ... he never was much good, by all accounts.

A woman I know, who shall be nameless, was expecting a baby late in life and he told her she had wind. She found another doctor forthwith."

Jim grinned. "I can believe it," he said.

The boy, Terence, came hurtling through the door then, bringing with him a blast of icy air. A thin, pale boy, he looked consumptive, Jim had thought when he first set eyes on him.

"Shut that bloody door quick, Terry, my lad," Bill said. "There's a mug of tea for you, and take a chunk of that cake there that the missus made for us."

"Thank you, Mr. Green. Good morning, Mr. Langridge," Terry said, taking off the inadequate cap that did not cover his ears. The ritual was the same every morning.

"Morning, Terry," Jim said. "You get that tea inside you, then I'll take you around the greenhouses where it's warm." It often occurred to him that Terry probably did not get much of a breakfast at home, if anything.

"How are you, Mr. Langridge?" Terry asked quietly when they were standing side by side, as close as possible to the stove, sipping tea.

"Not as good as I could or should be," he said. "Keep that to yourself, as I don't want it generally spread around, although perhaps it's common knowledge here."

"I don't think so," the boy said.

"Do you want to be a gardener, Terry? Or is this just a stop-gap job for you?"

"I want to be a gardener ... a professional gardener. Perhaps I could go up to London and work at Kew Gardens one day. That's what I would like."

"Then you shall, my lad. You pay close attention to me and I'll do my best to teach you all that I know ... if I've got the time left. Even if I'm not employed here, I can come back."

"Thank you."

Later, when they were in one of the big greenhouses that held the grape vines, Jim hung on to a railing to catch his breath. "I've got congestive cardiac failure, Terry," he said, "the result of having had rheumatic fever when I was in the army in 1915. It damages the heart valves. It's progressive, it's going to be the end of me, I expect. Now, you go down to the cellar, check the furnace and the thermometer there, as you've seen me do, then check all the other thermometers around the place up here. We need to keep this place as close to the optimum temperature as possible."

"Yes, Mr. Langridge."

When the boy was out of sight, Jim took several deep breaths, feeling that he could not get enough air into his lungs after the slight exertion of mounting the few steps into the greenhouse. The cold made it worse. No doubt his lips were blue, his face an unnatural pale. His heart was thumping unevenly. It was a sobering realization when you knew that your active life was coming to an end, when your fireside chair was something to look forward to.

"Don't forget the old saying," he said to the boy when he came back up, "that a little knowledge is dangerous and that ignorance can indeed be bliss, until the truth comes out. Always go the extra mile in checking something to make sure it's accurate. That's lesson number one. You know the carpenter's rule ... 'measure twice, cut once'."

"I'll remember. You must have been in the Great War, then, Mr. Langridge?" The boy was generally quiet and shy, Jim had noted in the few weeks that Terry had been there, but sometimes found the courage to come out with questions of a more personal nature to satisfy his curiosity. He never over-stepped a certain polite boundary.

"I was ... so called. That was a case of ignorance. That war must seem like a very long time ago to you, here in 1952."

"No," the boy said, surprisingly, with a certain emphatic passion. "My mother's father was killed in that war, she never saw him. We have photographs. She talks about him all the time, as though she knows everything about him, as though he just went through the door ... so I feel I know him. I think she's woven a whole life for him in her mind, and what she didn't know, she made up, as though he had a real life."

To his consternation, Jim felt a spurt of tears. "Well ... there must have been a big hole in her life," he managed to get out.

"That's it ... and she's been trying to fill it."

"I hope you manage to get through your life, Terry, without being in another war," he said, feeling inadequate.

"I've been through one. I'll never forget it. I know what to do ... and what not to do."

Out of the mouths of babes and sucklings hast thou ordained strength. "Well, my lad, I won't be doing all the teaching where you are concerned, I can see that."

They walked along frosty paths to that part of the spacious vegetable garden that contained the Brussels sprouts, where they could see that the few remaining leaves that clung to the tall stalks had been turned dark red by cold.

"Beautiful, isn't it?" Jim said to the boy. "It never ceases to amaze me. At times like this I wish I could draw and paint."

"I sometimes paint ... water colours."

"There you are, then, a subject for you."

"I can do it from memory."

With gloves on, they pulled the cold sprouts off the stalks, as yet undamaged by frost, and put them into baskets, moving quickly. It was not difficult work, walking along rows of stalks, bending a little, or squatting. The tangy, crisp air reddened their faces. Before long, two of the other gardeners came to help them. "What'cher!" they called out. The bare stalks were like blasted trees in a battlefield, imagery that would never leave him.

It was four o'clock when they were back in their potting shed, drinking a last mug of tea, the only two left of the gardeners. Jim banked up the stove to sustain some warmth there for part of the night, while Terry brought in more wood from a stack outside.

"How's your father, Terry?"

"Oh ... he doesn't change much. He's all right."

The father, Jim knew, had shell-shock from the recent war that prevented him from working in any capacity, a man fearful and damaged, who could only sleep when he was under a shelter of some sort. The boy's mother took care of him, day and night.

"Take some vegetables home for your mother, Terry ... fill a small sack. If anyone questions you, say I said so. Then get on home before it gets much darker."

When he was the only one remaining, he adjusted the damper on the stove so that it would burn slowly, barely alight. Then he lit his paraffin lantern, put on his outdoor clothing, locked the shed door and left the big iron key on a ledge under the eaves.

At the gate to the gardens he paused to gain his breath, standing in the yellow circle of light from the lantern, his surroundings partially hidden in darkness. All in all, his life had not been too bad, lived as it had been in an era of war and exceptional human folly that had not been of his making in any way. It was a time of which he could not pretend to make sense, he reflected, his interaction with the boy making him think of his young self at the same age, eager to work hard and to please.

He had worked with teams of horses, helping to train them to the plough and to the wagon. How he had loved those gentle creatures who responded to his kindness with loyalty and willingness to obey his commands. More than many men could say, he had known the love of two good women other than his mother and his sisters. *Consider a good woman; her price is above rubies* ... He remembered that line from his early readings of the bible, an exercise foisted upon him by church and school, by those who concerned themselves with the morals of the poor. In his experience, they did not adequately look to their own morals or to the morals of those above them on the social scale. Perhaps they were assumed capable of policing their own. Now he enjoyed those sayings when they manifested themselves unheralded in his mind at odd moments.

All he could feel sure of now was that there were good people in the world, and there were bad, as he had concluded long ago, with many in between. The word "evil" was gradually going out of modern parlance, he had observed, as though it frightened people, and if they did not use it, the actions that came from it could be attributed to something else. It was an uncompromising word. To be sure, some church ministers still pounded on the pulpit and bellowed over the heads of the congregations about it, but not in such a way that one could identify with evil in what, and who, they saw around them. Yet evil was something that one could recognize when one saw it, sometimes instantaneously.

All one could do was align oneself with the good. True goodness was without subterfuge. Perhaps that was God, that collective goodness, which sometimes came together as a whole when needed, a coalescing of many small lights in darkness to make a brilliance. Without conceit, he felt that he had succeeded in that, to some degree, as one makes a pact with oneself and does not break it. At the very least, he had tried. He was shifting now, thinking of himself in the past tense, yet frightened to project himself forward mentally. *Old soldiers never die ... they just fade away* — another line came to him unbidden, dredged up from his memory.

He moved onto the dark path that would take him through the small wood, then on to home, the lantern lighting up the discarded yellow and brown leaves from the beech and the horse-chestnut that crackled with frost as he stepped on them.

Once home, he would sit by the fire in his favourite chair where the newspaper was waiting for him, and where he would ease off his boots from swollen feet and ankles. Then May or Lizzie would bring him a bowl of warm water for his feet, as Mary Magdalene had brought water for Jesus, so the Word said. He would lean back and close his eyes, feeling the blessed warmth from the fire and the water creep into his frozen body.

Soon, he and his family would eat together, the rabbit pie or the beef and vegetable stew that May would have made. Bought meat was in short supply, for once a week, that small piece of beef or mutton that the village butcher delivered to the house. The scent of her cooking emanated from the cast-iron cooking range near where he sat. Sitting there in the orange firelight, they would be grateful for the food before them and the fuel for the warmth that they enjoyed. There he would think of Terence again, giving the vegetables to his mother: "Mr. Langridge let me have these; I didn't steal them."

"You be sure to thank him again tomorrow, from me," his mother would say, while his father would handle the potatoes, carrots, onions, as though they were artefacts from long ago, from a world where he had once walked and dug in the soil, being a countryman, a world of action and coherent thought which had receded far away from him.

As he walked he thought of the man who owned the land on which he moved. You could never really own land, because it was eternal and man was mortal. You could not possess it, as you desired to possess it, to somehow incorporate it into yourself; you could only borrow it for a span. Men moved over the face of the earth, both rich and poor, trying to make their mark on the implacable soil.

"Can I dry your feet for you, Dad?" Lizzie would say.

"Not with your hair," he would reply, to which she would smile, understanding. She would not comment on the swelling, the mottled skin, bending her head lest he see the fear in her eyes.

Often it was difficult to believe that he had helped to create this girl, so like himself, yet so much herself, a mystery. It takes a lifetime to know oneself, even partially. How then can one ever know another? One went by instinct, for the most part, by observation over time and by putting two and two together. *By their fruit shall ye know them* ... She would kneel on the rug by the fire and take his feet gently into her hands, onto the soft towel. Where there is love, one does not have to know, because love it at once part of the mystery and the answer.

∼ He could smell the smoke from the chimney before he could see the light at the front window, or the garden gate. Almost there. Still he tried to walk like a soldier, albeit pausing more often than he cared to notice, to slow the fast beating of his heart, to draw breath, no longer swinging his arms joyfully, no longer counting left, right, left, right, left, left ... left, right, left ...

Tomorrow he would take Terence to the greenhouse where they grew the potted plants that were for the market, for Christmas and beyond, that would be taken to towns large and small, would be taken by train up to London. He would name names for the boy: the beautiful gloxinia, the Jerusalem Cherry, the forced azaleas, the sprouting narcissus bulbs in flattish pots, the hyacinths, and all those other things that would not appear naturally in gardens for months, if at all in the English climate. The boy would commit some things to memory, would jot down a few notes, avid for knowledge while he would dream of working in Kew Gardens.

He closed his garden gate behind him, stood for a few minutes on the brick path, encompassed by a sense of sanctuary.

"What's your name?" The ambulance man, who appeared elderly to her, turned to Lizzie as she stood at the back of the ambulance just after he and his colleague, who looked just as old, loaded her father into the vehicle, having carried him from the house.

"Lizzie."

"All right, Lizzie. So you're coming to the hospital with us, not your mother?"

"Yes. She's not feeling well." Lizzie felt her face flush a little at the lie. Her mother's hands had trembled as she helped her father into his overcoat for the journey.

"Can you go to the hospital with him?" May had asked. "I can't stand the thought of it."

She had nodded, saying nothing, then had put on her own coat.

"You'll sit in the back with me and your dad," the young-old man said, he with the tired face under a peaked uniform cap. "Hop up the stairs, Lizzie, and take a seat by the driver's cab."

The double doors of the ambulance made a clunking sound as they were closed and locked, trapping them inside, it seemed to her, so that a sense of panic rose up in her like a physical sensation in her chest.

"I'm going to give you a bit of oxygen, Mr. Langridge," the man said, his voice calm, "which will entail having a rubber mask over your nose and mouth. Just breathe normally; don't be afraid of it. The oxygen will help you."

"All right, dear?" He turned to Lizzie after he had placed the mask over her dad's pale face and turned a knob on a cylinder at the head of the bed on which her father lay.

Nodding, she whispered: "Yes." Another lie.

First, the doctor had come to the house, old Dr. Ramsay, after her father had turned pale and bluish about the face that Saturday morning and she had run to the public telephone box on the main road to summon him. After giving her father an injection of something, he had turned to her and her mother and announced: "He must go to a hospital. He is in no immediate danger. I will return to the surgery and telephone from there. That will give you enough time in which to be ready."

Once the doctor had gone, she had ridden to the village on her ancient bicycle, going at break-neck speed, taking short cuts along footpaths and tracks over fields, to buy her father a pair of pyjamas from Miss Styles' drapery shop, because he did not have a pair suitable for a hospital stay. The ones she bought were striped, made of flannelette. She rode back as quickly as she had come, bumping over field and lane. "Don't die, Dad, don't die," she whispered as she leaned forward over the handlebars, the pyjamas in a paper carrier bag.

Now in the ambulance she sat clutching the bag, to which her father's shaving things and minimal toilet articles had been hastily added. The flannelette gave off that rare scent of newness, signifying a beginning of something, an interlude, and perhaps an ending. Her mind shied away from that. The motion of the wheels over the bumpy lane, together with anxiety, made her feel faint and sick. In moments they would be on the smooth main road. From where she sat behind the driver's cab she could see her father's forehead and the black rubber mask, as he lay with his feet towards the ambulance door.

Men of her father's generation, she knew, equated the journey to a hospital as the final journey for the living, a place of last resort. Most strove to die at home in their own beds. "Don't die, Dad." Her mind continued the litany, a prayer lifted up to a silent deity who did not reveal himself just then. Her father lay just as silently, his eyes closed. A faint hissing sound came from the oxygen tank. She wished she could hold his hand, but the ambulance man had taken possession of the one nearest her, by keeping his fingers on the pulse at the wrist.

It seemed very strange to her that the larger world continued on in all its drama and equal triviality at the same time that her own world as she had known it was approaching an end. For the first time she felt more fully the impersonal and arbitrary nature of the circumstances of human life, trapped as they were in the span of their mortality, like the birds, the foxes, and all the other creatures around them who shared their days. This was manifest in the pain that she felt in her chest, in the constriction of her throat, in her helplessness.

"How old are you, Lizzie?" the man asked, very quietly.

"Fourteen."

The man shook his head. "Like the bad old days of child labour," he said. "Leaving school at fourteen, growing up over the space of a single weekend, leaving on the Friday, starting work on the Monday."

Although his words did not apply directly to her, she knew exactly what he meant.

"We're taking him to a very good hospital," he said. "He'll get the best of care. You stand up for yourself, my girl ... and your father, if need be. Don't let them brow-beat you. Take your time while he's being admitted, then when you're ready we'll take you back home. We have to go that way anyhow."

~ At the hospital he was put in a room by himself, an admission room, and he would be moved to a big open ward later. A woman who looked plain and sloppy, not in uniform, with messy hair, as though she might be a floor cleaner but obviously was not, asked Lizzie a few basic questions about her father, writing down the answers. "And his religion?" she asked. Then when Lizzie took a few seconds to consider her reply, the woman opened her mouth as though she would suggest the answer. Lizzie responded quickly: "Church of England, I think." The woman smiled and acknowledged by a look that she thought Lizzie not, after all, a country bumpkin.

The ambulance men were ready to leave, so Lizzie went to the door of her father's room. "Goodbye, Dad," she whispered from the doorway. How could anyone else who did not know her or her father understand the depth of her sorrow? Such a private thing, the depth of great love. She held it to her closely, so that the sloppy woman with her sharp, impersonal eyes would not see her innermost being.

Her father gestured for her to come close, he sitting up in the bed looking small, thin and wiry, wearing his new striped pyjamas. Those garments formed an added bond between them just then, for they reminded her of her dash to the village on the rusty bicycle.

At the bedside she put her face down to his so that he could kiss her on the cheek. "Goodbye, Dad," she whispered again.

From the door she glanced back quickly, to see that his lips quivered as he looked at her disappearing through the door. Like hers, his love a private thing. *Don't die, Dad, don't die.*

The ambulance took her home, she sitting silently as the green countryside went by the windows, her heart with him who lay there in an alien bed, with fear in him.

Before going into the house she walked around the side of it, and stood by the lilac bush that grew next to the chimney. There she cried, alone.

There were intimations of spring when he sat in his own garden, breathing in the scents of moist soil, old rotting leaves, and of sunlight on tentatively growing things. The quality of light had changed from winter to an opalescent softness that promised warmth.

Having expected to die, here he was. Sometimes he felt disembodied, looking out at this familiar world as though from far away. He had come back home after three weeks, looking and feeling fitter and stronger. There at the hospital the young doctors, who had let go of an old fatalism, gave him digitalis and other drugs. They understood the damaged heart, what could be done for it with modern medicine. Far from leaving him in a corner to die, they had laboured over him day and night. That much he understood as he surveyed his own humble domain on his return; they had given him a little more time than he might otherwise have been able to expect. It would not last long, he sensed, this reprieve. If it lasted long enough for him to see his children out of childhood, into that premature adulthood that was the lot of the working class to which they belonged, he would have a measure of contentment.

Like an ox plodding under a yoke, inscrutable, enduring, he had maintained his role, had kept his pact to support and succour.

Since returning, he had gone back to work on the estate, had shown the boy how to plant seeds in flat boxes in greenhouses, how to keep them watered and to place them where they would get warmth and natural light. Soon they would plant seedlings out in the newly tilled vegetable gardens, in neat rows where they would be nurtured. He would teach Terence about the life cycle of a plant, when to harvest, how to collect seeds, how to preserve, how to fertilize the soil with dung and other compost.

"You are my eyes and ears, my strength, Terry," he would say at work. "I'm very lucky to have you." And he would transfer that edict to Lizzie at home.

More lines from his childhood learning came back to him as he directed Terence in the bending and planting work, pointing and explaining. "*But at my back I always hear Time's winged chariot hurrying near, and yonder all before us lie deserts of vast eternity*," he said out loud. At which Terence straightened up and remarked: "I live by that, Mr. Langridge."

Now in the quiet of his own garden his thoughts seemed to thunder in his brain, forcing themselves upon his consciousness. You went to the next stage in your life not necessarily by choice but by default. He was conscious of being at a time in his life when he did not believe much of what other people said to him. He often believed the opposite of what they said, divining their true meaning from the inversion of their words.

Bill Green and the boy were straight-forward. There was no flattery or subterfuge in Terence, who would listen to what he had to say, would then ask pertinent questions. Sometimes Terence would pull a battered and soiled notebook from his pocket and write in it with a pencil. "I'm immortalizing you in words, Mr. Langridge," he said once.

"Jolly good. I don't suppose anyone else will."

Lizzie came out to the garden. "We've made some tea, Dad. Do you want it out here?"

"I'll come in."

"Where did you go for your walk?" She sat down near him on a bench.

"Oh, I just went along to the church."

"You went into the church?"

"No. I just went to the bone yard to see where I'm going to doss."

"Oh, Dad!"

There had always been something about him that had intrigued her, difficult to explain; a strong sense of self, an awareness, a sense of "I-ness", seeing himself moving through time, she assumed, as though he were moving through his landscape like an actor against the backdrop of his stage, totally present there, completely alive.

"One of the Trust houses is empty, Dad," Lizzie said, coming into the sitting room of their cottage, where he sat by the fire in his usual place. "I went for a walk by there today, and I took the liberty of sneaking through a hole in the hedge to look at the gardens at the back. There's lots of land, some of it very overgrown."

"Did you now! I'll have to remind old Dr. Ramsay. He did put in a word for us. I'll be sorry to leave my garden. I suppose really it's his Lordship's garden."

"We'll make a new one."

So it was that they moved shortly afterwards, to a house in the middle of a row of six, with a green expanse of common at the front and the open countryside beyond the boundaries of the back gardens. It had electricity but no bathroom. There was a cold tap in the kitchen, no hot water tank. The lavatory was in the substantial brick shed across the yard from the back door. Nonetheless, the houses were solidly built, as though they would withstand hurricane and tempest for hundreds of years.

Jim surveyed the tangled blackberry brambles, the self-seeded saplings, the clumps of stinging nettles, and the elderberry shrubs that inhabited the former back gardens that no one had had the strength to wrest back from nature. It was time to consolidate the work and home assets of Terence and Lizzie — his eyes, ears, and strength — to shape a new garden. Somehow he would find a way to pass a few shillings to Terence for some hours of work on Sundays. They would hack brambles, saw down saplings, pull up weeds. When it was all dried out they would have a celebratory bonfire. They would stand and watch the white smoke billow out over the fields.

In this Trust house they would be safe, so long as they could come up with the token rent. The spirit of Miss Maude Histcott watched over them benignly, it seemed to him, the terms of her will and trust worded in such a way that no one could divest her legacy of the purpose for which it was intended. The yoke of the ox had been taken off, almost too late, but not quite, and this ox had wandered out into the field of freedom, although he did not own the field to pass to his children.

The great leveller of death would come to both landlord and tenant, and the land-owner would lie buried in the bone yard across the way next to the humble man who had been his beast of burden. For a man will be buried where he falls for the most part, and the stone mason would pay homage to them both in his carving, according to the directives of those left behind to mourn, the difference being that the labourer might lie in a unmarked grave, to all outward appearances as though he had never been.

∽ Chapter 30

On a particular day Lizzie came home from school and saw that her father's chair, the big wicker arm chair by the fire, was empty. "Where's Dad?" she asked May, hearing the high-pitched tone of anxiety in her own voice.

"He's lying down."

That was something new. Quickly she went up the stairs to look in his bedroom. "Anything you want, Dad?"

"Not just now."

Downstairs, she put her arms around their dog, a sweet mongrel that looked like an old English sheep dog. "I'm taking the dog for a walk," she called out to her mother.

When sadness descended, she went out with the dog, basking in his love. As they walked, she considered that both her parents must be depressed, in despair, albeit hidden from her as much as possible. After all, the things that had happened to them of a negative nature were not of their making. In many things they had given up. They did not celebrate Christmas any more; it was like any other day to them. Over the grass of the common they walked, she and the dog, while she sifted through her thoughts and feelings.

Terence still came to their house to help with the gardening, while her Dad talked to him from a chair where he sat outside. It was unthinkable that they would not have a garden. At the front of the house roses grew, the cream-coloured Peace rose, and the montbretia, both of which had been planted by someone else.

They were at peace in the Trust house, sheltered in that solid edifice of red brick, with its orange coloured hung tiles in the upper part, topped by the orange clay roof tiles. The doors were sturdy and thick, as were the window frames, the whole place put together by skilled men long ago, who had not apparently understood the word "shoddy" as applied to themselves.

She walked and walked, following on behind the dog, through grass and purple heather. He would take her on a circular route back to the house, so she did not have to think of where to go.

∼ One day, unannounced, a Youth Employment Officer came to her school, an overdressed woman with immaculate permed hair, exquisite heavy make-up, and red finger nails. To the children of that school, who were regularly shunted off to work in the metal box factory, it appeared that she presented herself in such a way as to be as different from them as possible. Accordingly, they were cowed in her presence, in their jumble-sale clothing, their mish-mash of items handed down from older brothers and sisters.

"And what do you want to do when you leave school?" the woman said to Lizzie, simpering at the outset of the two-minute interview that was allotted to her.

"I want to be a nurse," she piped up, having been briefed by her mother. May herself had yearned to train as a nurse at a time when the training had to be paid for and her father had not wanted her to do such a hard and difficult job, although he could have raised the money. She felt as though her mother were standing behind her right shoulder, prodding her with a finger into speech.

"Oh!" the YEO said, looking stunned. "Well!"

Lizzie did not retreat. A sense of change was strong in her, even though evidence of it in their daily lives was barely perceptible. It was a delicate sense of hope for better things, for a widening of horizons, for courage to grasp what was yet scarcely tangible.

As she stood there in her jumble sale clothing which was, of course, perfectly all right, she could not have guessed that she might as well have had a fairy godmother there with a magic wand, that the YEO would utter the words that would change her life for the better, and set her on a new path that would take her away from the one that led to the metal box factory and places of that ilk. "There's a new course starting up next January," the woman said, "for girls who want to enter nursing, at the Queen Victoria Hospital. It's called a pre-nursing course, from age sixteen to age eighteen, so that you can decide if you want to go on to a full training for a further three years to become a State Registered Nurse. Is that what you would like?"

"Yes. Thank you."

"During this pre-nursing course — if you are accepted for it, you will attend the local grammar school part-time, attend lectures at the hospital also, and work in the wards for a small salary."

Heaven seemed to open up to her then. That was perhaps the most that the Youth Employment Officer had ever said to a child at that school, she thought, committing the words to memory.

"You must apply in writing to the Matron of the hospital," the woman added. She did not give Lizzie the Matron's name, or the street address of the hospital or, heaven forbid, an introductory letter. That would have made it too easy; Lizzie was on her own.

Interview over.

"Thank you very much," Lizzie said, as she stood up to go.

Outside the room she saw one of her friends, Shirley, who had already been inside. "What did you say to that woman?" she whispered.

"My Mum told me to say I wanted to be a pastry cook, so I did."

"Do you want to?"

"No. I want to wear lovely clothes. That woman told me to apply to the kitchens at the Clarendon Hotel."

"They'll have you doing the washing up."

"I know. That won't lead to anything."

Shirley was a beautiful girl, willowy and graceful, a fast runner on sports days, intelligent and witty.

∼ At home, Lizzie wrote a careful letter of application, having found the address of the hospital.

~ Just before the summer holiday, 1953, Lizzie was accosted on her way home from school by the middle-aged chauffeur-handyman of a family who lived in a house along the road. They needed, he told her, a girl to work for them as a nanny for their three-year-old daughter and had asked him to approach her.

Lizzie had supposed herself more or less invisible as she walked home along the country road, having been dropped off half a mile back by the school bus. Mentally in a private world, it did not occur to her that others she did not know would be observing her progress and making assumptions about her. Dreamily she had been thinking about the poetry of D.H. Lawrence that her favourite English teacher, Mr. Pool, he with the fiery red hair, had recited to the class that day. Particularly she had liked the poem "Snake" in which the poet had written about a snake that had come to his well for a drink at a place in New Mexico, and he had, in a cowardly fashion, thrown a stone at it, then immediately regretted his action. With the poems in her head, she had walked down the toffee-papered lane from the school to the waiting buses that would take them near home, and those words had remained in her head.

But no, far from being invisible, her daily progress had been observed, her insouciant semi-freedom noted, for she was servant material, young, strong, and apparently healthy, with many years of servitude ahead of her. She listened, amazed, as the chauffeur, cross-eyed and totally without charm, stated the case for his employers.

After the approach, the mother and father of the child came to her cottage to see her. It was between them and her, as her parents had left her to make up her own mind. In an odd way she was flattered to be sought out, yet frightened at the age of fifteen to feel a trap closing around her, if only a temporary trap. Even so, there was a faith in her that the world had changed since the days of her mother's youth — her tired mother, now fifty-six — and that for herself there would be something different.

"I could do it for the summer," she said. "Later on, I'm going to be a nurse."

They took her on, showing little interest in her future plans, saying they would pay her two pounds a week. She watched them walk away, and she thought it would be nice to earn a little money. She would not be trapped there, for once she was sixteen she would start the pre-nursing course for which she had been accepted. May had gone with her to the hospital for the interview with Matron, an intimidating figure not without her benign aspects. "I'll be so proud of you," May whispered.

The letter of acceptance had come a week later, opening up a new world of possibility, a parallel world that she had not known existed. Dad had said to her, more than once: "You must get a training by which you can earn your living."

At about the same time, another family approached her, sending out their German butler to waylay her on the road, because they needed a maid. Lizzie wondered if the man had been a prisoner of war who had chosen to remain in England. "I'm afraid not," she said. "I'm going to be a nurse."

Nonetheless, she remained on warm speaking terms with this man and his plump German wife, who also worked at the big house. They seemed to be displaced persons, and a sadness for them came over her whenever she met them. In a way, she was like a displaced person in her own country, someone who worked in the land but never earned enough to own any of it. She and her family had lived in tied cottages, her father drawing pathetic wages for much work. Yet in another way the fields and woods belonged to her as much as they did to those who had title deed, for her kind wrested life from the land with their expertise, the wealthy depending on them. The ancient bridle paths that criss-crossed the land were open to all. As much as it was for the wild animals that survived there, who escaped the hounds, the hunt and the trap, it was hers. Other creatures had been hunted to extinction, the lovely sleek otter in the streams, the badgers, the harts, most of the deer, the hares. Still she clung to her green habitat, and schemed for her survival.

A reply letter had come first from the hospital matron, to whom she had written applying for a place in the pre-nursing course. It was one of her talents to be able to write a good letter in beautiful hand-writing. The letter from Matron was a call for an interview.

It was May who had elected to accompany her, not her own idea. She supposed it was acceptable, as she was still a child in the eyes of the law, if so old inside. Together they confronted the matron, who looked charming in a dark green dress and lacey cap, while they themselves wore their best, carefully ironed and polished. With her application she had had to submit an essay entitled "The Person I Most Admire." That was, she assumed, to make sure that she was fully literate and fully *compos mentis*. She had chosen Douglas Bader, the Second World War pilot, as the subject of her essay. After a crash, he had had his legs amputated, had been fitted with artificial legs. Even with this disability he had returned to flying and was subsequently shot down over enemy territory and had become a prisoner of war. All her admiration and respect had poured out into that essay. He had been to her the incarnation of Frederick George Decker, her mother's love who had been shot down over France in the First World War in his flimsy craft when there were no parachutes.

"Please, God," Lizzie had prayed silently, as she and May sat on the far side of Matron's spacious desk, "let Mum have cause to be proud of me." For she — unlike her father who had said: "When you're dead, you're dead," and presumably did not believe in God — did at that small moment in time believe fervently. How could there not be a God when the countryside was so beautiful, as were the flowers that her father grew in abundance, and the whole magnificence of nature, if there had been no intent in its creation? At that moment of suspended time she did not factor in the dread of the siren that she had known during the war, the army lorries full of young soldiers that had passed by their house, those young men who had smiled and waved at her as she stood watching. Neither had she seen the beautiful countryside turned into a corpse field, a sea of mud that sucked in the living and the dead. Even so, she knew of it. She had read Bertrand Russell's book, *The Scourge of the Swastika*, had seen the photographs in it. God could not be entirely responsible for the evil of man, if at all.

A more mature dissonance would come a little later for her; at least the process would start then, the start of a long, long journey of disengagement from her childhood faiths.

God must have been listening that day, for the interview with Matron went well. Although Matron did not mention the essay, she smiled frequently, so Lizzie got the impression that she was familiar with the pilot and approved of the choice of him as an object of admiration.

When the second letter came, accepting her into the program which would start the following January, she felt that heaven had truly opened up to her and the abyss had receded from her path, for now.

Sometimes she saw her father looking at her, pleased, she thought, as though she were a child of another world. Indeed, she was in many ways. Perhaps he had, in his way, perhaps inadvertently, helped to bring about those changes. By his suffering, his actions in the face of great odds, he had done something to ratchet up the speed of change from which he would not benefit much himself. Unlike the previous generations of men in his family, he had a small pension from the army to compensate for his deformity, and an old age pension, so he would not starve. Those simple privileges would die with him. All the efforts of working men like him had come together for her in goodness.

Throughout her childhood he had talked of politics, trades unions, world affairs, had sensitized her to the goings-on beneath the everyday machinations and surfaces of the world, as his own father, whom she had never met, had done for him.

~ At the start of the long summer holiday she began the job as nanny. She presented herself at the house where she was to work. Very shortly thereafter she found herself sweeping and washing floors, dusting, cleaning, washing dishes, even though there was a char lady who came every day on a bicycle from the village. Later she found herself doing the cooking, when her employers found out that she could cook well, a bonus from Domestic Science at school, her specialties being potato soup and chocolate butterfly cakes with butter icing, a dessert the family particularly enjoyed.

It wasn't that she was too proud to do this work. Oh, no! She believed that all work was valuable, that one should do a job to the best of one's ability, with a certain enthusiasm. It was the out and out deception of it that angered and saddened her.

"Back to the bad old days of child labour," the male half of her employer-couple remarked cheerfully one day as she kneeled to polish a floor, evidently not smitten by conscience. Although she wasn't exactly a child, she understood what he meant, as the drudgery of the work weighed heavily upon her.

While she was there, Lizzie honed her sense of humour, as one day, taking her by surprise, her employer announced that he intended to increase her wages. Like Bob Cratchett. waiting for Mr. Scrooge to make a pronouncement, she stood there expectantly. He added: "By two shillings a week."

Unable to help herself, she laughed in his face at the absurdity of it, eliciting from him a small, sheepish smile. Their worlds separated even further then.

Thinking of the letter from Matron, offering her a place at the Queen Victoria Hospital, to start in January, 1954, she felt that she could tolerate more or less anything until then, even her male employer's awakening sexual awareness of her as an attractive female, a realization as unwelcome to her as it was revolting. Thank God for that letter, she told herself several times a day.

She knew herself to be naïve in many ways, yet as old as the hills in others, sensing that her employer would be put off by the spontaneous look of horror and disgust that she knew would appear on her face if he made even the slightest move to bring his fantasies regarding her into fruition. Sometimes he trembled when he stood close to her, as she put wood into the stove that heated the water tank, or mixed the ingredients for the butterfly cakes. At those times she moved away, affronted, because he was so old, about thirty, twice her age, and there was a tired, used up aura about him. In his black hair there were threads of grey.

To a woman of his own age, he would no doubt appear very attractive, she could see that, but to a young person such as herself, little more than a child, he was of another world from which there could never be a bridge into her own in that regard. Boys of her own age, fresh and sweet, sheepish and humorous, without "side", were attractive to her, not the tired sophistication of the used-up and soon-to-be middle aged men. Arrogance, even the battened down kind, was repulsive. Here was a mediocre man who thought himself out of the ordinary. The boys she went to school with were the ones who would be called up for the army in a war, the sacrificial lambs. They would have duty thrust upon them.

The child, three years old, whom she cared for, was not difficult to manage, a neglected, sad child. The parents thought that all they had to do in the way of parental care was to give the girl a little attention once a day, call her "poppet" a few times, and then leave all the care to others who were strangers to her. Lizzie, who would never herself call a child "poppet", sympathized with the girl, yet was too close to her own struggles in childhood to feel that she could really stand up for her in many ways. Instead, she took the child walking in the fields where there were buttercups and butterflies, read to her at bedtime, knowing that when it was her time to depart from the house for her nursing career the child would miss her. Compassion held her to the girl. Already she felt herself entering that different world, with a sense of what she could do and what she could not in the here and now. In the time she was there she would try to bring a little joy into the girl's life.

With Matron's letter of acceptance in her hand, joy and vindication shifted her away from the world she had heretofore inhabited. New vistas opened up in her mind. Her mother, who read and re-read the letter, was duly proud — although the journey had only just begun towards that almost magical objective, the state registration — while her Dad smiled and said: "Jolly good!"

These days he was becoming more breathless, her dear Dad. Now she looked back more often to the days when, at three years of age, she had watched at their garden gate to see him coming home from work and had run to him, to reach up and put her hand in his. She thought of the times he had sung to them on winter evenings beside the fire. The one she liked best began with: "I am a poor maiden ...' and went on: "If I were a blackbird, I'd whistle and sing, and sail on the ship that my true love sails in, and on the top rigging I'd there build my nest, and pillow my head on his snowy white breast."

He had a good singing voice; he could make something soppy sound as dignified as a hymn and twice as emotive. Even with the sad and hard life that he had had, he was not what she could call cowed. Liberal-minded and humorous, he interpreted the world for her in a way that she liked.

Sometimes he was blue around the mouth when he exerted himself, and his finger nails were blue. She knew about the rheumatic fever, years before, that it damaged the heart, bringing about, eventually, gradual congestive cardiac failure. Like her first taste of dread at the screaming sirens during the war, a second source of dread took its place. The joy of having the acceptance letter in her hand was thus tempered by the reality of the approaching deterioration and death of Dad.

With his bravery, the bravery of the old soldier, he put her to shame. From then on, the anxiety of the orphan grew in her.

∼ On the day she told her employers that she definitely had been accepted for the pre-nursing education and training course, and that she must leave soon on a definite date, a grandmother was visiting the house. The old lady, tall and imperious, who often wore a long, purple crepe evening dress, had dirty hair that she braided and fixed to the top of her head like a European peasant. Lizzie longed to dunk the woman's head into a bowl of soapy water.

The grandmother cornered her and said accusingly: "How can you have been accepted into nursing? You haven't got Matric!"

"They have accepted me," she said. Even in her immaturity, she understood well the basic law of supply and demand, even though she could not have written a thesis on it at that moment.

"We love having you here," the old lady said. "We had hoped you would stay on and on."

"I must go," she said. With what they were paying her, she would never own any more than the clothes on her back. It was a dead-end job if ever there was one. Much of her money she gave to her mother. She wondered what the grandmother would say if she knew how her son-in-law trembled when he stood next to her, and how revolting she found him. She would not tell, because there was no point unless she became frightened of him.

The last blow from them had come when she heard the lady of the house refer to her as "the maid" to guests. For that, she felt demeaned. Not because such a job was without dignity, or beneath her. It was that she had clearly been hired to be a nanny.

When the day came for her to walk away from there for the last time, she grasped for the first time that the depth of one's relief was an accurate indicator of how wrong a situation was or could be.

That was not the last of the dealings she had with these people, as she found out that her employer had failed to keep up-to-date with the payments for her National Health Insurance stamps that he should have put on her card for the purpose. When she had asked for her cards on her departure, he said he would send them by post.

After she had started work at the hospital, she knew she had entered a new, civilized world when a woman working in the personnel office said: "Don't worry, dear, we'll get your cards from your former employer, paid up to date." There was a threat and a promise in the woman's tone that was on her behalf, Lizzie recognized, not against her. It was against the law not to stamp an employee's card for health and unemployment insurance. *Oh, brave new world, that hath such people in it*, she thought as she walked away from the office.

There began the happiest two years of her life. She knew that after the two years it would be necessary for her to leave that hospital, because it was not a large enough establishment to offer the three-year training for state registration. In the meantime, this two-year hiatus would see her move from childhood to early adulthood, in the company of others like herself, a band of young women who were moving on into that brave new world with their memories of war and a new sensibility that came out of it. They would never forget the war, because their experiences of it had been etched in their brains. There, she learned from observation and experience that the qualities of empathy and compassion were the most important, that they make us fully human.

Some of the ward orderlies, mostly men, and the nursing aids, who were women, had numbers tattooed on the inside of their forearms, evidence of their having been inmates of a Nazi concentration camp or a death camp. Thus the tentacles of the war stretched out into the nineteen fifties, into that place of sanctuary, into her own life as an observer now. She shared something of their sense of reprieve as they went about their work in caring for the sick as she did. Her compassion and grief reached out to them, although they did not speak of it.

Sadly she moved on when the time came, to another town, another hospital, to a world of extra hard work, long hours of day and night duty, often Dickensian in their harshness, to stress, study, examinations, duty, often wondering if she would ever get to the end of it. In her third year, she won a special prize as the best operating theatre nurse of the year. Thus, she discovered the speciality that would hold her interest for many years in the future.

May was duly proud of her again. Yet Lizzie realized that her mother could not understand her outward self-confidence, even though May deplored her own bowing and scraping on the occasions that she felt it necessary with her "betters." May did not notice any evidence of the seething of doubt inside that vied with a quiet certitude. The old adages that had been familiar to May when she was growing up were still there, in weaker form: *Self-praise is no recommendation,* and *Don't blow your own trumpet.*

Nonetheless, signs of that seething were there, had May been sensitive to them. Only just below the surface, sometimes, was Lizzie's sadness that erupted in sobs for that which was lost or never gained, an outpouring that seemed inexplicable to May who should, of all people, have understood. Forty-one years' difference in age, and different lessons from war, separated them. May saw the ashes; she herself saw the phoenix rising, but not without turmoil and doubting. Who could say what was right when there were no definitive answers, so many lies and half-truths?

Even so, even in May's depression and losses, there was not the fatalism of Granny who had said: "It is God's will" when certain things happened that she had not wanted, such as a fifth, then a sixth pregnancy. May had not once said that, Lizzie recalled. Neither had her father. They and she understood that much was the will of man, and man only, especially the will to destruction.

On days off she went home, walking in green and woodland places with the dog, where her soul was soothed. During the day, now, Dad spent more time in bed from where he could look to the window and see the blue of the sky and the moving clouds. Jo came home, too, from her job. Between them they ran errands for him, buying this and that small thing from the village shop or from the nearest town. One day he asked them to go to a chemist in the town and buy some spirits of nitre which, he said, was given to sick horses to make them sweat. From that remark, she concluded that his kidneys were failing.

"What are you going to do with this?" the chemist asked.

"My Dad wants it," she said.

"You be very careful," he said. "This is powerful and dangerous stuff."

Back at home she handed the small brown bottle over to Dad. He sat up in bed, propped up by pillows, his round-eyed, wire rimmed glasses on the end of his nose as he read the fine print on the bottle. On the counterpane were a newspaper and a book. "The chemist said this is dangerous," she said.

"I know ... I know how to us it. I need to sweat."

When she left the next day to go back to work, she said: 'Goodbye, Dad. See you soon." With such mundane words do we take our leave of those we love.

On the 23rd of November, 1957, a telegram came to her at work, sent by Jo. "Dad passed away," it said.

That evening she walked the dark streets near the hospital, walked and walked, until all her outward tears had dried.

At the end of the additional three years' training, after she had taken the final examinations and was waiting for the results, she was working in the Casualty Department of her training hospital when the official letter came and was delivered to her in the department.

"We are pleased to inform you," she read, stopping there. It was over ... the anxiety, the uncertainty of the future, and she felt herself step back once again from the edge of the abyss that at times re-formed and came closer. Now she was a professional woman who could pick and choose her work, who could stand up to bullies and to discrimination for being, perhaps, of the wrong social class in certain settings. She could make plans for her life instead of feeling herself blown by winds of circumstance. She could move to London, if she chose to do so.

She put her arms around Elsie, one of the cleaners, who stood near her. They had been talking before the letter came, and now she gave her a quick, fierce hug. "I've passed my finals," she said

Her father's words were in her mind again, as they so often had been over the years of hard work and uncertainty : "You must get a training by which you can earn a living, by which you can support yourself." She had affirmed those words, while from May she learned the many faces of bravery.

Now the best years were ahead, the years of independence, decisions that could be brought to fruition, adventures, expanded horizons, a going forward with courage. From within herself she had found the power of words.

Once, while on her knees in a garden planting flowers, it came to her that this skill she had in her hands and in her mind, this love of nurturing plants, and an empathy with animals, her nursing skills, were the inheritance from a father who had had little to give of a material nature. He had passed on his knowledge and skill in increments throughout the nineteen years that she had known him. It was as though that brief time had been lent to her by a benign deity. "You have a seriously green thumb," someone said to her.

Many years later she tried to get her mother's hospital records from the county hospital. Someone told her via e-mail that she should write to a particular person in a particular local government department, although he thought that the records of the hospital had been permanently closed. That government official did not acknowledge her letters. Permanently closed means forever. That indeed was the case. Was there something to be hidden? The records would have been taken away somewhere, the files placed on shelves in basement rooms of other institutions or offices, places seldom entered once the shelves were full. There they would remain hidden in dusty cardboard folders, the doors locked, the whereabouts of the keys not generally known.

She had read of men and women being driven mad by war, by terrible sights they had witnessed and events they had experienced, unnatural things that had to do with mass murder and maiming, and the destruction of love. They were hidden away, those who survived, in places far from sight, with damaged minds, their records inaccessible, as though they had never existed.

By up-to-date research methods she discovered that there had been a special railway line directly to the county hospital, so that trains did not have to pass through the nearby village station where the maimed in body and mind might be seen by the un-maimed and perhaps questions raised, a concept bringing with it shades of the concentration camps of the last war, death camps, prisoner of war camps, civilians in cattle trucks in Poland and Germany, all quiet and orderly in the beautiful countryside. Thus is history changed and lies told, the truth censored, memories discounted.

Words can shine a light into those dark places.

∽ Epilogue

*W*ill I come to beautiful France again, where wild flowers grow beside the wavy lines of shell craters, lined with brilliant green grass and moss, in the countryside in the east? Will I see again the rusted iron of barbed wire fences? Will I touch the etched names of the missing where wind and weather begin to obliterate them, as though challenging our will to remember?

Those thoughts came to her as she left the cemeteries and the fields of Loos to go on to the Somme and its haunted woods, its wind-swept fields of crops where the soil had been nurtured by blood of boys and men. There she saw school children gathering quietly, with their mentors, subdued by cruel history and the weight of their coming duty to maintain the peace.

In a book on recent archaeology of the Great War that she bought from a kiosk, put together by young archaeologists for whom the war was an anachronism, she read: "In a society increasingly preoccupied with the individual, the fact of sending an entire generation of men to their slaughter has become increasingly incomprehensible and generates a strong emotion and a duty to remember these soldiers sacrificed for illusory tactical objectives."

True, brave words from a new generation, and the photographs they chose revealed neat rows of skeletons, the Grimsby Chums among them, carefully buried, complete with leather boots, by their compatriots, in shallow graves near Arras. The graves were left open by this new generation, protected under glass, so that we might view those bones and ponder on lives and innocence callously squandered.

The power of the mute bones exhorts us to speak for them. Arise the dead through us and speak. Tell us your poems and your love letters, tell us your desires and joys, tell us the sadness of parting, your memories of childhood, your wisdom, your hopes, your work and your endeavours, your goodbyes. Let the regret be ours.

'Pool of Peace', a British mine crater, which undermined enemy lines, in the Ypres salient, Belgium.

○ Acknowledgements

I would like to acknowledge my editor, E. Alex Pierce, formerly of Cape Breton University, Nova Scotia, with many thanks, whose expertise, gentle critique and much encouragement kept me engaged. She is now senior editor with the Boularderie Island Press. Also I wish to thank my mentors at the writing studio at the Banff Centre for the Arts, Alberta — Greg Hollingshead and Edna Alford — who, in 2006, gave me much encouragement to make a start on the war stories.

↶ About the Author

Elizabeth Langridge was born in 1938 in the south of England, in the county of Kent, and grew up in Kent and Sussex, surrounded by beautiful countryside. Her earliest memories are of the Second World War. She lived in a rural area about thirty-five miles directly south of the east end of London, which was very heavily bombed because of the docks on the Thames. The enemy bombers went directly over her and her family. They could see London burning on the horizon at night. Their home was bombed in November, 1940. The family escaped with their lives, but not much else. The war was still on when, at age four, she started at the village school, where there was a bomb shelter in the playground. Those memories of war and how people dealt with it, their courage and bravery, their common sense, their humour, have remained with her.

She trained to be a nurse, although her first love was writing. In 1966 she married a Canadian who was in London working for two years. That year they came to Toronto to live. They have three children.

The story is for all those who suffered and endured during the two World Wars, which were not of their making. May they not be forgotten.